W9-BEJ-102

A NOTE FROM SUSAN ORLEAN

In *Life After Life,* Kate Atkinson brilliantly depicts the English wartime experience by presenting a looping tapestry of "what ifs" that I predict will engross you as much as it did me. It's a story that dares you to see the complexity and consequence of the directions we choose (or that fate chooses for us) at every juncture. This may be a distant hypothetical for me and you, but for the protagonist here, Ursula, it unfolds as a reality. As Ursula lives and dies again and again, she navigates a labyrinth of her own decisions, evading—and at times, succumbing to—the perils of 20th-century England. Atkinson manages to combine exquisite writing with the dizzying possibilities of quantum physics; is this the only life we could have lived? Or are there infinite ways our lives might have unfolded? This book turned me into a hard-core Atkinson fan; I knew I was meeting a master. I can't wait for you to experience it, too.

Susan Orlean

Also by Kate Atkinson

Behind the Scenes at the Museum

Human Croquet

Emotionally Weird

Not the End of the World

Case Histories

One Good Turn

When Will There Be Good News?

Started Early, Took My Dog

LIFE AFTER LIFE

A Novel

KATE ATKINSON

A REAGAN ARTHUR BOOK
LITTLE, BROWN AND COMPANY
NEW YORK BOSTON LONDON

Reagan Arthur Books/Little, Brown and Company
Hachette Book Group
1290 Avenue of the Americas, New York, NY 10104
www.hachettebookgroup.com

First United States Edition, April 2013

Originally published in the United Kingdom by Doubleday, March 2013

Reagan Arthur Books is an imprint of Little, Brown and Company, a division of Hachette Book Group, Inc. The Reagan Arthur Books name and logo are trademarks of Hachette Book Group, Inc.

Library of Congress Cataloging-in-Publication Data

Atkinson, Kate.
Life after life : a novel / Kate Atkinson.—First United States edition.
pages cm
ISBN 978-0-316-31236-3 (Luminary Edition)
1. Reincarnation—Fiction. 2. Great Britain—History—20th century—Fiction. I. Title.
PR6051.T56L54 2013
823'.914—dc23 2012046158

PRINTING 1, 2021

LSC-C

Printed in the United States of America

For Elissa

What if some day or night a demon were to steal after you into your loneliest loneliness and say to you: "This life as you now live it and have lived it, you will have to live once more and innumerable times more"... Would you not throw yourself down and gnash your teeth and curse the demon who spoke thus? Or have you once experienced a tremendous moment when you would have answered him: "You are a god and never have I heard anything more divine."

NIETZSCHE, *The Gay Science*

πάντα χωρεῖ καὶ οὐδὲν μένει
Everything changes and nothing remains still.

PLATO, *Cratylus*

"What if we had a chance to do it again and again, until we finally did get it right? Wouldn't that be wonderful?"

EDWARD BERESFORD TODD

Contents

BE YE MEN OF VALOR

November 1930

A fug of tobacco smoke and damp clammy air hit her as she entered the café. She had come in from the rain and drops of water still trembled like delicate dew on the fur coats of some of the women inside. A regiment of white-aproned waiters rushed around at tempo, serving the needs of the *Münchner* at leisure—coffee, cake and gossip.

He was at a table at the far end of the room, surrounded by the usual cohorts and toadies. There was a woman she had never seen before—a permed, platinum blonde with heavy makeup—an actress by the look of her. The blonde lit a cigarette, making a phallic performance out of it. Everyone knew that he preferred his women demure and wholesome, Bavarian preferably. All those dirndls and kneesocks, God help us.

The table was laden. *Bienenstich, Gugelhupf, Käsekuchen.* He was eating a slice of *Kirschtorte.* He loved his cakes. No wonder he looked so pasty, she was surprised he wasn't diabetic. The softly repellent body (she imagined pastry) beneath the clothes, never exposed to public view. Not a manly man. He smiled when he caught sight of her and half rose, saying, *"Guten Tag, gnädiges Fräulein,"* indicating the chair next to him. The bootlicker who was currently occupying it jumped up and moved away.

"Unsere Englische Freundin," he said to the blonde, who blew cigarette smoke out slowly and examined her without any interest before eventually saying, *"Guten Tag."* A Berliner.

She placed her handbag, heavy with its cargo, on the floor next to her chair and ordered *Schokolade.* He insisted that she try the *Pflaumen Streusel.*

"Es regnet," she said by way of conversation. "It's raining."

"Yes, it's raining," he said with a heavy accent. He laughed, pleased at his attempt. Everyone else at the table laughed as well. *"Bravo,"* someone said. *"Sehr gutes Englisch."* He was in a good mood, tapping the back of his index finger against his lips with an amused smile as if he was listening to a tune in his head.

The *Streusel* was delicious.

"Entschuldigung," she murmured, reaching down into her bag and delving for a handkerchief. Lace corners, monogrammed with her initials, "UBT"—a birthday present from Pammy. She dabbed politely at the *Streusel* flakes on her lips and then bent down again to put the handkerchief back in her bag and retrieve the weighty object nesting there. Her father's old service revolver from the Great War, a Webley Mark V.

A move rehearsed a hundred times. One shot. Swiftness was all, yet there was a moment, a bubble suspended in time after she had drawn the gun and leveled it at his heart when everything seemed to stop.

"Führer," she said, breaking the spell. *"Für Sie."*

Around the table guns were jerked from holsters and pointed at her. One breath. One shot.

Ursula pulled the trigger.

Darkness fell.

SNOW

11 February 1910

An icy rush of air, a freezing slipstream on the newly exposed skin. She is, with no warning, outside the inside and the familiar wet, tropical world has suddenly evaporated. Exposed to the elements. A prawn peeled, a nut shelled.

No breath. All the world come down to this. One breath.

Little lungs, like dragonfly wings failing to inflate in the foreign atmosphere. No wind in the strangled pipe. The buzzing of a thousand bees in the tiny curled pearl of an ear.

Panic. The drowning girl, the falling bird.

Dr. Fellowes should have been here," Sylvie moaned. "Why isn't he here yet? Where is he?" Big dewdrop pearls of sweat on her skin, a horse nearing the end of a hard race. The bedroom fire stoked like a ship's furnace. The thick brocade curtains drawn tightly against the enemy, the night. The black bat.

"Yer man'll be stuck in the snow, I expect, ma'am. It's sure dreadful wild out there. The road will be closed."

Sylvie and Bridget were alone in their ordeal. Alice, the parlor maid, was visiting her sick mother. And Hugh, of course, was chasing down Isobel, his wild goose of a sister, *à Paris*. Sylvie had no wish to involve Mrs. Glover, snoring in her attic room like a truffling hog. Sylvie imagined she would conduct proceedings like a parade-ground sergeant major. The baby was early. Sylvie was expecting it to be late like the others. The best-laid plans, and so on.

"Oh, ma'am," Bridget cried suddenly, "she's all blue, so she is."

"A girl?"

"The cord's wrapped around her neck. Oh, Mary, Mother of God. She's been strangled, the poor wee thing."

"Not breathing? Let me see her. We must do something. What can we do?"

"Oh, Mrs. Todd, ma'am, she's gone. Dead before she had a chance to live. I'm awful, awful sorry. She'll be a little cherub in heaven now, for sure. Oh, I wish Mr. Todd was here. I'm awful sorry. Shall I wake Mrs. Glover?"

The little heart. A helpless little heart beating wildly. Stopped suddenly like a bird dropped from the sky. A single shot.

Darkness fell.

SNOW

11 February 1910

"For God's sake, girl, stop running around like a headless chicken and fetch some hot water and towels. Do you know nothing? Were you raised in a field?"

"Sorry, sir." Bridget dipped an apologetic curtsy as if Dr. Fellowes were minor royalty.

"A girl, Dr. Fellowes? May I see her?"

"Yes, Mrs. Todd, a bonny, bouncing baby girl." Sylvie thought Dr. Fellowes might be over-egging the pudding with his alliteration. He was not one for bonhomie at the best of times. The health of his patients, particularly their exits and entrances, seemed designed to annoy him.

"She would have died from the cord around her neck. I arrived at Fox Corner in the nick of time. Literally." Dr. Fellowes held up his surgical scissors for Sylvie's admiration. They were small and neat and their sharp points curved upward at the end. "Snip, snip," he said. Sylvie made a mental note, a small, vague one, given her exhaustion and the circumstances of it, to buy just such a pair of scissors, in case of similar emergency. (Unlikely, it was true.) Or a knife, a good sharp knife to be carried on one's person at all times, like the robber girl in *The Snow Queen*.

"You were lucky I got here in time," Dr. Fellowes said. "Before the snow closed the roads. I called for Mrs. Haddock, the midwife, but I believe she is stuck somewhere outside Chalfont St. Peter."

"Mrs. *Haddock?*" Sylvie said and frowned. Bridget laughed out loud and then quickly mumbled, "Sorry, sorry, sir." Sylvie supposed that she and Bridget were both on the edge of hysteria. Hardly surprising.

"Bog Irish," Dr. Fellowes muttered.

"Bridget's only a scullery maid, a child herself. I am very grateful to her. It all happened so quickly." Sylvie thought how much she wanted to be alone, how she was never alone. "You must stay until morning, I suppose, doctor," she said reluctantly.

"Well, yes, I suppose I must," Dr. Fellowes said, equally reluctantly.

Sylvie sighed and suggested that he help himself to a glass of brandy in the kitchen. And perhaps some ham and pickles. "Bridget will see to you." She wanted rid of him. He had delivered all three (three!) of her children and she did not like him one bit. Only a husband should see what he saw. Pawing and poking with his instruments in her most delicate and secretive places. (But would she rather have a midwife called Mrs. Haddock deliver her child?) Doctors for women should all be women themselves. Little chance of that.

Dr. Fellowes lingered, humming and hawing, overseeing the washing and wrapping of the new arrival by a hot-faced Bridget. Bridget was the eldest of seven so she knew how to swaddle an infant. She was fourteen years old, ten years younger than Sylvie. When Sylvie was fourteen she was still in short skirts, in love with her pony, Tiffin. Had no idea where babies came from, even on her wedding night she remained baffled. Her mother, Lottie, had hinted but had fallen shy of anatomical exactitude. Conjugal relations between man and wife seemed, mysteriously, to involve larks soaring at daybreak. Lottie was a reserved woman. Some might have said narcoleptic. Her husband, Sylvie's father, Llewellyn Beresford, was a famous society artist but not at all Bohemian. No nudity or louche behavior in his household. He had painted Queen Alexandra, when she was still a princess. Said she was very pleasant.

They lived in a good house in Mayfair, while Tiffin was stabled in a mews near Hyde Park. In darker moments, Sylvie was wont to cheer herself up by imagining that she was back there in the sunny past, sitting neatly in her side-saddle on Tiffin's broad little back, trotting along Rotten Row on a clean spring morning, the blossom bright on the trees.

"How about some hot tea and a nice bit of buttered toast, Mrs. Todd?" Bridget said.

"That would be lovely, Bridget."

The baby, bandaged like a Pharaonic mummy, was finally passed to Sylvie. Softly, she stroked the peachy cheek and said, "Hello, little one," and Dr. Fellowes turned away so as not to be a witness to such syrupy demonstrations of affection. He would have all children brought up in a new Sparta if it were up to him.

"Well, perhaps a little cold collation wouldn't go amiss," he said. "Is there, by chance, any of Mrs. Glover's excellent piccalilli?"

FOUR SEASONS FILL THE MEASURE OF THE YEAR

11 February 1910

Sylvie was woken by a dazzling sliver of sunlight piercing the curtains like a shining silver sword. She lay languidly in lace and cashmere as Mrs. Glover came into the room, proudly bearing a huge breakfast tray. Only an occasion of some importance seemed capable of drawing Mrs. Glover this far out of her lair. A single, half-frozen snowdrop drooped in the bud vase on the tray. "Oh, a snowdrop!" Sylvie said. "The first flower to raise its poor head above the ground. How brave it is!"

Mrs. Glover, who did not believe that flowers were capable of courage, or indeed any other character trait, laudable or otherwise, was a widow who had only been with them at Fox Corner a few weeks. Before her advent there had been a woman called Mary who slouched a great deal and burned the roasts. Mrs. Glover tended, if anything, to undercook food. In the prosperous household of Sylvie's childhood, Cook was called "Cook" but Mrs. Glover preferred "Mrs. Glover." It made her irreplaceable. Sylvie still stubbornly thought of her as Cook.

"Thank you, Cook." Mrs. Glover blinked slowly like a lizard. "Mrs. Glover," Sylvie corrected herself.

Mrs. Glover set the tray down on the bed and opened the curtains. The light was extraordinary, the black bat vanquished.

"So bright," Sylvie said, shielding her eyes.

"So much snow," Mrs. Glover said, shaking her head in what could have been wonder or aversion. It was not always easy to tell with Mrs. Glover.

"Where is Dr. Fellowes?" Sylvie asked.

"There was an emergency. A farmer trampled by a bull."

"How dreadful."

"Some men came from the village and tried to dig his automobile out but in the end my George came and gave him a ride."

"Ah," Sylvie said, as if suddenly understanding something that had puzzled her.

"And they call it horsepower," Mrs. Glover snorted, bull-like herself. "That's what comes of relying on newfangled machines."

"Mm," Sylvie said, reluctant to argue with such strongly held views. She was surprised that Dr. Fellowes had left without examining either herself or the baby.

"He looked in on you. You were asleep," Mrs. Glover said. Sylvie sometimes wondered if Mrs. Glover was a mind reader. A perfectly horrible thought.

"He ate his breakfast first," Mrs. Glover said, displaying both approval and disapproval in the same breath. "The man has an appetite, that's for sure."

"I could eat a horse," Sylvie laughed. She couldn't, of course. Tiffin popped briefly into her mind. She picked up the silver cutlery, heavy like weapons, ready to tackle Mrs. Glover's devilled kidneys. "Lovely," she said (were they?) but Mrs. Glover was already busy inspecting the baby in the cradle. ("Plump as a suckling pig.") Sylvie idly wondered if Mrs. Haddock was still stuck somewhere outside Chalfont St. Peter.

"I hear the baby nearly died," Mrs. Glover said.

"Well..." Sylvie said. Such a fine line between living and dying. Her own father, the society portraitist, slipped on an Isfahan rug on a first-floor landing after some fine cognac one evening. The next morning he was discovered dead at the foot of the stairs. No one had heard him fall or cry out. He had just begun a portrait of the Earl of Balfour. Never finished. Obviously.

Afterward it turned out that he had been more profligate with his money than mother and daughter realized. A secret gambler, markers all over town. He had made no provision at all for unexpected death and soon there were creditors crawling over the nice house in Mayfair. A house of cards as it turned out. Tiffin had to go. Broke Sylvie's heart, the grief greater than any she felt for her father.

"I thought his only vice was women," her mother said, roosting temporarily on a packing case as if modeling for a pietà.

They sank into genteel and well-mannered poverty. Sylvie's mother grew pale and uninteresting, larks soared no more for her as she faded, consumed by consumption. Seventeen-year-old Sylvie was rescued from becoming an artist's model by a man she met at the post office counter. Hugh. A rising star in the prosperous world of banking. The epitome of bourgeois respectability. What more could a beautiful but penniless girl hope for?

Lottie died with less fuss than was expected and Hugh and Sylvie married quietly on Sylvie's eighteenth birthday. ("There," Hugh said, "now you will never forget the anniversary of our marriage.") They spent their honeymoon in France, a delightful *quinzaine* in Deauville, before settling in semirural bliss near Beaconsfield in a house that was vaguely Lutyens in style. It had everything one could ask for—a large kitchen, a drawing room with French windows onto the lawn, a pretty morning room and several bedrooms waiting to be filled with children. There was even a little room at the back of the house for Hugh to use as a study. "Ah, my growlery," he laughed.

It was surrounded at a discreet distance by similar houses. There was a meadow and a copse and a bluebell wood beyond with a stream running through it. The train station, no more than a halt, would allow Hugh to be at his banker's desk in less than an hour.

"Sleepy hollow," Hugh laughed as he gallantly carried Sylvie across the threshold. It was a relatively modest dwelling (nothing like Mayfair) but nonetheless a little beyond their means, a fiscal recklessness that surprised them both.

★ ★ ★

We should give the house a name," Hugh said. "The Laurels, the Pines, the Elms."

"But we have none of those in the garden," Sylvie pointed out. They were standing at the French windows of the newly purchased house, looking at a swath of overgrown lawn. "We must get a gardener," Hugh said. The house itself was echoingly empty. They had not yet begun to fill it with the Voysey rugs and Morris fabrics and all the other aesthetic comforts of a twentieth-century house. Sylvie would have quite happily lived in Liberty's rather than the as-yet-to-be-named marital home.

"Greenacres, Fairview, Sunnymead?" Hugh offered, putting his arm around his bride.

"No."

The previous owner of their unnamed house had sold up and gone to live in Italy. "Imagine," Sylvie said dreamily. She had been to Italy when she was younger, a grand tour with her father while her mother went to Eastbourne for her lungs.

"Full of Italians," Hugh said dismissively.

"Quite. That's rather the attraction," Sylvie said, unwinding herself from his arm.

"The Gables, the Homestead?"

"Do stop," Sylvie said.

A fox appeared out of the shrubbery and crossed the lawn. "Oh, look," Sylvie said. "How tame it seems, it must have grown used to the house being unoccupied."

"Let's hope the local hunt isn't following on its heels," Hugh said. "It's a scrawny beast."

"It's a vixen. She's a nursing mother, you can see her teats."

Hugh blinked at such blunt terminology falling from the lips of his recently virginal bride. (One presumed. One hoped.)

"Look," Sylvie whispered. Two small cubs sprang out onto the grass and tumbled over each other in play. "Oh, they're such handsome little creatures!"

"Some might say vermin."

"Perhaps they see *us* as verminous," Sylvie said. "Fox Corner—that's what we should call the house. No one else has a house with that name and shouldn't that be the point?"

"Really?" Hugh said doubtfully. "It's a little whimsical, isn't it? It sounds like a children's story. *The House at Fox Corner.*"

"A little whimsy never hurt anyone."

"Strictly speaking though," Hugh said, "can a house *be* a corner? Isn't it *at* one?"

So this is marriage, Sylvie thought.

Two small children peered cautiously round the door. "Here you are," Sylvie said, smiling. "Maurice, Pamela, come and say hello to your new sister."

Warily, they approached the cradle and its contents as if unsure as to what it might contain. Sylvie remembered a similar feeling when viewing her father's body in its elaborate oak-and-brass coffin (charitably paid for by fellow members of the Royal Academy). Or perhaps it was Mrs. Glover they were chary of.

"Another girl," Maurice said gloomily. He was five, two years older than Pamela and the man of the family for as long as Hugh was away. "On business," Sylvie informed people although in fact he had crossed the Channel posthaste to rescue his foolish youngest sister from the clutches of the married man with whom she had eloped to Paris.

Maurice poked a finger in the baby's face and she woke up and squawked in alarm. Mrs. Glover pinched Maurice's ear. Sylvie winced but Maurice accepted the pain stoically. Sylvie thought that she really must have a word with Mrs. Glover when she was feeling stronger.

"What are you going to call her?" Mrs. Glover asked.

"Ursula," Sylvie said. "I shall call her Ursula. It means little she-bear."

Mrs. Glover nodded noncommittally. The middle classes were a law unto themselves. Her own strapping son was a straightforward George. "Tiller of the soil, from the Greek," according to the vicar who christened him and George was indeed a plowman on the nearby Ettringham Hall estate farm, as if the very naming of him had formed his destiny. Not that Mrs. Glover was much given to thinking about destiny. Or Greeks, for that matter.

"Well, must be getting on," Mrs. Glover said. "There'll be a nice steak pie for lunch. And an Egyptian pudding to follow."

Sylvie had no idea what an Egyptian pudding was. She imagined pyramids.

"We all have to keep up our strength," Mrs. Glover said.

"Yes indeed," Sylvie said. "I should probably feed Ursula again for just the same reason!" She was irritated by her own invisible exclamation mark. For reasons she couldn't quite fathom, Sylvie often found herself impelled to adopt an overly cheerful tone with Mrs. Glover, as if trying to restore some kind of natural balance of humors in the world.

Mrs. Glover couldn't suppress a slight shudder at the sight of Sylvie's pale, blue-veined breasts surging forth from her foamy lace peignoir. She hastily shooed the children ahead of her out of the room. "Porridge," she announced grimly to them.

God surely wanted this baby back," Bridget said when she came in later that morning with a cup of steaming beef tea.

"We have been tested," Sylvie said, "and found not wanting."

"This time," Bridget said.

May 1910

"A telegram," Hugh said, coming unexpectedly into the nursery and ruffling Sylvie out of the pleasant doze she had fallen into while feeding Ursula. She quickly covered herself up and said, "A telegram? Is someone dead?" for Hugh's expression hinted at catastrophe.

"From Wiesbaden."

"Ah," Sylvie said. "Izzie has had her baby, then."

"If only the bounder hadn't been married," Hugh said. "He could have made an honest woman of my sister."

"An honest woman?" Sylvie mused. "Is there such a thing?" (Did she say that out loud?) "And anyway, she's so very *young* to be married."

Hugh frowned. It made him seem more handsome. "Only two years younger than you when you married me," he said.

"Yet so much older somehow," Sylvie murmured. "Is all well? Is the baby well?"

It had turned out that Izzie was already noticeably *enceinte* by the time Hugh caught up with her and dragged her onto the boat train back from Paris. Adelaide, her mother, said she would have preferred it if Izzie had been kidnapped by white slave traders rather than throwing herself into the arms of debauchery with such enthusiasm. Sylvie found the idea of the white slave trade rather attractive—imagined herself being carried off by a desert sheikh on an Arabian steed and then lying on a cushioned divan, dressed in silks and veils, eating sweetmeats and sipping on sherbets to the bubbling sound of rills and fountains. (She expected it wasn't really like that.) A harem of women seemed like an eminently good idea to Sylvie—sharing the burden of a wife's duties and so on.

Adelaide, heroically Victorian in her attitudes, had barred the door, literally, at the sight of her youngest daughter's burgeoning belly and dispatched her back across the Channel to wait out her shame abroad. The baby would be adopted as swiftly as possible. "A respectable German couple, unable to have their own child," Adelaide said. Sylvie tried to imagine giving away a child. ("And will we never hear of it again?" she puzzled. "I certainly hope not," Adelaide said.) Izzie was now to be packed off to a finishing school in Switzerland, even though it seemed she was already finished, in more ways than one.

"A boy," Hugh said, waving the telegram like a flag. "Bouncing, et cetera."

Ursula's own first spring had unfurled. Lying in her pram beneath the beech tree, she had watched the patterns that the light made flickering through the tender green leaves as the breeze delicately swayed the branches. The branches were arms and the leaves were like hands. The tree danced for her. *Rock-a-bye baby,* Sylvie crooned to her, *in the treetop.*

I had a little nut tree, Pamela sang lispingly, *and nothing would it bear, but a silver nutmeg and a golden pear.*

A tiny hare dangled from the hood of the carriage, twirling around, the sun glinting off its silver skin. The hare sat upright in a little basket and had once adorned the top of the infant Sylvie's rattle, the rattle itself, like Sylvie's childhood, long since gone.

Bare branches, buds, leaves—the world as she knew it came and went before Ursula's eyes. She observed the turn of seasons for the first time. She was born with winter already in her bones, but then came the sharp promise of spring, the fattening of the buds, the indolent heat of summer, the mold and mushroom of autumn. From within the limited frame of the pram hood she saw it all. To say nothing of the somewhat random embellishments the seasons brought with them—sun, clouds, birds, a stray cricket ball arcing silently overhead, a rainbow once or twice, rain more often than she would have liked. (There was sometimes a tardiness to rescuing her from the elements.)

Once there had even been the stars and a rising moon—astonishing and terrifying in equal measure—when she had been forgotten one autumn evening. Bridget was castigated. The pram was outside, whatever the weather, for Sylvie had inherited a fixation with fresh air from her own mother, Lottie, who when younger had spent some time in a Swiss sanatorium, spending her days wrapped in a rug, sitting on an outdoor terrace, gazing passively at snowy Alpine peaks.

The beech shed its leaves, papery bronze drifts filling the sky above her head. One boisterously windy November day a threatening figure appeared, peering into the baby carriage. Maurice, making faces at Ursula and chanting, "Goo, goo, goo," before prodding the blankets with a stick. "Stupid baby," he said before proceeding to bury her beneath a soft pile of leaves. She started to fall asleep again beneath her new leafy cover but then a hand suddenly swatted Maurice's head and he yelled, "Ow!" and disappeared. The silver hare pirouetted round and round and a big pair of hands plucked her from the pram and Hugh said, "Here she is," as if she had been lost.

"Like a hedgehog in hibernation," he said to Sylvie.

"Poor old thing," she laughed.

Winter came again. She recognized it from the first time around.

June 1914

Ursula entered her fifth summer without further mishap. Her mother was relieved that the baby, despite (or perhaps because of) her daunting start in life, grew, thanks to Sylvie's robust regime (or perhaps in spite of it) into a steady-seeming sort of child. Ursula didn't think too much, the way Pamela sometimes did, nor did she think too little, as was Maurice's wont.

A little soldier, Sylvie thought as she watched Ursula trooping along the beach in the wake of Maurice and Pamela. How small they all looked—they *were* small, she knew that—but sometimes Sylvie was taken by surprise by the breadth of her feelings for her children. The smallest, newest, of them all—Edward—was confined to a wicker Moses basket next to her on the sand and had not yet learned to cry havoc.

They had taken a house in Cornwall for a month. Hugh stayed for the first week and Bridget for the duration. Bridget and Sylvie managed the cooking between them (rather badly) as Sylvie gave Mrs. Glover the month off so that she could go and stay in Salford with one of her sisters who had lost a son to diphtheria. Sylvie sighed with relief as she stood on the platform and watched Mrs. Glover's broad back disappearing inside the railway carriage. "You had no need to see her off," Hugh said.

"For the pleasure of seeing her go," Sylvie said.

There was hot sun and boisterous sea breezes and a hard unfamiliar bed in which Sylvie lay undisturbed all night long. They bought meat pies and fried potatoes and apple turnovers and ate them sitting on a rug on the sand with their backs against the rocks. The rental of a beach hut took care of the always tricky problem of how to feed a baby in public. Sometimes Bridget and Sylvie took off their boots and daringly dabbled their toes in the water, other times they sat on the sand beneath enormous sunshades and read their books. Sylvie was reading Conrad, while Bridget had a copy of *Jane Eyre* that Sylvie had given her as she had not thought to bring one of her usual thrilling gothic romances. Bridget proved to be an animated reader, frequently gasping in horror or stirred to disgust and, at the end, delight. It made *The Secret Agent* seem quite dry by comparison.

She was also an inland creature and spent a lot of time fretting about whether the tide was coming in or going out, seemingly incapable of understanding its predictability. "It changes a little every day," Sylvie explained patiently.

"But what on earth for?" a baffled Bridget asked.

"Well..." Sylvie had absolutely no idea. "Why not?" she concluded crisply.

The children were returning from fishing with their nets in the rock pools at the far end of the beach. Pamela and Ursula stopped halfway along and began to paddle at the water's edge but Maurice picked up the pace, sprinting toward Sylvie before flinging himself down in a flurry of sand. He was holding a small crab by its claw and Bridget screeched in alarm at the sight of it.

"Any meat pies left?" he asked.

"Manners, Maurice," Sylvie admonished. He was going to boarding school after the summer. She was rather relieved.

Come on, let's go and jump over the waves," Pamela said. Pamela was bossy but in a nice way and Ursula was nearly always happy to fall in with her plans and even if she wasn't she still went along with them.

A hoop bowled past them along the sand, as if blown by the wind, and Ursula wanted to run after it and reunite it with its owner, but Pamela said, "No, come on, let's paddle," and so they put their nets down on the sand and waded into the surf. It was a mystery that no matter how hot they were in the sun the water was always freezing. They yelped and squealed as usual before holding hands and waiting for the waves to come. When they did they were disappointingly small, no more than a ripple with a lacy frill. So they waded out further.

The waves weren't waves at all now, just the surge and tug of a swell that lifted them and then moved on past them. Ursula gripped hard on to Pamela's hand whenever the swell approached. The water was already up to her waist. Pamela pushed further out into the water, a figurehead on a prow, plowing through the buffeting waves. The water was up to Ursula's armpits now and she started to cry and pull on Pamela's hand, trying to stop her from going any further. Pamela glanced back at her and said, "Careful, you'll make us both fall over," and so didn't see the huge wave cresting behind her. Within a heartbeat, it had crashed over both of them, tossing them around as lightly as though they were leaves.

Ursula felt herself being pulled under, deeper and deeper, as if she were miles out to sea, not within sight of the shore. Her little legs bicycled beneath her, trying to find purchase on the sand. If she could just stand up and fight the waves, but there was no longer any sand to stand on and she began to choke on water, thrashing around in panic. Someone would come, surely? Bridget or Sylvie, and save her. Or Pamela—where was she?

No one came. And there was only water. Water and more water. Her helpless little heart was beating wildly, a bird trapped in her chest. A thousand bees buzzed in the curled pearl of her ear. No breath. A drowning child, a bird dropped from the sky.

Darkness fell.

SNOW

11 February 1910

Bridget removed the breakfast tray and Sylvie said, "Oh, leave the little snowdrop. Here, put it on my bedside table." She kept the baby with her too. The fire was blazing now and the bright snowlight from the window seemed both cheerful and oddly portentous at the same time. The snow was drifting against the walls of the house, pressing in on them, burying them. They were cocooned. She imagined Hugh tunneling heroically through the snow to reach home. He had been away three days now, looking for his sister Isobel. Yesterday (how long ago that seemed now) a telegram had arrived from Paris, saying, THE QUARRY HAS GONE TO GROUND STOP AM IN PURSUIT STOP, although Hugh was not really a hunting man. She must send her own telegram. What should she say? Something cryptic. Hugh liked puzzles. WE WERE FOUR STOP YOU ARE GONE BUT WE ARE STILL FOUR STOP (Bridget and Mrs. Glover did not count in Sylvie's tally). Or something more prosaic. BABY HAS ARRIVED STOP ALL WELL STOP. Were they? All well? The baby had nearly died. She had been deprived of air. What if she wasn't quite right? They had triumphed over death this night. Sylvie wondered when death would seek his revenge.

Sylvie finally fell asleep and dreamed that she had moved to a new house and was looking for her children, roaming the unfamiliar rooms, shouting their names, but she knew they had disappeared forever and would never be found. She woke with a start and was relieved to see that at least the baby was still by her side in the great white snowfield of the bed. The baby. Ursula. Sylvie had had the name ready, Edward if it had turned out to be a boy. The naming of children was her preserve, Hugh seemed indifferent to what they were called although Sylvie supposed he had his limits. Scheherazade perhaps. Or Guinevere.

Ursula opened her milky eyes and seemed to fix her gaze on the weary snowdrop. *Rock-a-bye baby,* Sylvie crooned. How calm the house was. How deceptive that could be. One could lose everything in the blink of an eye, the slip of a foot. "One must avoid dark thoughts at all costs," she said to Ursula.

WAR

June 1914

Mr. Winton—Archibald—had set up his easel on the sand and was attempting to render a seascape in watery marine smears of blue and green—Prussians and Cobalt Blues, Viridian and Terre Verte. He daubed a couple of rather vague seagulls in the sky, sky that was virtually indistinguishable from the waves below. He imagined showing the picture on his return home, saying, "In the style of the Impressionists, you know."

Mr. Winton, a bachelor, was by profession a senior clerk in a factory in Birmingham that manufactured pins but was a romantic by nature. He was a member of a cycling club and every Sunday tried to wheel as far away from Birmingham's smogs as he could, and he took his annual holiday by the sea so that he could breathe hospitable air and think himself an artist for a week.

He thought he might try to put some figures in his painting, it would give it a bit of life and "movement," something his night-school teacher (he took an art class) had encouraged him to introduce into his work. Those two little girls down at the sea's edge would do. Their sun hats meant he wouldn't need to try and capture their features, a skill he hadn't yet quite mastered.

Come on, let's go and jump the waves," Pamela said.

"Oh," Ursula said, hanging back. Pamela took her hand and dragged her into the water. "Don't be a silly." The closer she got to the water the more Ursula began to panic until she was swamped with fear but Pamela laughed and splashed her way into the water and she could only follow. She tried to think of something that would make Pamela want to return to the beach—a treasure map, a man with a puppy—but it was too late. A huge wave rose, curling above their heads, and came crashing over them, sending them down, down into the watery world.

Sylvie was startled to look up from her book and see a man, a stranger, walking toward her along the sand with one of her girls tucked under each arm, as if he was carrying geese or chickens. The girls were sopping wet and tearful. "Went out a bit too far," the man said. "But they'll be fine."

They treated their rescuer, a Mr. Winton, a clerk ("senior") to tea and cakes in a hotel that overlooked the sea. "It's the least I can do," Sylvie said. "You have ruined your boots."

"It was nothing," Mr. Winton said modestly.

"Oh, no, it was most definitely *something,*" Sylvie said.

Glad to be back?" Hugh beamed, greeting them on the station platform.

"Are you glad to have us back?" Sylvie said, somewhat combatively.

"There's a surprise for you at home," Hugh said. Sylvie didn't like surprises, they all knew that.

"Guess," Hugh said.

They guessed a new puppy which was a far cry from the Petter engine that Hugh had had installed in the cellar. They all trooped down the steep stone staircase and stared at its oily throbbing presence, its rows of glass accumulators. "Let there be light," Hugh said.

It would be a long time before any of them were able to snap a light switch without expecting to be blown up. Light was all it could manage, of course. Bridget had hoped for a vacuum cleaner to replace her Ewbank but there wasn't enough voltage. "Thank goodness," Sylvie said.

July 1914

From the open French windows Sylvie watched Maurice erecting a makeshift tennis net, which mostly seemed to involve whacking everything in sight with a mallet. Small boys were a mystery to Sylvie. The satisfaction they gained from throwing sticks or stones for hours on end, the obsessive collection of inanimate objects, the brutal destruction of the fragile world around them, all seemed at odds with the men they were supposed to become.

Noisy chatter in the hallway announced the jaunty arrival of Margaret and Lily, once school friends and now infrequent acquaintances, bearing gaily beribboned gifts for the new baby, Edward.

Margaret was an artist, militantly unmarried, conceivably someone's mistress, a scandalous possibility that Sylvie hadn't mentioned to Hugh. Lily was a Fabian, a society suffragette who risked nothing for her beliefs. Sylvie thought of women being restrained while tubes were pushed down their throats and raised a reassuring hand to her own lovely white neck. Lily's husband, Cavendish (the name of a hotel, not a man, surely), had once cornered Sylvie at a tea dance, pressing her up against a pillar with his goatish, cigar-scented body, suggesting something so outrageous that even now she felt hot with embarrassment at the thought of it.

"Ah, the fresh air," Lily exclaimed when Sylvie led them out into the garden. "It's so *rural* here." They cooed like doves—or pigeons, that lesser species—over the pram, admiring the baby almost as much as they applauded Sylvie's svelte figure.

"I'll ring for tea," Sylvie said, already tired.

They had a dog. A big, brindled French mastiff called Bosun. "The name of Byron's dog," Sylvie said. Ursula had no idea who the mysterious Byron was but he showed no interest in reclaiming his dog from them. Bosun had soft loose furry skin that rolled beneath Ursula's fingers and his breath smelled of the scrag end that Mrs. Glover, to her disgust, had to stew for him. He was a good dog, Hugh said, a responsible dog, the kind that pulled people from burning buildings and rescued them from drowning.

Pamela liked to dress Bosun up in an old bonnet and shawl and pretend that he was her baby, although they had a real baby now—a boy, Edward. Everyone called him Teddy. Their mother seemed taken by surprise by the new baby. "I don't know where he came from." Sylvie had a laugh like a hiccup. She was taking tea on the lawn with two school friends "from her London days" who had come to inspect the new arrival. All three of them wore lovely flimsy dresses and big straw hats and sat in the wicker chairs, drinking tea and eating Mrs. Glover's sherry cake. Ursula and Bosun sat on the grass a polite distance away, hoping for crumbs.

Maurice had put up a net and was trying, not very enthusiastically, to teach Pamela how to play tennis. Ursula was occupied in making a daisy-chain coronet for Bosun. She had stubby, clumsy fingers. Sylvie had the long, deft fingers of an artist or a pianist. She played on the piano in the drawing room ("Chopin"). Sometimes they sang rounds after tea but Ursula never managed to sing her part at the right time. ("What a dolt," Maurice said. "Practice makes perfect," Sylvie said.) When she opened the lid of the piano there was a smell that was like the insides of old suitcases. It reminded Ursula of her grandmother, Adelaide, who spent her days swathed in black, sipping Madeira.

The new arrival was tucked away in the huge baby carriage under the big beech tree. They had all been occupants of this magnificence but none of them could remember it. A little silver hare dangled from the hood and the baby was cozy beneath a coverlet "embroidered by nuns," although no one ever explained who these nuns were and why they had spent their days embroidering small yellow ducks.

"Edward," one of Sylvie's friends said. "Teddy?"

"Ursula and Teddy. My two little bears," Sylvie said and laughed her hiccup laugh. Ursula wasn't at all sure about being a bear. She would rather be a dog. She lay down on her back and stared up at the sky. Bosun groaned mightily and stretched out beside her. Swallows were knifing recklessly through the blue. She could hear the delicate chink of cups on saucers, the creak and clatter of a lawn mower being pushed by Old Tom in the Coles' garden next door, and could smell the peppery-sweet perfume of the pinks in the border and the heady green of new-mown grass.

"Ah," said one of Sylvie's London friends, stretching out her legs and revealing graceful white-stockinged ankles. "A long, hot summer. Isn't it delicious?"

The peace was broken by a disgusted Maurice throwing his racquet onto the grass where it bounced with a thump and a squeak. "I can't teach her—she's a girl!" he yelled and stalked off into the shrubbery where he began to bash things with a stick, although in his head he was in the jungle with a machete. He was going to boarding school after the summer. It was the same school that Hugh had been to, and his father before *him*. ("And so on, back to the Conquest probably," Sylvie said.) Hugh said it would be "the making" of Maurice but he seemed quite made already to Ursula. Hugh said when he first went to the school he cried himself to sleep every night and yet he seemed more than happy to subject Maurice to the same torture. Maurice puffed out his chest and declared that *he* wouldn't cry.

("And what about us?" a worried Pamela asked. "Shall we have to go away to school?"

"Not unless you're very naughty," Hugh said, laughing.)

A pink-cheeked Pamela balled up her fists and, planting them on her hips, roared, "You're such a pig!" after Maurice's indifferent, retreating back. She made "pig" sound like a much worse word than it was. Pigs were quite nice.

"Pammy," Sylvie said mildly. "You sound like a fishwife."

Ursula edged nearer to the source of cake.

"Oh, come here," one of the women said to her, "let me look at you." Ursula tried to shy away but was held firmly in place by Sylvie. "She's quite pretty, isn't she?" Sylvie's friend said. "She takes after you, Sylvie."

"Fish have wives?" Ursula said to her mother and Sylvie's friends laughed, lovely bubbling laughs. "What a funny little thing," one of them said.

"Yes, she's a real hoot," Sylvie said.

Yes, she's a real hoot," Sylvie said.

"Children," Margaret said, "they are droll, aren't they?"

They are so much more than that, Sylvie thought, but how do you explain the magnitude of motherhood to someone who has no children? Sylvie felt positively matronly in her present company, the friends of her brief girlhood curtailed by the relief of marriage.

Bridget came out with the tray and started to take away the tea things. In the mornings Bridget wore a striped print dress for housework but in the afternoons she changed into a black dress with white cuffs and collar and a matching white apron and little cap. She had been elevated out of the scullery. Alice had left to get married and Sylvie had engaged a girl from the village, Marjorie, a boss-eyed thirteen-year-old, to help with the rough work. ("We couldn't get by with just two of them?" Hugh queried mildly. "Bridget and Mrs. G.? It's not as if they're running a mansion."

"No, we can't," Sylvie said and that was the end of that.)

The little white cap was too big for Bridget and was forever slipping over her eyes, like a blindfold. On her way back across the lawn she was suddenly blinkered by the cap and tripped, a music-hall tumble that she rescued just in time and the only casualties were the silver sugar bowl and tongs that went shooting through the air, lumps of sugar scattering like blind dice across the green of the lawn. Maurice laughed extravagantly at Bridget's misfortune, and Sylvie said, "Maurice, stop playing the fool."

She watched as Bosun and Ursula picked up the jettisoned sugar lumps, Bosun with his big pink tongue, Ursula, eccentrically, with the tricky tongs. Bosun swallowed his quickly without chewing. Ursula sucked hers slowly, one by one. Sylvie suspected that Ursula was destined to be the odd one out. An only child herself, she was frequently disturbed by the complexity of sibling relationships among her own children.

"You should come up to London," Margaret said suddenly. "Stay with me for a few days. We could have such fun."

"But the children," Sylvie said. "The baby. I can hardly leave them."

"Why not?" Lily said. "Your nanny can manage for a few days, surely?"

"But I have no nanny," Sylvie said. Lily cast her eyes around the garden as if she was looking for a nanny lurking in the hydrangeas. "Nor do I want one," Sylvie added. (Or did she?) Motherhood was her responsibility, her destiny. It was, lacking anything else (and what else could there be?), her life. The future of England was clutched to Sylvie's bosom. Replacing her was not a casual undertaking, as if her absence meant little more than her presence. "And I am feeding the baby myself," she added. Both women seemed astonished. Lily unconsciously clasped a hand to her own bosom as if to protect it from assault.

"It's what God intended," Sylvie said, even though she hadn't believed in God since the loss of Tiffin. Hugh rescued her, striding across the lawn like a man with a purpose. He laughed and said,

"What's going on here, then?" picking up Ursula and tossing her casually in the air, only stopping when she started to choke on a sugar lump. He smiled at Sylvie and said, "Your friends," as if she might have forgotten who they were.

"Friday evening," Hugh said, depositing Ursula back on the grass, "the working man's labors are over and I believe the sun is officially over the yardarm. Would you lovely ladies like to move on to something stronger than tea? Gin slings perhaps?" Hugh had four younger sisters and felt comfortable with women. That in itself was enough to charm them. Sylvie knew his instincts were to chaperone, not to court, but she did occasionally wonder about his popularity and where it might lead. Or, indeed, have already led.

A détente was brokered between Maurice and Pamela. Sylvie asked Bridget to drag a table out onto the small but useful terrace so that the children could eat their tea outside—herring roe on toast and a pink shape that was barely set and quivered without restraint. The sight of it made Sylvie feel slightly queasy. "Nursery food," Hugh said with relish, observing his children eating.

"Austria has declared war on Serbia," Hugh said conversationally and Margaret said, "How silly. I spent a wonderful weekend in Vienna last year. At the Imperial, do you know it?"

"Not intimately," Hugh said.

Sylvie knew it but did not say so.

The evening turned into gossamer. Sylvie, drifting gently on a mist of alcohol, suddenly remembered her father's cognac-induced demise and clapped her hands as if killing a small annoying fly and said, "Time for bed, children," and watched as Bridget pushed the heavy pram awkwardly across the grass. Sylvie sighed and Hugh helped her up from her chair, bussing her cheek once she was on her feet.

* * *

Sylvie propped open the tiny skylight window in the baby's stuffy room. They called it the "nursery" but it was no more than a box tucked into a corner of the eaves, airless in summer and freezing in winter, and thereby totally unsuitable for a tender infant. Like Hugh, Sylvie considered that children should be toughened up early, the better to take the blows in later life. (The loss of a nice house in Mayfair, a beloved pony, a faith in an omniscient deity.) She sat on the button-backed velvet nursing chair and fed Edward. "Teddy," she murmured fondly as he gulped and choked his way to sated sleep. Sylvie liked them all best as babies, when they were shiny and new, like the pink pads on a kitten's paw. This one was special though. She kissed the floss on his head.

Words floated up in the soft air. "All good things must come to an end," she heard Hugh say as he escorted Lily and Margaret indoors to dinner. "I believe the poetically inclined Mrs. Glover has baked a skate. But first, perhaps you would care to see my Petter engine?" The women twittered like the silly schoolgirls they still were.

Ursula was woken by an excited shouting and clapping of hands. "Electricity!" she heard one of Sylvie's friends exclaim. "How wonderful!"

She shared an attic room with Pamela. They had matching small beds with a rag rug and a bedside cabinet in between. Pamela slept with her arms above her head and sometimes cried out as if pricked with a pin (a horrible trick Maurice was fond of). On one side of the bedroom wall was Mrs. Glover who snored like a train and on the other side Bridget muttered her way through the night. Bosun slept outside their door, always on guard even when asleep. Sometimes he whined softly but whether in pleasure or pain they couldn't tell. The attic floor was a crowded and unquiet sort of place.

Ursula was woken again later by the visitors taking their leave. ("That child is an unnaturally light sleeper," Mrs. Glover said, as if it were a flaw in her character that should be corrected.) She climbed out of bed and padded over to the window. If she stood on a chair and looked out, something they were all expressly forbidden to do, then she could see Sylvie and her friends on the lawn below, their dresses fluttering like moths in the encroaching dusk. Hugh stood at the back gate, waiting to escort them along the lane to the station.

Sometimes Bridget walked the children to the station to meet their father off the train when he came home from work. Maurice said he might be an engine driver when he was older, or he might become an Antarctic explorer like Sir Ernest Shackleton who was about to set sail on his grand expedition. Or perhaps he would simply become a banker, like his father.

Hugh worked in London, a place they visited infrequently to spend stilted afternoons in their grandmother's drawing room in Hampstead, a quarrelsome Maurice and Pamela "fraying" Sylvie's nerves so that she was always in a bad mood on the train home.

When everyone had left, their voices fading into the distance, Sylvie walked back across the lawn toward the house, a darkening shadow now as the black bat unfolded his wings. Unseen by Sylvie, a fox trotted purposefully in her footsteps before veering off and disappearing into the shrubbery.

Did you hear something?" Sylvie asked. She was propped up on pillows, reading an early Forster. "The baby perhaps?"

Hugh cocked his head to one side. For a moment he reminded Sylvie of Bosun.

"No," he said.

The baby slept all through the night usually. He was a cherub. But not in heaven. Thankfully.

"The best one yet," Hugh said.

"Yes, I think we should keep this one."

"He doesn't look like me," Hugh said.

"No," she agreed amiably. "Nothing like you at all."

Hugh laughed and, kissing her affectionately, said, "Good night, I'm turning out my light."

"I think I'll read a little longer."

One afternoon of heat a few days later they went to watch the harvest being brought in.

Sylvie and Bridget walked across the fields with the girls, Sylvie carrying the baby in a sling that Bridget fashioned from her shawl and tied around Sylvie's torso. "Like a Hibernian peasant," Hugh said, amused. It was a Saturday and, freed from the gloomy confines of banking, he was lying on the wicker chaise longue on the terrace at the back of the house, cradling *Wisden Cricketers' Almanack* like a hymnal.

Maurice had disappeared after breakfast. He was a nine-year-old boy and free to go where he pleased with whomsoever he pleased, although he tended to keep to the exclusive company of other nine-year-old boys. Sylvie had no idea what they did but at the end of the day he would return, filthy from head to toe and with some unappetizing trophy, a jar of frogs or worms, a dead bird, the bleached skull of some small creature.

The sun had long since started on its steep climb into the sky by the time they finally set off, awkwardly encumbered with the baby, and picnic baskets, sunbonnets and parasols. Bosun trotted along at their side like a small pony. "Goodness, we're burdened like refugees," Sylvie said. "The Jews leaving Israel, perhaps."

"Jews?" Bridget said, screwing up her plain features in distaste.

Teddy slept throughout the trek in his makeshift papoose while they clambered over stiles and stumbled on muddy ruts made hard by the sun. Bridget tore her dress on a nail and said she had blisters on her feet. Sylvie wondered about removing her corsets and leaving them by the wayside, imagined someone's puzzlement when they came across them. She had a sudden memory, unexpected in the dazzling daylight in a field of cows, of Hugh unlacing her stays on honeymoon in their hotel in Deauville while sounds drifted in from the open window—gulls screeching on the wing and a man and a woman arguing in rough, rapid French. On the boat home from Cherbourg Sylvie was already carrying the tiny homunculus that would become Maurice, although she had been blissfully unaware of this fact at the time.

"Ma'am?" Bridget said, breaking this reverie. "Mrs. Todd? They're not *cows*."

They stopped to admire George Glover's plow horses, enormous Shires called Samson and Nelson who snorted and shook their heads when they caught sight of company. They made Ursula nervous but Sylvie fed them an apple each and they picked the fruit delicately from her palm with their big pink-velvet lips. Sylvie said they were dappled grays and much more beautiful than people and Pamela said, "Even children?" and Sylvie said, "Yes, especially children," and laughed.

They found George himself helping with the harvest. When he caught sight of them he strode across the field to greet them. "Ma'am," he said to Sylvie, removing his cap and wiping the sweat off his forehead with a big red-and-white-spotted handkerchief. Tiny pieces of chaff were stuck to his arms. Like the chaff, the hairs on his arms were golden from the sun. "It's hot," he said unnecessarily. He looked at Sylvie from beneath the long lock of hair that always fell in his handsome blue eyes. Sylvie appeared to blush.

As well as their own lunch—bloater-paste sandwiches, lemon

curd sandwiches, ginger beer and seed cake—they had carried the remains of yesterday's pork pie that Mrs. Glover had sent for George, along with a little jar of her famous piccalilli. The seedcake was already stale because Bridget had forgotten to put it back in the cake tin and it was left out in the warm kitchen overnight. "I wouldn't be surprised if the ants had laid eggs in it," Mrs. Glover said. When it came to eating it, Ursula had to pick out the seeds, which were legion, checking each one to make sure it wasn't an ant egg.

The workers in the field stopped to have their lunch, bread and cheese and beer mainly. Bridget turned red and giggled as she handed over the pork pie to George. Pamela told Ursula that Maurice said Bridget had a pash on George, although it seemed to both of them that Maurice was an unlikely source of information on affairs of the heart. They ate their picnic at the edge of the stubble, George sprawled casually as he took great horse-sized bites out of the pork pie, Bridget gazing at him in admiration as if he were a Greek god, while Sylvie fussed with the baby.

Sylvie traipsed off to find a discreet spot in order to feed Teddy. Girls brought up in nice houses in Mayfair did not generally duck behind hedges to suckle infants. Like Hibernian peasants, no doubt. She thought fondly of the beach hut in Cornwall. By the time she found a suitable covert in the lee of a hedge, Teddy was bawling his head off, little pugilistic fists clenched against the injustice of the world. Just as he settled at the breast she happened to glance up and caught sight of George Glover coming out of the trees at the far end of the field. Spotting her, he stopped, staring at her like a startled deer. For a second he didn't move but then he doffed his cap and said, "Still hot, ma'am."

"It certainly is," Sylvie said briskly and then watched as George

Glover hastened toward the five-bar gate that broke the hedgerow in the middle of the field and leapt over it as easily as a big hunter over a hurdle.

From a safe distance they watched the enormous harvester noisily eating the wheat. "Hypnotic, isn't it?" Bridget said. She had recently learned the word. Sylvie took out her pretty little gold fob watch, an article much coveted by Pamela, and said, "Heavens above, look at the time," although none of them did. "We must be getting back."

Just as they were leaving, George Glover shouted, "Heyathere!" and cantered toward them across the field. He was carrying something cuddled in his cap. Two baby rabbits. "Oh," Pamela said, tearful with excitement.

"Conies," George Glover said. "All huddled up in the middle of the field. Their mother gone. Take them, why don't you? One each."

On the way home, Pamela carried both baby rabbits in her pinafore, holding it out proudly in front of her like Bridget with a tea tray.

Look at you," Hugh said when they walked wearily through the garden gate. "Golden and kissed by the sun. You look like real countrywomen."

"More red than gold, I'm afraid," Sylvie said ruefully.

The gardener was at work. He was called Old Tom ("Like a cat," Sylvie said. "Do you think he was once called Young Tom?"). He worked six days a week, sharing his time between them and another house nearby. These neighbors, the Coles, addressed him as "Mr. Ridgely." He gave no indication which he preferred. The Coles lived in a very similar house to the Todds' and Mr. Cole, like Hugh, was a banker. "Jewish," Sylvie said in the same voice she would use for "Catholic"—intrigued yet unsettled by such exoticism.

"I don't think they practice," Hugh said. Practice what? Ursula wondered. Pamela had to practice her piano scales every evening before tea, a *plinking* and *plonking* that wasn't very pleasant to listen to.

Mr. Cole had been born with a quite different name, according to their eldest son, Simon, something far too complicated for English tongues. The middle son, Daniel, was friends with Maurice, for although the grown-ups weren't friends the children were familiar with each other. Simon, "a swot" (Maurice said), helped Maurice every Monday evening with his maths. Sylvie was unsure how to reward him for this disagreeable task, perplexed seemingly by his Jewishness. "Perhaps I might give him something that would offend them?" she speculated. "If I give money they might think I'm referring to their well-known reputation for miserliness. If I give sweets they might not fit their dietary strictures."

"They don't practice," Hugh repeated. "They're not *observant.*"

"Benjamin's very observant," Pamela said. "He found a blackbird's nest yesterday." She glared at Maurice when she said this. He had come upon them marveling at the beautiful eggs, blue and freckled brown, and had grabbed them and cracked them open on a stone. He thought it was a great joke. Pamela threw a small (well, smallish) rock at him that hit him on the head. "There," she said. "How does it feel to have *your* shell broken open?" Now he had a nasty cut and a bruise on his temple. "Fell," he said shortly when Sylvie inquired how he came by the injury. He would, by nature, have told on Pamela, but the initial sin would have come to light and Sylvie would have punished him soundly for breaking the eggs. She had caught him stealing eggs before now and had boxed his ears. Sylvie said they should "revere" nature, not destroy it, but reverence was not in Maurice's own nature, unfortunately.

"He's learning the violin, isn't he—Simon?" Sylvie said. "Jews are usually very musical, aren't they? Perhaps I could give him some sheet music, something like that." This discussion of the perils of offending Judaism had taken place around the breakfast table. Hugh always looked vaguely startled to find his children at the same table as him. He hadn't eaten breakfast with his parents until he was twelve years old and deemed fit to leave the nursery. He was the robust graduate of an efficient nanny, a household within a household in Hampstead. The infant Sylvie, on the other hand, had dined late, on *Canard à la presse,* perched precariously on cushions, lulled by flickering candles and twinkling silverware, while her parents' conversation floated above her head. It was not, she now suspected, an entirely regular childhood.

Old Tom was double-digging a trench, he said, for a new asparagus bed. Hugh had long since abandoned *Wisden* and had been picking raspberries to fill a big white enamel bowl that both Pamela and Ursula recognized as the one that Maurice had until recently been keeping tadpoles in, although neither of them mentioned this fact. Pouring himself a glass of beer, Hugh said, "Thirsty work, this agricultural labor," and they all laughed. Except for Old Tom.

Mrs. Glover came out to demand that Old Tom dig up some potatoes to go with her beef collops. She huffed and puffed at the sight of the rabbits, "Not enough even for a stew." Pamela screamed and had to be calmed down with a sip of Hugh's beer.

Pamela and Ursula made a nest, in a lost corner of the garden, out of grass and cotton wool, decorated with fallen rose petals, and carefully placed the baby rabbits in it. Pamela sang them a lullaby, she could keep a tune nicely, but they had been asleep ever since George Glover had handed them over.

"I think they might be too small," Sylvie said. Too small for what? Ursula wondered but Sylvie didn't say.

They sat on the lawn and ate the raspberries with cream and sugar. Hugh looked up into the blue, blue sky and said, "Did you hear that thunder? There's going to be a tremendous storm, I can feel it coming. Can't you, Old Tom?" he raised his voice so that Old Tom, far away in the vegetable bed, could hear. Hugh believed that, as a gardener, Old Tom must know about weather. Old Tom said nothing and carried on digging.

"He's deaf," Hugh said.

No, he isn't," Sylvie said, making a Rose Madder by mashing raspberries, beautiful like blood, into thick cream, and she thought, unexpectedly, about George Glover. A son of the soil. His strong square hands, his beautiful dappled grays, like big rocking horses, and the way he had lolled on the grassy bank eating his lunch, posed rather like Michelangelo's Adam in the Sistine Chapel but reaching for another slice of pork pie rather than the hand of his Creator. (When Sylvie had accompanied her father, Llewellyn, to Italy she had been astonished by the amount of male flesh available to view as art.) She imagined feeding George Glover apples from her hand and laughed.

"What?" Hugh said and Sylvie said, "What a handsome boy George Glover is."

"He must be adopted then," Hugh said.

In bed that night Sylvie abandoned Forster for less cerebral pursuits, entwining overheated limbs in the marital bed, more a panting hart than a soaring lark. She found herself thinking not of Hugh's smooth, wiry body but of the great burnished centaureal limbs of George Glover. "You're very..." a spent Hugh said, gazing at the bedroom cornice as he searched for an appropriate word. "Lively," he concluded finally.

"It must be all that fresh air," Sylvie said.

Golden and kissed by the sun, she thought as she drifted comfortably off to sleep and then Shakespeare came unwontedly to mind.

Golden lads and girls all must, / as chimney-sweepers, come to dust, and she felt suddenly afraid.

"There's the storm rolling in at last," Hugh said. "Shall I turn out the light?"

Sylvie and Hugh were ejected from their Sunday-morning slumber by a wailing Pamela. She and Ursula had woken early with excitement and rushed outside to find that the rabbits had disappeared, only the fluffy pom-pom of one tiny tail remaining, white smudged with red.

"Foxes," Mrs. Glover said, with some satisfaction. "What did you expect?"

January 1915

"Did you hear the latest news?" Bridget asked.

Sylvie sighed and put down the letter from Hugh, its pages as brittle as dead leaves. It was only a matter of months since he had left for the Front yet she could hardly remember being married to him anymore. Hugh was a captain in the Ox and Bucks. Last summer he was a banker. It seemed absurd.

His letters were cheerful and guarded (*the men are wonderful, they have such character*). He used to mention these men by name ("Bert," "Alfred," "Wilfred") but since the Battle of Ypres they had become simply "men" and Sylvie wondered if Bert and Alfred and Wilfred were dead. Hugh never mentioned death or dying, it was as if they were away on a jaunt, a picnic (*An awful lot of rain this week. Mud everywhere. Hope you are enjoying better weather than we are!*).

"To war? You are going to war?" she had shouted at him when he enlisted and it struck her that she had never shouted at him before. Perhaps she should have.

If there was to be a war, Hugh explained to her, he didn't want to look back and know that he had missed it, that others had stepped forward for their country's honor and he had not. "It may be the only adventure I ever have," he said.

"Adventure?" she echoed in disbelief. "What about your children, what about your *wife?*"

"But it's for you that I am doing this," he said, looking exquisitely pained, a misunderstood Theseus. Sylvie disliked him intensely in that moment. "To protect hearth and home," he persisted. "To defend everything we believe in."

"And yet I heard the word *adventure,*" Sylvie said, turning her back on him.

Nonetheless, she had, of course, gone up to London to see him off. They had been jostled by an enormous flag-waving throng who were cheering as if a great victory had already been won. Sylvie was surprised by the rabid patriotism of the women on the platform, surely war should make pacifists of all women?

Hugh had held her close to him as if they were new sweethearts and only jumped on the train at the very last moment. He was instantly swallowed by the crush of uniformed men. *His regiment,* she thought. How odd. Like the crowd, he had seemed immensely, stupidly cheerful.

When the train began to heave itself slowly out of the station the excitable crowd roared their approval, frantically waving their flags and throwing caps and hats in the air. Sylvie could only stare blindly at the carriage windows as they passed by, first slowly and then more and more rapidly until they were no more than a blur. She could see no sign of Hugh, nor, she supposed, could he see her.

She remained on the platform after everyone else had left, staring at the spot on the horizon where the train had disappeared.

Sylvie abandoned the letter and took up her knitting needles instead.

"*Did* you hear the news?" Bridget persisted. She was placing the cutlery on the tea table. Sylvie frowned at the knitting on her needles and wondered if she wanted to hear any news that had Bridget as its provenance. She cast off a stitch on the raglan sleeve of the serviceable gray jersey that she was knitting for Maurice. All the women of the household now spent an inordinate amount of time knitting—mufflers and mittens, gloves and socks and hats, vests and sweaters—to keep their men warm.

Mrs. Glover sat by the kitchen stove in the evening and knitted huge gloves, big enough to fit over the hooves of George's plow horses. They were not for Samson and Nelson, of course, but for George himself, one of the first to volunteer, Mrs. Glover said proudly at every opportunity, making Sylvie quite crotchety. Even Marjorie, the scullery maid, had been taken by the knitting fad, laboring after lunch on something that looked like a dishcloth, although to call it "knitting" was generous. "More holes than wool" was Mrs. Glover's verdict, before boxing her ears and telling her to get back to work.

Bridget had taken to making misshapen socks—she could not turn a heel for the life of her—for her new love. She had "given her heart" to a groom from Ettringham Hall called Sam Wellington. "Oh, for sure, he's an old boot," she said and laughed her head off at her joke, several times a day, as if telling it for the first time. Bridget sent Sam Wellington sentimental postcards in which angels hovered in the air over women who wept while sitting at chenille-covered tables in domestic parlors. Sylvie had hinted to Bridget that perhaps she should send more cheerful missives to a man at war.

Bridget kept a photograph, a studio portrait, of Sam Wellington on her rather poorly appointed dressing table. It took pride of place next to the old enameled brush and comb set that Sylvie had given her when Hugh had bought her a silver vanity set for her birthday.

A similar obligatory likeness of George adorned Mrs. Glover's bedside table. Trussed in uniform and uncomfortable before a studio backdrop that reminded Sylvie of the Amalfi coast, George Glover no longer resembled a Sistine Adam. Sylvie thought of all the enlisted men who had already undergone the same ritual, a keepsake for mothers and sweethearts, the only photograph that would ever be taken of some of them. "He could be killed," Bridget said of her beau, "and I might forget what he looked like." Sylvie had plenty of photographs of Hugh. He led a well-documented life.

All of the children, except for Pamela, were upstairs. Teddy was asleep in his cot, or perhaps he was awake in his cot, whichever state he was in, he was not complaining. Maurice and Ursula were doing Sylvie knew-not-what and she was not interested in it as it meant that tranquillity reigned in the morning room, apart from the occasional suspicious thud on the ceiling and the metallic report of heavy pans in the kitchen where Mrs. Glover was making her feelings about something known—the war or Marjorie's incompetence, or both.

Ever since the fighting on the continent began they had been taking their meals in the morning room, abandoning the Regency Revival dining table as too extravagant for wartime austerity and instead espousing the little parlor table. ("Not using the dining room isn't going to win the war," Mrs. Glover said.)

Sylvie gestured to Pamela who obediently followed her mother's mute orders and trailed round the table after Bridget, turning the cutlery the right way round. Bridget couldn't tell her right from her left or her up from her down.

Pamela's support for the expeditionary force had taken the form of a mass production of dun-colored mufflers of extraordinary and impractical lengths. Sylvie was pleasantly surprised by her elder daughter's capacity for monotony. It would stand her in good stead for her life to come. Sylvie lost a stitch and muttered an oath that startled Pamela and Bridget. "What news?" she asked at last, reluctantly.

"Bombs have been dropped on Norfolk," Bridget said, proud of her information.

"Bombs?" Sylvie said, looking up from her knitting. "In *Norfolk?*"

"A Zeppelin raid," Bridget said authoritatively. "That's the Hun for you. They don't care who they kill. They're wicked, so they are. They eat Belgian babies."

"Well..." Sylvie said, hooking the lost stitch, "that might be a slight exaggeration."

Pamela hesitated, dessert fork in one hand, spoon in the other, as if she was about to attempt an attack on one of Mrs. Glover's heavy-weight puddings. "Eat?" she echoed in horror. "Babies?"

"No," Sylvie said crossly. "Don't be silly."

Mrs. Glover shouted for Bridget from the depths of the kitchen and Bridget flew to her command. Sylvie could hear Bridget yelling, in turn, up the stairs to the other children, "Yer tea is on the table!"

Pamela sighed the sigh of someone with a lifetime behind them already and sat at the table. She stared blankly at the cloth and said, "I miss Daddy."

"Me too, darling," Sylvie said. "Me too. Now don't be a goose, go and tell the others to wash their hands."

At Christmas, Sylvie had packaged up a great box of goods for Hugh: the inevitable socks and gloves, one of Pamela's endless mufflers and, as an antidote to this, a two-ply cashmere comforter knitted by Sylvie and baptized with her favorite perfume, La Rose Jacqueminot, to remind him of home. She imagined Hugh on the battlefield wearing the comforter next to his skin, a gallant jousting knight sporting a lady's favor. This daydream of chivalry was a comfort in itself, preferable to the glimpses of something darker. They had spent a wintry weekend in Broadstairs, bundled in gaiters, bodices and balaclavas, and heard the booming of the great guns across the water.

The Christmas box also contained a plum cake baked by Mrs. Glover, a tin of somewhat misshapen peppermint creams made by Pamela, cigarettes, a bottle of good malt whisky and a book of poetry—an anthology of English verse, mostly pastoral and not too taxing—as well as little handmade gifts from Maurice (a balsa-wood plane) and a drawing from Ursula of blue sky and green grass and the tiny distorted figure of a dog. "Bosun," Sylvie wrote helpfully across the top. She had no idea whether or not Hugh had received the box.

Christmas was a dull affair. Izzie came and talked a great deal about nothing (or rather herself) before announcing that she had joined the Voluntary Aid Detachment and was leaving for France as soon as the festivities were over.

"But, Izzie," Sylvie said, "you can't nurse or cook or type or do anything useful." The words came out harsher than she intended, but really Izzie was such a cuckoo. ("Flibbertigibbet" was Mrs. Glover's verdict.)

"That's it then," Bridget said when she heard of Izzie's call to alms, "we'll have lost the war by Lent." Izzie never mentioned her baby. He had been adopted in Germany and Sylvie supposed he was a German citizen. How strange that he was only a little younger than Ursula but, officially, he was the enemy.

Then at New Year, one by one, all the children came down with chicken pox. Izzie was on the next train to London as soon as the first spot erupted on Pamela's face. So much for Florence Nightingale, Sylvie said irritably to Bridget.

Ursula, despite her clumsy, stubby fingers, had now joined in the household's knitting frenzy. For Christmas she received a wooden French knitting doll called La Reine Solange which Sylvie said meant "Queen Solange" although she was "doubtful" that there ever was a Queen Solange in history. Queen Solange was painted in regal colors and wore an elaborate yellow crown, the points of which held her wool. Ursula was a devoted subject and spent all of her spare time, of which she had oceans at her disposal, creating long serpentine lengths of wool that had no purpose except to be coiled into mats and lopsided tea cozies. ("Where are the holes for the spout and the handle?" Bridget puzzled.)

"Lovely, dear," Sylvie said, examining one of the little mats that was slowly uncurling in her hands, like something waking from a long sleep. "Practice makes perfect, remember."

Yer tea is on the table!"

Ursula ignored the call. She was in thrall to majesty, sitting on her bed, features scrunched up in concentration as she hooked wool around Queen Solange's crown. It was an old bit of fawn worsted but "needs must," Sylvie said.

Maurice should have been back at school but his chicken pox had been the worst of all of them and his face was still covered in little scars as if a bird had pecked at him. "Another few days at home, young man," Dr. Fellowes said, but, in Ursula's eyes, Maurice seemed bursting with rude health.

He paced restlessly round the room, bored as a caged lion. He found one of Pamela's slippers beneath the bed and kicked it around like a football. Then he picked up a china ornament, the figure of a crinolined lady that was precious to Pamela, and tossed it so high in the air that it glanced off the vaseline glass shade of the light with an alarming *ting.* Ursula dropped her knitting, her hands flying to her mouth in horror. The crinolined lady found a soft landing on the pouchy quilt of Pamela's satin eiderdown but not before Maurice had snatched up the discarded knitting doll instead and started running around with it, pretending it was an airplane. Ursula watched as poor Queen Solange flew round the room, the tail of wool that protruded from her innards streaming out behind her like a thin banner.

And then Maurice did something truly wicked. He opened the attic window, letting in a blast of unwelcome cold air, and sent the little wooden doll soaring out into the hostile night.

Ursula immediately hauled a chair over to the window, climbed aboard and peered out. Illuminated in the pool of light that flooded from the window, she spotted Queen Solange, stranded on the slates in the valley between the two attic roofs.

Maurice, a Red Indian now, was jumping from one bed to the other, emitting war whoops. "Yer tea is on the table!" Bridget bellowed more urgently from the foot of the stairs. Ursula ignored both of them, her heroine heart beating loudly as she clambered out of the window—no easy task—determined to rescue her sovereign. The slates were slick with ice and Ursula had barely placed her small, slippered foot on the slope beneath the window before it slid out from under her. She let out a little cry, held out a hand toward the knitting queen as she raced past her, feet first, a tobogganer without a toboggan. There was no parapet to buffer her descent, nothing at all to stop her being propelled into the black wings of night. A kind of rush, a thrill almost, as she was launched into the bottomless air and then nothing.

Darkness fell.

SNOW

11 February 1910

The piccalilli was the lurid color of jaundice. Dr. Fellowes ate at the kitchen table by the light of an annoyingly smoky oil lamp. He smeared the piccalilli onto buttered bread and topped it with a thick slice of fatty ham. He thought of the flitch of bacon resting coolly in his own pantry. He had chosen the pig himself, pointing it out to the farmer, seeing not a living creature but an anatomy lesson—an assembly of loin chops and hock, cheek and belly and huge joints of gammon for boiling. Flesh. He thought of the baby he had rescued from the jaws of death with a snip of his surgical scissors. "The miracle of life," he said dispassionately to the rough little Irish maid. ("Bridget, sir.") "I am to stay the rest of the night," he added. "On account of the snow."

He could think of many places he would rather be than Fox Corner. Why was it called that? Why would you celebrate the habitation of such a wily beast? Dr. Fellowes had ridden with the hunt, dashing in scarlet, when a young man. He wondered if the girl would skip into his room in the morning with a tray of tea and toast. Imagined her pouring hot water from the jug into the washbasin and soaping him down in front of the bedroom fire the way his mother had done, decades ago. Dr. Fellowes was obstinately faithful to his wife but his thoughts roamed far and wide.

Bridget led him upstairs with a candle. The candle flared and flickered wildly as he followed the maid's scrawny backside up to a chilly guest room. She lit him his own candle on top of the pot cupboard and then disappeared into the dark maw of the hall with a hasty "Good night, sir."

He lay in the cold bed, the piccalilli repeating unpleasantly. He wished he was at home, next to the slack, warm body of Mrs. Fellowes, a woman to whom nature had denied elegance and who always smelled vaguely of fried onions. Not necessarily a disagreeable thing.

WAR

20 January 1915

"Will yer get a move on?" Bridget said crossly. She was standing impatiently in the doorway, holding Teddy. "How many times do I have to tell you, *yer tea is on the table*." Teddy squirmed in the tight brace of her arms. Maurice paid no heed, deeply involved as he was in the intricacies of a Red Indian war dance. "Get down from that window, Ursula, for the love of God. And why is it open? It's freezing, you'll catch yer death."

Ursula had been about to plunge out of the window in Queen Solange's wake, intent on delivering her from the no man's land of the roof, when something made her hesitate. A little doubt, a faltering foot and the thought that the roof was very high and the night very wide. And then Pamela had appeared and said, "Mummy says you're to wash your hands for tea," closely followed by Bridget stomping up the stairs with her unyielding refrain, *Yer tea's on the table!* and all hope of royal rescue was lost. "And as for you, Maurice," Bridget continued, "you're little more than a savage."

"I *am* a savage," he said. "I'm an Apache."

"You could be the King of the Hottentots as far as I'm concerned but YER TEA IS STILL ON THE TABLE."

Maurice gave a last defiant battle cry before clattering noisily down the stairs and Pamela used an old lacrosse-net tied on to a walking cane to trawl Queen Solange back from the icy depths of the roof.

Tea was a boiled chicken. Teddy had a coddled egg. Sylvie sighed. Many meals involved chickens in one way or another now that they kept their own. They had a henhouse and a wired run on what was to have been an asparagus bed before the war. Old Tom had left them now, although Sylvie heard that "Mr. Ridgely" still worked for their neighbors, the Coles. Perhaps, after all, he did not like being called "Old Tom."

"This isn't one of our chickens, is it?" Ursula asked.

"No, darling," Sylvie said. "It isn't."

The chicken was tough and stringy. Mrs. Glover's cooking hadn't been the same since George was injured in a gas attack. He was still in a field hospital in France and when Sylvie inquired how badly he was injured she said she didn't know. "How awful," Sylvie said. Sylvie thought that if she had a wounded son, far from home, she would have to go on a quest to find him. Nurse and heal her poor boy. Perhaps not Maurice, but Teddy, certainly. The thought of Teddy lying wounded and helpless made her eyes prick with tears.

"Are you all right, Mummy?" Pamela asked.

"Absolutely," Sylvie said, fishing the wishbone out of the chicken carcass and offering it to Ursula, who said she didn't know how to wish. "Well, generally speaking, we wish for our dreams to come true," Sylvie said.

"But not my dreams?" Ursula said, a look of alarm on her face.

But not my dreams?" Ursula said, thinking of the giant lawn mower that chased her through the night and the Red Indian tribe that tied her to stakes and surrounded her with bows and arrows.

"This *is* one of our chickens, isn't it?" Maurice said.

Ursula liked the chickens, liked the warm straw and featheriness of the henhouse, liked reaching under the solid warm bodies to find an even warmer egg.

"It's Henrietta, isn't it?" Maurice persisted. "She was old. Ready for the pot, Mrs. Glover said."

Ursula inspected her plate. She was particularly fond of Henrietta. The tough white slice of meat gave no clues.

"Henrietta?" Pamela squeaked in alarm.

"Did you kill her?" Maurice asked Sylvie eagerly. "Was it very bloody?"

They had already lost several chickens to the foxes. Sylvie said she was surprised at how stupid chickens were. No more stupid than people, Mrs. Glover said. The foxes had taken Pamela's baby rabbit too, last summer. George Glover had rescued two and Pamela had insisted on making a nest for hers out in the garden but Ursula had rebelled and brought her little rabbit inside and placed it in the dolls' house where it knocked everything over and left droppings like tiny licorice balls. When Bridget discovered it she removed it to an outhouse and it was never seen again.

For pudding they had jam roly-poly and custard, the jam from the summer's raspberries. The summer was a dream now, Sylvie said.

"Dead baby," Maurice said, in that horribly off-hand manner that boarding school had only served to foster. He shoveled pudding into his mouth and said, "That's what we call jam roly-poly at school."

"Manners, Maurice," Sylvie warned. "And please, don't be so vile."

"Dead baby?" Ursula said, putting her spoon down and gazing in horror at the dish in front of her.

"The Germans eat them," Pamela said gloomily.

"Puddings?" Ursula puzzled. Didn't everyone eat puddings, even the enemy?

"No, *babies,*" Pamela said. "But only Belgian ones."

Sylvie looked at the roly-poly, the round, red seam of jam like blood, and shivered. This morning she had watched Mrs. Glover snapping poor old Henrietta's neck backward over a broom handle, the bird dispatched with the indifference of a state executioner.

Needs must, I suppose, Sylvie thought. "We're at war," Mrs. Glover said, "it's not the time to be squeamish."

Pamela would not let the subject rest. "*Was* it, Mummy?" she insisted quietly. "Was it Henrietta?"

"No, darling," Sylvie said. "On my word of honor, that was not Henrietta."

An urgent rapping at the back door prevented further discussion. They all sat still, staring at each other, as if they had been caught in the middle of a crime. Ursula didn't really know why. "Don't let it be bad news," Sylvie said. It was. Seconds later there was a terrible scream from the kitchen. Sam Wellington, the old boot, was dead.

"This terrible war," Sylvie murmured.

Pamela gave Ursula the remains of one of her dun-colored balls of four-ply lamb's wool and Ursula promised that Queen Solange would be delivered of a little mat for Pamela's water glass in gratitude for her rescue.

When they went to bed that night they placed the crinoline lady and Queen Solange side by side on the bedside cabinet, valiant survivors of an encounter with the enemy.

ARMISTICE

June 1918

Teddy's birthday. Born beneath the sign of the crab. An enigmatic sign, Sylvie said, even though she thought such things were "bunkum." "For you are four," Bridget said, which was perhaps a kind of joke.

Sylvie and Mrs. Glover were preparing a little tea party, "a surprise." Sylvie liked all her children, Maurice not so much perhaps, but she doted entirely on Teddy.

Teddy didn't even know it was his birthday as for days now they had been under strict instructions not to mention it. Ursula couldn't believe how difficult it was to keep a secret. Sylvie was an adept. She told them to take "the birthday boy" out while she got things ready. Pamela complained that *she* had never had a surprise party and Sylvie said, "Of course you have, you just don't remember." Was this true? Pamela frowned at the impossibility of knowing. Ursula had no idea whether or not she had ever had a surprise party or even a party that wasn't a surprise. The past was a jumble in her mind, not the straight line that it was for Pamela.

Bridget said, "Come on, we'll all go for a walk," and Sylvie said, "Yes, take some jam to Mrs. Dodds, why don't you?" Sylvie, sleeves rolled up, hair scarved, had spent all day yesterday helping Mrs. Glover make jam, boiling up copper pans of raspberries from the garden with the sugar that they had been hoarding from their ration. "Like working in a munitions factory," Sylvie said, as she funneled the boiling jam into one glass jar after another. "Hardly," Mrs. Glover muttered to herself.

The garden had produced a bumper crop, Sylvie had read books on how to cultivate fruit and declared that she was quite the gardener now. Mrs. Glover said darkly that berries were easy, wait until she tried her hand at cauliflowers. For the heavy work in the garden Sylvie employed Clarence Dodds, once a pal of Sam Wellington's, the old boot. Before the war Clarence had been an under-gardener at the Hall. He had been invalided out of the army and now wore a tin mask on half of his face and said he wanted to work in a grocer's shop. Ursula first came across him when he was preparing a bed for carrots and she gave an impolite little scream when he turned round and she saw his face for the first time. The mask had one wide-open eye painted blue to match the real one. "Enough to frighten the horses, isn't it?" he said and smiled. She wished he hadn't because his mouth wasn't covered by the mask. His lips were puckered and strange as if they were an afterthought, stitched on after he was born.

"One of the lucky ones," he said to her. "Artillery fire, it's the devil." It didn't look very lucky to Ursula.

The carrots had barely sprigged their feathery tops aboveground when Bridget started walking out with Clarence. By the time Sylvie was grubbing up the first of the King Edwards, Bridget and Clarence were engaged and, as Clarence couldn't afford a ring, Sylvie gave Bridget a gypsy ring that she said she'd "had forever" and never wore. "It's just a trinket really," she said, "it's not worth much," although Hugh had bought it for her in New Bond Street after Pamela was born and had not stinted on the cost.

Sam Wellington's photograph was banished to an old wooden crate in the shed. "I can't keep it," Bridget said fretfully to Mrs. Glover, "but I can hardly throw it away, can I now?"

"You could bury it," Mrs. Glover suggested but the idea gave Bridget the shivers. "Like black magic."

They set off for Mrs. Dodds's house, laden with jam, as well as a magnificent bouquet of maroon sweet peas that Sylvie was very proud of having grown. "The variety is 'Senator,' in case Mrs. Dodds is interested," she told Bridget.

"She won't be," Bridget said.

Maurice wasn't with them, of course. He had set off on his bicycle after breakfast, a picnic lunch in his knapsack, and had disappeared for the day with his friends. Ursula and Pamela took very little interest in Maurice's life and he took none whatsoever in theirs. Teddy was a quite different kind of brother, loyal and affectionate as a dog and petted accordingly.

Clarence's mother was still employed at the Hall in "a semi-feudal capacity," according to Sylvie, and had a cottage on the estate, a cramped, ancient thing that smelled of stale water and old plaster. Distemper on the damp ceiling ballooned like loose skin. Bosun had died of distemper the previous year and was buried beneath a Bourbon rose that Sylvie had ordered especially to mark his grave. "It's called 'Louise Odier,'" she said. "If you're interested." They had another dog now, a wriggly black lurcher puppy called Trixie who might as well have been called Trouble because Sylvie was always laughing and saying, "Uh-oh, here comes trouble." Pamela had seen Mrs. Glover giving Trixie a well-aimed kick with her big-booted foot and Sylvie had "to have a word." Bridget wouldn't let Trixie come to Mrs. Dodds's house, she said she would never hear the end of it. "She doesn't believe in dogs," Bridget said.

"Dogs are hardly an article of faith," Sylvie said.

Clarence met them at the entrance gate to the estate. The Hall itself was miles away, at the end of a long avenue of elms. The Daunts had lived there for centuries and popped up occasionally to open fetes and bazaars and fleetingly grace the annual Christmas party in the village hall. They had their own chapel so were never seen in church, although now they were never seen at all because they had lost three sons, one after the other, to the war and had more or less retreated from the world.

It was impossible not to stare at Clarence's tin face ("galvanized copper," he corrected them). They lived in terror that he would remove the mask. Did he take it off to go to bed at night? If Bridget married him would she see the horror beneath? "It's not so much what's there," they had overhead Bridget say to Mrs. Glover, "as what's *not* there."

Mrs. Dodds ("Old Mother Dodds" Bridget called her, like something from a nursery rhyme) made tea for the grown-ups, tea that Bridget later reported to be "as weak as lamb's water." Bridget liked her tea "strong enough for the teaspoon to stand up in it." Neither Pamela nor Ursula could decide what lamb's water might be but it sounded nice. Mrs. Dodds gave them creamy milk, ladled from a big enamel pitcher and still warm from the Hall's dairy. It made Ursula feel sick. "Lady Bountiful," Mrs. Dodds muttered to Clarence when they handed her the jam and the sweet peas and he said, *"Mother,"* chidingly. Mrs. Dodds passed the flowers over to Bridget, who remained holding the sweet peas like a bride until Mrs. Dodds said to her, "Put them in water, you daft girl."

Cake?" Clarence's mother said and doled out thin slices of gingerbread that seemed as damp as her cottage. "It's nice to see children," Mrs. Dodds said, looking at Teddy as if he were a rare animal. Teddy was a steadfast little boy and was not put off his milk and cake. He had a mustache of milk and Pamela wiped it off with her handkerchief. Ursula suspected that Mrs. Dodds didn't really think it was nice to see children, indeed she suspected that on the subject of children she was in agreement with Mrs. Glover. Except for Teddy, of course. Everyone liked Teddy. Even Maurice. Occasionally.

Mrs. Dodds examined the gypsy ring newly adorning Bridget's hand, pulling Bridget's finger toward her as if she was pulling a wishbone. "Rubies and diamonds," she said. "Very fancy."

"Tiny stones," Bridget said defensively. "Just a trinket really."

The girls helped Bridget wash the tea things and left Teddy to fend for himself with Mrs. Dodds. They washed up in a big stone sink in the scullery that had a pump instead of a tap. Bridget said that when she was a girl "in County Kilkenny" they had to walk to a well to get water. She arranged the sweet peas prettily in an old Dundee marmalade jar and left it on the wooden draining board. When they had dried the crockery with one of Mrs. Dodds's thin, worn tea towels (damp, of course), Clarence asked them if they would like to go over to the Hall to see the walled garden. "You should stop going back over there, son," Mrs. Dodds said to him, "it only upsets you."

They entered via an old wooden door in a wall. The door was stiff and Bridget gave a little scream when Clarence took his shoulder to it and shoved it open. Ursula was expecting something wonderful—sparkling fountains and terraces, statues, walks and arbors and flowerbeds as far as the eye could see—but it wasn't much more than an overgrown field, brambles and thistles rambling everywhere.

"Aye, it's a jungle," Clarence said. "This used to be the kitchen garden, twelve gardeners worked at the Hall before the war." Only the roses climbing on the walls were still flourishing, and the fruit trees in the orchard that were laden with fruit. Plums were rotting on the branches. Excited wasps darted everywhere. "They haven't picked this year," Clarence said. "Three sons at the Hall, all dead in this bloody war. I suppose they didn't much feel like plum pie."

"Tsk," Bridget said. "Language."

There was a glasshouse with hardly any glass and inside it they could see the withered peach and apricot trees. "Damned shame," Clarence said and Bridget tsked again and said, "Not in front of the children," just like Sylvie did. "Everything gone to seed," Clarence said, ignoring her. "I could weep."

"Well, you could get your job back here at the Hall," Bridget said. "I'm sure they'd be glad. It's not as if you can't work just as well with..." She hesitated and gestured vaguely in the direction of Clarence's face.

"I don't want my job back," he said gruffly. "My days as some rich nob's servant are over. I miss the garden, not the life. The garden was a thing of beauty."

"We could get our own little garden," Bridget said. "Or an allotment." Bridget seemed to spend a lot of time trying to cheer Clarence up. Ursula supposed she was rehearsing for marriage.

"Yes, why don't we do that?" Clarence said, sounding grim at the prospect. He picked up a small, sour apple that had fallen early and bowled it hard overarm like a cricketer. It landed on the glasshouse and shattered one of the few remaining panes. "Bugger," Clarence said and Bridget flapped her hand at him and hissed, "Children."

("A thing of beauty," Pamela said appreciatively that night, as they flannelled their faces before bed with the heavy bar of carbolic. "Clarence is a poet.")

As they trailed their way home Ursula could still smell the scent of the sweet peas they had left behind in Mrs. Dodds's kitchen. It seemed an awful waste to leave them there unappreciated. By then Ursula had forgotten all about the birthday tea and was almost as surprised as Teddy when they got back to the house and found the hallway decorated with flags and bunting and a beaming Sylvie bearing a gift-wrapped present that was unmistakably a toy airplane.

"Surprise," she said.

11 November 1918

"Such a melancholy time of year," Sylvie said to no one in particular.

The leaves still lay thick on the lawn. The summer was a dream again. Every summer, it was beginning to seem to Ursula, was a dream. The last of the leaves were falling and the big beech was almost a skeleton. The Armistice seemed to have made Sylvie even more despondent than the war. ("All those poor boys, gone forever. The peace won't bring them back.")

They had the day off school because of the great victory and they were turned outside into the morning drizzle to play. They had new neighbors, Major and Mrs. Shawcross, and they spent a good deal of the damp morning peering through gaps in the holly hedge trying to get a glimpse of the Shawcrosses' daughters. There were no other girls their age in the neighborhood. The Coles only had boys. They weren't rough like Maurice, they had nice manners and were never horrible to Ursula and Pamela.

"I think they're playing hide-and-seek," Pamela reported back from the Shawcross front. Ursula tried to see through the hedge and got scratched in the face by the vicious holly. "I think they're the same age as us," Pamela said. "There's even a little one for you, Teddy." Teddy raised his eyebrows and said, "Oh." Teddy liked girls. Girls liked Teddy. "Oh, wait, there's another one," Pamela said. "They're multiplying."

"Bigger or smaller?" Ursula asked.

"Smaller, another girl. More of a baby. Being carried by an older one." Ursula was growing confused by the mathematics of so many girls.

"Five!" Pamela said breathlessly, reaching a final total apparently. "Five girls."

By this time Trixie had managed to wriggle through the bottom of the hedge and they heard the excited squeals that accompanied her appearance on the other side of the holly.

"I say," Pamela said, raising her voice, "can we have our dog back?"

Lunch was boiled toad in the hole and a queen of puddings. "Where have you been?" Sylvie asked. "Ursula, you have twigs in your hair. You look like a pagan."

"Holly," Pamela said. "We've been next door. We met the Shawcross girls. Five of them."

"I know." Sylvie counted them off on her fingers. "Winnie, Gertie, Millie, Nancy and..."

"Beatrice," Pamela supplied.

"Were you invited in?" Mrs. Glover, a stickler for propriety, asked.

"We found a hole in the hedge," Pamela said.

"That's where those damn foxes are getting through," Mrs. Glover grumbled, "they're coming from the copse," and Sylvie frowned at Mrs. Glover's language but said nothing as, officially, they were in celebration mood. Sylvie, Bridget and Mrs. Glover were "toasting the peace" with glasses of sherry. Neither Sylvie nor Mrs. Glover seemed to have much of a taste for jubilation. Both Hugh and Izzie were still away at the Front and Sylvie said she wouldn't believe Hugh was safe until he walked through the door. Izzie had driven an ambulance throughout the war but none of them could imagine this. George Glover was being "rehabilitated" in a home somewhere in the Cotswolds. Mrs. Glover had traveled to visit him but was disinclined to talk about what she had found, other than to say that George was no longer really George. "I don't think any of them are themselves anymore," Sylvie said. Ursula tried to imagine not being Ursula but was defeated by the impossibility of the task.

Two girls from the Women's Land Army had taken George's place on the farm. They were both horsey types from Northamptonshire and Sylvie said that if she'd known they were going to let women work with Samson and Nelson she would have applied for the job herself. The girls had come to tea on several occasions, sitting in the kitchen in their muddy puttees, to Mrs. Glover's disgust.

* * *

Bridget had her hat on ready to go out when Clarence appeared shyly at the back door, mumbling a greeting to Sylvie and Mrs. Glover. The "happy couple," as Mrs. Glover referred to them without any hint of congratulation, were catching the train up to London to take part in the victory celebrations. Bridget was giddy with excitement. "Sure now you don't want to come with us, Mrs. Glover? I'll bet there'll be some high jinks to be had." Mrs. Glover rolled her eyes like a discontented cow. She was "avoiding crowds" on account of the influenza epidemic. She had a nephew who had dropped dead in the street, perfectly healthy at breakfast and "dead by noon." Sylvie said they mustn't be scared of the influenza. "Life must go on," she said.

After Bridget and Clarence left for the station, Mrs. Glover and Sylvie sat at the kitchen table and drank another sherry. "High jinks, indeed," Mrs. Glover said. By the time Teddy appeared, Trixie eager on his tail, and announced that he was starving and "Had they forgotten lunch?" the meringue on top of the queen of puddings had collapsed and was all burned. The final casualty of the war.

They had tried, and failed, to stay awake for Bridget's return, falling asleep over their bedtime reading. Pamela was in the spell of *At the Back of the North Wind* while Ursula was working her way through *The Wind in the Willows.* She was particularly fond of Mole. She was a mysteriously slow reader and writer ("Practice makes perfect, dear") and liked it best when Pamela read out loud to her. They both liked fairy stories and had all of the Andrew Lang books, all twelve colors, bought by Hugh for birthdays and Christmases. "Things of beauty," Pamela said.

Bridget's noisy return woke Ursula and she, in turn, roused

Pamela and they both tiptoed downstairs where a merry Bridget and a more sober Clarence regaled them with tales of the festivities, of the "sea of people" and of the gay crowd shouting themselves hoarse for the King ("We want the King! We want the King!" Bridget demonstrated enthusiastically) until he appeared on the balcony of Buckingham Palace. "And the bells," Clarence added, "never heard anything like it. All the bells of London ringing out the peace."

"A thing of beauty," Pamela said.

Bridget had lost her hat somewhere amid the throng as well as several hairpins and the top button of her blouse. "Lifted off my feet in the crush," she said happily.

"Goodness, what a racket," Sylvie said, appearing in the kitchen, sleepy and lovely in her lacy wrap, her hair in a great fraying rope down her back. Clarence blushed and looked at his boots. Sylvie made cocoa for them all and listened indulgently to Bridget until even the novelty of being up at midnight couldn't keep any of them awake.

"Back to normal tomorrow," Clarence said, giving Bridget a daring peck on the cheek before making his way back to his mother. It was, altogether, a day out of the ordinary.

"Do you think Mrs. Glover will be cross that we didn't wake her?" Sylvie whispered to Pamela on the way up the stairs.

"Furious," Pamela said and they both laughed like conspirators, like women.

When she fell asleep again Ursula dreamed of Clarence and Bridget. They were walking in an overgrown garden, looking for Bridget's hat. Clarence was crying, real tears on the good side of his face, while on the mask there were painted tears, like artificial raindrops on a picture of a windowpane.

When Ursula woke up the next morning she was burning hot

and aching all over and "Boiling, like a lobster," Mrs. Glover said, brought in for a second opinion by Sylvie. Bridget was also laid up in bed. "Hardly surprising," Mrs. Glover said, folding disapproving arms beneath her ample yet uninviting bosom. Ursula hoped she would never have to be nursed by Mrs. Glover.

Ursula's breathing was harsh and raspy, her breath thickening in her chest. The world boomed and receded like the sea in a giant shell. Everything was rather pleasantly fuzzy. Trixie lay on the bed at her feet while Pamela read to her from *The Red Fairy Book,* but the words came and went meaninglessly. Pamela's face loomed in and out of focus. Sylvie came and tried to feed her beef tea but her throat felt too small and she sputtered it out, all over the bedsheets.

There was the sound of tires on gravel and Sylvie said to Pamela, "That will be Dr. Fellowes," and rose swiftly, adding, "Stay with Ursula, Pammy, but don't let Teddy in here, will you?"

The house was more silent than usual. When Sylvie didn't come back, Pamela said, "I'll go and look for Mummy. I won't be long." Ursula heard murmurings and cries drifting from somewhere in the house but they meant nothing to her.

She was sleeping a strange restless kind of sleep when Dr. Fellowes appeared suddenly by the side of the bed. Sylvie sat on the other side of the bed and held Ursula's hand, saying, "Her skin is lilac. Like Bridget's." Lilac skin sounded rather nice, like *The Lilac Fairy Book.* Sylvie's voice seemed funny, choked up and panicked like the time she saw the telegram boy coming up the path but it turned out to be only a telegram from Izzie wishing Teddy a happy birthday. ("Thoughtless," Sylvie said.)

Ursula couldn't breathe and yet she could smell her mother's perfume and hear her voice murmuring gently in her ear like a bee-buzz on a summer's day. She was too tired to open her eyes. She heard Sylvie's skirts rustle as she left her bedside, followed by the sound of the window opening. "I'm trying to get you some air," Sylvie said, returning to Ursula's side and holding her against her crisp seersucker blouse with its safe scents of laundry starch and roses. The woody fragrance of bonfire smoke drifted through the window and into the little attic room. She could hear the clopping of hooves followed by the rattle of the coal as the coalman emptied his sacks into the coal shed. Life was going on. A thing of beauty.

One breath, that was all she needed, but it wouldn't come.

Darkness fell swiftly, at first an enemy, but then a friend.

SNOW

11 February 1910

A big woman with the forearms of a stoker woke Dr. Fellowes by clattering a cup and saucer down on the pot table next to his bed and yanking open the curtains even though it was still dark outside. It took him a moment to remember that he was in the freezing-cold guest bedroom at Fox Corner and that the rather intimidating woman bearing the cup and saucer was the Todds' cook. Dr. Fellowes searched the dusty archive of his brain for a name that he knew had come to him easily a few hours earlier.

"It's Mrs. Glover," she said, as if reading his mind.

"So it is. She of the excellent pickles." His head felt full of straw. He was uncomfortably aware that beneath the frugal covers he was wearing only his combinations. The bedroom grate, he noted, was cold and empty.

"You're needed," Mrs. Glover said. "There's been an accident."

"An accident?" Dr. Fellowes echoed. "Something has happened to the baby?"

"A farmer trampled by a bull."

ARMISTICE

12 November 1918

Ursula woke up with a start. It was dark in the bedroom but she could hear noises somewhere downstairs. A door closing, giggling and shuffling. She caught the high-pitched cackle that was Bridget's unmistakable laugh and the rumbling bass note of a man. Bridget and Clarence back from London.

Ursula's first instinct was to clamber out of bed and shake Pamela awake so that they could go downstairs and interrogate Bridget about the high jinks, but something stopped her. As she lay listening to the dark, a wave of something horrible washed over her, a great dread, as if something truly treacherous were about to happen. The same feeling she had had when she'd followed Pamela into the sea when they were on holiday in Cornwall, just before the war. They had been rescued by a stranger. After that Sylvie made sure they all went to the swimming baths in town and took lessons, from an ex-major in the Boer War who barked orders at them until they were too frightened to sink. Sylvie often retold the tale as if it were a hilarious escapade ("The heroic Mr. Winton!") when in fact Ursula still clearly recalled the terror.

Pamela mumbled something in her sleep and Ursula said, "Shh." Pamela mustn't wake up. They mustn't go downstairs. They mustn't see Bridget. Ursula didn't know why this was so, where this awful sense of dread came from, but she pulled the blankets over her head to hide from whatever was out there. She hoped it was out there and not inside her. She thought she would feign sleep but within minutes the real thing came.

In the morning they ate in the kitchen because Bridget was in bed, feeling ill. "Hardly surprising," Mrs. Glover said unsympathetically, doling out porridge. "I dread to think what time she staggered in."

Sylvie came down from upstairs with a tray that hadn't been touched. "I really don't think Bridget is well, Mrs. Glover," she said.

"Too much drink," Mrs. Glover scoffed, cracking eggs as if she were punishing them. Ursula coughed and Sylvie glanced sharply at her. "I think we should call Dr. Fellowes out," Sylvie said to Mrs. Glover.

"For Bridget?" Mrs. Glover said. "The girl's as healthy as a horse. Dr. Fellowes will give you short shrift when he smells the alcohol on her."

"Mrs. Glover," Sylvie said in the tone she used when she was being very serious about something and wanted to make sure people were listening (*Don't trail muddy footprints into the house, never be unkind to other children, no matter how provoking they are*). "I really do think Bridget is ill." Mrs. Glover seemed suddenly to understand.

"Can you see to the children?" Sylvie said. "I am going to telephone for Dr. Fellowes and then I'll go up and sit with Bridget."

"Aren't the children going to school?" Mrs. Glover asked.

"Yes, of course they are," Sylvie said. "Although perhaps not. No—yes—they are. Or should they?" She hovered, fretfully indecisive, in the kitchen doorway while Mrs. Glover waited with surprising patience for her to come to a conclusion.

"I think keep them at home, for today," Sylvie said finally. "Crowded schoolrooms and so on." She took a deep breath and stared at the ceiling. "But keep them down here, just now." Pamela raised her eyebrows at Ursula. Ursula raised hers back although she wasn't sure what they were trying to communicate to each other. Horror mainly, she supposed, at being put in Mrs. Glover's care.

They had to sit at the kitchen table so Mrs. Glover could "keep an eye on them" and then, despite their violent protests, she bade them get out their schoolbooks and do work—sums for Pamela, letters for Teddy (*Q is for quail, R is for rain*) and Ursula was set to practice her "atrocious" handwriting. Ursula thought it vastly unfair that someone who wrote nothing more than shopping lists in a blunt hand (*suet, stove blacking, mutton chops and Dinneford's magnesia*) should be passing judgment on her own painful script.

Mrs. Glover meanwhile was more than fully occupied with pressing a calf's tongue, removing the gristle and bone and rolling it up before squeezing it into the tongue press, an altogether more fascinating activity to observe than writing out *Quick wafting zephyrs vex bold Jim* or *The five boxing wizards jumped quickly.* "I would hate to be in any school where she was mistress," Pamela muttered, wrestling with equations.

They were all distracted by the advent of the butcher's boy, ringing his bicycle bell noisily to announce his arrival. He was a fourteen-year-old called Fred Smith whom both the girls and Maurice admired tremendously. The girls signaled their ardor by calling him "Freddy" while Maurice called him "Smithy" in comradely approval. Pamela had once declared that Maurice had a pash on Fred and Mrs. Glover, who happened to hear, slapped Pamela in passing on the back of her legs with a balloon whisk. Pamela was very put out and had no idea what she had been punished for. Fred Smith himself addressed the girls deferentially as "Miss" and Maurice as "Master Todd," although he took no interest in any of them. To Mrs. Glover he was "young Fred" and to Sylvie he was "the butcher's boy," sometimes "that nice butcher's boy" to distinguish him from the previous butcher's boy, Leonard Ash, "a sneaky rogue" according to Mrs. Glover, who had caught him stealing eggs from the henhouse. Leonard Ash died in the Battle of the Somme after lying about his age when he enlisted and Mrs. Glover said he got what was coming to him, which seemed a rough kind of justice.

Fred handed over a white-paper package to Mrs. Glover and said, "Your tripe," and then deposited the long soft body of a hare on the wooden draining board. "Hung for five days. It's a beauty, Mrs. Glover," and even Mrs. Glover, disinclined to praise in the best of circumstances, acknowledged the hare's superiority by opening a cake tin and allowing Fred to choose the biggest rock bun from within its usually clam-like innards.

Mrs. Glover, her tongue now safely in the press, immediately began skinning the hare, a distressing yet hypnotic process to witness, and it was only when the poor creature was stripped of its fur and exposed, naked and shiny, that anyone noticed Teddy's absence.

"Go and fetch him," Mrs. Glover said to Ursula. "And you can all have a glass of milk and a rock bun, although goodness knows you've done nothing to deserve it."

Teddy was fond of hide-and-seek and, when he didn't respond to his name being called, Ursula looked in his secret places, behind the drawing room curtains, beneath the dining room table, and when she could find no sign of him she set off up the stairs to the bedrooms.

A forceful clanging of the front doorbell echoed up the stairs in her wake. From the turn in the stairs she saw Sylvie appear in the hallway and open the door to Dr. Fellowes. Ursula supposed her mother must have come down the back stairs rather than appearing by magic. Dr. Fellowes and Sylvie engaged in an intense, whispered conversation, about Bridget, presumably, but Ursula couldn't catch any of the words.

Not in Sylvie's room (they had long ago ceased to think of it as a room that belonged to two parents). Not in Maurice's room, so generously sized for someone who spent more than half his life living at school. Not in the guest bedroom or the second guest bedroom nor in Teddy's own little back bedroom that was almost entirely taken up with his train set. Not in the bathroom or the linen cupboard. Nor was there any sign of Teddy under the beds or in the wardrobes or in the many cupboards, nor—his favorite trick—as still as a corpse beneath Sylvie's big eiderdown.

"There's cake downstairs, Teddy," she offered up to the empty rooms. The promise of cake, true or not, was normally enough to flush Teddy out from cover.

Ursula trudged up the dark narrow wooden staircase that led to the attic bedrooms and as soon as she had placed her foot on the first tread she experienced a sudden pinch of fear in her insides. She had no idea where it came from, or why.

"Teddy! Teddy, where are you?" Ursula tried to raise her voice but the words came out in a whisper.

Not in the bedroom she shared with Pamela, not in Mrs. Glover's old room. Not in the boxroom, once a nursery and now home to chests and trunks and packing cases of old clothes and toys. Only Bridget's room remained unexplored.

The door was ajar and Ursula had to force her feet to walk toward it. Something terrible was beyond that open door. She didn't want to see it, but she knew she must.

"Teddy!" she said, overcome with relief at the sight of him. Teddy was sitting on Bridget's bed, his birthday airplane on his knee. "I've been looking everywhere for you," Ursula said. Trixie was lying on the floor next to the bed and sprang up eagerly when she saw her.

"I thought it might make Bridget feel better," Teddy said, stroking the plane. Teddy had great faith in the healing power of toy trains and airplanes. (He was, he assured them, going to be a pilot when he grew up.) "I think Bridget's asleep but her eyes are open," he said.

They were. Wide open, staring sightlessly at the ceiling. There was a watery blue film across those disturbing eyes and her skin had a strange lilac hue. Cobalt Violet in Ursula's Winsor & Newton watercolor set. She could see the tip of Bridget's tongue sticking out of her mouth and had a momentary vision of Mrs. Glover pushing the calf's tongue into the press.

Ursula had never seen a dead body but she knew without any doubt that Bridget had now become one. "Get off the bed, Teddy," she said cautiously, as if her brother were a wild creature about to bolt. She started to tremble all over. It wasn't just that Bridget was dead, although that was bad enough, but there was something more perilous here. The unadorned walls, the thin jacquard bedspread on the iron bedstead, the enameled brush-and-comb set on the dressing table, the rag rug on the floor, all suddenly grew immensely threatening as if they were not really the objects they seemed. Ursula heard Sylvie and Dr. Fellowes on the stairs. Sylvie's tones were urgent, Dr. Fellowes's less concerned.

Sylvie came in and gasped, "Oh dear God," when she saw them in Bridget's room. She snatched Teddy off the bed and then pulled Ursula by the arm out into the passage. Trixie, tail wagging eagerly at the excitement, bounded after them. "Go to your room," Sylvie said. "No, go to Teddy's room. No, go to my room. Go *now,*" she said, sounding frantic, not at all the Sylvie they were used to. Sylvie went back into Bridget's room and closed the door decisively. They could hear only murmured exchanges between Sylvie and Dr. Fellowes and eventually Ursula said, "Come on," to Teddy and took his hand. He allowed her to lead him docilely back down the stairs to Sylvie's bedroom. "Did you say cake?" he asked.

Teddy's skin is the same color as Bridget's," Sylvie said. Her stomach hollowed out with terror. She knew what she was looking at. Ursula was merely pale, although her closed eyelids were dark and her skin glistened with a strange, sickly sheen.

"Heliotrope cyanosis," Dr. Fellowes said, taking Teddy's pulse.

"And see those mahogany spots on his cheeks? This is the more virulent strain, I'm afraid."

"Stop, please stop," Sylvie hissed. "Do not lecture me like a medical student. I am their *mother.*" How she hated Dr. Fellowes at that moment. Bridget was lying in her bed upstairs, still warm but as dead as the marble on a tomb. "The influenza," Dr. Fellowes continued relentlessly. "Your maid was mixing with crowds of people yesterday in London—perfect conditions for the infection to spread. It can take them in the blink of an eye."

"But not this one," Sylvie said fiercely, clutching Teddy's hand. "Not my child. Not my children," she amended, reaching across to stroke Ursula's burning forehead.

Pamela hovered in the doorway and Sylvie shooed her away. Pamela started to cry but Sylvie had no time for tears. Not now, not in the face of death.

"There must be something I can do," she said to Dr. Fellowes.

"You can pray."

"Pray?"

Sylvie did not believe in God. She considered the biblical deity to be an absurd, vengeful figure (Tiffin and so on), no more real than Zeus or the great god Pan. She went to church dutifully every Sunday, however, and avoided alarming Hugh with her heretical thoughts. Needs must, and so on. She prayed now, with desperate conviction but no faith, and she suspected it made no difference either way.

When a pale bloody kind of froth, like cuckoo-spit, bubbled from Teddy's nostrils Sylvie made a noise like a wounded animal. Mrs. Glover and Pamela were listening at the other side of the door and in a rare moment of unity they clutched each other's hands. Sylvie snatched Teddy from the bed and held him tightly to her breast and howled with pain.

Dear God, Dr. Fellowes thought, the woman grieved like a savage.

They sweated together in a tangle of Sylvie's linen bedsheets. Teddy was spread-eagled across the pillows. Ursula wanted to hold him close but he was too hot so she held one of his ankles instead, as if she was trying to stop him running away. Ursula's lungs felt as if they were full of custard, she imagined it thick and yellow and sweet.

Teddy was gone by nightfall. Ursula knew the moment he died, she felt it inside her. She heard just one wretched moan from Sylvie and then someone lifted Teddy out of the bed and even though he was just a little boy it was as if something weighty had gone from her side and Ursula was alone in the bed. She could hear Sylvie's choking sobs, an awful noise, as if someone had hacked off one of her limbs.

Every breath squeezed the custard stuff in her lungs. The world was fading and she began to have a stirring sense of anticipation, as if it were Christmas or her birthday, and then the black bat night approached and enfolded her in his wings. One last breath and then no more. She held out a hand to Teddy, forgetting that he wasn't there anymore.

Darkness fell.

SNOW

11 February 1910

Sylvie lit a candle. Winter dark, five o'clock in the morning by the little gold carriage clock on the bedroom mantelpiece. The clock, an English one ("Better than a French one," her mother had instructed), had been one of her parents' wedding presents. When the creditors came to call after the society portraitist's death his widow hid the clock beneath her skirts, bemoaning the passing of the crinoline. Lottie appeared to chime on the quarter, disconcerting the creditors. Luckily they were not in the room when she struck the hour.

The new baby was asleep in her cradle. Words from Coleridge suddenly came into Sylvie's mind: *Dear Babe, that sleepest cradled by my side.* Which poem was that?

The fire in the grate had died down, leaving only the smallest flame still dancing on the coals. The baby began to make mewling sounds and Sylvie climbed gingerly out of bed. Childbirth was a brutal affair. If she had been in charge of designing the human race she would have gone about things quite differently. (A golden shaft of light through the ear for conception perhaps and a well-fitting hatch somewhere modest for escape nine months later.) She left the warmth of her bed and retrieved Ursula from the cradle. And then, suddenly, breaking the snow-muffled silence, she thought she heard the soft nicker of a horse and felt a little buzz of electric pleasure in her soul at this unlikely sound. She carried Ursula over to the window and drew one of the heavy curtains back far enough to see out. The snow had obliterated everything familiar, the world outside was shawled in white. And there below was the fantastic sight of George Glover riding bareback on one of his great Shires (Nelson, if she wasn't mistaken) up the wintry drive. He looked magnificent, like a hero of old. Sylvie closed the curtains and decided that the tribulations of the night had probably affected her brain and were making her hallucinate.

She took Ursula back into bed with her and the baby rooted around for her nipple. Sylvie believed in wet-nursing her own children. The idea of glass bottles and rubber teats seemed unnatural somehow but that didn't mean that she didn't feel like a cow being milked. The baby was slow and floundering, confounded by the new. How long before breakfast? Sylvie wondered.

ARMISTICE

11 November 1918

Dear Bridget, I have locked and bolted the doors. There is a gang of thieves—should the "i" come before the "e"? Ursula chewed the end of her pencil until it splintered. Undecided, she crossed out "thieves" and wrote "robbers" instead. *There is a gang of robbers in the village. Please can you stay with Clarence's mother?* For good measure she added *and also I have a headache so don't knock.* She signed it *Mrs. Todd.* Ursula waited until there was no one in the kitchen and then went outside and pinned the note to the back door.

"What are you doing?" Mrs. Glover asked as she came back inside. Ursula jumped, Mrs. Glover could move as quietly as a cat.

"Nothing," Ursula said. "Looking to see if Bridget was coming yet."

"Heavens," Mrs. Glover said, "she'll be back on the last train, not for hours yet. Now shift yourself, it's long past your bedtime. It's Liberty Hall here."

Ursula didn't know what Liberty Hall meant but it sounded like rather a good place to live.

Next morning there was no Bridget in the house. Nor, more puzzlingly, was there any sign of Pamela. Ursula felt overwhelmed by a relief as inexplicable as the panic that had led her to write the note the previous night.

"There was a silly note on the door last night, a prank," Sylvie said. "Bridget was locked out. You know, it looks just like your handwriting, Ursula, I don't suppose you can explain that?"

"No, I can't," Ursula said stoutly.

"I sent Pamela to Mrs. Dodds to fetch Bridget home," Sylvie said.

"You sent *Pamela?*" Ursula echoed in horror.

"Yes, Pamela."

"Pamela is with *Bridget?*"

"Yes," Sylvie said. "Bridget. What is the matter with you?"

Ursula ran out of the house. She could hear Sylvie shouting after her but she didn't stop. She had never run so fast in all of her eight years, not even when Maurice was chasing her to give her a Chinese burn. She ran up the lane in the direction of Mrs. Dodds's cottage, splashing through the mud so that by the time Pamela and Bridget were in sight ahead of her she was filthy from head to toe.

"What *is* the matter?" Pamela asked anxiously. "Is it Daddy?" Bridget made the sign of the cross. Ursula threw her arms round Pamela and collapsed in tears.

"Whatever is it? *Tell* me," Pamela said, caught up now in the dread.

"I don't know," Ursula sobbed. "I just felt so worried about you."

"What a goose," Pamela said affectionately, hugging her.

"I have a bit of a headache," Bridget said. "Let's get back to the house."

Darkness soon fell again.

SNOW

11 February 1910

"A miracle, says the Fellowes feller," Bridget said to Mrs. Glover as they toasted the new baby's arrival over their morning teapot. As far as Mrs. Glover was concerned miracles belonged inside the pages of the Bible, not amid the carnage of birth. "Maybe she'll stop at three," she said.

"Now why would she be going and doing that when she has such lovely healthy babies and there's enough money in the house for anything they want?"

Mrs. Glover, ignoring the argument, heaved herself up from the table and said, "Well, I must get on with Mrs. Todd's breakfast." She took a bowl of kidneys soaking in milk from the pantry and commenced removing the fatty white membrane, like a caul. Bridget glanced at the milk, white marbled with red, and felt uncharacteristically squeamish.

Dr. Fellowes had already breakfasted—on bacon, black pudding, fried bread and eggs—and left. Men from the village had arrived and tried to dig his car out and when that had failed someone ran for George and he had come to the rescue, riding on the back of one of his big Shires. St. George slipped briefly into Mrs. Glover's mind and hastily slipped out again as being too fanciful. With not inconsiderable difficulty, Dr. Fellowes was hoisted up behind Mrs. Glover's son and the pair had ridden off, plowing snow, not earth.

A farmer had been trampled by a bull, but was alive still. Mrs. Glover's own father, a dairyman, had been killed by a cow. Mrs. Glover, young but doughty and not yet acquainted with Mr. Glover, had come across her father lying dead in the milking shed. She could still see the blood on the straw and the surprised look on the face of the cow, her father's favorite, Maisie.

Bridget warmed her hands on the teapot and Mrs. Glover said, "Well, I'd better to see to my kidneys. Find me a flower for Mrs. Todd's breakfast tray."

"A flower?" Bridget puzzled, looking through the window at the snow. "In this weather?"

ARMISTICE

11 November 1918

"Oh, Clarence," Sylvie said, opening the back door. "Bridget's had a bit of an accident, I'm afraid. She tripped and fell over the step. Just a sprained ankle, I think, but I doubt that she'll be able to go up to London for the celebrations."

Bridget was sipping a brandy, sitting in Mrs. Glover's chair, a big high-backed Windsor, by the stove. Her ankle was propped up on a stool, and she was enjoying the drama of her tale.

"I was just coming in the kitchen door, so I was. I'd been hanging out washing although I don't know why I bothered because it started to rain again, when I felt hands shoving me in the back. And then there I was, sprawled all over the ground, in agony. Small hands," she added. "Like the hands of a little ghost child."

"Oh, really," Sylvie said. "There are no ghosts in this house, children or otherwise. Did you see anything, Ursula? You were in the garden, weren't you?"

"Oh, the silly girl just tripped," Mrs. Glover said. "You know how clumsy she is. Well, anyway," she said with some satisfaction, "that's put paid to your London high jinks."

"Not so," Bridget said stoutly. "I'm not missing this day for anything. Come on, Clarence. Give me your arm. I can *hobble.*"

Darkness, and so on.

SNOW

11 February 1910

" 'Ursula,' before you ask," Mrs. Glover said, dumping spoonfuls of porridge into bowls in front of Maurice and Pamela, who were sitting at the big wooden table in the kitchen.

"Ursula," Bridget said appreciatively. "That's a good name. Did she like the snowdrop?"

ARMISTICE

11 November 1918

Everything familiar somehow. "It's called *déjà vu,*" Sylvie said. "It's a trick of the mind. The mind is a fathomless mystery." Ursula was sure that she could recall lying in the baby carriage beneath the tree. "No," Sylvie said, "no one can remember being so small," yet Ursula remembered the leaves, like great green hands, waving in the breeze and the silver hare that hung from the carriage hood, turning and twisting in front of her face. Sylvie sighed. "You do have a very vivid imagination, Ursula." Ursula didn't know whether this was a compliment or not but it was certainly true that she often felt confused between what was real and what was not. And the terrible fear—fearful terror—that she carried around inside her. The dark landscape within. "Don't dwell on such things," Sylvie said sharply when Ursula tried to explain. "Think sunny thoughts."

And sometimes, too, she knew what someone was about to say before they said it or what mundane incident was about to occur—if a dish was about to be dropped or an apple thrown through a glasshouse, as if these things had happened many times before. Words and phrases echoed themselves, strangers seemed like old acquaintances.

"Everyone feels peculiar from time to time," Sylvie said. "Remember, dear—sunny thoughts."

Bridget lent a more willing ear, declaring that Ursula "had the second sight." There were doorways between this world and the next, she said, but only certain people could pass through them. Ursula didn't think that she wanted to be one of those people.

Last Christmas morning, Sylvie had handed Ursula a box, nicely wrapped and ribboned, the contents quite invisible, and said,

"Happy Christmas, dear," and Ursula said, "Oh, good, a dining set for the dolls' house," and was immediately in trouble for having sneaked a preview of the presents.

"But I never," she insisted obstinately to Bridget later in the kitchen, where Bridget was trying to affix little white-paper crowns on the footless legs of the Christmas goose. (The goose made Ursula think of a man in the village, a boy really, who had had both his feet blown off at Cambrai.) "I didn't look, I just *knew.*"

"Ah, I know," Bridget said. "For sure, you have the sixth sense."

Mrs. Glover, wrestling with the plum pudding, snorted her disapproval. She was of the opinion that five senses were too many, let alone adding on another one.

They were shut out in the garden for the morning. "So much for victory celebrations," Pamela said as they sheltered from the drizzle beneath the beech tree. Only Trixie was having a good time. She loved the garden, mainly because of the number of rabbits which, despite the best attentions of the foxes, continued to enjoy all the benefits of the vegetable garden. George Glover had given two babies to Ursula and Pamela before the war. Ursula convinced Pamela that they had to keep them indoors and they hid them in their bedroom cupboard and fed them with an eyedropper they found in the medicine cabinet until they hopped out one day and frightened Bridget out of her wits.

"A *fait accompli,*" Sylvie said when she was presented with the rabbits. "You can't keep them in the house though. You'll have to ask Old Tom to build a hutch for them."

The rabbits had escaped long ago, of course, and had multiplied happily. Old Tom had laid down poison and traps to little avail. ("Goodness," Sylvie said, looking out one morning at the rabbits contentedly breakfasting on the lawn. "It's like Australia out there.") Maurice, who was learning to shoot in the junior ATC at school, had spent all of last summer's long holiday taking potshots at them from his bedroom window with Hugh's neglected old Westley Richards wild-fowler. Pamela was so furious with him that she put some of his own itching powder (he was forever in joke shops) in his bed. Ursula immediately got the blame and Pamela had to own up, even though Ursula had been quite ready to take it on the chin. That was the kind of person Pamela was—always very stuck on being fair.

They heard voices in the garden next door—they had new neighbors they were yet to meet, the Shawcrosses—and Pamela said, "Come on, let's go and see if we can catch a look. I wonder what they're called."

Winnie, Gertie, Millie, Nancy and baby Bea, Ursula thought but said nothing. She was getting as good at keeping secrets as Sylvie.

Bridget gripped her hatpin between her teeth and lifted her arms to adjust her hat. She had sewn a new bunch of paper violets onto it, especially for the victory. She was standing at the top of the stairs, singing "K-K-Katy" to herself. She was thinking of Clarence. When they were married ("in the spring," he said, although it had been "before Christmas" not so long ago) she would be leaving Fox Corner. She would have her own little household, her own babies.

Staircases were very dangerous places, according to Sylvie. People died on them. Sylvie always told them not to play at the top of the stairs.

Ursula crept along the carpet runner. Took a quiet breath and then, both hands out in front of her, as if trying to stop a train, she threw herself at the small of Bridget's back. Bridget whipped her head round, mouth and eyes wide in horror at the sight of Ursula.

Bridget went flying, toppling down the stairs in a great flurry of arms and legs. Ursula only just managed to stop herself from following in her wake.

Practice makes perfect.

The arm's broken, I'm afraid," Dr. Fellowes said. "You took quite a tumble down those stairs."

"She's always been a clumsy girl," Mrs. Glover said.

"*Someone* pushed me," Bridget said. A great bruise bloomed on her forehead, she was holding her hat, the violets crushed.

"Someone?" Sylvie echoed. "Who? Who would push you downstairs, Bridget?" She looked around the faces in the kitchen. "Teddy?" Teddy put his hand over his mouth as if he was trying to stop words escaping. Sylvie turned to Pamela. "Pamela?"

"Me?" Pamela said, piously holding both of her outraged hands over her heart like a martyr. Sylvie looked at Bridget, who made a little inclination of her head toward Ursula.

"Ursula?" Sylvie frowned. Ursula stared blankly ahead, a conscientious objector about to be shot. "Ursula," Sylvie said severely, "do you know something about this?"

Ursula had done a wicked thing, she had pushed Bridget down the stairs. Bridget might have died and she would have been a murderer now. All she knew was that she *had* to do it. The great sense of dread had come over her and she had to do it.

She ran out of the room and hid in one of Teddy's secret hiding places, the cupboard beneath the stairs. After a while the door opened and Teddy crept in and sat on the floor next to her. "I don't think you pushed Bridget," he said and slipped his small, warm hand into hers.

"Thank you. I did though."

"Well, I still love you."

She might never have come out of that cupboard but the front doorbell clanged and there was a sudden great commotion in the hallway. Teddy opened the door to see what was happening. He ducked back in and reported, "Mummy's kissing a man. She's crying. He's crying as well." Ursula put her head out of the cupboard to witness this phenomenon. She turned in astonishment to Teddy. "I think it might be Daddy," she said.

PEACE

February 1947

Ursula traversed the street cautiously. The road surface was treacherous—crimped and rucked by ridges and crevasses of ice. The pavements were even more perilous, no more than massifs of ugly, hard-packed snow, or, worse, toboggan runs ironed by the neighborhood children who had nothing better to do than enjoy themselves because the schools were closed. Oh, God, Ursula thought, how mean-spirited I've become. The bloody war. The bloody peace.

By the time she had put her key in the lock of the street door she was exhausted. A shopping trip had never seemed such a challenge previously, even in the worst days of the Blitz. The skin on her face was whipped raw by the biting wind and her toes were numb with cold. The temperature hadn't risen above zero for weeks, colder even than '41. Ursula imagined at some future date trying to recall this glacial chill and knew she would never be able to conjure it up. It was so *physical,* you expected bones to shatter, skin to crackle. Yesterday she had seen two men trying to open a manhole in the road with what looked like a flamethrower. Perhaps there would be no future of thaw and warmth, perhaps this was the beginning of a new Ice Age. First fire and then ice.

It was as well, she thought, that the war had robbed her of any care for fashion. She was wearing, in order, from inner to outer—a short-sleeved vest, a long-sleeved vest, a long-sleeved pullover, a cardigan and stretched on top of it all her shabby old winter coat, bought new in Peter Robinson's two years before the war. Not to mention, of course, the usual drab underwear, a thick tweed skirt, gray wool stockings, gloves *and* mittens, a scarf, a hat and her mother's old fur-lined boots. Pity any man who was suddenly moved to ravish her. "Chance'd be a fine thing, eh?" Enid Barker, one of the secretaries, said over the balm and succor of the tea urn. Enid had auditioned for the part of plucky young London woman somewhere around 1940 and had been playing it with gusto ever since. Ursula chided herself for more unkind thoughts. Enid was a good sort. Terrifically skilled at typing tabulations, something Ursula had never quite got the hang of when she was at secretarial college. She had done a typing and shorthand course, years ago now—everything before the war seemed like ancient history (her own). She had been surprisingly adept. Mr. Carver, the man who ran the secretarial college, had suggested that her shorthand was good enough for her to train as a court reporter at the Old Bailey. That would have been a quite different life, perhaps a better one. Of course, there was no way of knowing these things.

She trudged up the unlit stairs to her apartment. She lived on her own now. Millie had married an American USAF officer and moved to New York State ("Me—a war bride! Who'd a thunk it?"). A thin layer of soot and what seemed to be grease coated the walls of the stairway. It was an old building, in Soho of all places ("needs must" she heard her mother's voice say). The woman who lived upstairs had a great many gentleman callers and Ursula had become accustomed to the creaking bedsprings and strange noises that came through the ceiling. She was pleasant though, always ready with a cheery greeting and never missed her turn at sweeping the stairs.

The building had been Dickensian in its dinginess to begin with and was now even more neglected and unloved. But then, the whole of London looked wretched. Grimy and grim. She remembered Miss Woolf saying that she didn't think "poor old London" would ever be clean again. ("Everything is so awfully *shabby*.") Perhaps she was right.

"You wouldn't think we had *won* the war," Jimmy said when he came to visit, spiffy in his American clothes, shiny and bright with promise. She readily forgave her little brother his New World élan, he had had a hard war. Hadn't they all? "A long and hard war," Churchill had promised. How right he had been.

It was a temporary billet. She had the money for something better but the truth was she didn't really care. It was just one room, a window above the sink, a hot-water geyser, shared toilet down the hall. Ursula still missed the old apartment in Kensington that she had shared with Millie. They had been bombed out in the big raid of May '41. Ursula had thought of Bessie Smith singing *like a fox without a hole* but she had actually moved back in for a few weeks, living without a roof. It was chilly but she was a good camper. She had learned with the Bund Deutscher Mädel, although it wasn't the kind of fact that you bandied about in those dark days.

But here was a lovely surprise waiting for her. A gift from Pammy—a wooden crate filled with potatoes, leeks, onions, an enormous emerald-green Savoy cabbage (a thing of beauty) and on the top, half a dozen eggs, nestled in cotton wool inside an old trilby of Hugh's. Lovely eggs, brown and speckled, as precious as unpolished gemstones, tiny feathers stuck here and there. *From Fox Corner, with love* the label attached to the crate read. It was like receiving a Red Cross parcel. How on earth had it got here? There were no trains running and Pamela was almost certainly snowed in. Even more puzzling was how her sister had managed to dig up this wintry harvest when *Earth stood hard as iron.*

When she opened the door she found a scrap of paper on the floor. She had to put her spectacles on to read it. It was a note from Bea Shawcross. *Visited but you weren't in. Will pop by again. Bea.* Ursula was sorry she had missed Bea's visit, it would have been a nicer way to spend a Saturday afternoon than wandering in the dystopian West End. She was immensely cheered by nothing more than the sight of a cabbage. But then the cabbage—unexpectedly as was always the wont of these moments—uprooted an unwanted memory of the little parcel in the cellar at Argyll Road and she was plunged back into gloom. She was so up and down these days. Honestly, she chided herself, buck up, for heaven's sake.

It felt even colder inside the apartment. She had developed chilblains, horrid painful things. Even her ears were cold. She wished she had some earmuffs, or a balaclava, like the gray woolen ones that Teddy and Jimmy used to wear to school. There was a line in "The Eve of St. Agnes," what was it? Something about the stone effigies in the church *in icy hoods and mails.* It used to make her feel cold every time she recited it. Ursula had learned the whole poem at school, a feat of memory that was probably beyond her now, and what, after all, had been the point if she couldn't even remember a complete line? She had a sudden longing for Sylvie's fur coat, a neglected mink, like a large friendly animal, that now belonged to Pamela. Sylvie had chosen death on VE Day. While other women were scratching together food for tea parties and dancing in the streets of Britain, Sylvie had lain down on the bed that had been Teddy's when he was a child and swallowed a bottle of sleeping pills. No note, but her intention and motivation were quite clear to the family that she left behind. There had been a horrible funeral tea for her at Fox Corner. Pamela said it was the coward's way out, but Ursula wasn't so sure. She thought it showed a rather admirable clarity of purpose. Sylvie was another casualty of war, another statistic.

"You know," Pamela said, "I used to argue with her because she said science had made the world a worse place, that it was all about men inventing new ways to kill people. But now I wonder if she wasn't right." And that was before Hiroshima, of course.

Ursula lit the gas fire, a rather pathetic little Radiant that looked as if it dated from the turn of the century, and fed the meter. The rumor was that pennies and shillings were running out. Ursula wondered why they couldn't melt down armaments. Guns into plowshares, and so on.

She unpacked Pammy's box, laying everything out on the little wooden draining board like a poor man's still life. The vegetables were dirty but there wasn't much hope of washing the soil off as the pipes were frozen, even in the little Ascot, although the gas pressure was so low that it could barely heat the water anyway. *Water like a stone.* At the bottom of the crate she found a half bottle of whisky. Good old Pammy, ever the thoughtful one.

She scooped some water from the bucket that she'd filled from the standpipe in the street and put a pan of water on the gas ring, thinking she might boil one of the eggs, although it would take forever as there was only the tiniest frill of blue around the burner. There were warnings to be vigilant about the gas pressure—in case the gas came back on when the pilot light had gone out.

Would it be so bad to be gassed? Ursula wondered. *Gassed.* She thought of Auschwitz. Treblinka. Jimmy had been a Commando and at the end of the war he had become attached, rather haphazardly according to him (although everything to do with Jimmy was always slightly haphazard), to the antitank regiment that liberated Bergen-Belsen. Ursula insisted that he tell her what he had found there. He was reluctant and had probably withheld the worst but it was necessary to know. One must bear witness. (She heard Miss Woolf's voice in her head, *We must remember these people when we are safely in the future.*)

The toll of the dead had been her business during the war, the endless stream of figures that represented the blitzed and the bombed passed across her desk to be collated and recorded. They had seemed overwhelming, but the greater figures—the six million dead, the fifty million dead, the numberless infinities of souls—were in a realm beyond comprehension.

Ursula had fetched water yesterday. They—who *were* "they"?

After six years of war everyone had become accustomed to following "their" orders, what an obedient lot the English were—*they* had set up a standpipe in the next street and Ursula had filled up a kettle and bucket from the tap. The woman ahead of her in the queue was terrifically smart in an enviable floor-length sable, silver-gray, and yet there she was, waiting patiently in the bitter cold with her buckets. She looked out of place in Soho but then who knew her story?

The women at the well. Ursula seemed to remember that Jesus had a particularly confrontational conversation with the woman at the well. A woman of Samaria—no name, of course. She had had five husbands, Ursula recalled, and was living with a man who wasn't her husband, but the King James Bible never said what had happened to those five. Perhaps she had poisoned the well.

Ursula remembered Bridget telling them that when she was a girl in Ireland she had walked to a well every day to draw water. So much for progress. How quickly civilization could dissolve into its more ugly elements. Look at the Germans, the most cultured and well mannered of people, and yet... Auschwitz, Treblinka, Bergen-Belsen. Given the same set of circumstances it could just as well have been the English, but that was something else you couldn't say. Miss Woolf had believed that, she'd said—

"I say," the woman in sable said, interrupting her thoughts. "Do you understand why my water is frozen solid and yet this isn't?" She had a cut-glass accent.

"I don't know," Ursula said. "I know nothing." The woman laughed and said, "Oh, I feel the same way, believe me," and Ursula thought that perhaps this was someone she would like as a friend but then a woman behind them said, "Get a move on, love," and the sable-furred woman hefted her buckets, as strapping as a Land Girl, and said, "Well, must be off, cheerio."

* * *

She turned on the wireless. Transmission of the Third Program had been suspended for the duration. The war against the weather. You were lucky if you got the Home or the Light, there were so many electricity cuts. She needed noise, the sound of a familiar life. Jimmy had given her his old gramophone before he left, hers had been lost in Kensington along, sadly, with most of her records. She had managed to rescue a couple, miraculously unbroken, and placed one on the turntable now. "I'd Rather Be Dead and Buried in My Grave." Ursula laughed. "Cheerful or what?" she said out loud. She listened to the scratch and hiss of the old record. Was that how she felt?

She glanced at the clock, Sylvie's little gold carriage clock. She had brought it home after the funeral. Four o'clock only. Ye gods, how the days dragged. She caught the pips, turned off the news. What was the point?

She had spent the afternoon trawling Oxford Street and Regent Street, for something to do—really it was just to get out of her monastic cell of a bedsit. All the shops were dim and dismal. Paraffin lamps in Swan & Edgar's, candles in Selfridge's—the drawn, shadowy faces of people like something from a painting by Goya. There was nothing to buy, or certainly nothing that she wanted, and anything she did want, like a lovely cozy-looking pair of fur-topped bootees, was outrageously expensive (fifteen guineas!). So depressing. "Worse than the war," Miss Fawcett at work said. She was leaving to get married, they had all clubbed together for her wedding present, a rather uninspiring vase, but Ursula wanted to get her something more personal, more special, but she couldn't think what and had hoped that the West End department stores might have just the thing. They didn't.

She'd gone into a Lyons for a pale cup of tea, like lamb's water, Bridget would have said. And a utilitarian tea cake, she counted just two hard dry raisins, and a scraping of margarine, and tried to imagine she was eating something wonderful—a luscious *Creme-schnitte* or a slice of *Dobostorte.* She supposed the Germans weren't getting much in the way of pastries at the moment.

She murmured *Schwarzwälder Kirschtorte* accidentally out loud (such an extraordinary name, such an extraordinary cake) and attracted the unwanted attention of a neighboring table, a woman stoically working her way through a large iced bun. "Refugee, love?" she asked, surprising Ursula with her sympathetic tone.

"Something like that," Ursula said.

While she was waiting for the egg to boil—the water still only lukewarm—she rooted among her books, never unpacked after Kensington. She found the Dante that Izzie had given her, nicely tooled red leather but the pages all foxed, a copy of Donne (her favorite), *The Waste Land* (a rare first edition purloined from Izzie), a *Collected Shakespeare,* her beloved metaphysical poets and, finally, at the bottom of the box, her battered school copy of Keats, with an inscription that read *To Ursula Todd, for good work.* It would do for an epitaph too, she supposed. She flicked through the neglected pages until she found "The Eve of St. Agnes."

Ah, bitter chill it was!
The owl, for all his feathers, was a-cold;
The hare limp'd trembling through the frozen grass,
And silent was the flock in woolly fold.

She read out loud and the words made her shiver. She should read something warming, Keats and his bees—*For Summer has o'er-brimm'd their clammy cells.* Keats should have died on English soil. Asleep in an English garden on a summer's afternoon. Like Hugh.

She ate the egg while reading a copy of yesterday's *Times,* given to her by Mr. Hobbs in the post room when he had finished with it, a little daily ritual they had acquired. The paper's newly shrunk dimensions made it seem ridiculous somehow, as if the news itself was less important. Although really it was, wasn't it?

Snow like flakes of gray, soapy ash was falling outside the window. She thought of the Coles' relatives in Poland—rising above Auschwitz like a volcanic cloud, circling the Earth and blotting out the sun. Even now, after everything people had learned about the camps and so on, anti-Semitism was still rife. "Jewboy" she'd heard someone being called yesterday, and when Miss Andrews ducked out of contributing to Miss Fawcett's wedding present Enid Barker had made a joke of it and said, "What a Jew," as if it were the mildest of insults.

The office was a tedious, rather irritable place these days—fatigue, probably, due to the cold and the lack of good, nourishing food. And the work was tedious, an endless compilation and permutation of statistics to be filed away in the archives somewhere—to be pored over by the historians of the future, she supposed. They were still "clearing up and putting their house in order," as Maurice would have it, as if the casualties of war were clutter to be put away and forgotten. Civil Defense had been stood down for over a year and a half yet she still hadn't rid herself of the minutiae of bureaucracy. The mills of God (or the government) did indeed grind extremely small and slow.

The egg was delicious, it tasted as if it had been laid that very morning. She found an old postcard, a picture of the Brighton Pavilion (bought on a day trip with Crighton) that she'd never sent, and scrawled a thank-you to Pammy—*Wonderful! Like a Red Cross package*—and propped it up on the mantelpiece next to Sylvie's clock. Next to Teddy's photo too. Teddy and his Halifax crew taken one sunlit afternoon. They were lounging in an assortment of old chairs. Forever young. The dog, Lucky, stood as proud as a little figurehead on Teddy's knee. How cheering it would be to still have Lucky. She had Teddy's DFC, propped up on the glass of the photo frame. Ursula had a medal too but it meant nothing to her.

She would put the postcard in with the afternoon post tomorrow. It would take an age to reach Fox Corner, she supposed.

Five o'clock. She took her plate over to the sink to join the other unwashed dishes. The gray ash was a blizzard in the dark sky now and she pulled the flimsy cotton curtain to try to make it disappear. It tugged hopelessly on its wire and she gave up before she brought the whole thing down. The window was old and ill fitting and let in a piercing draft.

The electricity went off and she fumbled for the candle on the mantelpiece. Could it get any worse? Ursula took the candle and the whisky bottle to bed, climbed under the covers still in her coat. She was so tired.

The flame on the little Radiant fire quivered alarmingly. Would it be so very bad? *To cease upon the midnight with no pain.* There were worse ways. Auschwitz, Treblinka. Teddy's Halifax going down in flames. The only way to stop the tears was to keep drinking the whisky. Good old Pammy. The flame on the Radiant flickered and died. The pilot light too. She wondered when the gas would come back on. If the smell would wake her, if she would get up and relight it. She hadn't expected to die like a fox frozen in its den. Pammy would see the postcard, know that she'd been appreciated. Ursula closed her eyes. She felt as though she had been awake for a hundred years and more. She really was so very, very tired.

Darkness began to fall.

SNOW

11 February 1910

Warm and milky and new, the smell was a siren call to Queenie the cat. Queenie, strictly speaking, belonged to Mrs. Glover, although she was aloofly unaware that she was anyone's possession. An enormous tortoiseshell, she had arrived on the doorstep with Mrs. Glover, carried in a carpet bag, and had taken up residence in her own Windsor chair, a smaller version of Mrs. Glover's, next to the big kitchen range. Having her own chair didn't stop her leaving her fur on every other available seat in the house, including the beds. Hugh, no great lover of cats, complained continually about the mysterious way that the "mangy beast" managed to deposit its hairs on his suits.

More malevolent than most cats, she had a way of simply punching you, like a fighting hare, if you got close to her. Bridget, also no great cat lover, declared the cat to be possessed by a demon.

Where was that delicious new scent coming from? Queenie padded up the stairs and into the big bedroom. The room was warmed by the embers of a hot fire. This was a good room, the thick, soft quilt on the bed and the gentle rhythms of sleeping bodies. And there—a perfect little cat-sized bed, already warmed by a perfect little cat-sized cushion. Queenie kneaded her paws on the soft flesh, carried suddenly back to kittenhood. She settled herself down more comfortably, a deep bass purr of happiness rumbling in her throat.

Sharp needles in the soft skin pricked her into consciousness. Pain was a new, unwelcome thing. But then suddenly she was muffled, her mouth full of something, stoppering her, suffocating her. The more she tried to breathe the less it became possible. She was pinned down, helpless, no breath. Falling, falling, a bird shot.

Queenie had already purred herself into a pleasant oblivion when she was woken by a shriek and found herself being grabbed and thrown across the room. Growling and spitting, she backed out of the door, sensing this was a fight she would lose.

Nothing. Slack and still, the little ribcage not moving. Sylvie's own heart was knocking in her chest as if a fist was inside her, punching its way out. Such danger! Like a terrible thrill, a tide washing through her.

Instinctively, she placed her mouth over the baby's face, covering the little mouth and nose. She blew gently. And again. And again.

And the baby came back to life. It was that simple. ("I'm sure it was a coincidence," Dr. Fellowes said, when told of this medical miracle. "It seems very unlikely that you could revive someone using that method.")

Bridget returned to the kitchen from upstairs where she had been delivering beef tea and reported faithfully to Mrs. Glover, "Mrs. Todd says to tell Cook—that's you, Mrs. Glover—that you have to get rid of the cat. That it would be better if you had it killed."

"Killed?" Mrs. Glover said, outraged. The cat, now reinstated in her usual place by the stove, raised her head and stared balefully at Bridget.

"I'm just telling you what she said."

"Over my dead body," Mrs. Glover said.

Mrs. Haddock sipped a glass of hot rum, in what she hoped was a ladylike way. It was her third and she was beginning to glow from the inside out. She had been on her way to help deliver a baby when the snow had forced her to take refuge in the snug of the

Blue Lion, outside Chalfont St. Peter. It was not the kind of place she would ever have considered entering, except out of necessity, but there was a roaring fire in the snug and the company was proving surprisingly convivial. Horse brasses and copper jugs gleamed and twinkled. Visible from the snug, on the other side of the counter, was the public bar, where the drink seemed to flow particularly freely. It was an altogether rowdier place. A sing-song was currently in progress there and Mrs. Haddock was surprised to find her toe tapping in accompaniment.

"You should see the snow," the landlord said, leaning across the great polished depth of the brass bar counter. "We could all be stuck here for days."

"Days?"

"You may as well have another tot of rum. You won't be going anywhere in a hurry tonight."

LIKE A FOX IN A HOLE

September 1923

"And so you don't see Dr. Kellet at all now?" Izzie asked, snapping open her enameled cigarette case and displaying a neat row of Black Russian cigarettes. "Gasper?" she offered, holding out the case. Izzie addressed everyone as if they were the same age as herself. It was both seductive and lazy.

"I'm thirteen years old," Ursula said. Which as far as she could see answered both questions.

"Thirteen is quite grown-up nowadays. And life can be very short, you know," Izzie added, taking out a long ebony-and-ivory cigarette holder. She cast vaguely around the restaurant for a waiter to produce a light. "I rather miss those little visits of yours to London. Chaperoning you to Harley Street and then on to the Savoy for tea. A treat for both of us."

"I haven't seen Dr. Kellet for over a year," Ursula said. "I'm considered cured."

"Jolly good. I, on the other hand, am considered by *la famille* to be incurable. You are, of course, a *jeune fille bien élevée* and will never know what it is like to be the scapegoat for everyone else's sins."

"Oh, I don't know. I think I have an idea."

It was Saturday lunchtime and they were in Simpson's. "Ladies at leisure," Izzie said, over great slices of bloody beef carved off the bone before their eyes. Millie's mother, Mrs. Shawcross, was a vegetarian and Ursula imagined her horror at the sight of the great haunch of meat. Hugh called Mrs. Shawcross (Roberta) "a Bohemian," Mrs. Glover called her mad.

Izzie leaned toward the young waiter who had scurried over to light her cigarette. "Thank you, darling," she murmured, gazing directly up into his eyes in a way that made him grow suddenly as pink as the roast beef on her plate. *"Le rosbif,"* she said to Ursula, dismissing the waiter with an indifferent flap of her hand. She was always peppering her conversation with French words ("I spent some time in Paris when I was younger. And, of course, the war..."). "Do you speak French?"

"Well, we do it at school," Ursula said. "But that doesn't mean I can speak it."

"You're a droll little thing, aren't you?" Izzie inhaled deeply on her cigarette holder and then puckered up her (astonishingly) red cupid's bow as if she were about to play the trumpet before exhaling a stream of smoke. Several men seated nearby turned to stare at her in fascination. She winked at Ursula. "I bet the first French words you learned were *déjà vu.* Poor old thing. Maybe you were dropped on your head as a baby. I expect I was. Come on, let's tuck in, I'm ravenous, aren't you? I'm supposed to be banting but really there's only so much one can take," Izzie said, cutting enthusiastically into the beef.

This was an improvement, when she had met Ursula on the platform at Marylebone Izzie had looked green and said she was "a tad queasy" on account of the oysters and rum ("never a good combination") after a "disreputable" night in a club in Jermyn Street. Now, oysters apparently forgotten, she was eating as if she were starving even though she claimed, as usual, to be "watching her figure." She also claimed to be "stony broke" yet was wildly extravagant with her money. "What's life worth if you can't have some fun?" she said. ("Her life is nothing but fun as far as I can see," Hugh grumbled.)

Fun—and the concomitant treats—were necessary, Izzie claimed, to sweeten the fact that she had now "joined the ranks of the workers," and had to "pound away" on a typewriter to earn her keep. "Goodness, you would think she was hewing coal," Sylvie said crossly after a rare and rather embattled family luncheon at Fox Corner. After Izzie had gone, Sylvie banged down the Worcester fruit plates she was helping Bridget to clear and said, "All she's doing is producing drivel, which is something she's been doing since she first learned to talk."

"Heirlooms," Hugh murmured, rescuing the Worcester.

Izzie had managed to get a job ("God knows how," Hugh said) writing a weekly column for a newspaper—*Adventures of a Modern Spinster,* the column was called—on the subject of being a "singleton." "Everyone knows that there simply aren't enough men to go round anymore," she said, tearing into a bread roll at Fox Corner's Regency Revival dining table. ("*You* don't seem to have any trouble finding them," Hugh muttered.) "The poor boys are all dead," Izzie continued, ignoring him. Butter was plastered onto the roll with no regard for the hard labor of the cow. "There's nothing can be done about it, we have to move on as best we can without them. The modern woman must fend for herself without the prospect of the succor of hearth and home. She must learn to be independent, emotionally, financially and, most importantly, in her *spirit.*" ("Rot." Hugh again.) "The men are not the only ones who had to sacrifice themselves in the Great War." ("They're dead, you're not, that's the difference." This from Sylvie. Coldly.)

"Of course," Izzie said, mindful of Mrs. Glover at her elbow with a tureen of Brown Windsor, "the women of the lower classes have always known what it is to work." Mrs. Glover gave her a baleful look and tightened her grip on the soup ladle. ("Brown Windsor, how delicious, Mrs. Glover. What do you put in it to make it taste this way? Really? How *interesting.*") "We're moving toward a classless society, of course," a remark directed at Hugh but which earned a snort of derision from an unappeased Mrs. Glover.

"Are you a Bolshevik this week then?" Hugh asked.

"We're all Bolsheviks now," Izzie said blithely.

"And at my table!" Hugh said and laughed.

"She's such a fool," Sylvie said when Izzie had finally departed for the station. "And so much makeup! You would think she was on the stage. Of course, in her head she's always on the stage. She *is* her own theater."

"The hair," Hugh said regretfully. It went without saying that Izzie had bobbed her hair before anyone else they knew. Hugh had expressly forbidden the women in his family to cut their hair. Almost as soon as he had issued this paternal edict the normally unrebellious Pamela had gone into town with Winnie Shawcross and the pair of them had returned shingled and shorn. ("It's just easier for games" was Pamela's rational explanation.) Pamela had saved her heavy plaits, whether as relics or trophies, it was hard to say. "Mutiny in the ranks, eh?" Hugh said. Neither of them being the argumentative sort, that was the end of the conversation. The plaits now lived at the back of Pamela's underwear drawer. "You never know, they might come in useful for something," she said. No one in the family could imagine what that something might be.

Sylvie's feelings about Izzie went deeper than hair or makeup. She had never forgiven Izzie for the baby. He would be thirteen now, the same age as Ursula. "A little Fritz or Hans," she said. "My own children's blood running through his veins. But, of course, the only thing of any interest to Izzie is Izzie."

"Still, she can't be entirely shallow," Hugh said. "I expect she saw some awful things in the war." As if he hadn't.

Sylvie tossed her head. There might have been a halo of gnats around her own lovely hair. She was rather envious of Izzie's war, even the awfulness. "She's still a fool," she said and Hugh laughed and said, "Yes, she is."

Izzie's column seemed for the most part to be nothing more than a diary of her own hectic personal life with the odd social comment thrown in. Last week it had been "How high can they go?"

and was about "the rise of the emancipated female hemline," but consisted mostly of Izzie's tips to acquire the necessary shapely ankles. *Stand backward, on tiptoe, on the bottom step of a staircase and let your heels drop over the edge.* Pamela practiced all week on the attic staircase and declared no improvement at all.

Much against his will, Hugh felt it necessary to buy Izzie's newspaper every Friday and read it on the train home, "just to keep an eye on what she's saying" (and then jettison the offending item on the hall table, from where Pamela was able to rescue it). Hugh harbored a particular horror that Izzie would write about *him* and his only comfort was that she wrote under the pseudonym Delphine Fox, which was "the silliest name" that Sylvie had ever heard. "Well," Hugh said, "Delphine is her middle name, from her godmother. And Todd is an old word for fox, so I suppose there is some logic in it. Not that I'm defending her."

"But it's my *name,* it's on my birth certificate," Izzie said, looking hurt when attacked over the preprandial decanter. "And it's from Delphi, you know, the oracle, and so on. So rather fitting, I would have said." ("She's an oracle now?" from Sylvie. "If she's an oracle then I'm the high priestess of Tutankhamen.")

Izzie, in the person of Delphine, had already on more than one occasion mentioned "my two nephews" ("Terrific rascals, both of them!") but had not cited any names. "So far," Hugh said darkly. She had made up a few "amusing anecdotes" about these clearly fictional nephews. Maurice was eighteen (Izzie's "sturdy little chaps" were nine and eleven), still away at boarding school and had spent no more than ten minutes in Izzie's company in as many years. As for Teddy, he tended to avoid situations that might evolve into anecdotes.

"Who *are* these boys?" Sylvie quizzed over Mrs. Glover's surprisingly capricious interpretation of sole Véronique. She had the folded newspaper on the table next to her and tapped Izzie's column with her forefinger as if it might be impregnated with germs. "Are they supposed to be based in some way on Maurice and Teddy?"

"What about Jimmy?" Teddy said to Izzie. "Why don't you write about *him?*" Jimmy, perky in a sky-blue knitted jumper, was spooning mashed potato into his mouth and didn't look too bothered about being written out of great literature. He was a child of the peace, the war to end all wars had, after all, been fought for Jimmy. Yet again, Sylvie claimed to be taken by surprise by the newest addition to the family ("Four had seemed like the complete set"). Once, Sylvie had had no idea how children were started, now she seemed uncertain as to how you might stop them. ("Jimmy's an afterthought, I suppose," Sylvie said.

"I wasn't *thinking* much," Hugh said and they both laughed and Sylvie said, "Really, Hugh.")

Jimmy's arrival had the effect of making Ursula feel as if she was being pushed further away from the heart of the family, like an object at the edge of an overcrowded table. A cuckoo, she had overheard Sylvie say to Hugh. *Ursula's a bit of an awkward cuckoo.* But how could you be a cuckoo in your own nest? "You are my real mother, aren't you?" she asked Sylvie and Sylvie laughed and said, "Incontrovertibly, dear."

"The odd one out," she said to Dr. Kellet.

"Well, there always has to be one," he said.

Don't write about my children, Isobel," Sylvie said heatedly to Izzie.

"They're *imaginary,* for heaven's sake, Sylvie."

"Don't even write about my imaginary children." She lifted the tablecloth and peered at the floor. "What *are* you doing with your feet?" she said testily to Pamela, who was sitting opposite her.

"I'm making circles with my ankles," Pamela said, unconcerned by Sylvie's irritability. Pamela was quite bold these days but also rather reasonable, a combination that seemed designed to annoy Sylvie. ("You are so like your father," she had said to Pamela only this morning over some trifling difference of opinion. "But why would that be a bad thing?" Pamela said.) Pamela wiped gluey potato from Jimmy's pink cheeks and said, "Clockwise, then anticlockwise. It's the way to a shapely ankle, according to Aunt Izzie."

"Izzie is not a person from whom anyone with any sense would take advice." ("Excuse me?" Izzie said.) "Besides which, you're too young for shapely ankles."

"Well," Pamela said, "I'm nearly the same age as you were when you married Daddy."

"Oh, splendid," Hugh said, relieved at the sight of Mrs. Glover waiting in the doorway to make a grand entrance with a *Riz impératrice.* "The ghost of Escoffier is at your back today, Mrs. Glover." Mrs. Glover couldn't help but glance behind her.

Oh, splendid," Izzie said. "A cabinet pudding. You can rely on Simpson's for nursery food. We had a nursery, you know, it took up the whole top floor of the house."

"In Hampstead? Grandmama's house?"

"The very same. I was the baby. Like Jimmy." Izzie wilted a little, as if she were remembering some hitherto long-forgotten sadness. The ostrich feather on her hat trembled in sympathy. She revived at the sight of the silver sauceboat of custard. "And so you don't have those odd feelings anymore? The *déjà vu* and so on?"

"Me?" Ursula said. "No. Sometimes. Not so much, I suppose. It was before, you know. Now it's gone. Sort of." Had it? She was never sure. Her memories seemed like a cascade of echoes. Could echoes cascade? Perhaps not. She had tried (and largely failed) to learn to be precise with language under Dr. Kellet's guidance. She missed that cozy hour (*tête-à-tête,* he called it. More French) on a Thursday afternoon. She was ten years old when she first went to see him and had enjoyed being liberated from Fox Corner, in the company of someone who gave his full attention to her and only her. Sylvie, or more often than not Bridget, put Ursula on the train and she was met at the other end by Izzie even though both Sylvie and Hugh doubted that Izzie was sufficiently reliable to be in charge of a child. ("Expediency," Izzie said to Hugh, "generally trumps ethics, I've noticed. Personally, if I had a ten-year-old child I don't think I would feel entirely comfortable allowing it to travel all on its own." "You *do* have a ten-year-old child," Hugh pointed out. The little Fritz. "Couldn't we try and find him?" Sylvie asked. "Needle in a haystack," Hugh said. "The Hun are legion.")

So I rather miss seeing you," Izzie said, "which is why I asked if you could come up for the day. To be frank, I was surprised Sylvie agreed. There's always been a certain, shall we say, *froideur* between your mother and myself. I, of course, am considered mad, bad and dangerous to know. Anyway I thought I should try to single you out from the herd, as it were. You remind me a little of me." (Was that a good thing? Ursula wondered.) "We could be special chums, what do you think? Pamela's a little dull," Izzie continued. "All that tennis and cycling, no wonder she has such sturdy ankles. *Très sportive,* I'm sure, but still. And science! No fun in that. And the boys are, well . . . boys, but you're interesting, Ursula. All that funny stuff in your head about knowing the future. Quite the little clairvoyant. Perhaps we should set you up in a gypsy caravan, get you a crystal ball, Tarot cards. *The drowned Phoenician sailor* and all that. You can't see anything in my future, can you?"

"No."

Reincarnation," Dr. Kellet had said to her. "Have you heard of that?" Ursula, aged ten, shook her head. She had heard of very little. Dr. Kellet had a nice set of rooms in Harley Street. The one that he showed Ursula into was half paneled in mellow oak, with a thick carpet figured in red and blue on the floor and two large leather armchairs either side of a well-stoked coal fire. Dr. Kellet himself wore a three-piece Harris tweed suit strung with a large gold fob watch. He smelled of cloves and pipe tobacco and had a twinkly look about him as if he were going to toast muffins or read a particularly good story to her, but instead he beamed at Ursula and said, "So, I hear you tried to kill your maid?" (Oh, that's why I'm here, Ursula thought.)

He offered her tea which he brewed in something called a samovar in the corner of the room. "Although I'm not Russian, far from it, I'm from Maidstone, I visited St. Petersburg before the Revolution." He was like Izzie in that he treated you as a grown-up, or at least he appeared to, but that was where the resemblance ended. The tea was black and bitter and only drinkable with the aid of heaps of sugar and the contents of the tin of Huntley and Palmers Marie biscuits that sat between them on a little table.

He had trained in Vienna ("where else?") but trod, he said, his own path. He was no one's disciple, he said, although he had studied "at the feet of all of the teachers. One must nose forward," he said. "Nudge one's way through the chaos of our thoughts. Unite the divided self." Ursula had no idea what he was talking about.

"The maid? You pushed her down the stairs?" It seemed a very direct question for someone who talked about nosing and nudging.

"It was an accident." She didn't think of Bridget as "the maid," she thought of her as Bridget. And it was ages ago now.

"Your mother is worried about you."

"I just want you to be happy, darling," Sylvie said after she had made the appointment with Dr. Kellet.

"Aren't I happy?" Ursula puzzled.

"What do you think?"

Ursula didn't know. She wasn't sure that she had a yardstick against which to measure happiness or unhappiness. She had obscure memories of elation, of falling into darkness, but they belonged to that world of shadows and dreams that was ever present and yet almost impossible to pin down.

"As if there is another world?" Dr. Kellet said.

"Yes. But it's this one as well."

("I know she says the oddest things, but a *psychiatrist?*" Hugh said to Sylvie. He frowned. "She's only small. She's not *defective*."

"Of course not. She just needs a little fixing.")

And, hey presto, you're fixed! How marvelous," Izzie said. "He was an odd little bod, that mind doctor, wasn't he? Shall we essay the cheese board—the Stilton's so ripe it looks as if it's about to walk away of its own accord—or shall we tootle off and go to mine?"

"I'm stuffed," Ursula said.

"Me too. Tootle off it is then. Shall I pick up the bill?"

"I have no money. I'm thirteen," Ursula reminded her.

They left the restaurant and, to Ursula's astonishment, Izzie sauntered a few yards up the Strand and climbed into the driver's seat of a gleaming open-top car, parked, rather carelessly, outside the Coal Hole. "You have a car!" Ursula exclaimed.

"Good, isn't it? Not *exactly* paid for. Hop in. A Sunbeam, sports model. Certainly beats driving an ambulance. Wonderful in this weather. Shall we take the scenic route, go along the Embankment?"

"Yes, please."

"Ah, the Thames," Izzie said when the river came into view. "The nymphs, sadly, are all departed." It was a lovely late-September afternoon, crisp as an apple. "London's glorious, isn't it?" Izzie said. She drove as if she were on the circuit at Brooklands. It was both terrifying and exhilarating. Ursula supposed that if Izzie had managed to drive throughout the war unscathed then they would probably make it along the Victoria Embankment without coming to grief.

As they approached Westminster Bridge they had to slow down on account of the crowds of people whose flow had been interrupted by a largely silent demonstration of unemployed men. *I fought overseas,* a placard held aloft read. Another proclaimed *Hungry and wanting to work.* "They're so meek," Izzie said dismissively. "There'll never be a revolution in this country. Not another one at any rate. We chopped the head off a king once and felt so guilty about it that we've been trying to make up for it ever since." A shabby-looking man came up alongside the car and shouted something incomprehensible at Izzie, although the meaning was clear.

"*Qu'ils mangent de la brioche,*" Izzie murmured. "You know she never said that, don't you? Marie-Antoinette? She's a rather maligned figure in history. You must never believe everything they say about a person. Generally speaking, most of it will be lies, half-truths at best." It was hard to figure out whether Izzie was a royalist or a republican. "Best not to adhere too closely to one side or the other really," she said.

Big Ben tolled a solemn three o'clock as the Sunbeam pushed its way through the throng. "*Si lunga tratta di gente, ch'io non avrei mai creduto che morte tanta n'avesse disfatta.* Have you read Dante? You should. He's very good." How did Izzie know so much? "Oh," she said airily. "Finishing school. And I spent some time in Italy after the war. I took a lover, of course. An impoverished count, it's more or less *de rigueur* when you're over there. Are you shocked?"

"No." She was. Ursula wasn't surprised there was a *froideur* between her mother and Izzie.

Reincarnation is at the heart of Buddhist philosophy," Dr. Kellet would say, sucking on his meerschaum pipe. All conversations with Dr. Kellet were punctuated by this object, whether by gesture—a great deal of pointing with both mouthpiece and Turk's-head bowl (fascinating in itself)—or the necessary ritual of emptying, filling, tamping, lighting and so on. "Have you heard of Buddhism?" She hadn't.

"How old are you?"

"Ten."

"Still quite new. Perhaps you're remembering another life. Of course, the disciples of the Buddha don't believe that you keep coming back as the *same* person in the *same* circumstances, as you feel you do. You move on, up or down, sideways occasionally, I expect. Nirvana is the goal. Non-being, as it were." At ten it seemed to Ursula that perhaps *being* should be the goal. "Most ancient religions," he continued, "adhered to an idea of circularity—the snake with its tail in its mouth, and so on."

"I've been confirmed," she said, trying to be helpful. "Church of England."

Dr. Kellet had come to Sylvie recommended by Mrs. Shawcross via Major Shawcross, their next-door neighbor. Kellet had done a lot of good work, the major said, with men who "needed help" after they returned from the war (there was a suggestion that the major himself had "needed help"). Ursula's path crossed occasionally with some of these other patients. Once there was a dejected young man who stared at the carpet in the waiting room speaking quietly to himself, another who tapped his foot restlessly in time to something only he could hear. Dr. Kellet's receptionist, Mrs. Duckworth, who was a war widow and had been a nurse during the war, was always very nice to Ursula, offering her peppermints and asking her about her family. One day a man blundered into the waiting room, although the doorbell downstairs had never rung. He looked bewildered and a little wild but he just stood stock still in the middle of the room, staring at Ursula as if he'd never seen a child before, until Mrs. Duckworth led him to a chair and sat down next to him and then put her arm round him and said, "Now, now, Billy, what is it?" the way a nice mother would have done and Billy laid his head on her chest and began to sob.

If Teddy ever cried when he was younger, Ursula could never bear it. It seemed to open up a chasm inside, something deep and dreadful and full of sorrow. All she ever wanted was to make sure he never felt like crying again. The man in Dr. Kellet's waiting room had the same effect on her. ("That's how motherhood feels every day," Sylvie said.)

Dr. Kellet came out of his room at that moment and said, "Come along, Ursula, I'll see to Billy later," but when Ursula finished her appointment Billy was no longer in the waiting room. "Poor man," Mrs. Duckworth said sadly.

The war, Dr. Kellet said to Ursula, had made many people search for meaning in new places—"Theosophy, Rosicrucianism, anthroposophy, spiritualism. Everyone needs to make sense of their loss." Dr. Kellet himself had sacrificed a son, Guy, a captain in the Royal West Surreys, lost at Arras. "One must hold on to the idea of sacrifice, Ursula. It can be a higher calling." He showed her a photograph, not one taken in uniform, just a snapshot really, of a boy in cricket whites, standing proudly behind his bat. "Could have played for the county," Dr. Kellet said sadly. "I like to think of him—of all of them—playing a never-ending game in heaven. A perfect afternoon in June, always just before they break for tea."

It seemed a shame for all the young men never to have their tea. Bosun was in heaven, along with Sam Wellington, the old boot, and Clarence Dodds, who had died with astonishing speed of the Spanish flu the day after the Armistice. Ursula couldn't imagine any of them playing cricket.

"Of course, I don't believe in God," Dr. Kellet said. "But I believe in heaven. One has to," he added, rather bleakly. Ursula wondered how all of this was supposed to fix her.

"From a more scientific point of view," he said, "perhaps the part of your brain responsible for memory has a little flaw, a neurological problem that leads you to think that you are repeating experiences. As if something had got stuck." She wasn't really dying and being reborn, he said, she just *thought* she was. Ursula couldn't see what the difference was. *Was* she stuck? And if so, where?

"But we don't want it to result in you killing the poor servants, do we?"

"But it was such a long time ago," Ursula said. "It's not as if I've tried to kill anyone since."

"Down in the dumps," Sylvie said at their first meeting with Dr. Kellet, the only time she had been to the Harley Street rooms with Ursula although she had clearly already talked to him *without* Ursula. Ursula wondered very much what had been said about her. "And she's rather forlorn all the time," Sylvie continued. "I can understand an adult feeling like that—"

"Can you?" Dr. Kellet said, leaning forward, the meerschaum indicating interest. "Do *you?*"

"I'm not the problem," Sylvie said with her most gracious smile.

I'm a problem? Ursula thought. And anyway she hadn't been *killing* Bridget, she was *saving* her. And if she wasn't saving her perhaps she was sacrificing her. Hadn't Dr. Kellet himself said sacrifice was a higher calling?

"If I were you I would stick to traditional moral guidelines," he said. "Fate isn't in your hands. That would be a very heavy burden for a little girl." He got up from his chair and put another shovel of coal on the fire.

"There are some Buddhist philosophers (a branch referred to as Zen) who say that sometimes a bad thing happens to prevent a worse thing happening," Dr. Kellet said. "But, of course, there are some situations where it's impossible to imagine anything worse."

Ursula supposed he was thinking of *Guy, lost at Arras* and then denied his tea and cucumber sandwiches for eternity.

Try this," Izzie said, squirting a perfume atomizer in Ursula's direction. "Chanel Number 5. It's quite the thing. *She's* quite the thing. *Her strange, synthetic perfumes.*" She laughed as if she had made a great joke and sprayed another invisible cloud around the bathroom. It was quite different from the flowery scents that Sylvie anointed herself with.

They had finally arrived at Izzie's apartment in Basil Street ("rather a dull *endroit* but handy for Harrods"). Izzie's bathroom was pink-and-black marble ("I designed it myself, delicious, isn't it?") and was all sharp lines and hard corners. Ursula hated to think what would happen if you slipped and fell in here.

Everything in the apartment seemed to be new and shiny. It was nothing like Fox Corner, where the slow-seeming tick of the grandfather clock in the hall counted time and the patina of years shone on the parquet floors. The Meissen figures with their missing fingers and chipped toes, the Staffordshire dogs with accidentally lopped-off ears, bore no resemblance to the Bakelite bookends and onyx ashtrays in Izzie's rooms. In Basil Street everything looked so new it seemed to belong in a shop. Even the books were new, novels and volumes of essays and poetry by writers Ursula had never heard of. "One must keep up with the times," Izzie said.

Ursula regarded herself in the bathroom mirror. Izzie stood behind her, Mephistopheles to her Faustus, and said, "Goodness, you're turning out to be quite pretty," before rearranging her hair into different styles. "You must have it cut," she said, "you should come to my *coiffeur*. He's really very good. You're in danger of looking like a milkmaid, when really I think you're going to turn out to be deliciously wicked."

★ ★ ★

Izzie danced around the bedroom singing *I wish I could shimmy like my sister Kate.* "Can you shimmy? Look, it's easy." It wasn't and they collapsed in laughter on the satin eiderdown of the bed. "Gort to 'ave fun, 'aven't yew?" Izzie said in an atrocious mock-Cockney accent. The bedroom was a terrible mess, clothes everywhere, satin petticoats, *crêpe de Chine* nightdresses, silk stockings, partnerless shoes lying abandoned on the carpet, a dusting of Coty powder over everything. "You can try things on if you want," Izzie said carelessly. "Although you're rather small compared to me. *Jolie et petite.*" Ursula declined, fearing enchantment. They were the kind of clothes that might turn you into someone else.

"What shall we do?" Izzie said, suddenly bored. "We could play cards? Bezique?" She danced through to the living room and tripped her way toward a large shining chrome object that looked as if it belonged on the bridge of an ocean liner and turned out to be a cocktail cabinet. "A drink?" She looked doubtfully at Ursula. "No, don't tell me, you're only thirteen." She sighed, lit a cigarette and looked at the clock. "We're too late to catch a matinee, too early for an evening performance. *London Calling!* is on at the Duke of York's, it's supposed to be very amusing. We could go, you could get a later train home."

Ursula fingered the keys on the Royal typewriter that sat on a desk at the window. "My trade," Izzie said. "Perhaps I should put you in this week's column."

"Really? What would you say?"

"I don't know, make something up, I expect," she said. "That's what writers do." She took out a record from the cabinet of the gramophone and put it on the turntable. "Listen to this," she said. "You've never heard anything like it."

It was true, she hadn't. It started with a piano, but nothing like the Chopin and Liszt that Sylvie played so nicely (and Pamela in such a pedestrian fashion).

"They call it honky-tonk, I believe," Izzie said. A woman began to sing, raw and American. She sounded as if she had spent her life in a prison cell. "Ida Cox," Izzie said. "She's a Negress. Isn't she extraordinary?"

She was.

"Singing about how wretched it is to be a woman," Izzie said, lighting up another cigarette and sucking hard. "If only one could find someone really filthy rich to marry. *A large income is the best recipe for happiness I ever heard of.* Do you know who said that? No? Well you should." She was suddenly irritable, a not completely domesticated animal. The phone rang and she said, "Saved by the bell," and proceeded to have a feverishly animated conversation with the unseen, unheard caller. She ended the call by saying, "That would be delish, darling, meet you in half an hour." And to Ursula, "I would offer you a lift but I'm going to Claridge's and it's simply *miles* from Marylebone and after that I have a party to go to in Lowndes Square so I can't possibly see you to the station. You can Tube it to Marylebone, can't you? You know how? The Piccadilly line to Piccadilly Circus and then change to the Bakerloo to Marylebone. Come on, I'll walk out with you."

When they reached the street Izzie breathed deeply as if she'd been released from unwanted confinement. "Ah, twilight," she said. "The violet hour. Lovely, isn't it?" She kissed Ursula on the cheek and said, "It was marvelous seeing you, we have to do this again. Are you all right from here? *Tout droit* onto Sloane Street, turn left and Bob's your uncle, there's Knightsbridge Tube station. Toodle-oo, then."

Amor fati," Dr. Kellet said, "have you heard of that?" It sounded like he had said, "A more fatty." Ursula was puzzled—both herself and Dr. Kellet were on the lean side. Nietzsche ("a philosopher"), he said, was drawn to it. "A simple acceptance of what comes to us, regarding it as neither bad nor good."

"*Werde, der du bist,* as he would have it," Dr. Kellet continued, knocking the ashes from his pipe onto the hearth from where Ursula supposed someone else would sweep them up. "Do you know what that means?" Ursula wondered how many ten-year-old girls Dr. Kellet had actually encountered before. "It means become who you are," he said, adding more shreds of tobacco to the meerschaum. (The being before the non-being, Ursula supposed.) "Nietzsche got that from Pindar. γένοι' οἷος ἐσσὶ μαθών. Do you know Greek?" He had quite lost her now. "It means—become such as you are, having learned what that is."

Ursula thought he said "from Pinner," which was where Hugh's old nanny had retired to, living with her sister above a shop in an old building on the high street. Hugh had driven Ursula and Teddy out there in his splendid Bentley one Sunday afternoon. Nanny Mills was rather frightening (although not to Hugh apparently), spending a lot of time quizzing Ursula about her manners and inspecting Teddy's ears for dirt. Her sister was nicer and plied them with glasses of elderflower cordial and slices of milk fadge spread with blackberry jelly. "How is Isobel?" Nanny Mills asked, her mouth set like a prune. "Izzie is Izzie," Hugh said, which if you repeated it very quickly, as Teddy did later, sounded like a small swarm of wasps. Izzie, apparently, had become herself a long time ago.

It seemed unlikely that Nietzsche had obtained anything from Pinner, least of all his beliefs.

Nice time with Izzie?" Hugh asked when he picked her up from the station. There was something reassuring about the sight of Hugh in his gray homburg and long dark-blue wool overcoat. He scrutinized her for any visible change. She thought it best not to tell him that she had taken the Tube on her own. It had been a terrifying adventure, a dark night in the forest, but one which, like any good heroine, she had survived. Ursula shrugged. "We went to Simpson's for lunch."

"Hmm," Hugh said as if trying to decipher a meaning from this.

"We listened to a Negress singing."

"In Simpson's?" Hugh puzzled.

"On Izzie's gramophone."

"Hmm," again. He opened the car door for her and she settled into the lovely leathery seat of the Bentley, almost as reassuring as Hugh himself. Sylvie regarded the car as "ruinously" extravagant. It *was* breathtakingly expensive. The war had made Sylvie parsimonious: slivers of soap were collected and boiled down for the laundry, sheets turned side to middle, hats refurbished. "We would live on eggs and chickens if she had her way," Hugh laughed. He, on the other hand, had become less prudent since the war, "perhaps not the best trait for a banker to develop," Sylvie said. "*Carpe diem,*" Hugh said and Sylvie said, "You were never one for seizing."

"Izzie has a car now," Ursula offered.

"Does she?" Hugh said. "I'm sure it's not as splendid as this beast." He patted the dashboard of the Bentley fondly. As they drove away from the station he said quietly, "She's not to be trusted."

"Who?" (Mother? The car?)

"Izzie."

"No, you're probably right," Ursula agreed.

"How did you find her?"

"Oh, you know. Incurable. Izzie is Izzie, after all."

When they returned to the house they found Teddy and Jimmy playing a tidy game of dominos on the table in the morning room while Pamela was next door with Gertie Shawcross. Winnie was slightly older than Pamela and Gertie slightly younger and Pamela divided her time equally between them but rarely both at the same time. Ursula, devoted to Millie, found it an odd arrangement. Teddy loved all the Shawcross girls but his heart was in Nancy's small hands.

Of Sylvie there was no sign. "Don't know," Bridget said, rather indifferently, when Hugh inquired.

Mrs. Glover had left them a rather utilitarian mutton stew keeping warm in the range. Mrs. Glover no longer lived with them at Fox Corner. She rented a little house in the village so that she could look after George as well as them. George hardly ever left the house. Bridget referred to him as a "poor soul" and it was hard to disagree with that description. If it was good weather (or even not particularly good weather at all) he sat in a big ugly bath chair at the front door and watched the world pass him by. His handsome head ("Leonine, once," Sylvie said sadly) hung down on his chest and a long thread of drool dangled from his mouth. "Poor devil," Hugh said. "Better off if he'd been killed."

Sometimes one or other of them tagged along when Sylvie—or a more reluctant Bridget—visited him during the day. It seemed odd that they would go to his home to see him while his own mother stayed in their home looking after them. Sylvie would fuss with the blanket across his legs and fetch him a glass of beer and then wipe his mouth the way you did with Jimmy.

There were other war veterans in the neighborhood, visible thanks to their limps or missing limbs. All those unclaimed arms and legs lost in the fields of Flanders—Ursula imagined them pushing roots down into the mud and shoots up to the sky and growing once again into men. An army of men marching back for revenge. ("Ursula has morbid thoughts," she heard Sylvie say to Hugh. Ursula had become a great eavesdropper, it was the only way to find out what people were really thinking. She didn't hear Hugh's answer as Bridget came crashing into the room in a fury because the cat—Hattie, one of Queenie's offspring, possessed of the same character as her mother—had stolen the poached salmon that was to have been their lunch.)

There were those, too, who, like the men in Dr. Kellet's waiting room, had less visible injuries. There was an ex-soldier in the village called Charles Chorley who had served with the Buffs and had come through the war without a scratch and then one day in the spring of 1921 he had stabbed his wife and three children where they lay sleeping in their beds and then shot himself in the head with a Mauser he had taken from a German soldier he had killed at Bapaume. ("Terrible mess," Dr. Fellowes reported. "These chaps should think about the people who have to clean up afterward.")

Bridget, of course, had her "own cross to bear," having lost Clarence. Like Izzie, Bridget was resigned to spinsterhood although she embraced it in a less giddy fashion. They had all attended Clarence's funeral, even Hugh. Mrs. Dodds had been her usual restrained self and had flinched when Sylvie placed a comforting hand on her arm, but after they had shuffled away from the gaping hole of the grave (not a thing of beauty, not at all) Mrs. Dodds said to Ursula, "Part of him died during the war. This was just the rest of him catching up," and she put her finger to the corner of her eye and dabbed at a trace of moisture there—a tear would have been too generous a description. Ursula didn't know why she had been chosen for this confidence, possibly simply because she was the nearest person. Certainly no response was expected, or received.

"Ironic, one might say," Sylvie said, "for Clarence to have survived the war and to die of an illness." ("What would I have done if one of you had caught the influenza?" she often said.)

Ursula and Pamela had spent a considerable amount of time discussing whether Clarence had been buried with his mask on or off.

(And if off, where might it be now?) They didn't feel it was the kind of thing that they could ask Bridget. Bridget said bitterly that Old Mrs. Dodds had finally got her son to herself and stopped another woman taking him away from her. ("A little harsh, perhaps," Hugh murmured.) Clarence's photograph, a print of the one taken for his mother, before Bridget knew him, before he marched off to his destiny, had now joined that of Sam Wellington in the shed. "The endless ranks of the dead," Sylvie said angrily. "Everyone wants to forget them."

"Well, I certainly do," Hugh said.

Sylvie returned in time for Mrs. Glover's apple charlotte. Their own apples—a small orchard that Sylvie had planted at the end of the war was beginning to bear fruit. When Hugh wondered where she had been she said something indistinct about Gerrards Cross. She sat at the dining table and said, "I'm not really terribly hungry."

Hugh caught her eye and, nodding in Ursula's direction, said, "Izzie." An exquisite shorthand communication.

Ursula had expected an inquisition but all Sylvie said was "Good lord, I had quite forgotten that you had been to London. You've returned in one piece, I'm glad to see."

"Untainted," Ursula said brightly. "Do you, by the way, know who it was who said, *A large income is the best recipe for happiness I ever heard of?*" Sylvie's knowledge, like Izzie's, was random yet far-ranging, "the sign that one has acquired one's learning from novels, rather than an education," according to Sylvie.

"Austen," Sylvie said promptly. "*Mansfield Park.* She puts the words in Mary Crawford's mouth, for whom she professes disdain, of course, but really I expect dear Aunt Jane rather believed those words. Why?"

Ursula shrugged. "Nothing."

"*Till I came to Mansfield, I had not imagined a country parson ever aspired to a shrubbery, or anything of the kind.* Wonderful stuff. I always think the word 'shrubbery' denotes a certain kind of person."

"We have a shrubbery," Hugh said but Sylvie ignored him and continued to Ursula, "You really should read Jane Austen. You're surely the right age by now." Sylvie seemed quite gay, a mood somehow at odds with the mutton that was still sitting on the table in its dull brown pot, little ponds of white fat congealing on the surface. "Really," Sylvie said sharply, turning suddenly like the weather. "Standards are falling everywhere, even in one's own home." Hugh raised his eyebrows and before Sylvie had a chance to call on Bridget he got up from the table and took the stewpot back to the kitchen himself. Their little maid-of-all-work, Marjorie, no longer so little, had recently decamped and Bridget and Mrs. Glover were left to shoulder the burden of looking after them. ("It's not as if we're demanding in any way," Sylvie said crossly when Bridget mentioned that she hadn't had a pay rise since the end of the war. "She should be grateful.")

In bed that night—Ursula and Pamela still shared the cramped quarters of the attic bedroom ("like prisoners in a cell" according to Teddy)—Pamela said, "Why didn't she invite me as well as you, or even instead of you?" This, being Pamela, was said with genuine curiosity rather than malice.

"She thinks I'm interesting."

Pamela laughed and said, "She thinks Mrs. Glover's Brown Windsor is *interesting.*"

"I know. I'm not flattered."

"It's because you're pretty and clever," Pamela said, "while I am merely clever."

"That's not true and you know it," Ursula said, hotly defensive of Pamela.

"I don't mind."

"She says she'll put me in her newspaper next week but I don't suppose she will."

Ursula, in her account to Pamela of the day's adventures in London, had omitted a scene she had witnessed, unseen by Izzie, who had been preoccupied with turning the car round in the middle of the road outside the Coal Hole. A woman wearing a mink coat had come out of the entrance to the Savoy, on the arm of a rather elegant man. The woman was laughing in a carefree way at something the man had just said but then she broke away from his arm to search in her handbag for her purse in order to drop a handful of coins into the bowl of an ex-soldier who was sitting on the pavement. The man had no legs and was perched on some kind of makeshift wooden trolley. Ursula had seen another limbless man on a similar contraption outside Marylebone station. Indeed, the more she had looked on the London streets, the more amputees she had seen.

A doorman from the hotel darted out of Savoy Court and advanced on the legless man, who quickly scooted away using his hands as oars on the pavement. The woman who had given him money remonstrated with the doorman—Ursula could make out her handsome, impatient features—but then the elegant man took her gently by the elbow and guided her away up the Strand. The remarkable thing about this scene was not the content but the characters. Ursula had never seen the elegant man before but the agitated woman was—quite unmistakably—Sylvie. If she hadn't recognized Sylvie, she would have recognized the mink, given to her by Hugh for their tenth wedding anniversary. She seemed a long way from Gerrards Cross.

"Well," Izzie said when the car was finally facing the right way, "that was a tricky maneuver!"

★ ★ ★

When it came to the next week Ursula was indeed absent from Izzie's column, even in fictional form. She had written instead about the freedom that the single woman could obtain from ownership of "a little car." "The joys of the open road far surpass being trapped on a filthy omnibus or being followed down a dark street by a stranger. One has no need to glance nervously over one's shoulder at the wheel of a Sunbeam."

"I say, that's grim," Pamela said. "Do you think she has? Been followed down a street by a stranger?"

"Lots of times, I expect."

Ursula was not called upon again to be Izzie's "special chum," indeed none of them heard from her again until she turned up on the doorstep on Christmas Eve (invited but not expected) and declared herself to be "in a bit of a jam," a state which necessitated her being closeted in the growlery with Hugh, to emerge an hour later looking almost chastened. She had brought no presents with her and smoked throughout Christmas dinner, picking listlessly at her food. "Annual income twenty pounds," Hugh said when Bridget brought the brandy-soaked pudding to the table. "Annual expenditure twenty pounds ought and six, result misery."

"Oh, do shut up," Izzie said and flounced off before Teddy could put a match to the pudding.

"Dickens," Sylvie said to Ursula.

"J'étais un peu dérangée," Izzie said to Ursula, rather contritely, next morning by way of explanation.

"Silly of me, really," Izzie said. "I got in a bit of a muddle."

In the new year the Sunbeam disappeared and the Basil Street address was exchanged for a less salubrious one in Swiss Cottage (an even duller *endroit*) but nonetheless Izzie remained undeniably Izzie.

December 1923

Jimmy had a cold so Pammy said she would stay at home with him and make decorations from silver milk-bottle tops while Ursula and Teddy tramped along the lane in search of holly. Holly was abundant in the copse but the copse was further away and the weather was so wretched that they wanted to be outside for as little time as possible. Mrs. Glover, Bridget and Sylvie were confined to the kitchen, caught up in the afternoon drama of Christmas cooking.

"Don't pick any branches without berries," Pamela instructed as they left the house. "And don't forget to look for some mistletoe as well."

They went prepared with pruning shears and a pair of Sylvie's leather gardening gloves, having learned the painful lesson of previous Christmas foraging expeditions. They had their sights set on the big holly tree in the field at the far end of the lane, having been deprived of the handy holly hedge in the garden, which had been replaced by a more biddable privet after the war. The whole neighborhood was tamer and more suburban. Sylvie said it would not be long before the village had spread so much that they would be surrounded by houses. "People must live somewhere," Hugh said reasonably. "But not here," Sylvie said.

It was unpleasantly windy and spitting with rain and Ursula would have much preferred to stay by the fire in the morning room with the festive promise of Mrs. Glover's mince pies scenting the whole house. Even Teddy, usually the one to find a silver lining, trudged disconsolately along beside her, hunched against the weather, a small, stalwart Knight Templar in his knitted gray balaclava. "This is beastly," he said. Only Trixie relished the outing, ferreting in the hedgerows and delving in the ditch as if she had been sent on a mission to unearth treasure. She was a noisy dog, much given to barking for reasons apparent only to herself, so when, way ahead of them in the lane, she began to yap deliriously they took little notice.

Trixie had quietened down a bit by the time they caught up with her. She was standing sentinel over her prize, and Teddy said, "Something dead, I expect." Trixie was particularly skilled at truffling out half-rotted birds and the desiccated corpses of larger mammals. "A rat or a vole, probably," Teddy said. And then an eloquent "Oh," when he saw the true nature of the trove in the ditch.

"I'll stay here," Ursula said to Teddy, "and you run back to the house and fetch someone," but then as she watched his vulnerable little figure setting off, running alone along the deserted lane, the early winter dark already closing in around him, she had shouted at him to wait for her. Who knew what terror lay in wait? For Teddy, for all of them.

There was confusion as to what to do with the body over the holiday and eventually it was decided to keep it in the ice house at Ettringham Hall until after Christmas.

Dr. Fellowes, who had arrived along with a police constable, said the child had died of unnatural causes. A girl, eight or nine years old; her second set of front teeth had grown in although they had been knocked out before death. There were no little girls reported missing, the police said, certainly not locally. They speculated she might be a gypsy, although Ursula thought that gypsies *took* children, rather than left them behind.

It was almost New Year before a reluctant Lady Daunt was willing to give her up. When they removed her from the ice house they found her decorated like a relic—flowers and little tokens on her body, her skin bathed and her hair brushed and beribboned. As well as their three sons sacrificed to the Great War, the Daunts had also once had a girl, dead in infancy, and her custody of the little corpse had caused Lady Daunt to revisit her old grief and she had gone out of her mind for a while. She wanted to bury the girl in the grounds of the Hall but there was a rebellious murmuring from the villagers who insisted that she be buried in the churchyard, "Not hidden away as Lady Daunt's pet," someone said. A strange kind of pet, Ursula thought.

Neither her identity nor that of her murderer was ever discovered. The police questioned everyone in the neighborhood. They had come to Fox Corner one evening and Pamela and Ursula had almost hung themselves from the banisters in an attempt to hear what was said. From this eavesdropping they learned that no one in the village was a suspect and that "terrible things" had been done to the child.

In the end she was buried on the last day of the old year but not before the vicar had christened her, as the general feeling was that although the girl was determined to remain an enigma she should not be buried without a name. No one seemed to know how "Angela" was arrived at but it seemed appropriate. Nearly the whole village turned out for the funeral and many wept more heartily for Angela than they had ever done for their own flesh and blood. There was sadness rather than fear and Pamela and Ursula often discussed why it was, exactly, that everyone they knew was regarded as innocent.

Lady Daunt was not the only one to be strangely affected by the murder. Sylvie was particularly disturbed, more by anger, it seemed, than sadness. "It's not," she fumed, "that she was killed, although heaven knows that's terrible enough, it's that *no one missed her.*"

Teddy had nightmares for weeks afterward, creeping into bed beside Ursula in the dead of night. They would forever be the ones who found her, the ones who had seen the little shoeless, sockless foot—bruised and grubby, poking out from the dead branches of an elm, her body shrouded with a cold coverlet of leaves.

11 February 1926

"Sweet sixteen," Hugh said, kissing her affectionately. "Happy birthday, little bear. Your future's all ahead of you." Ursula still harbored the feeling that some of her future was also behind her but she had learned not to voice such things. They were to have gone up to London for afternoon tea at the Berkeley (it was half term), but Pamela had recently twisted her ankle in a hockey game and Sylvie was recovering from an attack of pleurisy that had seen her spend a night in the cottage hospital ("I suspect I have my mother's lungs," a remark that Teddy found funny every time he thought about it). And Jimmy was only just over a bout of the tonsillitis he was prone to. "Going down like flies," Mrs. Glover said, beating butter into sugar for the cake. "Who's next, I wonder?"

"Who needs to go to a hotel for a decent tea anyway?" Bridget said. "Just as good here."

"Better," Mrs. Glover said. Although, of course, neither Bridget nor Mrs. Glover had been invited to the Berkeley and indeed Bridget had never been inside a London hotel, or a hotel anywhere come to that, apart from having gone into the Shelbourne to admire the foyer before catching the ferry at Dún Laoghaire to come to England, "a lifetime ago." Mrs. Glover, on the other hand, declared herself to be "quite familiar" with the Midland in Manchester where one of her nephews (of which, it seemed, she had an endless supply) had taken her and her sister for dinner "on more than one occasion."

Coincidentally, Maurice was down for the weekend, although he had forgotten ("if he ever knew" Pamela said) that it was Ursula's birthday. He was in his last year at Balliol where he was reading law and was "more of a prig than ever" according to Pamela. His parents didn't seem particularly taken with him either. "He *is* mine, isn't he?" Ursula had overheard Hugh say to Sylvie. "You didn't have a dalliance in Deauville with that terrifically boring chap from Halifax, the one who owned the mill?"

"What a memory you have," Sylvie laughed.

Pamela had taken time out from her studies to make a lovely card, a *découpage* of flowers cut out from Bridget's magazines, as well as baking a batch of her famous (in Fox Corner anyway) "piccaninny" biscuits. Pamela was studying for the entrance exam for Girton. "A Girton girl," she said, her eyes alight, "imagine." As Pamela prepared to leave the sixth form of the school they both attended, Ursula was about to enter it. She was good at Classics. Sylvie said that she couldn't see the point of Latin and Greek (she had never been taught them and seemed to feel the lack). Ursula, on the other hand, was rather attracted to words that were now only whispers from the necropoles of ancient empires. ("If you mean 'dead' then say 'dead,'" Mrs. Glover said irritably.)

Millie Shawcross was also invited to tea and had arrived early, her usual chirpy self. Her present was an assortment of lovely velvet hair ribbons, bought with her own money from the haberdasher's in town. ("Now you'll never be able to cut your hair," Hugh said to Ursula, with some satisfaction.)

Maurice had brought two friends to stay for the weekend, Gilbert and an American, Howard ("Call me Howie, everyone does"), who were going to have to double up in the spare-room bed, a fact that seemed to make Sylvie uneasy. "You can go top to tail," she told them briskly. "Or one of you can sleep on a cot with the Great Western Railway," which was their name for Teddy's Hornby train set that took up all of Mrs. Glover's old room in the attic. Jimmy was allowed to share this pleasure. "Your sidekick, huh?" Howie said to Teddy, ruffling Jimmy's hair so vigorously that Jimmy was knocked off balance. The fact that Howie was an American gave him a special kind of glamour, although it was Gilbert who had the brooding, rather exotic, movie star looks. His name—Gilbert Armstrong—and his father (a high court judge) and his education (Stowe) pointed to impeccably English credentials but his mother was the scion of an old Spanish aristocratic family ("Gypsies," Mrs. Glover concluded, which was pretty much what she considered all foreigners to be).

"Oh, my," Millie whispered to Ursula, "the gods walk among us." She crossed her hands over her heart and flapped them like wings. "Not Maurice," Ursula said. "He would have been kicked off Olympus for getting on everyone's nerves."

"The self-importance of gods," Millie said, "what a wonderful title for a novel." Millie, needless to say, wanted to be a writer. Or an artist, or a singer, or a dancer, or an actress. Anything where she might be the center of attention.

"What are you little girls chattering about?" Maurice said. Maurice was very sensitive, some might have said oversensitive, to criticism.

"You," Ursula said. Girls did find Maurice attractive, a fact that continually surprised the women in his own family. He had fair hair that looked as if it had been marcelled and a strapping physique from rowing but it was hard to overlook his charmlessness. Gilbert, however, was even now kissing Sylvie's hand ("Oh," said Millie, "can it *get* any better?"). Maurice had introduced Sylvie as "My old mater," and Gilbert said, "You're too young to be anyone's mother."

"I know," Sylvie said.

("A rather louche fellow" was Hugh's verdict. "A Lothario," Mrs. Glover said.)

The three young men seemed to fill Fox Corner as if the house had suddenly shrunk, and both Hugh and Sylvie were relieved when Maurice suggested that they go outside for "a tour of the grounds." "Good idea," Sylvie said, "work off some of that surplus energy." The three of them ran out into the garden in Olympian fashion (sportive rather than sacred) and commenced a hearty kick-about with a ball that Maurice had found in the hall cupboard. ("Mine, actually," Teddy pointed out to no one in particular.) "They'll ruin the lawn," Hugh said, observing them howling like hooligans as they chewed up the grass with their muddy brogues.

"Oh," Izzie said, when she arrived and caught sight of this athletic trio through the window, "I say, they're rather gorgeous, aren't they? Can I have one?"

Izzie, swathed from head to toe in fox fur, said, "I brought gifts," an unnecessary announcement as she was laden with all kinds of different-shaped parcels in expensive wrapping "for my favorite niece." Ursula glanced at Pamela and gave a rueful shrug. Pamela rolled her eyes. Ursula hadn't seen Izzie in months, not since a fleeting visit to Swiss Cottage in the car with Hugh to drop off a crate full of vegetables from Fox Corner's bountiful late-summer garden. ("A marrow?" Izzie said, inspecting the contents of the box. "What on earth am I supposed to do with that?")

Prior to that she had visited for a long weekend but had more or less ignored everyone except Teddy, whom she took off for long walks and quizzed relentlessly. "I think she's singled him out from the herd," Ursula told Pamela. "Why?" Pamela said. "So she can eat him?"

When questioned (closely by Sylvie), Teddy was mystified as to why he had received special attention. "She just asked me what I did, what school was like, what my hobbies were, what I liked to eat. My friends. Stuff like that."

"Maybe she wants to adopt him," Hugh said to Sylvie. "Or sell him. I'm sure Ted would bring a good price." And Sylvie, fiercely,

"Don't say things like that, not even in jest." But then Teddy was dropped by Izzie as swiftly as he'd been picked up by her and they had thought no more of it.

The first of Ursula's presents to be unwrapped was a recording by Bessie Smith which Izzie immediately placed on the gramophone, home usually to Elgar and, Hugh's favorite, *The Mikado*. "The 'St. Louis Blues,'" Izzie said instructively. "Listen to that cornet! Ursula loves this music." ("Do you?" Hugh asked Ursula. "I had no idea.") Then a lovely tooled red-leather edition of Dante in translation was produced. This was followed by a satin-and-lace bed jacket from Liberty's—"as you know, a shop of which your mother is inordinately fond." This was pronounced "far too grown-up" by Sylvie, "Ursula wears flannelette." Next a bottle of Shalimar ("new by Guerlain, divine") which received a similar verdict from Sylvie.

"So speaks the child bride," Izzie said.

"I was eighteen, not sixteen," a tight-lipped Sylvie said. "One day we must talk about what *you* got up to at sixteen, Isobel."

"What?" Pamela said eagerly.

"Il n'avait pas d'importance," Izzie said dismissively. Finally, from this cornucopia, a bottle of champagne. ("And definitely far too young for that!")

"Better get that on ice," Izzie said, handing it to Bridget.

A perplexed Hugh glared at Izzie. "Did you steal all this?" he asked.

Hey, darkie music," Howie said when the three boys returned from the outdoors, crowding into the drawing room and smelling vaguely of bonfires and something else, less definable ("Essence of stag," Izzie murmured, sniffing the air). Bessie Smith was now on her third go-round and Hugh said, "It begins to grow on one after a while." Howie did some kind of odd dance to the music, vaguely barbaric, and then whispered something in Gilbert's ear. Gilbert laughed, rather crudely for someone with blue blood, albeit foreign, and Sylvie clapped her hands and said, "Boys, how about some potted shrimps?" and marshaled them into the dining room when she noticed, too late, the dirty footprints they had tracked through the house.

"They didn't fight in the war," Hugh said, as if that explained their muddy spoor.

"And that's a good thing," Sylvie said firmly. "No matter how unsatisfactory they turn out."

Now," Izzie said when the cake was cut and apportioned, "I have one last gift—"

"For goodness' sake, Izzie," Hugh interrupted, unable to contain his exasperation any longer. "Who is paying for this? You have no money, your debts are piled to the rafters. You promised you would learn economy."

"Please," Sylvie said. Any discussion of money (even Izzie's) in front of strangers filled her with reticent horror. A sudden dark cloud passed over her heart. It was Tiffin, she knew.

"*I* am paying," Izzie said, very grandly. "And this is not a present for Ursula, it is for Teddy."

"Me?" Teddy said, startled onto center stage. He had been thinking what a jolly good cake it was and wondering what the chances of a second piece were and certainly had no desire to be pushed into the limelight.

"Yes, you, darling boy," Izzie said. Teddy visibly shrank away from both Izzie and the present that she put on the table in front of him. "Go on," Izzie said encouragingly, "unwrap it. It won't explode." (But it would.)

Gingerly, Teddy removed the expensive paper. Unwrapped, the

present turned out to be exactly what it looked like when wrapped—a book. Ursula, sitting opposite, tried to decipher the upside-down title. *The Adventures of...*

"The Adventures of Augustus," Teddy read out loud, "by Delphie Fox." ("Delphie?" Hugh queried.)

"Why is everything an 'adventure' with you?" Sylvie said irritably to Izzie.

"Because life is an adventure, of course."

"I would say it was more of an endurance race," Sylvie said. "Or an obstacle course."

"Oh, my dear," Hugh said, suddenly solicitous, "not that bad, surely?"

"Anyway," Izzie said, "back to Teddy's present."

The thick card of the cover was green, the lettering and line drawings were gold—illustrations of a boy, roughly Teddy's age, wearing a schoolboy's cap. He was accompanied by a catapult and a small dog, a scruffy West Highland terrier. The boy was disheveled and had a wild look on his face. "That's Augustus," Izzie said to Teddy. "What do you think? I've based him on you."

"Me?" Teddy said, horrified. "But I don't look like that. It's not even the right dog."

Something astonishing. "Give anyone a lift back to town?" Izzie asked casually.

"You haven't got another car?" Hugh moaned.

"I parked it at the foot of the drive," Izzie said sweetly, "so as not to annoy you." They all trooped down the drive to inspect the car, Pamela, still on her crutches, hobbling tardily behind. "The poor and the maimed, the halt and the blind," she said to Millie and Millie laughed and said, "For a scientist you know your Bible."

"Best to know your enemy," Pamela said.

It was cold and none of them had thought to put their coats on. "But really quite mild for this time of year," Sylvie said. "Not like when you were born. Goodness, I've never seen snow like that."

"I know," Ursula said. The snow the day she was born was a legend in the family. She had heard the story so often that she thought she could remember it.

"It's just an Austin," Izzie said. "An open-road tourer—four doors though—but nowhere near as costly as a *Bentley,* goodness, it's positively a vehicle for hoi polloi compared to *your* indulgence, Hugh." "On tick, no doubt," Hugh said. "Not at all, paid up in full, *in cash.* I have a *publisher,* I have *money,* Hugh. You don't need to worry about me anymore."

While everyone was admiring (or not, in the case of Hugh and Sylvie) the cherry-bright vehicle, Millie said, "I have to go, I have a dancing exhibition tonight. Thank you very much for a lovely tea, Mrs. Todd."

"Come on, I'll walk you back," Ursula said.

On the return home, through the well-worn shortcut at the bottom of the gardens, Ursula had an unexpected encounter—this was the something amazing, not the Austin tourer—when she almost tripped over Howie, on his hands and knees, rooting among the bushes. "Looking for the ball," he said apologetically. "It was your kid brother's. I think we lost it in the"—he sat back on his heels and looked around helplessly at the berberis and buddleia—"Shrubbery," Ursula supplied. "We aspire to it."

"Huh?" he said, standing up in one clean move and suddenly towering above her. He looked as though he boxed. Indeed there was a bruise below his eye. Fred Smith, who used to be the butcher's boy but now worked on the railways, was a boxer. Maurice had taken a couple of his pals to cheer Fred on in an amateur bout in the East End. Apparently it had dissolved into a boozy riot. Howie smelled of bay rum—Hugh's scent—and there was something polished and new about him, like a freshly minted coin.

"Did you find it?" she asked. "The ball?" She sounded squeaky to her own ears. She had thought Gilbert was the handsome one out of the two but faced with Howie's clean-limbed, uncomplicated strength, like a large animal, she felt stupid.

"How old are you?" he asked.

"Sixteen," she said. "It's my birthday. You ate cake." Clearly she wasn't the only stupid one.

"Hoo-ee," he said, an ambiguous kind of word (closely related to his own name, she noted) although it seemed to signal amazement as if reaching sixteen was a feat. "You're shivering," he said.

"It's freezing out here."

"I can warm you up," he said and then—the something astonishing—he took her by the shoulders and pulled her toward him and—an action that necessitated bending down quite a bit—pushed his big lips against hers. "Kiss" seemed too courtly a word for what Howie was doing. He prodded his enormous tongue, like an ox's, against the portcullis of her teeth and she was amazed to realize that he was expecting her to open her mouth and let the tongue in. She would choke, for sure. Mrs. Glover's tongue press in the kitchen came unwontedly to mind.

Ursula was debating what to do, the bay rum and the lack of oxygen were making her dizzy, when they heard Maurice shouting, quite nearby, "Howie! Leaving without you, chum!" Ursula's mouth was released and, without a word to her, Howie yelled, "Coming!" so loudly that her ears hurt. Then he let go of her and set off, crashing through the bushes, leaving Ursula gasping for air.

She wandered back to the house in a daze. Everyone was still on the drive, even though it felt like hours had passed but she supposed it was only minutes really, like in the best fairy stories. In the dining room, the ruins of the cake were being licked delicately by Hattie. *The Adventures of Augustus,* lying on the table, had a smear of icing on it. Ursula's heart was still palpitating from the shock of Howie's advances. To be kissed on her sixteenth birthday, and in such an unlooked-for way, seemed a considerable accomplishment. She was surely passing beneath the triumphal arch that led to womanhood. If only it had been Benjamin Cole, then it would have been perfect!

Teddy, "the kid," himself appeared, very browned off and said, "They lost my ball."

"I know," Ursula said.

He opened the book at the title page where, in a flamboyant hand, Izzie had inscribed, *To my nephew, Teddy. My own darling Augustus.*

"What rot," Teddy said, scowling. Ursula picked up a half-drunk glass of champagne the rim of which was adorned with red lipstick and poured half of it into a jelly glass that she handed to Teddy. "Cheers," she said. They chinked their glasses and drained them to the dregs.

"Happy birthday," Teddy said.

May 1926

By the beginning of the month, Pamela, off her crutches and back to playing tennis, had learned that she had failed her Cambridge exam. "I panicked," she said, "I saw questions I didn't know and I went to pieces and flunked it. I should have swotted more or if I'd just stayed calm and thought it through I could probably have made a good fist of it."

"There are other universities if you're so set on being a bluestocking," Sylvie said. Sylvie, although she never quite came out and said it, thought academia was pointless for girls. "After all, woman's highest calling is to be a mother and a wife."

"You'd have me slave over a hot stove rather than a Bunsen burner?"

"What did science ever do for the world, apart from make better ways of killing people?" Sylvie said.

"Well, it's a crying shame about Cambridge," Hugh said. "Maurice is set to get a first and he's a complete dolt." To make up for Pamela's disappointment he bought her a Raleigh loop-frame roadster and Teddy asked what he would get if *he* failed an exam. Hugh laughed and said, "Careful, that's Augustus talk."

"Oh, please, don't," Teddy said, mortified at any mention of the book. *The Adventures of Augustus* had, to everyone's chagrin but particularly Teddy's, proved a roaring success, "flying off the bookshelves" and reprinted three times so far, according to Izzie who had already earned a "fat little royalty check" and moved into an apartment in Ovington Square. She had also done an interview for a newspaper in which she mentioned her "prototype," her "charming rogue of a nephew."

"But not my *name,*" Teddy said, hanging on to hope. He got a conciliation gift from Izzie in the shape of a new dog. Trixie had died a few weeks previously and Teddy had been in mourning ever since. The new dog was a Westie, like Augustus's dog—not a breed that any of them would have chosen. He had already been christened by Izzie—Jock, naturally, the name engraved on the tag on his expensive collar.

Sylvie suggested changing his name to Pilot ("Charlotte Brontë's dog," she said to Ursula. "One day," Ursula said to Pamela, "my communion with our mother will consist entirely of the names of the great writers of the past," and Pamela said, "I think it probably already does.")

The little dog already answered to Jock and it seemed wrong to confuse him, so Jock he remained, and in time they all grew to love him best of any of their dogs despite his annoying provenance.

Maurice turned up on a Saturday morning, this time with only Howie in tow and no sign of Gilbert, who had been sent down for "an indiscretion." When Pamela said, "What indiscretion?" Sylvie said that it was the definition of an indiscretion that you didn't speak of it afterward.

Ursula had thought of Howie quite often since their last encounter. It was not so much the physical Howie—the Oxford bags, the soft-collared shirt, the brilliantined hair—but the fact that he had been thoughtful enough to try to find Teddy's lost ball. Being kind modified the extraordinary, alarming *otherness* of him, which was threefold—large, male and American. Despite her ambivalent feelings she couldn't help but experience a slight thrill when she saw him hop effortlessly out of his open-top car, parked outside the front door of Fox Corner.

"Hey," he said when he caught sight of her and she realized her imaginary beau didn't even know her name.

A pot of coffee and a plate of scones were hastily conjured up by Sylvie and Bridget. "We're not staying," Maurice said to Sylvie, who said, "Thank goodness, I don't have enough to stretch to feed two hulking young men."

"We're going up to London to help out with the strike," Maurice said. Hugh expressed surprise. He hadn't realized, he said, that Maurice's politics put him on the side of the workers and Maurice in turn expressed surprise that his father could even think this was the case. They were going to drive buses and trains, and whatever else it took "to keep the country running."

"I didn't know you knew how to drive a train, Maurice," Teddy said, suddenly finding his brother interesting.

"Well, a stoker, then," Maurice said irritably, "it can't be that difficult."

"They're not called stokers, they're called firemen," Pamela said, "and it's a very skilled job. Ask your friend Smithy." A remark which for some reason got Maurice even hotter under the collar.

"You're trying to shore up a civilization that's in its death throes," Hugh said, as casually as if he were remarking on the weather. "There's really no point."

Ursula left the room at this juncture. If there was one thing she found more tedious than thinking about politics it was *talking* about politics.

And then. Astonishing. Again. As she was skipping up the back stairs on her way to the attic bedroom to fetch something, something innocent—a book, a handkerchief, afterward she would never remember what—she was almost sent flying by Howie on his way down. "I was looking for a bathroom," he said.

"Well, we only have one," Ursula said, "and it's not up these—" but before the sentence was finished she found herself pinned awkwardly against the neglected floral wallpaper of the back stairs, a pattern that had been up since the house was built. "Pretty girl," he said. His breath smelled of mint. And then she was again subjected to pushing and shoving from the outsized Howie. But this time it was not his tongue trying to jam its way into her mouth but something inexpressibly more intimate.

She tried to say something but before a sound came out his hand clamped over her mouth, over half her face in fact, and he grinned and said, "Shh," as if they were conspirators in a game. With his other hand he was fiddling with her clothes and she squealed in protest. Then he was butting up against her, the way the bullocks in the Lower Field did against the gate. She tried to struggle but he was twice, three times her size even and she might as well have been a mouse in Hattie's jaws.

She tried to see what he was doing but he was pressed so tightly against her that all she could see was his big square jaw and the slight brush of stubble, unnoticeable from a distance. Ursula had seen her brothers naked, knew what they had between their legs—wrinkled cockles, a little spout—and it seemed to have little to do with this painful piston-driven thing that was now ramming inside her like a weapon of war. Her own body breached. The arch that led to womanhood did not seem so triumphal anymore, merely brutal and completely uncaring.

And then Howie gave a great bellow, more ox than Oxford man, and was hitching himself back together and grinning at her. "English girls," he said, shaking his head and laughing. He wagged his finger at her, almost disapproving, as if she had engineered the disgusting thing that had just happened and said, "You really are something!" He laughed again and bounded down the stairs, taking them three at a time, as though his descent had been barely interrupted by their strange tryst.

Ursula was left to stare at the floral wallpaper. She had never noticed before that the flowers were wisteria, the same flower that grew on the arch over the back porch. This must be what in literature was referred to as "deflowering," she thought. It had always sounded like a rather pretty word.

When she came back downstairs a half hour later, a half hour of thoughts and emotions considerably more intense than was usual for a Saturday morning, Sylvie and Hugh were on the doorstep waving a dutiful good-bye to the disappearing rear end of Howie's car.

"Thank goodness they weren't staying," Sylvie said. "I don't think I could have been bothered with Maurice's bluster."

"Imbeciles," Hugh said cheerfully. "All right?" he said, catching sight of Ursula in the hallway.

"Yes," she said. Any other answer would have been too awful.

* * *

Ursula found it easier than she had expected to lock this occurrence away. After all, hadn't Sylvie herself said that the definition of an indiscretion was that you didn't speak of it afterward? Ursula imagined a cupboard in her mind, a corner one, in simple pitch pine. Howie and the back stairs were put on a high shelf and the key was firmly turned in the lock.

A girl surely should know better than to be caught on those back stairs—or in the shrubbery—like the heroine in a gothic novel, the kind that Bridget was so fond of. But who would have suspected that the reality of it would be so sordid and bloody? He must have sensed something in her, something unchaste, that even she was unaware of. Before locking it away she had gone over the incident again and again, trying to see in what way she had been to blame. There must be something written on her skin, in her face, that some people could read and others couldn't. Izzie had seen it. Something wicked this way comes. And the something was herself.

The summer unrolled. Pamela was given a place at Leeds University to read chemistry and said she was glad because people would be "more straightforward" in the provinces and not as snobbish. She played a lot of tennis with Gertie and championship mixed doubles with Daniel Cole and his brother Simon, and often let Ursula borrow her bike so that she could go for long rides with Millie, both of them shrieking as they freewheeled down hills. Sometimes Ursula went for lazy walks through the lanes with Teddy and Jimmy, Jock running rings around them. Neither Teddy nor Jimmy seemed to need to keep their lives secret from their sisters in the way that Maurice had done.

Pamela and Ursula took Teddy and Jimmy up to London for day trips, to the Natural History Museum, to the British Museum, to Kew, but they never told Izzie when they were in town. She had moved yet again, to a large house in Holland Park ("a rather artistic *endroit*"). One day as they wandered along Piccadilly they spied a pile of *The Adventures of Augustus* in a bookshop window, accompanied by "a photograph of the author—Miss Delphie Fox, taken by Mr. Cecil Beaton" in which Izzie looked like a film star or a society beauty. "Oh, God," Teddy said and Pamela, despite being *in loco parentis,* didn't correct his language.

There was a fete once more in the grounds of Ettringham Hall. The Daunts had gone, after a thousand years, Lady Daunt never having recovered from the murder of little Angela, and the Hall was now owned by a rather mysterious man, a Mr. Lambert who some said was Belgian, some Scottish, but no one had had a long enough conversation with him to discover his origins. Rumor said he had made his fortune during the war but everyone reported him shy and difficult to talk to. There were dances, too, in the village hall on Friday evenings and at one of these Fred Smith appeared, scrubbed clean of his daily soot, and asked, in turn, Pamela, Ursula and the three eldest Shawcrosses to dance. There was a gramophone, not a band, and they danced only old-fashioned dances, no Charleston or Black Bottom, and it was pleasant to be waltzed safely around the room, with surprising skill, by Fred Smith. Ursula thought it would be rather nice to have someone like Fred as a beau, although obviously Sylvie would never have tolerated such a thing. ("A *railwayman?*")

As soon as she thought about Fred in this way, the cupboard door sprang open and the whole appalling scene on the back stairs tumbled out.

"Steady on," Fred Smith said, "you've gone a bit green round the gills, Miss Todd," and Ursula had to blame it on the heat and insist on taking some fresh air on her own. She had in fact been feeling quite queasy lately. Sylvie put it down to a summer cold.

Maurice had gained his expected first ("How?" Pamela puzzled) and came home for a few weeks to lounge around before taking up a place in chambers in Lincoln's Inn, to train as a barrister. Howie, apparently, had returned to "his people" at their summer home on Long Island Sound. Maurice seemed a little miffed that he had not been invited to join them.

"What happened to you?" Maurice said to Ursula one afternoon as he sprawled on a deckchair on the lawn reading *Punch,* cramming nearly an entire slice of Mrs. Glover's marmalade cake into his mouth at once.

"What do you mean what happened to me?"

"You've turned into a heifer."

"A heifer?" It was true she was filling out her summer frocks rather alarmingly, even her hands and feet seemed to have plumped up. "Puppy fat, dear," Sylvie said, "even I had it. Less cake and more tennis, that's the remedy."

"You look hellish," Pamela said to her, "what's wrong with you?"

"I have no idea," Ursula said.

And then something truly terrible dawned on her, so awful, so shameful, so *irretrievable,* that she felt something catch fire and burn inside her at the very thought. She hunted down Sylvie's copy of *The Teaching of Young Children and Girls as to Reproduction* by Dr. Beatrice Webb, which, theoretically, Sylvie kept under lock and key in a chest in her bedroom, but the chest was never locked because Sylvie had long ago lost the key. Reproduction seemed to be the last thing on the author's mind. She advised distracting young girls by giving them plenty of "homemade bread, cake, porridge, puddings and cold water splashed regularly onto the parts." It was clearly no help. Ursula shuddered at the memory of Howie's "parts" and how they had come together with hers in one vile conjugation. Was this what Sylvie and Hugh did? She couldn't imagine her mother putting up with such a thing.

She sneaked a look at Mrs. Shawcross's medical encyclopedia.

The Shawcrosses were on holiday in Norfolk but their maid thought nothing of it when Ursula appeared at the back door saying she had come to look at a book.

The encyclopedia explained the mechanics of "the sexual act," something which appeared to take place only within the "loving confines of the marital bed" rather than on the back stairs when you were on your way to fetch a handkerchief, a book. The encyclopedia also detailed the consequences of failing to retrieve that handkerchief, that book—the missed monthlies, the sickness, the weight gain. It took nine months apparently. And now they were already well into July. Before long she would be squeezing herself back into her navy-blue gymslip and catching the bus to school every morning with Millie.

Ursula began to take long solitary walks. There was no Millie to confide in (and would she have anyway?) and Pamela had decamped to Devon with her Girl Guide patrol. Ursula had never taken to the Guides, now she rather regretted that—they might have given her the gumption to deal with Howie. A Guide would have retrieved that handkerchief, that book, without being hindered on the journey.

"Is there anything the matter, dear?" Sylvie asked as they darned stockings together. Sylvie's children only really came into focus for her when in isolation. Together they were an unwieldy flock, singly they had character.

Ursula imagined what she could say. *You remember Maurice's friend Howie? I appear to be the mother of his child.* She glanced at Sylvie, serenely wefting and warping her little woolen patch on the hole in the toe of one of Teddy's socks. She did not look like a woman who had had her parts breached. (A "vagina," apparently, according to Mrs. Shawcross's encyclopedia—not a word that had ever been uttered in the Todds' household.)

"No, nothing at all," Ursula said. "I'm fine. Absolutely fine."

* * *

That afternoon she walked to the station and sat on a bench on the platform and contemplated throwing herself under the express when it came hurtling through, but the next train turned out to be for London, huffing slowly to a halt in front of her in a way that seemed so familiar that it made her want to cry. She spotted Fred Smith climbing down from the cab, oily overalls and face smutty with coal dust. Spotting her, he came over and said, "Here's a coincidence, are you catching our train?"

"I haven't got a ticket," Ursula said.

"That's all right," Fred said, "nod and a wink from me and the ticket inspector'll see a friend of mine all right." Was she a friend of Fred Smith? It was comforting to think so. Of course, if he knew about her condition he would no longer be a friend. No one would.

"Yes, all right, thank you," she said. Not having a ticket seemed such a *little* problem.

She watched Fred climb back into the cab of his locomotive. The stationmaster stalked along the platform, slamming the carriage doors with a finality that suggested they would never be opened again. Steam flared from the funnel and Fred Smith stuck his head out of the cab and shouted, "Look smart there, Miss Todd, or you'll be left behind," and she stepped obediently on board.

The stationmaster's whistle chirped, short at first and then a longer call, and the train shuffled out of the station. Ursula sat on the warm plush of the seats and contemplated the future. She supposed she could get lost among the other fallen women crying woe on the streets of London. Curl up on a park bench and freeze to death overnight, except that it was the height of summer and she was unlikely to freeze. Or wade into the Thames and drift gently on the tide, past Wapping and Rotherhithe and Greenwich and on to Tilbury and out to sea. How puzzled her family would be if her drowned body was hooked from the deep. She imagined Sylvie, frowning over her darning, *But she only went for a walk, she said she was going to pick the wild raspberries in the lane.* Ursula thought guiltily of the white china pudding basin she had abandoned in the hedgerow, intending to collect it on her return. It was half full of the sour little berries and her fingers were still stained red.

She spent the afternoon walking through the great parks of London, through St. James's and Green Park, past the Palace and into Hyde Park and on to Kensington Gardens. It was extraordinary how far you could go in London and barely touch a pavement or cross a road. She had no money on her, of course—a ridiculous mistake, she realized now—and couldn't even buy a cup of tea in Kensington. There was no Fred Smith here to "see her all right." She was hot and tired and dusty and felt as parched as the grass in Hyde Park.

Could you drink the water in the Serpentine? Shelley's first wife had drowned herself here but Ursula supposed that on a day like this—crowds of people enjoying the sunshine—it would be almost impossible to avoid another Mr. Winton jumping in and rescuing her.

She knew where she was going, of course. It was inevitable somehow.

Good God, what happened to you?" Izzie said, throwing her front door wide dramatically as if she had been expecting someone more interesting. "You look a fright."

"I've been walking all afternoon," Ursula said. "I have no money," she added. "And I think I'm going to have a baby."

"You'd better come in then," Izzie said.

And now here she was, sitting on an uncomfortable chair in a large house in Belgravia in what must have once been the dining room. Now, devoid of any purpose except waiting, it was nondescript. The Dutch still life above the fireplace and the bowl of dusty-looking chrysanthemums on a Pembroke table provided no clue as to what might happen elsewhere in the house. It was hard to connect any of this to the odious rendezvous with Howie on the back stairs. Who would have thought it could be so easy to slip from one life to another. Ursula wondered what Dr. Kellet would have made of her predicament.

After her unexpected arrival in Melbury Road, Izzie had put her to bed in her spare bedroom and Ursula had lain sobbing beneath the shiny satin cover, trying not to listen to Izzie's unlikely lies on the phone in the hallway—*I know! She just turned up on the doorstep, the lamb... wanted to see me... pay a visit, museums and so on, the theater, nothing risqué... now don't be a termagant, Hugh...* It was just as well that Izzie hadn't spoken to Sylvie, she would have been given short shrift there. The upshot was that she was to be allowed to stay for a few days for *museums and so on.*

Phone call finished, Izzie came into the bedroom carrying a tray.

"Brandy," she said. "And buttered toast. All I could rustle up at short notice, I'm afraid. You are such a fool," she sighed. "There are ways, you know, things that one can do, prevention better than cure and so on." Ursula had no idea what Izzie was talking about.

"And you must get rid of it," Izzie continued. "We are agreed on that, aren't we?" A question which produced a heartfelt "yes" from Ursula.

A woman in a nurse's uniform opened the door of the Belgravia waiting room and looked in. Her uniform was so starched it would have stood up quite well without her inside it.

"This way," she said stiffly, without addressing Ursula by name. Ursula followed as meek as a lamb to the slaughter.

Izzie, efficient rather than sympathetic, had dropped her off in the car ("Good luck") with a promise that she would return "later." Ursula had no idea what was to happen in the interim between Izzie's "Good luck" and her "later" but she presumed it would be unpleasant. A foul-tasting syrup or a kidney dish full of large pills perhaps. And undoubtedly a good talking-to about her morals and her character. She hardly cared, as long as in the end the clock could be put back. How big was the baby? she wondered. Her brief research in the Shawcrosses' encyclopedia had given few clues. She supposed it would come out with a certain amount of difficulty and be wrapped in a shawl before being placed in a cradle and tended carefully until it was ready to be given to a nice couple who longed to have a baby as much as Ursula longed not to have one. And then she would be able to catch the train home, walk along Church Lane and retrieve the white china bowl with its harvest of raspberries, before entering Fox Corner as if nothing had happened beyond *museums and so on.*

It was a room like any other really. There were curtains, swagged and tasseled, at the tall windows. The curtains looked as though they were left over from the previous life of the house, as did the marble fireplace that now held a gas fire and, on the mantelpiece, a plain-faced clock with large numbers. The green linoleum underfoot and the operating table in the middle of the room were equally incongruous. The room smelled like the science laboratory at school. Ursula wondered about the brutish array of shining metal instruments that were laid out on a linen cloth on a trolley. They seemed to have more to do with butchery than babies. There was no sign of a cradle waiting anywhere. Her heart began to flutter.

A man, older than Hugh, in a long white doctor's smock hurried into the room as if he were on his way somewhere else and ordered Ursula up onto the operating table with her feet "in the stirrups."

"Stirrups?" Ursula repeated. Surely horses were not involved. The request was baffling until the starched nurse pushed her down and hooked her feet up. "I'm having an operation?" Ursula protested. "But I'm not ill." The nurse placed a mask over her face. "Count from ten down to one," she said. "Why?" Ursula tried to ask, but the word had barely formed in her brain before the room and everything in it disappeared.

The next thing she knew she was in the passenger seat of Izzie's Austin, gazing woozily through the windscreen.

"You'll be right as rain in no time," Izzie said. "Don't worry, they've doped you up. You'll feel queer for a bit." How did Izzie know so much about this appalling process?

Back in Melbury Road, Izzie helped her into bed and she slept deeply beneath the shiny satin cover in the spare bedroom. It was dark outside when Izzie came in with a tray. "Oxtail soup," she said cheerfully. "I got it from a tin." Izzie smelled of alcohol, something sweet and cloying, and underneath her makeup and her bright demeanor she looked exhausted. Ursula supposed she must be a terrible burden to her. She struggled to sit up. The smell of the alcohol and the oxtail was too much and she vomited all over the shiny satin.

"Oh, God," Izzie said, holding her hand over her mouth. "I'm really not cut out for this kind of thing."

"What happened to the baby?" Ursula asked.

"What?"

"What happened to the baby?" Ursula repeated. "Did they give it to someone nice?"

She woke in the night and vomited again and fell back to sleep without either cleaning it up or calling out to Izzie. When she woke in the morning she was too hot. Far too hot. Her heart was knocking in her chest and each breath was hard to come by. She tried to get out of bed but her head was swimming and her legs wouldn't hold her. After that everything was a blur. Izzie must have called Hugh because she felt a cool hand on her clammy forehead and when she opened her eyes he was smiling reassuringly at her. He was sitting on the bed, still in his overcoat. She was sick all over it.

"We'll get you to a hospital," he said, unperturbed by the mess. "You've got a bit of an infection." Somewhere in the background Izzie was putting up a fierce protest. "I'll be prosecuted," she hissed at Hugh and Hugh said, "Good, I hope they put you in jail and throw away the key." He lifted Ursula up in his arms and said, "Quicker to take the Bentley, I think." Ursula felt weightless, as if she was going to float away. The next thing she knew she was on a cavernous hospital ward and Sylvie was there, her face tight and awful. "How could you?" she said. She was glad when evening came and Sylvie changed places with Hugh.

It was Hugh who was with her when the black bat came. The hand of night was held out to her and Ursula rose to meet it. She was relieved, almost glad, she could feel the shining, luminous world beyond calling, the place where all the mysteries would be revealed. The darkness enveloped her, a velvet friend. Snow was in the air, as fine as talcum, as icy as the east wind on a baby's skin—but then Ursula fell back into the hospital bed, her hand rejected.

There was a brilliant slant of light across the pale green of the hospital counterpane. Hugh was asleep, his face slack and tired. He was sitting in an awkward position in a chair next to the bed. One trouser leg had ridden up slightly and Ursula could see a wrinkled gray lisle sock and the smooth skin of her father's shin. He had once been like Teddy, she thought, and one day Teddy would be like him. The boy within the man, the man within the boy. It made her want to weep.

Hugh opened his eyes and when he saw her he smiled weakly and said, "Hello, little bear. Welcome back."

August 1926

The pen should be held lightly, and in such a manner as to permit of the shorthand characters being easily written. The wrist must not be allowed to rest on the notebook or desk.

The rest of the summer was wretched. She sat beneath the apple trees in the orchard and tried to read a Pitman's shorthand instruction book. It had been decided she would do a typing and shorthand course rather than return to school. "I can't go back," she said. "I just can't."

There was little escape from the chill that Sylvie brought with her every time she entered a room and discovered Ursula in it. Both Bridget and Mrs. Glover were puzzled as to why the "serious illness" that Ursula had contracted in London while staying with her aunt seemed to have made Sylvie so distant from her daughter when they might have expected the opposite. Izzie, of course, was barred forever. *Persona non grata in perpetuam.* No one knew the truth of what had happened except for Pamela who had wormed the whole story out of Ursula, bit by bit.

"But he *forced* himself on you," she fumed, "how can you think it was your fault?"

"But the consequences . . ." Ursula murmured.

Sylvie blamed her entirely, of course. "You've thrown away your virtue, your character, everyone's good opinion of you."

"But no one knows."

"*I* know."

"You sound like someone in one of Bridget's novels," Hugh said to Sylvie. Had Hugh read one of Bridget's novels? It seemed unlikely. "In fact," Hugh said, "you sound rather like my own mother." ("It seems dreadful now," Pamela said, "but this too will pass.")

Even Millie was fooled by her lies. "Blood poisoning!" she said. "How dramatic. Was hospital ghastly? Nancy said that Teddy told her that you nearly died. I'm sure nothing so exciting will ever happen to me."

What a world of difference there was between dying and nearly dying. One's whole life, in fact. Ursula felt she had no use for the life she had been saved for. "I'd like to see Dr. Kellet again," she said to Sylvie.

"He's retired, I believe," Sylvie said indifferently.

Ursula still wore her hair long, mostly to please Hugh, but one day she went into Beaconsfield with Millie and had her hair chopped short. It was a penitent act that made her feel rather like a martyr or a nun. She supposed that was how she would live out the rest of her life, somewhere between the two.

Hugh seemed surprised rather than saddened. She supposed a haircut was a mild travesty compared to Belgravia. "Good gracious," he said, when she sat down at the dinner table to unappetizing veal cutlets *à la Russe.* ("Looks like the dog's dinner," Jimmy said, although Jimmy, a boy of magnificent appetite, would have quite happily eaten Jock's dinner.)

"You look like a completely different person," Hugh said.

"That can only be a good thing, can't it?" Ursula said.

"I liked the old Ursula," Teddy said.

"Well, it seems as though you're the only one who does," Ursula muttered. Sylvie made a noise that fell short of a word and Hugh said to Ursula, "Oh, come, I think you're—"

But she never did find out what Hugh thought of her because the loud rapping of the front-door knocker announced a rather anxious Major Shawcross inquiring as to whether Nancy was with them. "Sorry to interrupt your dinner," he said, hovering in the doorway of the dining room.

"She isn't here," Hugh said, although Nancy's absence was obvious.

Major Shawcross frowned at the cutlets on their plates. "She went to gather some leaves in the lane," he said. "For her scrapbook. You know what she's like." This addressed to Teddy, Nancy's twin soul. Nancy loved nature, forever collecting twigs and pine cones, shells and stones and bones, like the totems of an ancient religion. "A child of nature," Mrs. Shawcross called her ("As if that were a good thing," Sylvie said).

"She wanted oak leaves," Major Shawcross said. "We don't have any oaks in our garden."

There was a short discussion about the demise of the English oak, followed by a thoughtful silence. Major Shawcross cleared his throat. "She's been gone about an hour, according to Roberta. I've walked the length of the lane, up and back, shouting her name. I can't think where she might be. Winnie and Millie are out searching as well." Major Shawcross was beginning to look rather sick. Sylvie poured a glass of water and handed it to him. "Sit down," she said. He didn't. Of course, Ursula thought, he was thinking of Angela.

"I expect she'll have found something interesting," Hugh said, "a bird's nest or a farm cat with kittens. You know what she's like." They were all now quite in agreement that they knew what Nancy was like.

Major Shawcross picked up a spoon from the dining room table and gazed at it absently. "She's missed her dinner."

"I'll come and help you look for her," Teddy said, jumping up from the table. He knew what Nancy was like too, knew she never missed her dinner.

"Me too," Hugh said, giving Major Shawcross an encouraging pat on the back, the veal cutlets abandoned.

"Shall I come?" Ursula asked.

"No," Sylvie said. "Nor Jimmy either. Stay here, we'll look in the gardens."

No ice house this time. A hospital mortuary for Nancy. Still warm and soft when they found her, pushed into an empty old cattle trough. "Interfered with," Hugh told Sylvie while Ursula lurked like a spy behind the morning room door. "Two little girls in three years, it can't be a coincidence, can it? Strangled like Angela before her."

"A monster is living among us," Sylvie said.

It was Major Shawcross who found her. "Thank God, it wasn't poor old Ted this time," Hugh said. "He couldn't have borne it." Teddy couldn't bear it anyway. He barely spoke for weeks. His soul had been cut away, he said, when he did eventually speak. "Scars heal," Sylvie said. "Even the worst ones."

"Do you think that's true?" Ursula said, thinking about the wisteria wallpaper, the waiting room in Belgravia, and Sylvie said, "Well, not always," not even bothering to lie.

They heard Mrs. Shawcross screaming all through the first night. Afterward her face never looked right and Dr. Fellowes reported that she'd had a "small stroke."

"Poor, poor woman," Hugh said.

"She never knows where those girls are," Sylvie said. "She just lets them run wild. Now she's paying the price of her carelessness."

"Oh, Sylvie," Hugh said sadly. "Where is your heart?"

Pamela left for Leeds. Hugh drove her there in the Bentley. Her trunk was too massive for the boot and had to be sent by train.

"Big enough to hide a body in," Pamela said. She was bound for a women's hall of residence and had already been informed that she was to share the small room with a girl called Barbara, from Macclesfield. "It'll be just like being at home," Teddy said encouragingly, "except that Ursula will be someone else."

"Well, that rather makes it *nothing* like home," Pamela said. She clung to Ursula a little too fiercely before climbing into the car and sitting next to Hugh.

"I can't wait to go," Pamela said to Ursula in bed on her last night, "but I feel bad at leaving you."

When she didn't go back to school for the autumn term, no one questioned Ursula's decision. Millie was too grief-stricken over Nancy's death to care much about anything.

Ursula traveled on the train to High Wycombe every morning to attend a private secretarial college. "College" was a fancy word for two rooms, a cold scullery and a colder cupboard containing a WC above a greengrocer's on the high street. The college was run by a man called Mr. Carver whose lifelong passions were Esperanto and Pitman's shorthand, the latter more useful than the former. Ursula rather liked shorthand, it was akin to a secret code, with a whole new vocabulary—aspirates and shun hooks, compound consonants, special contractions, halving and doubling—the language of neither the dead nor the living but the strangely inert. There was something soothing about listening to Mr. Carver's monotonous intonation of word lists—*iterate, iteration, reiteration, reiterated, reiterating, prince, princely, princes, princess, princesses...*

The other girls on the course were all very pleasant and friendly—sanguine, practical sorts who always remembered their shorthand notebooks and rulers and never had fewer than two different-colored inks in their bags.

At lunchtime when the weather was bad they stayed in, sharing their packed lunches and darning stockings among the banks of typewriters. They had spent their summer hiking and swimming and camping and Ursula wondered if they could tell just by looking at her how different her own summer had been. "Belgravia" had become her shorthand for what had happened. ("An abortion," Pamela said. "An illegal abortion." Pamela was never one to avoid a blunt vocabulary. Ursula very much wished that she would.) She envied the ordinariness of their lives. (How Izzie would scorn such an idea.) Ursula's own chance at ordinariness seemed lost forever.

What if she had thrown herself beneath the express train or had died after Belgravia, or, indeed, what if she were simply to open her bedroom window and throw herself out, head first? Would she really be able to come back and start again? Or was it, as everyone told her, and as she must believe, all in her head? And so what if it was—wasn't everything in her head real too? What if there was no demonstrable reality? What if there was nothing beyond the mind? Philosophers "came to grips" with this problem a long time ago, Dr. Kellet had told her, rather wearily, it was one of the very first questions they addressed, so there was really no point in her fretting over it. But surely, by its very nature, everyone wrestled with this dilemma anew every time?

("Forget typing," Pamela wrote from Leeds, "you should read philosophy at university, you have the right kind of mind for it. Like a terrier with a terrifically tedious bone.")

She had, eventually, gone in search of Dr. Kellet and found his rooms occupied by a steel-haired, steel-spectacled woman who informed her that Dr. Kellet had indeed retired and did she wish to make an appointment with herself? No, Ursula said, she didn't. It was the first time she had been to London since Belgravia and she had a panic attack on the Bakerloo line on the way back from Harley Street and had to run out of the station at Marylebone, gasping for air. A newspaper seller said, "Are you all right, miss?" and she said, yes, yes, quite all right, thank you.

Mr. Carver liked touching the girls ("my girls") lightly on their shoulders, stroking the angora of a bolero cardigan or the lamb's wool of a sweater as if they were animals he was fond of.

In the morning they practiced their typing skills on the big Underwoods. Sometimes Mr. Carver made them practice with blindfolds on as this was, he claimed, the only way to stop them looking at the keys and slowing down their speeds. Wearing the blindfold made Ursula feel like a soldier about to be shot for desertion. On these occasions she often heard him making odd noises, muffled wheezes and grunts, but didn't like to peek from the blindfold to see what he might be doing.

In the afternoons they did shorthand—soporific dictation exercises that encompassed every kind of business letter. *Dear-Sir, I-brought your letter before-the Board-of-Directors at their-meeting yesterday, but after some discussion they-were obliged to postpone further-consideration of-the-matter until the next Directors'-meeting, which-will-be held on-the last Tuesday*... The content of these letters was tedious in the extreme and was a strange contrast to the furious flow of ink across their pads as they struggled to keep up.

One afternoon, while he was dictating to them, *We-fear there-is-no prospect of success for-those-who raise objection to-the appointment,* Mr. Carver passed behind Ursula and gently touched the nape of her neck, no longer protected by long hair. A shiver rippled right through her. She stared at the keys of her Underwood on the table in front of her. Was it something in her that attracted this kind of attention? Was she not a good person?

June 1932

Pamela had chosen a white brocade for herself and yellow satin for her bridesmaids. The yellow was on the acidic side and made all of the bridesmaids look slightly liverish. There were four of them—Ursula, Winnie Shawcross (chosen over Gertie) and Harold's two youngest sisters. Harold came from a large noisy family in the Old Kent Road that Sylvie considered to be "inferior." The fact that Harold was a doctor didn't seem to mitigate his circumstances (Sylvie was curiously averse to the medical profession). "I thought your own family were somewhat *déclassé,* weren't they?" Hugh said to Sylvie. He liked his new son-in-law-to-be, found him "refreshing." He liked Harold's mother, Olive, too. "She says what she means," he said to Sylvie. "And means what she says. Unlike some people."

"I thought it looked nice in the pattern book," Pamela said doubtfully at Ursula's third and final fitting, in a dressmaker's front room in Neasden, of all places. The bias-cut dress stretched tightly across Ursula's midriff.

"You've put on weight since the last fitting," the dressmaker said.

"Have I?"

"Yes," Pamela said. Ursula thought of the last time she had put on weight. Belgravia. It was certainly not the reason this time. She was standing on a chair, the dressmaker moving in a circle around her, a pincushion attached to her wrist. "You still look nice though," Pamela added.

"I sit all day at my work," Ursula said. "I should walk more, I expect." It was so easy to be lazy. She lived on her own but no one knew. Hilda, the girl she was supposed to share the apartment with—a top floor in Bayswater—had moved out, although she still paid the rent, thank goodness. Hilda was living in Ealing in a "regular little pleasure palace" with a man called Ernest whose wife wouldn't grant him a divorce, and she had to pretend to her parents that she was still in Bayswater, living the life of a single and virtuous woman. Ursula supposed it would only be a matter of time before Hilda's parents turned up unexpectedly on the door-step and she would have to spin a lie, or several, to explain their daughter's absence. Hugh and Sylvie would have been horrified if they thought Ursula was living on her own in London.

"Bayswater?" Sylvie said doubtfully when Ursula announced she was moving out of Fox Corner. "Is that really necessary?" Hugh and Sylvie had vetted the apartment, and they had also vetted Hilda, who stood up well to Sylvie's inquisition. Nonetheless Sylvie found both the apartment and Hilda somewhat wanting.

"Ernest from Ealing," as Ursula always thought of him, was the one who paid the rent ("a kept woman," Hilda laughed) but Hilda herself came by every couple of weeks to pick up her post and pay the rent money over. "I can find someone else to share with," Ursula offered, although she hated the idea.

"Let's wait a bit," Hilda said, "see if it all works out for me. That's the beauty about living in sin, you can always just get up and leave."

"So can Ernest (from Ealing)."

"I'm twenty-one, he's forty-two, he's not about to leave, trust me."

It had been a relief when Hilda had moved out. Ursula was able to lounge around all evening in her dressing gown, with her curl-ers in, eating oranges and chocolates and listening to the wireless. Not that Hilda would have objected to any of these things, would have enjoyed them in fact, but Sylvie had instilled decorum in the presence of others from an early age and it was hard to shake it off.

After a couple of weeks of being on her own, it struck her that she had hardly any friends and those that she did have she never seemed to care enough about to keep in touch with. Millie had become an actress, and was away almost all the time with a touring theater company. She sent the odd postcard from places she would probably never have visited otherwise—Stafford, Gateshead, Grantham—and drew funny cartoons of herself in various roles ("Me as Juliet, what a hoot!"). Their friendship hadn't really survived Nancy's death. The Shawcross family had turned inward with grief and when Millie finally started to live her life again she found Ursula had stopped living hers. Ursula often wished that she could explain Belgravia to Millie but didn't want to risk what was left of their fragile attachment.

She worked for a big importing company and sometimes when Ursula listened to the girls in the office chatting about what they'd been doing and with whom, she found herself wondering how on earth they met all these people, these Gordons, Charlies, Dicks, Mildreds, Eileens and Veras—a gay, restless flock with whom they frequented variety palaces and cinemas, went skating, swam in lidos and baths and drove out to Epping Forest and Eastbourne. Ursula did none of these things.

Ursula craved solitude but she hated loneliness, a conundrum that she couldn't even begin to solve. At work, they regarded her as a person apart, as if she were senior to them in every way, even though she wasn't. Occasionally one or other of the office coterie would say to her, "Do you want to come out with us after work?" It was meant kindly and felt like charity, which it probably was. She never took them up on their offers. She suspected, no, she knew, that they talked about her behind her back, nothing nasty, just curiosity really. They imagined there must be more to her. *A dark horse.* And *still waters run deep.* They would be disappointed to know that there *was* no more, that even clichés were more interesting than the life she lived. No depths, no darkness (in the past perhaps, but not the present). Unless you counted the drink. Which she supposed they would.

The work was a chore—endless bills of lading and customs forms and balance sheets. The goods themselves—rum, cocoa, sugar—and the exotic places they came from seemed at odds with the daily tedium of the office. She supposed she was a little cog in the big wheel of Empire. "Nothing wrong with being a cog," Maurice said, himself a big wheel now in the Home Office. "The world needs cogs." She didn't want to be a cog, but Belgravia seemed to have put paid to anything grander.

Ursula knew how the drinking had started. Nothing dramatic, just something as small and domestic as a *boeuf bourguignon* she had planned for Pamela when she came to stay for the weekend a few months ago. She was still working in the lab in Glasgow and wanted to do some shopping for her wedding. Harold hadn't moved yet either, he was due to take up his post at the Royal London in a few weeks. "We'll have a nice weekend, just the two of us," Pamela said.

"Hilda's away," Ursula lied easily. "Gone to Hastings for the weekend with her mother." There was no reason not to tell Pamela the truth of her arrangement with Hilda, Pamela had always been the one person she could be honest with, and yet something held her back.

"Splendid," Pamela said. "I'll drag Hilda's mattress through to your bedroom and it'll be like old times."

Are you looking forward to being married?" Ursula asked as they lay in bed. It wasn't really like old times at all.

"Of course I am, why would I be doing it otherwise? I like the idea of marriage. There is something smooth and round and solid about it."

"Like a pebble?" Ursula said.

"A symphony. Well, more of a duet, I suppose."

"It's not like you to wax poetic."

"I like what our parents have," Pamela said simply.

"Do you?" It was a while since Pamela had spent much time with Hugh and Sylvie. Perhaps she didn't know what they had these days. Dissonance rather than harmony.

"Have you met anyone?" Pamela asked cautiously.

"No. No one."

"Not yet," Pamela said in her most encouraging manner.

The *boeuf bourguignon* had, naturally, required burgundy and in her lunch hour Ursula had dropped into the wine merchant's that she passed every day on her way to work in the City. It was an ancient place, the wood of the interior gave the impression that it had been soaked in wine over the centuries and the dark bottles with their beautiful labels seemed to hold out the promise of something that went beyond their contents. The wine merchant picked out a bottle for her, some people used inferior wine for cooking, he said, but the only use one should have for inferior wine was vinegar. He himself was acerbic and rather overwhelming. He afforded the bottle the tenderness of care due a baby, lovingly wrapping it in tissue paper and passing it to Ursula to cradle in her basket-weave shopper where her purchase remained concealed from the office during the afternoon, in case they suspected her of being a secret lush.

The burgundy was bought before the beef and that evening Ursula thought she would open the wine and try a glass, seeing as it had been lauded so highly by the wine merchant. Of course, she'd had alcohol before, she was no teetotaler, after all, but she had never drunk alone. Never uncorked an expensive bottle of burgundy and poured a glass just for herself (dressing gown, curlers, a cozy gas fire). It was like stepping into a warm bath on a cold night, the deep, mellow wine suddenly enormously comforting. This was Keats's *beaker full of the warm South,* was it not? Her habitual despondency seemed to evaporate a little so she had another glass. When she stood up she felt quite swimmy and laughed at herself. "Tiddly," she said to no one and found herself wondering about getting a dog. It would be someone to talk to. A dog like Jock would greet her every day with cheerful optimism and perhaps some of that would rub off on her. Jock was gone now, a heart attack, the vet said. "And he had such a strong little heart," Teddy said, himself heartbroken. He had been replaced by a sad-eyed whippet that seemed too delicate for the rough and tumble of a dog's life.

Ursula rinsed the glass and put the cork back in the bottle, leaving plenty for the beef tomorrow before tottering off to bed.

She fell fast asleep and didn't wake until the alarm, which made a change from the usual restlessness. *Drink, and leave the world unseen.* When she woke she realized that she couldn't possibly look after a dog.

Next day at work, the tedium of filling in ledgers all afternoon was cheered by the thought of the half bottle sitting on her kitchen draining board. After all, she could buy another bottle for the beef.

That good, eh?" the wine merchant said when she appeared again two days later.

"No, no," she laughed, "I haven't cooked the meal yet. It struck me that I should have something equally good to drink with it." She realized she couldn't come back here, to this lovely shop, there was a limit to how many *boeuf bourgignons* someone was likely to cook.

For Pamela, Ursula made an abstemious cottage pie, followed by baked apples and custard. "I brought you a present from Scotland," Pamela said and produced a bottle of malt whisky.

* * *

Once the malt had been drunk she found another wine merchant, one who treated his wares with less veneration. "For a *boeuf bourguignon,*" she said, although he showed no interest in its purpose. "I'll take two, actually. I'm cooking for a lot of people." A couple of bottles of Guinness from the public house on the corner, "For my brother," she said, "he popped in unexpectedly." Teddy wasn't quite eighteen, she doubted he was a drinker. A couple of days later the same. "Your brother round again, miss?" the publican said. He winked at her and she flushed.

An Italian restaurant in Soho that she "happened to be passing" happily sold her a couple of bottles of Chianti without question. "Sherry from the wood"—she could take a jug to the Co-op at the end of the road and they would fill it up from the barrel. ("For my mother.") Rum from public houses a long way from the apartment ("for my father"). She was like a scientist experimenting with the various forms of alcohol, but she knew what she liked best, that first bottle of blushful Hippocrene, the bloodred wine. She plotted how to get a case delivered ("for a family celebration").

She had become a secret drinker. It was a private act, intimate and solitary. The very thought of a drink made her heart thud with both fear and anticipation. Unfortunately, between the restrictive licensing laws and the horror of humiliation, a young woman from Bayswater could have considerable difficulty in supplying her addiction. It was easier for the rich, Izzie had an account somewhere, Harrods probably, that simply delivered the stuff to her door.

She had dipped her toe in the waters of Lethe and the next thing she knew she was drowning, from sobriety to being a drunkard in a matter of weeks. It was both shameful and a way of annihilating shame. Every morning she woke up and thought, not tonight, I won't take a drink tonight, and every afternoon the longing built as she imagined walking into her apartment at the end of the day and being greeted by oblivion. She had read sensationalist accounts of the opium dens of Limehouse and wondered if they were true. Opium sounded better than burgundy for eclipsing the pain of existence. Izzie could probably supply her with the location of a Chinese opium den, she had "kicked the gong around," she had reported blithely, but it wasn't really the kind of thing Ursula felt she could ask. It might not lead to Nirvana (she had proved an apt pupil of Dr. Kellet after all), it might lead to a new Belgravia.

Izzie was occasionally allowed back into the family fold ("Weddings and funerals only," Sylvie said. "Not christenings"). She had been invited to Pamela's wedding but to Sylvie's profound relief had sent her apologies. "Weekend in Berlin," she said. She knew someone with a plane (*thrilling*) who was going to fly her there. Ursula visited Izzie occasionally. They had the horror of Belgravia in common, a memory that would unite them forevermore, although they never spoke of it.

In her stead there was a wedding present, a box of silver cake forks, a gift that Pamela was amused by. "How mundane," she said to Ursula. "She never ceases to surprise."

"Nearly finished," the Neasden dressmaker said through a mouthful of pins.

"I suppose I am getting a bit plump," Ursula said, looking in the mirror at the yellow satin straining to accommodate her potbelly. "Perhaps I should join the Women's League of Health and Beauty."

Stone-cold sober, she tripped on her way home from work. It was a miserable November evening a few months after Pamela's wedding, wet and dark, and she simply hadn't seen the pavement slab the edge of which had been lifted slightly by a tree root. Her hands were full—books from the library and grocery shopping, all acquired hastily in a lunch hour—and her instinct was to save the groceries and the books rather than herself. The result was that her face slammed into the pavement, the full force taken by her nose.

The pain stunned her, she had never experienced anything that came close to it before. She knelt on the ground and held her arms around herself, shopping and books now abandoned to the wet pavement. She could hear herself moaning—keening—and could do nothing to stop the noise.

"Oh, my," a man's voice said, "how awful for you. Let me help you. You have blood all over your nice peach scarf. Is that the color, or is it salmon?"

"Peach," Ursula murmured, polite despite the pain. She had never given much thought to the mohair muffler around her neck. There seemed to be a lot of blood. She could feel her whole face swelling and could smell the blood, thick and rusty, in her nose but the pain had lessened a degree or two.

The man was rather nice-looking, not very tall but he had sandy hair and blue eyes, and clean, polished-looking skin stretched over good cheekbones. He helped her to her feet. His hand in hers was firm and dry. "My name's Derek, Derek Oliphant," he said.

"Elephant?"

"Oliphant."

Three months later they were married.

Derek's origins were in Barnet and as unremarkable to Sylvie as Harold's before him. That was, of course, the essence of his appeal for Ursula. He taught history at Blackwood, a minor public school for boys ("the children of aspirant shopkeepers," Sylvie said dismissively) and courted Ursula with concerts in the Wigmore Hall and walks on Primrose Hill. They took long bike rides that ended up in pleasant pubs in the outer suburbs, a half-pint of mild for him, a lemonade for her.

Her nose proved to be broken. ("Oh, poor you," Pamela wrote. "And you had such a nice nose.") Before he escorted her to a hospital, Derek had led her into a public house nearby to get cleaned up a little. "Let me get you a brandy," he said when she sat down and she said, "No, no, I'm fine, I'll just have a glass of water. I'm not much of a drinker," even though the previous evening she had blacked out on the floor of her bedroom in Bayswater, courtesy of a bottle of gin she had stolen from Izzie's house. She had no qualms about thieving from Izzie, Izzie had taken so much from her. Belgravia, and so on.

Ursula stopped drinking almost as suddenly as she had started. She supposed she had had a hollow inside her that had been scooped out in Belgravia. She had tried to fill it with alcohol but now it was being replenished with her feelings for Derek. What were those feelings? Mostly relief that someone wanted to look after her, someone who knew nothing of her shameful past. "I'm in love," she wrote rather deliriously to Pamela. "Hurrah," Pamela wrote back.

"Sometimes," Sylvie said, "One can mistake gratitude for love."

Derek's mother still lived in Barnet but his father was dead, as was a younger sister. "A horrible accident," Derek said. "She fell into the fire when she was four years old." Sylvie had always been very particular about fireguards. Derek himself had nearly drowned when he was a boy, he said after Ursula had offered up her own incident in Cornwall. It was one of the few adventures in her life where she felt she had played an almost entirely innocent part. And Derek? A rough tide, an upturned rowing boat, a heroic swim to shore. No Mr. Winton necessary. "I rescued myself," he said.

"He's not *entirely* ordinary then," Hilda said, offering Ursula a cigarette. She hesitated but declined, not ready to take on another addiction. She was in the middle of packing up her goods and chattels. She could hardly wait to leave Bayswater behind. Derek was in digs in Holborn but was finalizing the purchase of a house for them.

"I've written to the landlord, by the way," Hilda said. "Told him we're both moving out. Ernie's wife's giving him a divorce, did I say?" She yawned. "He's popped the question. Thought I might take him up on it. We'll both be respectable married women. I can come and visit you in—where is it again?"

"Wealdstone."

The wedding party, in a register office, was, according to Derek's wishes, restricted to his mother and to Hugh and Sylvie. Pamela was disconcerted not to be invited. "We didn't want to wait," Ursula said. "And Derek didn't want any fuss."

"And don't *you* want fuss?" Pamela asked. "Isn't that the point of a wedding?"

No, she didn't want a fuss. She was going to belong to someone, safe at last, that was all that counted. Being a bride was nothing, being a wife was everything. "We wanted it all to be simple," she said resolutely. ("And cheap, by the looks of it," Izzie said. Another set of mundane silver cake forks was dispatched.)

"He seems like a pleasant enough chap," Hugh said at what passed for a reception—a three-course luncheon in a restaurant close to the register office.

"He is," Ursula agreed. "Very pleasant."

"Still, it's a bit of a rum do, little bear," Hugh said. "Not like Pammy's wedding, is it? Half of the Old Kent Road seemed to turn out for that. And poor Ted was very put out not to be invited today. As long as you're happy, though," he added encouragingly, "that's the main thing."

Ursula wore a dove-gray suit for the ceremony. Sylvie had provided corsages for everyone made from hothouse roses from a florist. "Not my roses, sadly," she said to Mrs. Oliphant. "Gloire des Mousseux, if you're interested."

"Very nice, I'm sure," Mrs. Oliphant said, in a way that didn't sound much like a compliment.

"Marry in haste, repent at leisure," Sylvie murmured to no one in particular before a restrained sherry toast to the bride and bridegroom.

"Have *you?*" Hugh asked her mildly. "Repented?" Sylvie pretended not to hear. She was in a particularly discordant mood. "Change of life, I believe," an embarrassed Hugh whispered to Ursula.

"Me too," she whispered back. Hugh squeezed her hand and said, "That's my girl."

And does Derek know you're not intact?" Sylvie asked when she was alone with Ursula in the ladies' powder room. They were sitting on little padded stools, repairing their lipstick in the mirror. Mrs. Oliphant remained at the table, having no lipstick to repair.

"Intact?" Ursula echoed, staring at Sylvie in the mirror. What did that mean, that she was flawed? Or broken?

"One's maidenhood," Sylvie said. "Deflowering," she added impatiently when she saw Ursula's blank expression. "For someone who is far from innocent you seem remarkably naive."

Sylvie used to love me, Ursula thought. And now she didn't. "Intact," Ursula repeated again. She had never even considered this question. "How will he tell?"

"The blood, of course," Sylvie said, rather testily.

Ursula thought of the wisteria wallpaper. The deflowering. She hadn't known there was a connection. She thought the blood was a wound, not the breaching of the arch.

"Well, he might not realize," Sylvie sighed. "I'm sure he won't be the first husband to be deceived on his wedding night."

Fresh war paint?" Hugh said easily when they returned to the table. Ted had inherited Hugh's smile. Derek and Mrs. Oliphant shared the same frown. Ursula wondered what Mr. Oliphant had been like. He was seldom mentioned.

"Vanity, thy name is woman," Derek said with what seemed like a forced joviality. He was not, Ursula noticed, as comfortable in social situations as she had first thought. She smiled at him, feeling a new bond. She was marrying a stranger, she realized. ("Everyone marries a stranger," Hugh said.)

"The word is 'frailty,' actually," Sylvie said pleasantly. "*Frailty, thy name is woman.* Hamlet. Many people misquote it for some reason."

A shadow passed over Derek's face but then he laughed it off. "I bow to your superior learning, Mrs. Todd."

Their new house in Wealdstone had been chosen for its location, relatively near to the school where Derek taught. He had an inheritance, "a very small sum" from his seldom-mentioned father's investments. It was a "sound" terrace in Masons Avenue, half-timbered in the Tudor style with leaded lights and a stained-glass panel in the front door depicting a galleon in full sail, although Wealdstone seemed a long way from any ocean. The house had all modern conveniences as well as shops close by, a doctor, a dentist and a park for children to play in, in fact everything a young wife (and mother, "one day very soon," according to Derek) could want.

Ursula could see herself eating breakfast with Derek in the mornings before waving him off to work, could see herself pushing their children in prams then pushchairs then swings, bathing them in the evening and reading bedtime stories in their pretty bedroom. She and Derek would sit quietly in the lounge in the evenings listening to the wireless. He could work on the book he was writing, a school textbook—*From Plantagenets to Tudors.* ("Gosh," Hilda said. "Sounds thrilling.") Wealdstone was a long way from Belgravia. Thank goodness.

The rooms this married life was to be carried out in remained in her imagination until after their honeymoon, as Derek had bought and furnished the house without her ever having seen it.

"That's a bit odd, don't you think?" Pamela said. "No," Ursula said. "It's like a surprise gift. My wedding present from him."

When Derek finally carried her awkwardly over the Wealdstone threshold (a red-tiled porch that neither Sylvie nor William Morris would have approved of) Ursula couldn't help but feel a twinge of disappointment. The house proved to be more sparsely old-fashioned than the one in her imagination and there was a drabness about it that she supposed came from its not having had a woman's hand in the decor, so she was surprised when Derek said, "Mother helped me." But then there was, of course, a similar kind of occlusion in Barnet where a certain dinginess adhered to the dowager Mrs. Oliphant.

Sylvie had passed her honeymoon in Deauville, Pamela spent hers on a walking holiday in Switzerland, but Ursula began her own marriage with a rather wet week in Worthing.

She married one man ("a pleasant enough chap") and woke up with another, one as tightly wound as Sylvie's little carriage clock.

He changed almost immediately, as if the honeymoon itself was a transition, an anticipated rite of passage for him from solicitous suitor to disenchanted spouse. Ursula blamed the weather, which was wretched. The landlady of the boardinghouse where they were staying expected them to vacate the premises between breakfast and dinner at six and so they spent long days sheltering in cafés or in the art gallery and museum or fighting the wind on the pier. Evenings were spent playing partner whist with other (less dispirited) guests before retiring to their chilly bedroom. Derek was a poor card player, in more ways than one, and they lost nearly every hand. He seemed almost to willfully misread her attempts to indicate her hand to him.

"Why did you lead trumps?" she asked him later—genuinely curious—as they decorously removed their clothes in the bedroom. "You think that nonsense is important?" he said with a look of such deep contempt that she thought it might be best to avoid games of any kind with Derek in the future.

On the first night, blood, or the lack of it, passed unnoticed, Ursula was relieved to find. "I think you should know that I am not inexperienced," Derek said rather pompously as they climbed into bed together for the first time. "I believe it is the duty of a husband to know something of the world. How else can he protect the purity of his wife?" It sounded like a specious argument to Ursula but she was hardly in a position to argue.

Derek rose early each morning and did a relentless series of press-ups—as if he were in an army barracks rather than on honeymoon. *"Mens sana in corpora sana,"* he said. Best not to correct him, she thought. He was proud of his Latin, as well as his smattering of ancient Greek. His mother had scrimped and saved to make sure he had a good education, "nothing had been handed on a plate, unlike some." Ursula had been rather good at Latin, Greek too, but she thought it best not to crow. That was another Ursula, of course. A different Ursula, unmarked by Belgravia.

Derek's method of having conjugal relations was very similar to his method of exercise, even down to the same expression of pain and effort on his face. Ursula could have been part of the mattress for all he seemed to care. But what did she have to measure it against? Howie? She wished now that she had questioned Hilda about what went on in her "pleasure palace" in Ealing. She thought of Izzie's exuberant flirting and the warm affection between Pamela and Harold. It all seemed to indicate diversion if not downright happiness. "What's life worth if you can't have some fun?" Izzie used to say. Ursula sensed there was going to be a shortage of fun in Wealdstone.

As humdrum as her job had been, it was as nothing compared to the drudge work of keeping house, day in, day out. Everything had to be continually washed, scrubbed, dusted, polished and swept, not to mention the ironing, the folding, the hanging, the straightening. The *adjustments.* Derek was a man of right angles and straight lines. Towels, tea towels, curtains, rugs all needed constant alignment and realignment. (As did Ursula, apparently.) But this was her job, this was the arrangement and realignment of marriage itself, wasn't it? Although Ursula couldn't get over the feeling that she was on some kind of permanent probation.

It was easier to succumb to Derek's unquestioning belief in domestic order rather than to fight it. ("A place for everything and everything in its place.") Crockery had to be scoured clean of stains, cutlery had to be polished and straightened in drawers—knives adjusted like soldiers on parade, spoons spooning each other neatly. A housewife has to be the most observant worshipper at the altar of the Lares and Penates, he said. It should be "hearth," not "altar," she thought, the amount of time she spent sweeping out grates and rattling clinker out of the boiler.

Derek was particular about tidiness. He couldn't think, he said, if things were out of place or askew. "Tidy house, tidy mind," he said. He was, Ursula was learning, rather fond of aphorisms. He certainly couldn't work on *From Plantagenets to Tudors* in the kind of muddle that Ursula seemed to create simply by entering a room. They needed the income from this textbook—his first—which William Collins was to publish and to this end he commandeered the poky dining room (table, sideboard and all) at the back of the house as his "study" and Ursula was banished from Derek's company most evenings so that he could write. Two should live as cheaply as one, he said, and yet here they were, barely able to pay their bills because of her lack of domestic economy, so she could at least give him some peace to try to earn an extra crust. And no, thank you, he didn't want her help in typing up his manuscript.

Ursula's old household routines now seemed appallingly slovenly, even to her own eyes. In Bayswater her bed often went unmade and her pots unwashed. Bread and butter made a good breakfast and there was nothing wrong, as far as she could see, with a boiled egg for tea. Married life was more exacting. Breakfasts had to be cooked and on the table at just the right time in the morning. Derek couldn't be late for school and regarded his breakfast, a litany of porridge, eggs and toast, as a solemn (and solitary) communion. The eggs were cooked in rotation throughout the week, scrambled, fried, boiled, poached, and on Fridays the excitement of a kipper. At weekends Derek liked bacon, sausage and black pudding with his eggs. The eggs came not from a shop but a smallholding three miles away, to which Ursula had to trek on foot every week because Derek had sold their bikes when they moved to Wealdstone "to save money."

Tea was a different kind of nightmare as she had to think of new things to cook all the time. Life was an endless round of chops and steaks and pies and stews and roasts, not to mention the pudding that was expected every day and in great variety. *I'm a slave to recipe books!* she wrote with faux-cheerfulness to Sylvie, although cheerful was far from how she felt every day, poring over their demanding pages. She gained a new respect for Mrs. Glover. Of course, Mrs. Glover benefited from a large kitchen, a substantial budget and a full *batterie de cuisine,* whereas the Wealdstone kitchen was fitted out in a rather paltry fashion and Ursula's housekeeping allowance never seemed to stretch throughout the week so that she was continually chastised for overspending.

She had never bothered much about money in Bayswater, if she fell short she ate less and walked instead of taking the Tube. If she really needed topping up there had always been Hugh or Izzie to fall back on, but she could hardly go running to them for money now that she had a husband. Derek would have been mortified at this slur on his manhood.

After several months under the constraint of unending chores Ursula thought she might go mad if she couldn't find some kind of pastime to alleviate the long days. There was a tennis club that she passed en route to the shops every day. All she could see of it was the tall netting that rose behind a wooden fence and a green door in a white pebble-dash wall facing the street, but she could hear the familiar inviting summer sound of *thock* and *twang* and one day she found herself knocking on the green door and asking if she could join.

"I've joined the local tennis club," she said to Derek when he came home that evening.

"You didn't ask me," Derek said.

"I didn't think you played tennis."

"I don't," he said. "I meant you didn't ask me if you could join."

"I didn't know I had to ask." Something passed over his face, the same cloud she had briefly seen on their wedding day when Sylvie had corrected his Shakespeare. This time it took longer to pass and seemed to change him in some indefinable way, as though part of him had shriveled inside.

"Well, can I?" she said, thinking it would be better to be meek and keep the peace. Would Pammy have asked such a question of Harold? Would Harold have ever expected such a question? Ursula wasn't sure. She realized she knew nothing about marriage. And, of course, Sylvie and Hugh's alliance remained an ongoing enigma.

She wondered what argument Derek could possibly have against her playing tennis. He seemed to be having the same struggle and eventually said begrudgingly, "I suppose so. As long as you still have time to do everything in the house." Halfway through their tea—stewed lamb chops and mashed potatoes—he got up abruptly from the table, picked up his plate and threw it across the room and then walked out of the house without saying a word. He didn't come back until Ursula was getting ready for bed. He still wore the same thrawn expression on his face as when he had left and gave her a brief "good night" that almost choked him as they climbed into bed.

In the middle of the night she was woken by him clambering on top of her and hitching himself wordlessly inside her. Wisteria came to mind.

The thrawn face ("that look" was how she thought of it) now made regular appearances and Ursula surprised herself with how far she would go to appease it. But it was hopeless, once he was in this mood she got on his nerves, no matter what she did or said, in fact her attempts to placate him seemed to make the situation worse, if anything.

A visit was arranged to Mrs. Oliphant in Barnet, the first since the wedding. They had popped in briefly—tea and a stale scone—to announce their engagement, but hadn't been back since.

This time round Mrs. Oliphant fed them a limp ham salad and some small conversation. She had several odd jobs "saved up" for Derek and he disappeared, tools in hand, leaving his womenfolk to clear up. When the washing-up was done, Ursula said, "Shall I make a cup of tea?" and Mrs. Oliphant said, "If you like," without any great encouragement.

They sat awkwardly in the parlor, sipping their tea. There was a framed photograph hanging on the wall, a studio portrait of Mrs. Oliphant and her new husband on their wedding day, looking straitlaced in turn-of-the-century wedding garb. "Very nice," Ursula said. "Do you have any photographs of Derek when he was small? Or of his sister?" she added because it didn't seem right to exclude the girl from family history merely on account of her being dead.

"Sister?" Mrs. Oliphant said, frowning. "What sister?"

"His sister who died," Ursula said.

"Died?" Mrs. Oliphant looked startled.

"Your daughter," Ursula said. "She fell in the fire," she added, feeling foolish, it was hardly a detail you were likely to forget. She wondered if perhaps Mrs. Oliphant was a little simple. Mrs. Oliphant herself looked confused, as if she were trying to recollect this forgotten child. "I only ever had Derek," she concluded firmly.

"Well, anyway," Ursula said, as if this were a trivial subject to be lightly tossed away, "you must come and visit us in Wealdstone. Now that we're settled. We're very grateful, you know, for the money that Mr. Oliphant left."

"Left? He left money?"

"Some shares, I think, in the will," Ursula said. Perhaps Mrs. Oliphant hadn't been involved in the probate.

"Will? He left nothing but debts when he went. He's not dead," she added as if it were Ursula who was the simple one. "He's living in Margate."

What other lies and half-truths were there? Ursula wondered. Did Derek really nearly drown when he was younger?

"Drown?"

"Fall out of a rowing boat and swim to shore?"

"Whatever gave you that idea?"

"Now then," Derek said, appearing in the doorway and making them both jump, "what are you two gossiping about?"

You've lost weight," Pamela said.

"Yes, I suppose I have. I've been playing tennis." How normal that made her life sound. She doggedly attended the tennis club, it was the only relief she had from the claustrophobia of life in Masons Avenue, though she had to face a constant inquisition on the subject. Every evening when he came home Derek asked if she had played tennis today, even though she only played two afternoons a week. She was always interrogated about her partner, a dentist's wife called Phyllis. Derek seemed to despise Phyllis, even though he had never met her.

Pamela had traveled all the way from Finchley. "Obviously it was the only way I was ever going to see you. You must like married life. Or Wealdstone," she laughed. "Mother said that you put her off." Ursula had been putting everyone off since the wedding, rebuffing Hugh's offers to "pop in" for a cup of tea and Sylvie's hints that perhaps they should be invited to Sunday lunch. Jimmy was away at school and Teddy was in his first year at Oxford but he wrote lovely long letters to her, and Maurice, of course, had no inclination to visit anyone in his family.

"I'm sure she's not too bothered about visiting. Wealdstone and so on. Not her cup of tea at all."

They both laughed. Ursula had almost forgotten what it felt like to laugh. She felt tears start to her eyes and had to turn away and busy herself with the tea things. "It's so nice to see you, Pammy."

"Well, you know you're welcome in Finchley whenever you please. You should get a telephone, and then we could talk all the time." Derek thought a telephone was an expensive luxury but

Ursula suspected that he simply didn't want her speaking to anyone. She could hardly voice this suspicion (and to whom—Phyllis? the milkman?) as people would think she was off her head. Ursula had been looking forward to Pamela's visit the way people looked forward to holidays. On Monday she had said to Derek, "Pamela's coming on Wednesday afternoon," and he had said, "Oh?" He seemed indifferent and she was relieved that the thrawn face did not appear.

As soon as they were finished with them Ursula quickly cleared the tea things away, washed and dried them and put them back in their places.

"Golly," Pamela said, "when did you become such a neat little *Hausfrau?*"

"Tidy house, tidy mind," Ursula said.

"Tidiness is overrated," Pamela said. "Is anything the matter? You seem awfully down."

"Time of the month," Ursula said.

"Oh, rotten luck. I'm going to be free of that problem for a few months. Guess what?"

"You're having a baby? Oh, that's wonderful news!"

"Yes. Isn't it? Mother will be a grandmother again." (Maurice had already made a start on the next generation of Todds.) "Will she like that, do you suppose?"

"Who knows? She's rather unpredictable these days."

"Did you have a nice visit from your sister?" Derek asked when he came home that night.

"Lovely. She's having a baby."

"Oh?"

The next morning her poached eggs were not "up to scratch." Even Ursula had to admit that the egg she presented for Derek's breakfast was a sad sight, a sickly jellyfish deposited on toast to die. A sly smile appeared on his face, an expression that seemed to indicate a certain triumph in finding fault. A new look. Worse than the old.

"Do you expect me to eat that?" he asked.

Several answers to that question passed through Ursula's mind but she rejected them all as provocative. Instead she said, "I can do you another one."

"You know," he said, "I have to work all hours at a job I despise, just to keep you. You don't have to worry your silly little noggin about anything, do you? You do nothing all day—oh, no, forgive me," he said sarcastically, "I was forgetting you play tennis—and you can't even manage to cook me an egg."

Ursula hadn't realized he despised his job. He complained a great deal about the behavior of the Lower Third and talked incessantly about the headmaster's lack of appreciation of his hard work, but she hadn't thought that he *hated* teaching. He looked close to tears and she felt suddenly and unexpectedly sorry for him and said, "I'll poach another."

"Don't bother." She anticipated the egg would be thrown at the wall, Derek was given to tossing food around since she had joined the tennis club, but instead he delivered a massive open-handed slap to the side of her head that sent her reeling against the cooker and then to the floor where she remained, kneeling as though she were at prayer. The pain, more than the act, had taken her by surprise.

Derek walked across the kitchen and stood over her with the plate containing the offending egg. For a moment she thought he was going to bring it crashing down on her but instead he slid the egg off the plate and onto the top of her head. Then he stalked out of the kitchen and she heard the front door slam a minute later.

The egg slid off her hair, down her face and onto the floor, where it burst open in a quiet splash of yellow. She struggled to her feet and fetched a cloth.

That morning seemed to open up something in him. She broke rules she didn't know existed—too much coal on the fire, too much toilet paper used, a light accidentally left on. Receipts and bills were all scrutinized by him, every penny had to be accounted for and she never had any spare money.

He proved himself capable of the most enormous rants over the pettiest of things, once started he seemed unable to stop. He was angry all the time. *She* made him angry all the time. Every evening now he demanded an exacting account of her day. How many books did she change in the library, what did the butcher say to her, did anyone call at the house? She gave up tennis. It was easier.

He didn't hit her again but violence seemed to simmer constantly beneath his surface, a dormant volcano that Ursula had unwontedly brought back to life. She was wrong-footed by him all the time so that she never seemed to have a moment to clear the befuddlement in her brain. Her very existence seemed to be irksome to him. Was life to be lived as a continuous punishment? (Why not, didn't she deserve that?)

She began to live in a strange kind of malaise, as though her head was full of fog. She had made her bed, she supposed, and now she must lie on it. Perhaps that was another version of Dr. Kellet's *amor fati*. What would he say about her current predicament? More to the point, perhaps, what would he say about Derek's peculiar character?

She was to attend sports day. It was a big event in Blackwood's calendar and wives of masters were expected to attend. Derek had given her money for a new hat and said, "Make sure you look smart."

She went to a local shop that sold apparel for women and children, called A La Mode (although it really wasn't). It was here that she bought her stockings and undergarments. She had had no new clothes since her wedding. She didn't care enough about her appearance to badger Derek for the money.

It was a lackluster-looking shop in a row of other lackluster shops—a hairdressing salon, a fishmonger, a greengrocer's, a post office. She didn't have the heart or the stomach (or the budget) to bother going up to town to a smart London department store (and what would Derek say about such a jaunt?). When she worked in London, before the watershed of marriage, she had spent a lot of time in Selfridges and Peter Robinson's. Now those places seemed as distant as foreign countries.

The contents of the shop window were protected from the sun by a yellowy-orange screen, a kind of thick cellophane that reminded her of the wrapper on a bottle of Lucozade and made everything in the window completely undesirable.

It was not the most beautiful hat but she supposed it would do. She scrutinized her reflection unwillingly in the shop's floor-to-ceiling tripartite mirror. In triptych she looked three times worse than she did in the bathroom mirror (the only one in the house that she couldn't avoid). She no longer recognized herself, she thought. She had taken the wrong path, opened the wrong door, and was unable to find her way back.

Suddenly, horribly, she frightened herself by wailing, the wretched sound of utter despondency. The owner of the shop came rushing from behind the counter and said, "There, dear, don't get upset. Time of the month, is it?" She made her sit and have a cup of tea and a biscuit and Ursula couldn't begin to express her gratitude for this simple kindness.

The school was one stop on the train and then a short walk along a quiet road. Ursula joined the stream of parents flowing through Blackwood's gates. It was exciting—and slightly terrifying—to suddenly find herself among a crush. She had been married less than six months but had forgotten what it was like to be in a crowd.

Ursula had never been to the school before and was surprised by its commonplace red brick and its pedestrian herbaceous borders, quite unlike the ancient school that the men of the Todd family attended. Teddy and then Jimmy had followed in Maurice's footsteps to Hugh's old school, a lovely building of soft gray stone and as pretty as an Oxford college. ("Savage within," though, according to Teddy.) The grounds were particularly beautiful and even Sylvie admired the profusion of flowers in the beds. "Rather romantic planting," she said. No such romance at Derek's school, where the emphasis was on the playing fields. The boys at Blackwood were not particularly academic, according to Derek anyway, and were kept occupied by an endless round of rugby and cricket. More healthy minds in healthy bodies. Did Derek have a healthy mind?

It was too late to ask him about his sister and his father, Krakatoa would erupt, Ursula suspected. Why would you make up something like that? Dr. Kellet would know.

Trestle tables, bearing refreshments for parents and staff, were set up at one end of the athletics field. Tea and sandwiches and finger slices of dry Dundee cake. Ursula lingered by the tea urn looking for Derek. He had told her he wouldn't be able to talk much to her as he was needed to "help out" and when she did eventually spot him at the far end of the field he was diligently carrying an armful of large hoops, the purpose of which seemed mysterious to Ursula.

Everyone gathered around the trestles seemed to know each other, particularly the masters' wives, and it struck Ursula that there must be a great many more social events at Blackwood than Derek ever mentioned.

A couple of senior masters, gowned like bats, settled on the tea table and she caught the name "Oliphant." As inconspicuously as possible Ursula stepped a little closer to them, pretending a deep fascination with the crab paste in the sandwich on her plate.

"Young Oliphant's in trouble again, I hear."

"Really?"

"Hit a boy, I believe."

"Nothing wrong with hitting boys. I hit them all the time."

"Bad this time though, apparently. Parents are threatening to go to the police."

"He's never been able to control a class. Ruddy awful teacher, of course."

Plates now fully loaded with cake, the two men began to wander off, Ursula drifting in their wake.

"In debt up to his ears, you know."

"Perhaps he'll make some money from his book."

They both laughed heartily as if a great joke had been told.

"The wife's here today, I gather."

"Really? We'd better watch out. I hear she's very unstable." This, too, a great joke, seemingly. A sudden shot from the starting pistol signaling the beginning of a hurdles race made Ursula jump. She let the masters amble off. She had lost her appetite for eavesdropping.

She caught sight of Derek striding toward her, hoops now replaced by an unwieldy burden of javelins. He shouted to a couple of boys for help and they trotted up obediently. As they passed

Ursula, one of them sniggered, sotto voce, "Yes, Mr. Elephant, coming, Mr. Elephant." Derek dropped the javelins to the grass with a great clatter and said to the boys, "Carry them to the end of the field, come on, get a move on." He approached Ursula and kissed her lightly on the cheek, saying, "Hello, dear." She burst out laughing, she couldn't help herself. It was the nicest thing he had said to her in weeks and was voiced not to her but for the benefit of the two masters' wives who were standing nearby.

"Is there something funny?" he asked, studying her face a little too long for comfort. She could tell he was seething. She shook her head in answer. She was worried she might scream out loud, could feel her own volcano bubbling up, ready to explode. She supposed she was hysterical. *Unstable.*

"I have to see to the Upper School's high jump," Derek said, frowning at her. "I'll meet you shortly." He walked off, still frowning, and she started to laugh again.

"Mrs. Oliphant? Is it Mrs. Oliphant, it is, isn't it?" The two masters' wives pounced on her, lionesses sensing wounded prey.

She also traveled home alone as Derek had to supervise evening study and would eat at the school, he said. She made herself a scrappy tea of fried herring and cold potatoes and had a sudden longing for a bottle of good red wine. In fact one bottle after another until she had drunk herself to death. She scraped the herring bones into the bin. *To cease upon the midnight with no pain.* Anything was better than this ludicrous life.

Derek was a joke, to the boys, to the staff. *Mr. Elephant.* She could just imagine the unruly Lower Third driving him mad with rage. And his book, what of his book?

Ursula never bothered much with the contents of Derek's "study." She had never felt any great interest in the Plantagenets or Tudors either for that matter. She was under strict instructions not to move any of his papers or books when dusting and polishing in the dining room (as she still liked to think of it) but she didn't care to anyway, barely glancing at the progress of the great tome.

He had been working feverishly of late, the table was covered in a clutter of notes and scraps of paper. It was all disconnected sentences and thoughts—*rather amusing if somewhat primitive belief—planta genista, the common broom gives us the name Angevin—come of the devil, and to the devil they would go.* There was little sign of an actual manuscript, just corrections and re-corrections, the same paragraph written over and over with tiny changes each time, and endless trial pages, written in ruled exercise books with Blackwood's crest and motto (*A posse ad esse*—"from possibility to reality") on the cover. No wonder he hadn't wanted her to type up his manuscript. She had married a Casaubon, she realized.

Derek's whole life was a fabrication. From his very first words to her (*Oh, my, how awful for you. Let me help you*) he had not been genuine. What had he wanted from her? Someone weaker than himself? Or a wife, a mother of his children, someone running his house, all the trappings of the *vie quotidienne* but without any of its underlying chaos. She had married him in order to be safe from that chaos. He had married her, she now understood, for the same reason. They were the last two people on earth who could make anyone safe from anything.

Ursula rooted through the sideboard drawers and found a sheaf of letters, the top one with the letterhead of William Collins and Sons, Co. Ltd "regretfully" rejecting his idea for a book, in an "already oversubscribed area of history textbooks." There were similar letters from other educational publishers and, worse, there were unpaid bills and threatening final notices. A particularly harsh letter demanded immediate repayment of the loan taken out apparently to pay for the house. It was the kind of sour letter that she had typed up from dictation at her secretarial college, *Dear Sir, It has been brought to my notice—*

She heard the front door open and her heart jumped. Derek appeared in the doorway of the dining room, a Gothic intruder onstage. "What are you doing?"

She held up the letter from William Collins and said, "You're a liar, through and through. Why did you marry me? Why did you make us both so unhappy?" The look on his face. That look. She was asking to be killed, but wasn't that easier than doing it herself? She didn't care anymore, there was no fight in her.

Ursula was expecting the first blow but it still took her by surprise, his fist punching hard into the middle of her face as if he wanted to obliterate it.

She slept, or perhaps she passed out, on the kitchen floor and woke some time before six. She was sick and dizzy and every inch of her was sore and aching, her whole body made of lead. She was desperate for a drink of water but didn't dare turn the tap on for fear of waking Derek. Using first a chair, then the table, she hauled herself up to standing. She found her shoes and crept into the hallway where she took her coat and a head scarf from the peg. Derek's wallet was in his jacket pocket and she took a ten-shilling note, more than enough for the rail fare and then a cab onward. She felt exhausted just at the thought of this taxing journey—she wasn't even sure she could make it on foot as far as Harrow and Wealdstone station.

She slipped her coat on and pulled the head scarf over her face, avoiding the mirror in the hallstand. It would be too dreadful a sight. She left the front door slightly ajar in case the noise of it closing woke him up. She thought of Ibsen's Nora slamming the door behind her. Nora wouldn't have gone in for dramatic gestures if she had been trying to escape from Derek Oliphant.

It was the longest walk of her life. Her heart was beating so fast she thought it might give out. All the way she expected to hear his footsteps running up behind her and him yelling her name. At the ticket office she had to mumble "Euston" through a mouthful of bloody, broken teeth. The ticket clerk glanced at her and then glanced quickly away when he saw the state she was in. Ursula supposed he had no precedent for dealing with female passengers who looked as if they had been in bare-knuckle fights.

She had to wait for the first train of the day for another ten agonizing minutes in the ladies' waiting room but at least she was able to get a drink of water and remove some of the dried blood from her face.

In the carriage she sat with her head bowed, one hand shielding her face. The men in suits and bowlers studiously ignored her. As she waited for the train to pull away she risked a glance along the platform and was relieved beyond measure that there was still no sign of Derek. With any luck he hadn't missed her yet and was still doing his press-ups on the bedroom floor, presuming her to be down in the kitchen preparing his breakfast. Friday, kipper day. The kipper still lay on the pantry shelf, wrapped in newspaper. He would be furious.

When she got off the train at Euston her legs almost gave way. People gave her a wide berth and she worried that the cabdriver would refuse the fare, but when she showed him the money he took her. They drove in silence across London, bathed in rain overnight, and now the stones of the buildings were sparkling in the first rays of sun and the soft cloudy dawn was opalescent in pinks and blues. She had forgotten how much she liked London. Her heart rose. She had decided to live and now she wanted to very much.

The cabdriver helped her out at the end of the journey. "You're sure about this, miss, are you?" he said, looking doubtfully at the large redbrick house in Melbury Road. She nodded, mutely.

It was an inevitable destination.

She rang the bell and the front door opened. Izzie's hand flew to her mouth in horror at the sight of her face. "Oh, my God. What *happened* to you?"

"My husband tried to kill me."

"You'd better come in then," Izzie said.

The bruises healed, very slowly. "Battle scars," Izzie said.

Izzie's dentist fixed Ursula's teeth and she had to wear her right arm in a sling for a while. Her nose had been broken again and her cheekbones and jaw cracked. She was flawed, no longer *intact.* On the other hand, she felt as if she had been scourged clean. The past no longer weighed so heavily on the present. She sent a message to Fox Corner saying that she had gone away for the summer, "a touring holiday of the Highlands with Derek." She was fairly sure that Derek wouldn't contact Fox Corner. He would be licking his wounds somewhere. Barnet, maybe. He had no idea where Izzie lived, thank goodness.

Izzie was surprisingly sympathetic. "Stay as long as you like," she said. "It'll make a change from rattling around in here on my own. And God only knows, I've got more than enough money to keep you. Take your time," she added. "No rush. And you're only twenty-three, for heaven's sake." Ursula didn't know which was more surprising—Izzie's genuine hospitality or the fact that she knew how old she was. Perhaps Izzie had been changed by Belgravia too.

Ursula was in on her own one evening when Teddy turned up on the doorstep. "You're hard to find," he said, giving her an enormous hug. Ursula's heart bumped with pleasure. Teddy always seemed more real than other people somehow. He was brown and strong from spending the long summer vacation working on the Hall farm. He had announced recently that he wanted to be a farmer. "I'll have the money back that I spent on your education," Sylvie said—but smiling because Teddy was her favorite.

"I believe it was *my* money," Hugh said. (Did Hugh have a favorite? "You, I think," Pamela said.)

"What happened to your face?" Teddy asked her.

"Bit of an accident, you should have seen it before," she laughed.

"You're not in the Highlands," Teddy said.

"Doesn't seem so, does it?"

"You've left him then?"

"Yes."

"Good." Teddy, like Hugh, didn't go in for long narratives. "Where's the giddy aunt then?" he asked.

"Out giddying. The Embassy Club, I believe." They drank some of Izzie's champagne to celebrate Ursula's freedom.

"You'll be disgraced in Mother's eyes, I expect," Teddy said.

"Don't worry, I believe I already am."

Together they made an omelet and a tomato salad and ate with their plates on their knees listening to Ambrose and his orchestra on the wireless. When they finished their food, Teddy lit a cigarette. "You're so grown-up these days," Ursula laughed. "I have muscles," he said, demonstrating his biceps like a circus strongman. He was reading English at Oxford and said it was a relief to stop thinking and "be working on the land." He was writing poetry, too, he said. About the land, not about "feelings." Teddy's heart had been fractured by Nancy's death and once a thing was cracked, he said, it could never be repaired perfectly. "Quite Jamesian, isn't it?" he said ruefully. (Ursula thought of herself.)

A bereft Teddy carried his wounds on the inside, a scar across his heart where little Nancy Shawcross had been ripped away. "It's as if," he said to Ursula, "you walk into a room and your life ends but you keep on living."

"I think I understand. I do," Ursula said.

Ursula dozed off with her head on Teddy's shoulder. She was still tremendously tired. ("Sleep is a great healer," Izzie said, bringing her breakfast on a tray every morning.)

Eventually, Teddy sighed and stretched and said, "I suppose I should be getting back to Fox Corner. What's the story, did I see you? Or are you still in Brigadoon?" He took their plates through to the kitchen. "I'll clear up while you think about your answer."

When the doorbell rang Ursula presumed it was Izzie. Now that Ursula was living in Melbury Road she had grown careless about her door keys. "But you're always here, darling," she said when Ursula had to crawl out of bed at three in the morning to let her in.

It wasn't Izzie, it was Derek. She was so surprised she couldn't even speak. She had left him so firmly behind that she thought of him as someone who had ceased to exist. He didn't belong in Holland Park, but rather in some dark place of the imagination.

He twisted her arm behind her back and frog marched her down the hall into the drawing room. He glanced at the coffee table, a heavy wooden thing carved in the Oriental style. Seeing the empty champagne glasses still sitting on the coffee table and the big onyx ashtray containing Teddy's cigarette stubs, he hissed, "Who's been here with you?" He was incandescent with rage. "Who have you been fornicating with?"

"Fornicating?" Ursula said, surprised by the word. So biblical. Teddy came into the room, a dish towel casually over his shoulder. "What's all this?" he said, and then, "Get your hands off her."

"Is this him?" Derek asked Ursula. "Is this the man you're whoring around London with?" and without waiting for an answer he smashed her head onto the coffee table and she slid to the ground. The pain in her head was terrible and grew worse rather than lessened, as if she were in a vice being tightened all the time. Derek lifted the heavy onyx ashtray high as if it were a chalice, careless of the cigarette butts that showered onto the carpet. Ursula knew her brain wasn't working properly because she should have been cowering in terror but all she could think about was that this was rather like the incident with the poached egg and how silly life was. Teddy yelled something at Derek and Derek threw the ashtray at him instead of breaking open Ursula's skull with it. Ursula couldn't see whether or not the ashtray hit Teddy because Derek grabbed her by her hair, lifted her head up and cracked it back onto the coffee table. A bolt of lightning flashed in front of her eyes but the pain began to fade.

She slipped down onto the carpet, unable to move. There was so much blood in her eyes that she could barely see. The second time that her head hit the table she had felt something give way, the instinct to life perhaps. She knew from the awkward shuffling and grunting dance on the carpet around her that Derek and Teddy were fighting. At least Teddy was on his feet and not lying unconscious but she didn't want him to fight, she wanted him to run away, out of harm's way. She didn't mind dying, she really didn't, as long as Teddy was safe. She tried to say something but it came out as guttural nonsense. She was very cold and tired. She remembered feeling this way in the hospital, after Belgravia. Hugh had been there, he had held on to her hand and kept her in this life.

Ambrose was still on the wireless, Sam Browne was singing "The Sun Has Got His Hat On." It was a jolly song to leave life to. Not what you expected.

The black bat was coming for her. She didn't want to go. The blackness edged around her. *Easeful death.* It was so cold. It will snow tonight, she thought, even though it isn't winter yet. It was already snowing, cold flakes dissolving on her skin like soap. Ursula put out a hand for Teddy to hold but this time nothing could stop her fall into the dark night.

11 February 1926

"Ow! What d'ya do that for?" Howie yelled, rubbing his cheek where Ursula had punched him in a very unladylike way.

"You have one hell of a right cross for a little girl," Howie said, almost admiringly. He made another grab for her which she jinked as neatly as a cat. As she did so, she spotted Teddy's ball, lurking deep within the recesses of a cotoneaster. A well-aimed kick connected with Howie's shin and gave her enough time to rescue the ball from the clutches of the reluctant bush.

"I just wanted a kiss," Howie said, sounding absurdly hurt. "It wasn't like I was trying to *rape* you or anything." The brutal word hung in the chilly air. Ursula might have blushed, should have blushed at the word but she felt a certain possession of it. She sensed it was what boys like Howie did to girls like Ursula. All girls, especially those celebrating their sixteenth birthdays, had to be cautious when walking through the dark, wild wood. Or, in this case, the shrubbery at the bottom of Fox Corner's garden. Howie rewarded her by looking somewhat shamefaced.

"Howie!" they heard Maurice shouting. "Leaving without you, chum!"

"You had better go," Ursula said. A small triumph for her new womanhood.

* * *

I found your ball," she said to Teddy.

"Excellent," Teddy said. "Thank you. Shall we have more of your birthday cake?"

August 1926

Il se tenait devant un miroir long, appliqué au mur entre les deux fenêtres, et contemplait son image de très beau et très jeune homme, ni grand ni petit, le cheveu bleuté comme un plumage de merle.

She could barely keep her eyes open to read. It was beautifully hot and time treacled past every day with nothing more to do than read books and go for long walks—mainly in the vain hope of bumping into Benjamin Cole, or indeed any of the Cole boys, who had all grown into darkly handsome youths. "They could pass for Italian," Sylvie said. But why would they want to pass for anything other than themselves?

"You know," Sylvie said, discovering her lying beneath the apple trees, *Chéri* drowsily abandoned on the warm grass, "long, lazy days like these will never come again in your life. You think they will, but they won't."

"Unless I become incredibly rich," Ursula said. "Then I could be idle all day long."

"Perhaps," Sylvie said, unwilling to renounce her newly habitual dysphoric stance. "But summer would still come to an end one day." She sank down on the grass next to Ursula. Her skin was freckled from working in the garden. Sylvie was always up with the sun. Ursula would have been happy to sleep all day. Sylvie leafed idly through the Colette and said, "You should do more with your French."

"I could live in Paris."

"Perhaps not *that,*" Sylvie said.

"Do you think I should apply to university when I finish school?"

"Oh, really, dear, what's the point? It won't teach you how to be a wife and mother."

"What if I don't want to be a wife and mother?"

Sylvie laughed. "Now you're just talking nonsense to provoke." She stroked Ursula's cheek. "You always were such a funny little thing. There's tea on the lawn," she said, rousing herself reluctantly. "And cake. And, unfortunately, Izzie."

Darling," Izzie said when she saw Ursula coming across the lawn toward her. "You've quite grown since I last saw you. You're a woman now, and so pretty!"

"Not quite," Sylvie said. "We were just discussing her future."

"Were we?" Ursula said. "I thought we were discussing my French. I need more of an education," she said to Izzie.

"How serious," Izzie said. "At sixteen you should be head over heels in love with some unsuitable boy." I am, Ursula thought, I am in love with Benjamin Cole. She supposed he was unsuitable. ("A Jew?" she imagined Sylvie saying. Or a Catholic, or a coal miner—or anyone foreign—a shop assistant, a clerk, a groom, a tram-driver, a schoolteacher. The unsuitable males were legion.)

"Were *you?*" Ursula asked Izzie.

"Was I what?" Izzie puzzled.

"In love when you were sixteen?"

"Oh, tremendously."

"What about you?" Ursula said to Sylvie.

"Goodness, no," Sylvie said.

"But at *seventeen* you must have been in love," Izzie said to Sylvie.

"Must I?"

"When you met Hugh, of course."

"Of course."

Izzie leaned toward Ursula and dropped her voice to a conspirator's whisper. "I eloped when I was about your age."

"Nonsense," Sylvie said to Ursula. "She did no such thing. Ah, here comes Bridget with the tea tray." Sylvie turned to Izzie. "Was there a particular reason for your visit, or have you merely come to annoy?"

"I was driving nearby, I thought I'd drop in. I've got something I wanted to ask you."

"Oh, dear," Sylvie said wearily.

"I've been thinking," Izzie said.

"Oh, dear."

"*Would* you stop saying that, Sylvie."

Ursula poured tea and sliced cake. She sensed a battle. Izzie was rendered temporarily speechless by a mouthful of cake. It was not one of Mrs. Glover's airier sponges.

"As I said"—she swallowed with difficulty—"I've been thinking—and don't say anything, Sylvie. *The Adventures of Augustus* is still *wildly* successful, I'm writing a book every six months. It's quite crazy. And I have the house in Holland Park, and I have money, but of course no husband. Nor do I have a child."

"Really?" Sylvie said. "Are you sure?"

Izzie ignored her. "No one to share my good fortune with. So, I was thinking, why don't I adopt Jimmy?"

"I'm sorry?"

She's unbelievable," Sylvie hissed at Hugh. Izzie was still out on the lawn, entertaining Jimmy by reading from an unfinished manuscript she had in her oversized handbag. *Augustus Goes to the Seaside.*

"Why doesn't she want to adopt me?" Teddy said. "After all, it's me that's supposed to be Augustus."

"Do you want to be adopted by Izzie?" Hugh puzzled.

"Good lord, no," Teddy said.

"No one is being adopted," Sylvie said furiously. "Go and have a word with her, Hugh."

In the kitchen, Ursula went looking for an apple and found Mrs. Glover thumping slices of veal with a meat tenderizer. "I imagine that they're the heads of the Boche," she said.

"Really?"

"The ones that sent the gas over that did for poor George's lungs."

"What's for dinner? I'm starving." Ursula had grown rather callous about George Glover's lungs, she had heard so much of them that they seemed to have a life of their own, rather like Sylvie's mother's lungs, organs that seemed to have more character than their owner.

"Veal cutlets *à la Russe,*" Mrs. Glover said, flipping the meat over and pounding again. "The Ruskies are just as bad, mind you." Ursula wondered if Mrs. Glover had ever actually met anyone from another country.

"Well, there are a lot of Jews in Manchester," Mrs. Glover said.

"Did you meet any?"

"Meet? Why would I meet them?"

"Jews aren't necessarily foreign, though, are they? The Coles next door are Jewish."

"Don't be daft," Mrs. Glover said, "they're as English as you and me." Mrs. Glover had a certain fondness for the Cole boys, based on their excellent manners. Ursula wondered if it was worth arguing. She took another apple and Mrs. Glover returned to her pounding.

Ursula ate the apple sitting on a bench in a secluded corner of the garden, one of Sylvie's favorite hideaways. The words "Veal cutlets *à la Russe*" drifted sleepily through her brain. And then suddenly she was on her feet, her heart knocking in her chest, a sudden familiar but long-forgotten terror triggered—but by what? It was so at odds with the peaceful garden, the late-afternoon warmth on her face, Hattie, the cat, washing herself lazily on the sunny path.

There were no terrible portents of doom, nothing to suggest all was not well in the world but nonetheless Ursula flung the apple core into the bushes and fled from the garden, through the gate and into the lane, the old demons snapping at her heels. Hattie paused in her toilette and viewed the swinging gate with disdain.

Perhaps it was a train disaster, perhaps she would have to rip off her petticoats like the girls in *The Railway Children* to signal the driver, but no, as she reached the station the 5:30 to London was drawing quietly alongside the platform in the safe stewardship of Fred Smith and his driver.

"Miss Todd?" he said, tipping the brim of his railwayman's cap. "Are you all right? You look worried."

"I'm fine, Fred, thank you for asking." Just in a state of mortal dread, nothing to fret about. Fred Smith didn't look as if he had ever suffered a moment of mortal dread.

She walked back along the lane, still drenched with the nameless fear. Halfway along she met Nancy Shawcross and said, "Hello there, what are you up to?" and Nancy said, "Oh, just looking for things for my nature book. I've got some oak leaves and some tiny baby acorns."

The fear started to drain from Ursula's body and she said, "Come on, then, I'll walk back home with you."

As they approached the dairy herd's field a man climbed over the five-bar gate and landed heavily among the cow parsley. He tipped his cap at Ursula and mumbled, "Evening, miss," before carrying on in the direction of the station. He had a limp that made him walk rather comically, like Charlie Chaplin. Another veteran of the war perhaps, Ursula thought.

"Who was that?" Nancy asked.

"I have no idea," Ursula said. "Oh, look, there on the road, a dead devil's-coach-horse beetle. Is that any good to you?"

A LOVELY DAY TOMORROW

2 September 1939

"Maurice says it will be over in a few months." Pamela rested her plate on the neat dome that contained her next baby. She was hoping for a girl.

"You're going to go on forever until you produce one, aren't you?" Ursula said.

"Till the crack of doom," Pamela agreed cheerfully. "So, we were invited, *much* to my surprise. Sunday lunch in Surrey, the full works. Their rather strange children, Philip and Hazel—"

"I think I've only met them twice."

"You've probably met them more than that, you just didn't notice them. Maurice said he'd invited us over so that the 'cousins could get to know each other better' but the boys didn't take to them at all. Philip and Hazel have no idea how to *play.* And their mother was being a martyr to the roast beef and apple pie. Edwina's a martyr to Maurice as well. Martyrdom would suit her, of course, she's quite *violently* Christian considering she's C of E."

"I would hate to be married to Maurice, I don't know how she puts up with it."

"She's grateful to him, I think. He's given her Surrey. A tennis court, friends in the Cabinet, lots of roast beef. They *entertain* a lot—the great and the good. Some women would suffer for that. Even suffer Maurice."

"I expect he's a great test of her Christian tolerance."

"A great test of Harold's beliefs in general. He had a scrap with Maurice over welfare, another one with Edwina about predestination."

"She believes in that? I thought she was an Anglican."

"I know. She has no sense of logic though. She's remarkably stupid, I suppose that's why he married her. Why do you think

Maurice says the war will only last a few months? Is that just departmental bluster? Do we believe everything he says? Do we believe *anything* he says?"

"Well, generally speaking, no," Ursula said. "But he is a big chief in the Home Office, so he *ought* to know, presumably. Home Security, new department as of this week."

"You too?" Pamela asked.

"Yes, me too. The ARP Department is now a ministry, we're all still getting used to the idea of being grown-ups."

When Ursula left school at eighteen she had not gone to Paris, nor, despite the exhortations of some of her teachers, had she applied to Oxbridge and done a degree in any languages, dead or alive. She had not in fact gone further than High Wycombe and a small secretarial college. She was eager to *get on* and earn her independence rather than be cloistered in another institution. "*Time's winged chariot,* and all that," she said to her parents.

"Well, we all *get on,*" Sylvie said, "one way or another. And in the end we all arrive at the same place. I hardly see that it matters how we get there."

It seemed to Ursula that *how* you got there was the whole point but there was nothing to be gained from arguing with Sylvie on the days when she was mired in gloom. "I shall be able to get an interesting job," Ursula said, brushing off her parents' objections, "working in a newspaper office or perhaps a publishing house." She imagined a Bohemian atmosphere, men in tweed jackets and cravats, women smoking in a sophisticated manner while sitting at their Royals.

"Anyway, good for you," Izzie said to Ursula, over a rather superior afternoon tea at the Dorchester to which she had invited both Ursula and Pamela ("She must want something," Pamela said).

"And who wants to be a boring old bluestocking?" Izzie said.

"Me," Pamela said.

It turned out that Izzie did have an ulterior motive. Augustus was so successful that Izzie's publisher had asked her to produce "something similar" for girls. "But not books based on a *naughty* girl," she said. "That apparently won't do. They want a gung-ho sort, hockey-captain kind of thing. Lots of japes and scrapes but always toeing the line, nothing that will frighten the horses." She turned to Pamela and said sweetly, "So I thought of you, dear."

The college had been run by a man called Mr. Carver, a man who was a great disciple of both Pitman's and Esperanto and who tried to make his "girls" wear blindfolds when they were practicing their touch-typing. Ursula, suspecting there was more to it than monitoring their skills, led a revolt of Mr. Carver's "girls." "You're such a rebel," one of them—Monica—said admiringly. "Well, not really," Ursula said. "Just being sensible, you know."

She was. She had become a sensible sort.

At Mr. Carver's college Ursula had proved to have a surprising aptitude for typing and shorthand, although the men who interviewed her for the job in the Home Office, men she would never see again, clearly believed that her proficiency in the Classics would somehow stand her in better stead when opening and closing filing-cabinet drawers and conducting endless searches among a sea of buff-colored folders. It wasn't quite the "interesting job" she had envisaged but it kept her attention and over the next ten years she rose slowly through the ranks, in the bridled way that women did. ("One day a woman will be Prime Minister," Pamela said. "Maybe even in our lifetime.") Now Ursula had her own junior clericals to chase down the buff folders for her. She supposed that was progress. Since '36 she'd been working in the Air Raid Precautions Department.

"*You've* not heard rumors then?" Pamela said.

"I'm a lowly squaw, I hear nothing but rumors."

"Maurice can't say what he does," Pamela grumbled. "Couldn't possibly talk about what goes on within the 'hallowed walls.' He actually used that term—hallowed walls. You would think he had signed the Official Secrets Act with his blood and pledged his soul as warranty."

"Oh, well, we all have to do that," Ursula said, helping herself to cake. "*De rigueur,* don't you know. Personally, I suspect Maurice just goes around *counting* things."

"And feeling very pleased with himself. He's going to love the war, lots of power and no personal danger."

"*Lots* of things to count." They both laughed. It struck Ursula that they seemed very merry for people on the brink of dreadful conflict. They were in the garden of Pamela's house in Finchley, a Saturday afternoon with the tea things set out on a spindly bamboo table. They were eating cake, almond speckled with chopped-up pieces of chocolate, an old recipe of Mrs. Glover's handed down on a piece of paper that was covered in greasy fingerprints. In places, the paper was as transparent as a dirty windowpane.

"Make the most of it," Pamela said, "there'll be no more cake, I expect." She fed a piece to Heidi, an unprepossessing mongrel rescued from Battersea. "Did you know that people are putting their pets down, thousands of them?"

"That's horrible."

"As if they weren't part of the *family,*" Pamela said, rubbing the top of Heidi's head. "She's much nicer than the boys. Better behaved too."

"How were your evacuees?"

"Grubby." Despite her condition, Pamela had spent most of the morning organizing evacuees at Ealing Broadway while Olive, her mother-in-law, looked after the boys.

"You would be so much more help to the war effort than someone like Maurice," Ursula said. "If it were up to me I would make you Prime Minister. You'd make a much better job of it than Chamberlain."

"Well, that's true." Pamela put down her tea plate and took up her knitting—something pink and lacy. "If it's a boy I'm just going to *pretend* it's a girl."

"And aren't *you* going to leave?" Ursula asked. "You're not going to keep the boys in London, are you? You could go and stay at Fox Corner, I don't expect the Germans will be much bothered with bombing sleepy hollow."

"And stay with Mother? Lord, no. I have a friend from university, Jeanette, a vicar's daughter, not that that's relevant, I suppose. There's a cottage that belonged to her grandmother, up in Yorkshire, Hutton-le-Hole, dot on the map, that kind of place. She's going up there with her two boys and suggested I join her with my three." Pamela had given birth in quick succession to Nigel, Andrew and Christopher. She had taken to motherhood with gusto. "Heidi will love it too. It sounds utterly primitive, no electricity, no running water. Wonderful for the boys, they can run around like savages. It's hard to be a savage in Finchley."

"I expect some people manage," Ursula said.

How's 'the man'?" Pamela asked. " 'The Man from the Admiralty.' "

"You *can* use his name," Ursula said, brushing cake crumbs off her skirt. "The antirrhinums don't have ears."

"You never know these days. Has *he* said anything?"

Ursula had been involved with Crighton—"the Man from the Admiralty"—for a year now (she dated it from Munich). They had met at an interdepartmental meeting. He was fifteen years older than Ursula, rather dashing and with a vaguely wolfish air that was barely offset by his marriage to an industrious wife (Moira) and their clutch of three girls, all at a private school. "I shan't leave them, no matter what," he told her after the first time they had made love in the rather basic quarters of his "emergency bolt hole."

"But I don't want you to," Ursula said, although as a declaration of his intent she thought it might have been better if he had let it precede the act rather than provide its coda.

"The bolt hole" (she suspected that she was not the first woman to have seen the inside of it at Crighton's invitation) was an apartment provided by the Admiralty for the nights when Crighton stayed in town rather than "hiking" all the way back to Moira and the girls in Wargrave. The bolt hole wasn't his exclusively and when it wasn't available he "trekked out" to Ursula's apartment in Argyll Road where they spent long evenings in her single bed (he had a sailor's practical attitude toward confined spaces) or on her sofa, pursuing the "delights of the flesh" as he put it, before he "slogged his way" back to Berkshire. Any journey on land, even a couple of stops on the Tube, had an expeditionary quality for Crighton. He was a naval man at heart, Ursula supposed, and would have been happier sailing a skiff to the Home Counties rather than making his way overland. They did once take a little boat out to Monkey Island and have a picnic on the banks of the river. "Like a normal couple," he said apologetically.

"What then, if not love?" Pamela asked.

"I *like* him."

"I like the man who delivers my groceries," Pamela said. "But I don't share my bed with him."

"Well, I can assure you he means a good deal more to me than a tradesman." They were almost arguing. "And he's not a callow youth," she continued for the defense. "He's a proper person, he comes whole, all . . . ready-made. You know?"

"Ready-made with a family," Pamela said, rather crotchety now. She looked quizzical and said, "But doesn't your heart beat a little faster at the sight of him?"

"Perhaps a little faster," Ursula conceded generously, sidestepping the argument, suspecting that she would never be able to explain the forensics of adultery to Pamela. "Who would have thought that out of everyone in our family, you would turn out to be the romantic?"

"Oh, no, I think that's Teddy," Pamela said. "I just like to believe that there are nuts and bolts that hold our society together—especially now—and that marriage is part of that."

"Nothing romantic about nuts and bolts."

"I admire you, really," Pamela said. "Being your own woman. Not following the herd and so on. I just don't want you to be hurt."

"Believe me, neither do I. Pax?"

"Pax," Pamela agreed readily. Laughing, she said, "My life would be so dull without your salacious reports from the front line. What a deal of vicarious excitement I derive from your love life—or whatever you want to call it."

There had been nothing salacious about their outing to Monkey Island, they had sat chastely on a tartan blanket and eaten cold chicken and drunk warm red wine. *"The blushful Hippocrene,"* Ursula said and Crighton laughed and said, "That sounds suspiciously like literature to me. I have no poetry in me. You should know that."

"I do."

The thing about Crighton was that there always seemed to be more of him than he ever revealed. She had overheard someone in the office refer to him as "the Sphinx" and he did indeed wear an air of reticence that hinted at unexplored depths and suppressed secrets—some childhood harm, some magnificent obsession. His cryptic self, she thought, peeling a hard-boiled egg and dipping it into a little screw of paper that contained salt. Who had packed this picnic—not Crighton, surely? Not Moira, heaven forfend.

He had grown rather remorseful over the clandestine nature of their relationship. She had brought a little excitement into what had become a rather tedious life, he said. He had been at Jutland with Jellicoe, he had "seen much" and now he was "little better than a bureaucrat." He was restless, he said.

"You're either about to declare your love for me," Ursula said, "or tell me that it's all over." There was fruit—peaches nestling inside tissue paper.

"It's a fine balance," he said, with a rueful smile. "I am teetering." Ursula laughed, the word didn't suit him.

He embarked on a tale about Moira, something to do with her life in the village and her need for committee work, and Ursula drifted off, more interested in the discovery of a Bakewell tart that had apparently been magicked from a kitchen somewhere deep in the Admiralty. ("We're well looked after," he said. Like Maurice, she thought. The privileges of men in power, unavailable to those adrift on the sea of buff.)

If Ursula's older female colleagues had got wind of the affair, there would have been a stampede for the smelling salts, especially if they had known just who in the Admiralty it was that she was dallying with (Crighton was rather senior). Ursula was good, very good, at keeping secrets.

"Your reputation for discretion precedes you, Miss Todd," Crighton had said when introduced to her.

"Goodness," Ursula said, "that makes me sound so dull."

"Intriguing, rather. I suspect you would make a good spy."

And how *was* Maurice? In himself?" Ursula asked.

"Maurice is very well 'in himself,' in that he *is* himself and will never change."

"Invitations to Sunday lunch in Surrey never come *my* way."

"Count yourself lucky."

"In fact I hardly ever see him. You wouldn't think we worked in the same ministry. He walks the airy corridors of power—"

"The hallowed walls."

"The hallowed walls. And I scurry around in a bunker."

"Are you? In a bunker?"

"Well, it's aboveground. In South Ken, you know—in front of the Geological Museum. Not Maurice, he prefers his Whitehall office to our War Room."

When she had applied originally for a job in the Home Office, Ursula had rather presumed that Maurice would put in a good word for her but instead he had blustered on about nepotism and having to be seen to be above any suspicion of favoritism, "Caesar's wife and so on," he said. "And I take it Maurice is Caesar in this conceit, rather than Caesar's wife?" Pamela said. "Oh, don't put that idea into my head," Ursula laughed. "Maurice as a woman, imagine."

"Ah, but a *Roman* woman. That would suit him more. What was Coriolanus's mother called?"

"Volumnia."

"Oh, and I know what I had to tell you—Maurice invited a friend to lunch," Pamela said. "From his Oxford days, that big American chap. Do you remember?"

"I do!" Ursula struggled to come up with the name. "Oh, darn, what was he called…something American. He tried to kiss me on my sixteenth birthday."

"The swine!" Pamela laughed. "You never said."

"Hardly what you want from a first kiss. More like a rugby tackle. He was a bit of a lout." Ursula laughed. "I think I hurt his pride—or perhaps more than his pride."

"Howie," Pamela said. "Only now he's Howard—Howard S. Landsdowne III to give him his full title, apparently."

"Howie," Ursula mused. "I had quite forgotten. What's he doing now?"

"Something diplomatic. He's even more secretive than Maurice. At the embassy, Kennedy's a god to him. I think Howie rather admires old Adolf."

"Maurice, too, probably, if he weren't quite so *foreign*. I saw him once at a Blackshirt meeting."

"Maurice? Never! Perhaps he was spying, I can imagine him as an *agent provocateur.* What were *you* doing there?"

"Oh, you know, espionage, like Maurice. No, really just happenstance."

"So many startling revelations for one pot of tea. Are there more to come? Should I brew another pot?"

Ursula laughed. "No, I think that's it."

Pamela sighed. "It's bloody, isn't it?"

"What, about Harold?"

"Poor man, I suppose he'll have to stay here. They can't really call up hospital doctors, can they? They'll need them if we're bombed and gassed. We *will* be bombed and gassed, you do know that, don't you?"

"Yes, of course," Ursula said, as offhand as if they were talking about the weather.

"What an awful thought." Pamela sighed again, abandoning her needles and stretching her arms above her head. "It's such a glorious day. It's hard to believe this is probably the last ordinary day we'll have for a long time."

Ursula had been due to begin her annual leave on Monday. She had planned a week of leisurely day trips—Eastbourne and Hastings or perhaps as far afield as Bath or Winchester—but with war about to be declared it seemed impossible to think of going anywhere. She felt suddenly listless at the idea of what might lie ahead. She had spent the morning on Kensington High Street, stocking up—batteries for her torch, a new hot-water bottle, candles, matches, endless amounts of black paper, as well as tins of baked beans and potatoes, vacuum-packed coffee. She had bought clothes too, a good woolen frock for eight pounds, a green velvet jacket for six, stockings and a pair of nice tan leather brogues that looked made to last. She had felt pleased with herself for resisting a yellow *crêpe de Chine* tea dress, patterned with little black swallows. "My winter coat's only two years old," she said to Pamela, "it'll see the war out, surely?"

"Goodness, I would hope so."

"It's all so horrid."

"I know," Pamela said, cutting more cake. "It's vile. It makes me so *cross.* Going to war is madness. Have more cake, why don't you? May as well, while the boys are still at Olive's. They'll come in and go through the place like locusts. God knows how we'll manage with rationing."

"You'll be in the country—you can grow things. Keep chickens. A pig. You'll be all right." Ursula felt miserable at the thought of Pamela going away.

"You should come."

"I should stay, I'm afraid."

"Oh, good, here's Harold," Pamela said when Harold appeared, carrying a big bunch of dahlias wrapped in damp newspaper. She half rose to greet him and he kissed her on the cheek and said, "Don't get up." He kissed Ursula as well and presented the dahlias to Pamela.

"A girl was selling them on the street corner, in Whitechapel," he said. "Very *Pygmalion.* Said they came from her grandfather's allotment." Crighton had given Ursula roses once but they had quickly drooped and faded. She rather envied Pamela her robust allotment flowers.

"So, anyway," Harold said, when he had poured himself a

lukewarm cup of tea from the pot, "we're already evacuating patients who are well enough to be moved. They're definitely going to declare war tomorrow. In the morning. It's probably timed so that the nation can get down on its collective knees in church and pray for deliverance."

"Oh, yes, war is always so *Christian,* isn't it?" Pamela said sarcastically. "Especially when one is English. I have several friends in Germany," she said to Ursula. "Good people."

"I know."

"Are they the enemy now?"

"Don't get upset, Pammy," Harold said. "Why is it so quiet, what have you done with the boys?"

"Sold them," Pamela said, perking up. "Three for the price of two."

"You ought to stay the night, Ursula," Harold said kindly. "You shouldn't be on your own tomorrow. It'll be one of those awful days. Doctor's orders."

"Thanks," Ursula said. "But I've already got plans."

"Good for you," Pamela said, picking up her knitting again. "We mustn't behave as if the world is coming to an end."

"Even if it is?" Ursula said. She wished now that she'd bought the yellow *crêpe de Chine.*

November 1940

She was on her back, lying in a shallow pool of water, a fact that didn't worry her so much at first. The worst thing was the awful smell. It was a combination of different things, none of them good, and Ursula was trying to separate them into their components. The fetid stench of gas (domestic) for one, and, for another, the stink of sewage, disgustingly rank, that was making her gag. Added to that was a complex cocktail of damp, old plaster and brick dust, all mixed with the traces of human habitation—wallpaper, clothes, books, food—and the sour, alien smell of explosive. In short, the essence of a dead house.

It was as if she were lying at the bottom of a deep well. Through a hazy veil of dust, like fog, she could make out a patch of black sky and a pared fingernail of moon that she remembered noticing earlier in the evening when she had looked out of the window. That seemed a long time ago.

The window itself, or at least the frame, was still there, way, way above her, not where it should be at all. It was definitely her window, she recognized the curtains, charred rags now, flapping in the breeze. They were—had been—a thick jacquard brocade from John Lewis's that Sylvie had helped her pick out. The apartment in Argyll Road was rented as furnished but Sylvie declared the curtains and rugs to be "completely shoddy" and subbed Ursula for new ones when she moved in.

At the time Millie had suggested that she move in with her in Phillimore Gardens. Millie was still playing ingenues and said she expected to go from Juliet to the Nurse with nothing in between. "It would be fun," Millie said, "to share digs," but Ursula wasn't so sure that Millie's idea of fun coincided with her own. She often felt rather dull and sober against Millie's brightness. A dunnock keeping company with a kingfisher. And sometimes Millie burned just a little too brightly.

This was just after Munich and Ursula had already started her affair with Crighton and it seemed more practical to live on her own. Looking back, she realized that she had accommodated Crighton's needs a great deal more than he had hers, as if Moira and the girls somehow trumped her own existence.

Think about Millie, she told herself, think about the curtains, think about Crighton if you must. Anything except her present predicament. Especially the gas. It seemed particularly important to try to take her mind off the gas.

After their purchases in soft furnishings Sylvie and Ursula had taken afternoon tea in John Lewis's restaurant, served by a grimly efficient waitress. "I'm always so glad," Sylvie murmured, "that I don't have to take a turn at being other people."

"You're very good at being yourself," Ursula said, aware that it didn't necessarily sound like a compliment.

"Well, I've had years of practice."

It was a very good afternoon tea, the kind you couldn't get anymore in department stores. And then John Lewis itself was destroyed, no more than the black toothless skull of a building. ("How awful," Sylvie wrote, moved in a way that she didn't appear to have been by the dreadful raids on the East End.) It was up and running again in days, "Blitz spirit" everyone said, but really, what was the alternative?

Sylvie had been in a good mood that day, and they had drawn closer over the subject of curtains and the idiocy of people who thought that Chamberlain's silly little piece of paper meant anything at all.

It was very quiet and Ursula wondered if her eardrums were shattered. How did she get here? She remembered looking out of the window in Argyll Road—the window that was so far away now—and seeing the sickle moon. And before that she had been sitting on the sofa, doing some sewing, turning the collar on a blouse, with the wireless tuned to a shortwave German station. She was taking a German evening class (*know your enemy*) but was finding it difficult to decipher anything beyond the occasional violent noun (*Luftangriffe, Verluste*) in the broadcast. In despair at her lack of proficiency, she had turned the wireless off and put Ma Rainey on the gramophone. Before she left for America, Izzie had bequeathed Ursula her collection of records, an impressive archive of female American blues artistes. "I don't listen to that stuff anymore," Izzie said. "It's very *passé.* The future lies with something a little more *soigné.*" Izzie's Holland Park house was shut up now, everything covered in dust sheets. She had married a famous playwright and they had decamped to California in the summer. ("Cowards, the pair of them," Sylvie said.

"Oh, I don't know," Hugh said, "I'm sure if I could sit out the war in Hollywood I would.")

"That's interesting music I hear you listening to," Mrs. Appleyard said to Ursula one day as they passed on the stairs. The wall between their flats was paper thin and Ursula said, "I'm sorry. I don't mean to disturb you," although she could well have added that she heard Mrs. Appleyard's baby bawling its head off day and night and that was *very* disturbing. The baby at four months old was big for its age, fat and ruddy, as if it had leeched all the life out of Mrs. Appleyard.

Mrs. Appleyard—the deadweight of the baby asleep in her arms, its head on her shoulder—waved a dismissive hand and said, "Don't be concerned, it doesn't bother me." She was lugubriously East European, a refugee of some kind, Ursula supposed, although her English was precise. Mr. Appleyard had disappeared some months ago, gone for a soldier, perhaps, but Ursula hadn't asked as the marriage had been clearly (and audibly) unhappy. Mrs. Appleyard was pregnant when her husband left and, as far as Ursula could tell (or hear), he had never been back to meet his squawking infant.

Mrs. Appleyard must have been pretty once but day by day she grew thinner and sadder until it seemed as though only the (very) solid burden of the baby and its needs kept her tethered to everyday life.

In the bathroom that they shared on the first floor there was always an enamel pail in which the baby's foul-smelling nappies lay soaking before being boiled in a pan on Mrs. Appleyard's two-ring stove. On the neighboring ring there was usually to be found a pan of cabbage and, perhaps as a result of this twin boiling, she always carried on her person a faint perfume of old vegetables and damp laundry. Ursula recognized it, it was the smell of poverty.

The Misses Nesbit, nesting on the top floor, fretted a good deal about Mrs. Appleyard and the baby in the way that old maids were inclined to. The two Nesbits, Lavinia and Ruth, slight spinsters, lived in the attic rooms ("beneath the eaves, like swallows," they twittered). They might as well have been twins for all the difference between them and Ursula had to make a tremendous effort to remember which was which.

They were long retired—they had both been telephonists in Harrods—and were a frugal pair, their only indulgence being an impressive collection of costume jewelry, purchased mainly from Woolworths in their lunch hour, during their "working years." Their apartment smelled quite different to Mrs. Appleyard's, lavender water and Mansion House polish—the scent of old ladies. Ursula sometimes did shopping for both the Nesbits and Mrs. Appleyard. Mrs. Appleyard was always ready at the door with the exact money that she owed (she knew the price of everything) and a polite "thank you," but the Nesbits were forever trying to inveigle Ursula inside with weak tea and stale biscuits.

Below them, on the second floor, were to be found Mr. Bentley ("a queer fish," they were all agreed) whose apartment smelled (appropriately) of the finnan haddock he boiled in milk for his supper, and next door to him the aloof Miss Hartnell (whose apartment smelled of nothing at all) who was a housekeeper at the Hyde Park Hotel and rather severe, as if nothing could ever hope to meet her standards. She made Ursula feel distinctly wanting.

"Disappointed in love, I believe," Ruth Nesbit whispered in mitigation to Ursula, clamping her bird-boned hand on her chest as if her own frail heart might be about to jump ship and attach itself to someone unsuitable. Both the Misses Nesbit were deeply sentimental about love, never having experienced its rigors. Miss Hartnell looked more as if she would mete out disappointment than receive it.

"I also have some records," Mrs. Appleyard said with the earnestness of a conspirator. "But, alas, no gramophone." Mrs. Appleyard's "alas" seemed freighted with all the tragedy of a broken continent. It could hardly bear the weight it was asked to carry.

"Well, do please feel welcome to come and play them on mine," Ursula said, rather hoping that the downtrodden Mrs. Appleyard wouldn't take up the offer. She wondered what kind of music Mrs. Appleyard possessed. It seemed impossible that it could be anything very jolly.

"Brahms," Mrs. Appleyard said, answering the unasked question. "And Mahler." The baby shifted restlessly as if disturbed by the prospect of Mahler. Whenever Ursula met Mrs. Appleyard on the stairs or the landing, the baby was asleep. It was as if there were two babies, the one inside the apartment who never stopped crying and the one outside who never started.

"Would you mind holding Emil for a moment while I find my keys?" Mrs. Appleyard asked, handing the cumbersome child over without waiting for an answer.

"Emil," Ursula murmured. She hadn't thought of the baby as having a name. Emil was, as usual, dressed for some kind of Arctic winter, bulked out with nappies and rubber knickers and romper suits and all kinds of knitted and beribboned garments. Ursula wasn't a stranger to babies, both she and Pamela had mothered Teddy and Jimmy with the same enthusiasm they accorded puppies and kittens and rabbits, and she was the very picture of a doting aunt where Pamela's boys were concerned, but Mrs. Appleyard's baby was of a less appealing order. The Todd babies smelled sweetly of milk and talcum powder and the fresh air that their clothes were dried in, whereas Emil had a slightly gamey scent.

Mrs. Appleyard rummaged for her keys in her large battered handbag, an item that looked as if it, too, had crossed Europe from a faraway country (of which Ursula, patently, knew nothing). With a great sigh, Mrs. Appleyard finally located the keys at the bottom of the bag. The baby, perhaps sensing the proximity of the threshold, squirmed in Ursula's arms as if preparing itself for the transition. It opened its eyes and looked rather quarrelsome.

"Thank you, Miss Todd," Mrs. Appleyard said, reclaiming the baby. "It was nice talking to you."

"Ursula," Ursula said. "Do please call me Ursula."

Mrs. Appleyard hesitated before saying, almost shyly, "Eryka. E-r-y-k-a." They had lived next door to each other for a year now but this was the nearest they had come to intimacy.

Almost as soon as her door closed the baby began its customary roaring. "Does she stick pins in it?" Pamela wrote. Pamela produced placid babies. "They don't tend to turn feral until they're two," she said. She had given birth to another boy, Gerald, just before last Christmas. "Better luck next time," Ursula said when she saw her. She had taken a train north to visit the new arrival, a long and challenging journey, most of which was spent in the guard's van, on a train packed with soldiers on their way to a training camp. She had been subjected to a barrage of sexual innuendo which had started as amusing and ended as tedious. "Not exactly perfect gentle knights," she said to Pamela when she finally arrived, the last part of the journey being accomplished in a donkey cart as if time had slipped into some other century, some other country even.

Poor Pammy was bored with the phony war and with being shut up with so many little boys, "like being a matron in a boys' school." Not to mention Jeanette who had proved to be "a bit of a slacker" (not to mention a moaner and a snorer). "One expects better of a vicar's daughter," Pamela wrote, "although goodness knows why." She had decamped back to Finchley in the spring but since the nightly raids had started she had retreated with her brood to Fox Corner "for the duration," despite her previous misgivings about living with Sylvie. Harold, now at St. Thomas's, was working on the front line. The nurses' home there had been bombed a couple of weeks ago and five nurses killed. "Every night is hell," Harold reported. It was the same report that Ralph gave from the bombsites.

Ralph! Of course, Ralph. Ursula had quite forgotten him. He had been in Argyll Road too. Was he there when the bomb exploded? Ursula struggled to turn her head to look around, as if she would find him among the wreckage. There was no one, she was alone. Alone and corralled in a cage of smashed wooden beams and jagged rafters, the dust settling all around her, in her mouth, her nostrils, her eyes. No, Ralph had already left when the sirens went.

Ursula was no longer bedded by her man from the Admiralty. The declaration of war had brought on a sudden flush of guilt in her lover. They must stop their affair, Crighton said. The temptations of the flesh were apparently secondary to martial pursuits—as if she were Cleopatra about to destroy his Antony for love. There was enough excitement in the world now, it seemed, without the added hazards of "keeping a mistress." "I'm a mistress?" Ursula said. She had not thought of herself as sporting a scarlet letter, a rubric that belonged to a racier woman, surely?

The balance had shifted. Crighton had teetered. And apparently tottered. "Very well," she had said equably. "If that's what you want." She had begun to suspect by then that there was not, in fact, a different, more intriguing Crighton hidden beneath the enigmatic surface. He was not so very inscrutable, after all. Crighton was Crighton—Moira, the girls, Jutland, although not necessarily in that order.

Despite the fact that the end of the affair was at his instigation, he was cut up. Wasn't she? "You're very cool," he said.

But she had never been "in love" with him, she said. "And I expect we can still be friends."

"I don't think that we can, I'm afraid," Crighton said, already wistful for what was now history.

Nonetheless, she had spent the following day dutifully crying for her loss. Her *liking* for him had not been quite the negligent emotion that Pamela seemed to think. Then she dried her tears, washed her hair and went to bed with a plate of Bovril on toast and a bottle of 1929 Château Haut-Brion that she had filched from Izzie's excellent wine cellar, left casually behind in Melbury Road. Ursula had the keys to Izzie's house. "Just help yourself to anything you can find," Izzie had said. So she did.

It was rather a shame though, Ursula thought, that she no longer had assignations with Crighton. The war made indiscretions easier. The blackout was the perfect screen for illicit liaisons, and the disruption of the bombing—when it finally started—would have provided him with plenty of excuses for not being in Wargrave with Moira and the girls.

Instead, Ursula was having an entirely aboveboard relationship with a fellow student on her German course. After the initial class (*Guten Tag. Mein Name ist Ralph. Ich bin dreizig Jahre alt*) the two of them had retired to the Kardomah on Southampton Row, almost invisible behind a wall of sandbags these days. It turned out that he worked in the same building as she did, on the bomb-damage maps.

It was only as they left the class—held in a stuffy room, three floors up in Bloomsbury—that Ursula noticed that Ralph was limping. Wounded at Dunkirk, he said, before she could ask. Shot in the leg while waiting in the water to get into one of the little boats that were shuttling back and forth between the shore and the bigger boats. He was hauled on board by a fisherman from Folkestone who was shot in the neck minutes later. "There," he said to Ursula, "now we don't need to talk about it again."

"No, I don't suppose we do," Ursula said. "But how awful." She had watched the newsreels, of course. "We played a bad hand well," Crighton said. Ursula had run into him in Whitehall not long after the evacuation of the troops. He missed her, he said. (He was teetering again, she thought.) Ursula was determinedly nonchalant, said she had reports she needed to take to the War Cabinet Office, clutching buff folders to her chest like a cuirass. She had missed him too. It seemed important not to let him see that.

"You liaise with the War Cabinet?" Crighton said, rather impressed.

"Just an assistant to an undersecretary. Actually, not even to the assistant, just another 'girl' like me."

The conversation had gone on long enough, she decided. He was gazing at her in a way that made her want to feel his arms around her. "Must push off," she said brightly, "there's a war on, you know."

Ralph was from Bexhill, gently sardonic, left-wing, utopian. ("Aren't all socialists utopians?" Pamela said.) Ralph was nothing like Crighton, who with hindsight seemed rather too powerful.

"Being courted by a Red?" Maurice asked, coming across her within the hallowed walls. She felt sought out by him. "It might not look good for you if anyone knew."

"He's hardly a card-carrying communist," she said.

"Still," Maurice said, "at least he won't be betraying battleship positions in his pillow talk."

What did that mean? Did Maurice know about Crighton?

"Your personal life isn't personal, not while there's a war on," he said with a look of distaste. "And why, by the way, are you learning German? Are you awaiting the invasion? Getting ready to welcome the enemy?"

"I thought you were accusing me of being a communist, not a fascist," Ursula said crossly. ("What an ass," Pamela said. "He's just terrified of anything that might reflect badly on him. Not that I'm defending him. Heaven forbid.")

From her position at the bottom of the well, Ursula could see that most of the insubstantial wall between her apartment and Mrs. Appleyard's had disappeared. Looking up through the fractured floorboards and the shattered beams she could see a dress hanging limply on a coat hanger, hooked to a picture rail. It was the picture rail in the Millers' lounge on the ground floor, Ursula recognized the wallpaper of sallow, overblown roses. She had seen Lavinia Nesbit on the stairs wearing the dress only this evening, when it had been the color of pea soup (and equally limp). Now it was a gray bomb-dust shade and had migrated down a floor. A few yards from her head she could see her own kettle, a big brown thing, surplus to requirements in Fox Corner. She recognized it from the thick twine wound around the handle one day long ago by Mrs. Glover. Everything was in the wrong place now, including herself.

Yes, Ralph had been in Argyll Road. They had eaten—bread and cheese—accompanied by a bottle of beer. Then she had done the crossword, yesterday's *Telegraph*. Recently Ursula had been forced to buy a pair of spectacles for close work, rather ugly things. It was only after she had brought them home that she realized they were almost identical to the pair that one of the Misses Nesbit wore. Was this her fate too, she thought, contemplating her bespectacled reflection in the mirror above the fireplace? Would she, too, end up as an old maid? *The proper sport of boys and girls.* And could you be an old maid if you had worn the scarlet letter? Yesterday an envelope had mysteriously appeared on her desk while she was snatching a sandwich lunch in St. James's Park. She saw her name in Crighton's handwriting (he had a surprisingly nice italic hand) and tore the whole thing to bits and threw it in the bin without reading it. Later, when all the clerical assistants were flocking like pigeons around the tea trolley, she had retrieved the scraps and pieced them together.

I have mislaid my gold cigarette case. You know the one—my father gave it to me after Jutland. You wouldn't have come across it by any chance, would you?

Yours, C.

But he was never hers, was he? On the contrary, he belonged to Moira. (Or perhaps the Admiralty.) She dropped the pieces of paper back in the bin. The cigarette case was in her handbag. She had found it beneath her bed a few days after he had left her.

"Penny for them?" Ralph said.

"Not worth it, trust me."

Ralph was stretched out next to her, resting his head on the arm of the sofa, his socked feet in her lap. Although he looked as though he were asleep he gave a murmured response every time she tossed a clue in his direction. "*A Roland for an Oliver?* How about 'paladin'?" she said. "What do you think?"

An odd thing had happened to her yesterday. She had been on the Tube, she didn't like the Tube, before the bombing she cycled everywhere but it was difficult with so much glass and rubble around. She had been doing the *Telegraph* crossword, trying to pretend she wasn't underground. Most people felt safer underground but Ursula didn't like the idea of confinement. There had been an incident only a couple of days previously of a bomb falling onto an Underground entrance, the blast had traveled down and into the tunnels and the result was pretty awful. She wasn't sure that it had made the papers, these things were so bad for morale.

On the Tube, a man sitting next to her had suddenly leaned across—she had shrunk back—and, nodding at her half-filled grid, said, "You're rather good at that. Can I give you my card? Pop into my office if you like. I'm recruiting clever girls." I bet you are, she thought. He got off at Green Park, tipping his hat to her. The card had an address in Whitehall but she had thrown it away.

Ralph shook two cigarettes from a packet and lit them both. He passed one to her and said, "You're a clever thing, aren't you?"

"Pretty much," she said. "That's why I'm in the Intelligence Department and you're in the Map Room."

"Ha, ha, clever and funny."

There was an easy camaraderie between them, that of pals more than lovers. They respected each other's character and made few demands. It helped that they both worked in the War Room. There were a lot of things they never had to explain to each other.

He touched the back of her hand with his and said, "How are you?" and she said, "Very well, thank you." His hands were still those of the architect he had been before the war, unspoiled by battle. He had been safely away from the fighting, a surveyor in the Royal Engineers, poring over maps and photographs and so on and hadn't expected to become a combatant, wading through filthy, oily, bloody seawater being shot at from all quarters. (For he had, after all, spoken a little more of it.)

Although the bombing was awful, he said, you could see that something good could come out of it. He was hopeful about the future (unlike Hugh or Crighton). "All those hovels," he said. Woolwich, Silvertown, Lambeth, and Limehouse were being destroyed and after the war they would have to be rebuilt. It was an opportunity, he said, to build clean, modern homes with all the facilities—a community of glass and steel and air in the sky instead of Victorian slums. "A kind of San Gimignano for the future."

Ursula was unconvinced by this vision of modernist towers, if it were up to her she would rebuild the future as garden cities, comfortable little houses with cottage gardens. "What an old Tory you are," he said affectionately.

Yet he loved the old London too ("What architect wouldn't?")—Wren's churches, the grand houses and elegant public buildings—"the Stones of London," he said. One or two nights a week he was part of the St. Paul's night watch, men who were ready to climb into the rafters "if necessary" to keep the great church safe from incendiaries. The place was a firetrap, he said—old timbers, lead everywhere, flat roofs, a multitude of staircases and dark forgotten places. He had answered an advertisement in the Royal Institute of British Architects' journal, appealing for architects to volunteer to be firewatchers because they would "understand the plans, and so on." "We might have to be pretty nimble," he said and Ursula wondered how he would do that with his limp. She had visions of him beleaguered by flames on all those staircases and in the dark forgotten places. It seemed a chummy kind of watch—they played chess and had long conversations about philosophy and religion. She imagined that it suited Ralph very well.

Only a few weeks ago they had watched together, spellbound in horror, as Holland House burned. They had been in Melbury Road, raiding the wine cellar. "Why not stay in my house," Izzie had said casually before she embarked for America. "You can be my caretaker. You'll be safe here. I can't imagine the Germans will want to bomb Holland Park." Ursula thought that Izzie might be rather overestimating the Luftwaffe's precision with bombs. And if it was so safe why was Izzie turning tail and running?

"No thanks," she said. The house was too big and empty. She had taken the key though and occasionally foraged in the house for useful things. There was still some tinned food in the cupboards that Ursula was keeping for a last-ditch emergency, and, of course, the full wine cellar.

They were scanning the wine racks with their torches—the electricity had been turned off when Izzie left—and Ursula had just pulled a rather fine-looking bottle of Pétrus from the rack and said to Ralph, "Do you think this would go with potato scallops and Spam?" when there was a terrific explosion and, thinking the house had been hit, they had thrown themselves on the hard stone floor of the cellar with their hands over their heads. This was Hugh's advice, instilled in Ursula at a recent visit to Fox Corner. "Always protect your head." He had been in a war. She sometimes forgot. All the wine bottles had shaken and shivered in their racks and with hindsight Ursula dreaded to think what damage those bottles of Château Latour and Château d'Yquem could have done if they had rained down on them, the splintered glass like shrapnel.

They had run outside and watched Holland House turn into a bonfire, the flames eating everything, and Ursula thought, don't let me die in a fire. Let it be quick, please God.

She was tremendously fond of Ralph. Not hounded by love the way some women were. With Crighton she had been teased endlessly by the *idea* of it, but with Ralph it was more straightforward. Again not love, more like the feelings you would have for a favorite dog (and, no, she would never have said such a thing to him. Some people, a lot of people, didn't understand how attached one could be to a dog).

Ralph lit another cigarette and Ursula said, "Harold says smoking is very bad for people. Says he's seen lungs on operating tables that look like unswept chimneys."

"Of course it's not good for you," Ralph said, lighting one for Ursula too. "But being bombed and shot at by the Germans isn't good for you either."

"Don't you wonder sometimes," Ursula said. "If just one small thing had been changed, in the past, I mean. If Hitler had died at birth, or if someone had kidnapped him as a baby and brought him up in—I don't know, say, a Quaker household—surely things would be different."

"Do you think Quakers would kidnap a baby?" Ralph asked mildly.

"Well, if they knew what was going to happen they might."

"But nobody knows what's going to happen. And anyway he might have turned out just the same, Quakers or no Quakers. You might have to kill him instead of kidnapping him. Could you do that? Could you kill a baby? With a gun? Or what if you had no gun, how about with your bare hands? In cold blood."

If I thought it would save Teddy, Ursula thought. Not just Teddy, of course, the rest of the world, too. Teddy had applied to the RAF the day after war was declared. He had been working on a small farm in Suffolk. After Oxford he had done a year at an agricultural college and then had worked on different farms and smallholdings around the country. He wanted to know everything, he said, before he got his own place. ("A *farmer?*" Sylvie still said.) He didn't want to be one of those idealistic back-to-the-land types who ended up knee-deep in muddy yards with sickly cows and dead lambs, their crops not worth picking. (He had worked on one of those places apparently.)

Teddy still wrote poetry and Hugh said, "A poet farmer, eh? Like Virgil. We'll expect a new *Georgics* from you." Ursula wondered how Nancy felt about being a farmer's wife. She was awfully smart, doing research at Cambridge into some arcane and bewildering aspect of maths. ("All gibberish to me," Teddy said.) And now his childhood dream of becoming a pilot was suddenly and unexpectedly within reach. At the moment he was safe in Canada at an Empire Training School, learning to fly, sending home letters about how much food there was, how great the weather was, making Ursula green with envy. She wished he could stay over there forever, out of harm's way.

How did we end up talking about murdering babies in cold blood?" Ursula said to Ralph. "Mind you," she cocked her head toward the wall and the rise and fall of Emil's siren wail.

Ralph laughed. "He's not so bad tonight. Mind you, I'd go batty if my children made a racket like that."

Ursula thought it was interesting that he said "my children," not "our children." Strange to be thinking of having children at all during a time when the very existence of the future was in doubt. She stood up rather abruptly and said, "The raids will be starting soon." Back at the beginning of the Blitz they would have said, "They can't come *every* night," now they knew they could. ("Is this to be life forever," she wrote to Teddy, "to be harried without rest by the bombs?") Fifty-six nights in a row now so that it was beginning to seem possible that there really would be no end to it.

"You're like a dog," Ralph said. "You've got a sixth sense for the raiders."

"Well you'd better believe me then and go. Or you'll have to come down to the dark hole of Calcutta and you know you won't like that." The sprawling Miller family, Ursula had counted at least four generations, lived on the ground floor and in the semi-basement of the house in Argyll Road. They also had access down to a further level, a subterranean cellar that the residents of the house used as an air-raid shelter. It was a maze, a moldy, unpleasant space, full of spiders and beetles, and felt horribly crowded if they were all in there, especially once the Millers' dog, a shapeless rug of fur called Billy, was dragged reluctantly down the stairs to join them. They had also, of course, to put up with the tears and lamentations of Emil, who was passed around between the cellar occupants like an unwanted parcel in a futile attempt to pacify him.

Mr. Miller, in an effort to make the cellar "homely" (something it could never be), had taped some reproductions of "great English art," as he called it, against the sandbagged walls. These color plates—*The Haywain,* Gainsborough's *Mr. and Mrs. Andrews* (how smug they looked) and *Bubbles* (the most sickly Millais possible, in Ursula's opinion)—looked suspiciously as if they had been pilfered from expensive reference books on art. "Culture," Mr. Miller said, nodding sagely. Ursula wondered what she would have chosen to represent "great English art." Turner perhaps, the smudged, fugitive content of the late works. Not to the Millers' taste at all, she suspected.

She had sewn the collar on her blouse. She had switched off the *Sturm und Drang* of the wireless broadcast and listened instead to Ma Rainey singing "Yonder Come the Blues"—an antidote to all the easy sentiment that was beginning to pour out of the wireless. And she had eaten bread and cheese with Ralph, attempted the crossword and then hurried him out of the door with a kiss. Then she had turned off the light and moved the blackout aside so that she could catch a glimpse of him walking away down Argyll Road. Despite his limp (or perhaps because of it) he had a buoyant gait as if he was expecting something interesting to cross his path. It reminded her of Teddy.

He knew that she was watching him but he didn't look back, simply raised an arm in silent salute and was swallowed by the dark. There was some light though, a bright slice of crescent moon and a scattering of the faintest stars as though someone had flung a handful of diamond dust into the dark. The *Queen-Moon,* surrounded by *all her starry Fays,* although she suspected Keats was writing about a full moon and the moon above Argyll Road seemed more like a moon-in-waiting. She was in a—rather poor—poetic mood. It was the enormity of war, she thought, it left you scrabbling for ways to think about it.

Bridget always said it was bad luck to look at the moon through glass and Ursula let the blind fall back into place and closed the curtains tightly.

Ralph was casual with his safety. After Dunkirk, he said, he felt proofed against sudden violent death. It seemed to Ursula that in a time of war, when one was surrounded by an immense amount of sudden violent death, the odds were quite changed and it was impossible to be protected from anything.

As she knew it would, the caterwauling commenced, followed swiftly by the guns in Hyde Park starting up and the noise of the first bombs, over the docks again by the sound of it. She was galvanized into action, snatching her torch from the hook beside the front door where it lived like a holy relic, picking up her book, also kept by the door. It was her "shelter book"—*Du côté de chez Swann.* Now that the war looked as if it was going to last forever Ursula had decided she might as well embark on Proust.

The planes whined overhead and then she heard the fearsome *swish* of a bomb descending and then a walloping *thump!* as it landed somewhere nearby. Sometimes an explosion sounded much closer than it actually was. (How quickly one acquired new knowledge in the most unlikely subjects.) She looked for her shelter suit. She was wearing a rather flimsy dress considering the season and it was horribly cold and damp in the cellar. The shelter suit had been bought by Sylvie, up in town for the day not long before the bombing started. They had gone for a stroll along Piccadilly and Sylvie had spotted an advertisement in Simpson's window for "tailored shelter suits" and insisted that they go in and try them on. Ursula couldn't imagine her mother in a shelter, let alone a shelter suit, but it was clearly a garment, a uniform even, that attracted Sylvie. "It'll be rather good for mucking out hens," she said and bought them one each.

The next massive bang had an urgency to it and Ursula abandoned her search for the dratted suit and instead she grabbed the blanket of woolen squares crocheted by Bridget. ("I was going to parcel it up and send it off to the Red Cross," Bridget had written in her round schoolgirl's hand, "but then I thought you might need it more."

"You see, even within my own family I have the status of a refugee," Ursula wrote to Pamela.)

She passed the Nesbit sisters on the stairs. "Ooh, bad luck, Miss Todd," Lavinia giggled. "Crossing on the stairs, you know."

Ursula was going down, the sisters were coming up. "You're going the wrong way," she said, rather pointlessly.

"I forgot my knitting," Lavinia said. She was wearing an enamel brooch shaped like a black cat. A little rhinestone winked for an eye. "She's knitting leggings for Mrs. Appleyard's baby," Ruth said. "It's so cold in their apartment." Ursula wondered how many more knitted garments could be applied to the poor child before it resembled a sheep. Not a lamb. Nothing lamb-like about the Appleyard infant. Emil, she reminded herself.

"Well, do hurry, won't you?" she said.

Hail, hail, the gang's all here," Mr. Miller said as they trooped, one by one, into the cellar. A ragtag assortment of chairs and temporary bedding filled the dank space. There were two ancient army camp beds that Mr. Miller had scrounged from somewhere and on which the Nesbits were persuaded to rest their elderly bones. In the current absence of either sister, Billy the dog had installed himself on one of them. There was also a small spirit stove and an Aladdin paraffin stove, both of which seemed to Ursula extraordinarily dangerous items to be in such proximity when people were dropping bombs on you. (The Millers were effortlessly sanguine in the face of jeopardy.)

The roll call was almost complete—Mrs. Appleyard and Emil, the queer fish Mr. Bentley, Miss Hartnell and the full complement of Millers. Mrs. Miller voiced her concern for the whereabouts of the Nesbits and Mr. Miller volunteered to go and hurry them up ("ruddy knitting and all") but just then a tremendous explosion rocked the cellar. Ursula felt the foundations trembling as the blast moved through the earth beneath her. Obedient to Hugh's directive, she dropped to the floor with her hands over her head, grabbing the nearest of the smaller Miller boys ("Oi, get your hands off me!") on the way down. She crouched awkwardly over him but he wriggled away from her.

All went quiet.

"That wasn't our house," the boy said dismissively, swaggering a little to restore his wounded male dignity.

Mrs. Appleyard had also thrown herself to the floor, the baby soft-shelled beneath her. Mrs. Miller had clutched not one of her brood but the old Farrah's Harrogate Toffee tin that contained her savings and insurance policies.

Mr. Bentley, his voice sounding a quaver higher than normal, asked, "*Was* that us?" No, thought Ursula, we would be dead if it had been. She sat down again on one of the rickety bentwood chairs provided by Mr. Miller. She could feel her heart, too loud. She began to shiver and wrapped herself in Bridget's crochet.

"Nah, the boy's right," Mr. Miller said, "that sounded like Essex Villas." Mr. Miller always professed to know where the bombs were dropping. Surprisingly, he was often correct. All of the Millers were adept at wartime language as well as wartime spirit. They could all take it. ("And we can give it out too, can't we?" Pamela wrote. "You would think *we* had no blood on our hands.")

"The backbone of England, no doubt," Sylvie said to Ursula on first (and last) acquaintance with them. Mrs. Miller had invited Sylvie down to her kitchen for a cup of tea but Sylvie was still cross at the state of Ursula's curtains and rugs, for which she blamed Mrs. Miller, under the apprehension that she was the landlady and not merely another renter. (She was deaf to Ursula's explanations.) Sylvie behaved as though she were a duchess visiting the cottage of one of her rustic tenants. Ursula imagined Mrs. Miller later saying to Mr. Miller, "Hoity-toity, that one."

Up above, the racket of a steady bombardment was now under way, they could hear the timpani of the big bombs, the whistling of shells and the thunder of a nearby mobile artillery unit. Every now and then the foundations of the cellar shook with a *crump* and *thump* and *bump* as the bombs hammered down on the city. Emil howled, Billy the dog howled, a couple of the smallest Millers howled. All in discord with each other, an unwelcome counterpoint to the *Donner und Blitzen* of the Luftwaffe. A terrible, endless storm. *Despair behind, and death before.*

"Crikey, old Fritz is really trying to put the wind up us tonight," Mr. Miller said, calmly adjusting a lamp for all the world as if they were on a camping trip. He was responsible for morale in the cellar. Like Hugh, he had lived through the trenches and claimed that he was impervious to threats from Jerry. There was a whole club of them, Crighton, Ralph, Mr. Miller, even Hugh, who had undergone their ordeal by fire and mud and water and who presumed it was a once-in-a-lifetime experience.

"What's old Fritz up to, eh?" he said soothingly to one of the smaller, more frightened children. "Trying to stop me getting my beauty sleep?" The Germans always came singularly for Mr. Miller in the person of Fritz and Jerry, Otto, Hermann, Hans, sometimes Adolf himself was four miles up dropping his high explosive.

Mrs. Miller (Dolly), an embodiment of the triumph of experience over hope (unlike her spouse), was doling out "refreshments" of tea, cocoa, biscuits and bread and margarine. The Millers, a family of generous morals, were never short of rations thanks to Renee, their eldest daughter, who had "connections." Renee was eighteen and fully formed in every way and seemed to be a girl of most easy virtue. Miss Hartnell made it clear that she found Renee very wanting indeed although she was not averse to sharing in the provender that she brought home. Ursula got the impression that one of the smaller Miller children was actually Renee's rather than Mrs. Miller's and had, in a pragmatic way, simply been absorbed into the family pool.

Renee's "connections" were ambiguous but a few weeks ago Ursula had spotted her in the first-floor coffee lounge of the Charing Cross Hotel sipping daintily on gin in the company of a sleek and rather prosperous-looking man who had "racketeer" written all over him.

"There's a sleazy gent if ever I saw one," Jimmy had laughed. Jimmy, the baby produced to celebrate the peace after the war to end all wars, was about to fight in another one. He had a few days' leave from his army training and they had taken refuge in the Charing Cross Hotel while an unexploded bomb in the Strand was being dealt with. They could hear the naval guns that had been stationed on trolleys between Vauxhall and Waterloo—*boom-boom-boom*—but the bombers were looking for other targets and seemed to have moved on. "Doesn't it ever stop?" Jimmy asked.

"Apparently not."

"It's safer in the army," he laughed. He had joined the ranks as a private even though the army had offered him a commission. He wanted to be one of the chaps, he said. ("But someone has to be an officer, surely?" Hugh puzzled. "Better if it's someone with a bit of intelligence.")

He wanted the experience. He wanted to be a writer, he said, and what better than a war to reveal to him the heights and depths of the human condition? "A *writer?*" Sylvie said. "I fear the hand of the evil fairy rocked his cradle." She meant Izzie, Ursula supposed.

It had been lovely spending time with Jimmy. Jimmy was dashing in his battle dress and gained an entrance wherever they went—risqué venues in Dean Street and Archer Street, the Boeuf sur le Toit in Orange Street that was very risqué indeed (if not downright risky), places that made Ursula wonder about Jimmy. All in the pursuit of the human condition, he said. They got very drunk and a little silly and it was all rather a relief from cowering in the Millers' cellar. "Promise you won't die," she said to Jimmy as they groped like a blind couple along the Haymarket, listening to some other part of London being blown out of existence.

"Do my best," Jimmy said.

She was cold. The water she was lying in was making her even colder. She needed to move. Could she move? Apparently not. How long had she been lying here? Ten minutes? Ten years? Time had ceased. Everything seemed to have ceased. Only the awful concoction of smells remained. She was in the cellar. She knew that because she could see *Bubbles,* still miraculously taped to a sandbag near her head. Was she going to die looking at this banality? Then banality seemed suddenly welcome as a ghastly vision appeared at her side. A terrible ghost, black eyes in a gray face and wild hair, was clawing at her. "Have you seen my baby?" the ghost said. It took Ursula a few moments to realize that this was no ghost. It was Mrs. Appleyard, her face covered in dirt and bomb dust and streaked with blood and tears. "Have you seen my baby?" she said again.

"No," Ursula whispered, her mouth dry from whatever filth had been falling. She closed her eyes and when she opened them again Mrs. Appleyard had disappeared. She might have imagined her, perhaps she was delirious. Or perhaps it really had been the ghost of Mrs. Appleyard and they were both trapped in some desolate limbo.

Her attention was caught again by Lavinia Nesbit's dress hanging from the Millers' picture rail. But it wasn't Lavinia Nesbit's dress. A dress didn't have arms in it. Not sleeves, but *arms.* With *hands.* Something on the dress winked at Ursula, a little cat's eye caught by the crescent moon. The headless, legless body of Lavinia Nesbit herself was hanging from the Millers' picture rail. It was so absurd that a laugh began to boil up inside Ursula. It never broke because something shifted—a beam, or part of the wall—and she was sprinkled with a shower of talcum-like dust. Her heart thumped uncontrollably in her chest. It was sore, a time-delay bomb waiting to go off.

For the first time she felt panic. No one was coming to help her. Certainly not the deranged ghost of Mrs. Appleyard. She was going to die alone in the cellar of Argyll Road, with nothing but *Bubbles* and the headless Lavinia Nesbit for company. If Hugh were here, or Teddy or Jimmy, or even Pamela, they would be fighting to get her out of here, to *save* her. They would care. But there was no one here to care. She heard herself mewling like an injured cat. How sorry she felt for herself, as if she were someone else.

Mrs. Miller had said, "Well, I think we could all do with a nice cup of cocoa, don't you?" Mr. Miller was fretting about the Nesbits again and Ursula, utterly fed up with the claustrophobia of the cellar, said, "I'll go and look for them," and got up from the rickety dining chair just as the *swish* and *pheew* announced the arrival of a high explosive bomb. There was a giant thunderclap, a great cracking noise as the wall of hell suddenly split open and let all the demons out and then the tremendous suction and compression, as if her insides, her lungs, her heart and stomach, even her eyeballs were being sucked from her body. *Salute the last and everlasting day.* This is it, she thought. This is how I die.

A voice broke into the silence, almost next to her ear, a man's voice saying, "Come on then, miss, let's see if we can get you out of here, shall we?" Ursula could see his face, grimy and sweaty as if he had tunneled to reach her. (She supposed he had.) She was surprised to recognize him. It was one of their local ARP wardens, a new one.

"What's your name, miss? Can you tell me?" Ursula muttered her name but she knew it hadn't come out right. "Urry?" he queried. "What's that then—Mary? Susie?"

She didn't want to die as a Susie. But did it matter?

"Baby," she mumbled to the warden.

"Baby?" he said sharply. "You've got a baby?" He backed away slightly and shouted something to someone unseen. She heard other voices and realized there were lots of people now. As if to verify this the warden said, "We're all here to get you out. The gas boys have turned the gas off and we'll be moving you in a tick. Don't you worry. Now tell me about your baby, Susie. Were you holding him? Is he just a littl'un?" Ursula thought of Emil, as heavy as a bomb (who had been caught out holding him when the music stopped and the house exploded?), and tried to speak but found herself mewling again.

Something creaked and groaned overhead and the warden grabbed her hand and said, "It's all right, I'm here," and she felt immensely grateful to him, and to all the people toiling to get her out. And she thought how grateful Hugh would be too. The thought of her father made her start to cry and the warden said, "There, there, Susie, everything's all right, soon have you out of here, like a winkle out of a shell. Get you a nice cup of tea, eh? How does that sound? Lovely, eh? Fancy one myself."

Snow seemed to be falling, tiny icy needles on her skin. "So cold," she murmured.

"Don't worry, we'll have you out of here in two shakes of a lamb's tail, you'll see," the warden said. He struggled out of the coat he was wearing and covered her with it. There wasn't room for such a generous maneuver and he knocked something, causing a shower of debris to fall on them both.

"Oh," she said to the warden because she felt suddenly violently sick but it passed and she felt calmer. Leaves were falling now mixed with the dust and ash and flakes of the dead and suddenly she was blanketed in piles of wafery beech leaves. They smelled of mushrooms and bonfires and something sweet. Mrs. Glover's gingerbread. So much nicer than sewage and gas.

"Come on, girl," the warden said. "Come on, Susie, don't go to sleep on me now." He held her hand tighter but Ursula was looking at something glinting and twirling in the sunlight. A rabbit? No, a hare. A silver hare, spinning slowly in front of her eyes. It was mesmerizing. It was the prettiest thing she had ever seen.

She was flying off a roof into the night. She was in a cornfield with the sun beating down. Picking raspberries in the lane. Playing hide-and-seek with Teddy. *She's a funny little thing,* someone said. Not the warden, surely? And then the snow began to come down.

The night sky was no longer high above, it was all around her, like a warm dark sea.

She was floating into the blackout. She tried to say something to the warden. *Thank you.* But it didn't matter anymore. Nothing mattered. The darkness had fallen.

A LOVELY DAY TOMORROW

2 September 1939

"Don't get upset, Pammy," Harold said. "Why is it so quiet, what have you done with the boys?"

"Sold them," Pamela said, perking up. "Three for the price of two."

"You ought to stay the night, Ursula," Harold said kindly. "You shouldn't be on your own tomorrow. It'll be one of those awful days. Doctor's orders."

"Thanks," Ursula said. "But I've already got plans."

She tried on the yellow *crêpe de Chine* tea dress that she'd bought earlier that day in an eve-of-war spending spree on Kensington High Street. The *crêpe de Chine* had a pattern—tiny black swallows in flight. She admired it, rather admired herself, or what she could see in the dressing-table mirror as she had to stand on her bed in order to see her lower half.

Through Argyll Road's thin walls Ursula could hear Mrs. Appleyard having a row, in English, with a man—the mysterious Mr. Appleyard presumably—whose comings and goings at all times of the day and night kept no noticeable timetable. Ursula had encountered him in the flesh only once, in passing on the stairs, when he had glared moodily at her and hurried on without a greeting. He was a big man, ruddy and slightly porcine. Ursula could imagine him standing behind a butcher's counter or hauling brewery sacks, although according to the Misses Nesbit he was in fact an insurance clerk.

Mrs. Appleyard, in contrast, was thin and sallow and when her husband was out of the apartment Ursula could hear her singing mournfully to herself in a language that she couldn't place.

Something Eastern European by the sound of it. How useful Mr. Carver's Esperanto would be, she thought. (Only if everyone spoke it, of course.) And especially these days with so many refugees flooding into London. ("She's Czech," the Nesbits had eventually informed her. "We didn't used to know where Czechoslovakia was, did we? I wish we still didn't.") Ursula presumed Mrs. Appleyard was also some kind of refugee who, looking for safe harbor in the arms of an English gentleman, had found instead the pugnacious Mr. Appleyard. Ursula thought that if she ever heard Mr. Appleyard actually hitting his wife then she would have to knock on their door and somehow put a stop to it, although she had no idea how she would do that.

The dispute next door reached a crescendo and then the Appleyards' front door slammed decisively in conclusion and all went quiet. Mr. Appleyard, a great one for noisy exits and entrances, could be heard stomping down the stairs, a trail of profanity in his wake on the subject of women and foreigners, of which the oppressed Mrs. Appleyard was both.

The sour aura of dissatisfaction that seeped through the walls, along with the even less appetizing smell of boiled cabbage, was really quite depressing. Ursula wanted her refugees to be soulful and romantic—fleeing for their cultural lives—rather than the abused wives of insurance clerks. Which was ridiculously unfair of her.

She stepped down from the bed and did a little twirl for the mirror. The dress suited her, she decided, she still had her figure, even at nearly thirty. Would she one day develop Sylvie's matronly girth? It was beginning to seem unlikely now that she would ever have children of her own. She remembered holding Pamela's babies—remembered Teddy and Jimmy, too—how overwhelming the feelings of love and terror, the desperate desire to protect. How much stronger would those feelings be if it were her own child? Perhaps too strong to bear.

Over their afternoon tea in John Lewis, Sylvie had asked, "Do you never get broody?"

"Like your hens?"

"A 'career woman,'" Sylvie said, as if the two words had no place in the same sentence. "A spinster," she added, contemplating the word. Ursula wondered why her mother was working so hard to rile her. "Perhaps you will never marry," Sylvie said, as if in conclusion, as if Ursula's life was as good as over.

"Would that be such a bad thing? 'The unmarried daughter,'" Ursula said, tucking into an iced fancy. "It was good enough for Jane Austen."

She lifted the dress over her head and, in petticoat and stocking feet, padded through to the little scullery and filled a water glass at the tap before hunting down a cream cracker. Prison fare, she thought, good practice for what was to come. All she had had to eat since her breakfast toast was Pamela's cake. She was hoping to be stood, at the very least, a good dinner by Crighton tonight. He had asked her to meet him at the Savoy, they rarely had such public assignations, and she wondered if there was going to be drama, or if the shadow of war was drama enough and he wanted to talk to her about it.

She knew that war was to be declared tomorrow, even though she had played rather dumb with Pammy. Crighton told her all kinds of things he shouldn't, on the basis that they had "both signed the Official Secrets Act." (She, on the other hand, told him almost nothing.) He had been teetering again lately and Ursula wasn't at all sure which way he was going to fall, wasn't sure which way she wanted him to fall.

He had asked her to meet him for a drink, a request conveyed on an Admiralty docket that had arrived mysteriously while she was briefly out of the office. Not for the first time Ursula wondered who brought these notes that seemed to appear on her desk as if delivered by elves. *I think your department may be due an audit,* it read. Crighton liked code. Ursula hoped that the navy's encryptions weren't as rudimentary as Crighton's.

Miss Fawcett, one of her clerical assistants, spotted the note lying in full view and gave her a panic-stricken look. "Crikey," she said. "Are we? Due an audit?"

"Someone's idea of a joke," Ursula said, dismayed to find herself blushing. There was something un-Crighton-like about these salacious (if not downright filthy) but seemingly innocent messages. *I believe there is a shortage of pencils.* Or *Are your ink levels sufficiently topped up?* Ursula wished he would learn Pitman's, or more discretion. Or, better still, stop altogether.

When she was ushered inside the Savoy by a doorman, Crighton was waiting for her in the expansive foyer and instead of escorting her up to the American Bar he shepherded her up the stairs to a suite on the second floor. The bed seemed to dominate the room, enormous and pillowy. Oh, so this is why we're here, she thought.

The *crêpe de Chine* had been deemed unsuitable for the occasion and she had donned her royal-blue satin—one of her three good evening dresses—a decision she now regretted as Crighton, if form was anything to go by, would soon be divesting her of it rather than treating her to a slap-up meal.

He liked undressing her, liked looking at her. "Like a Renoir," he said, although he knew little about art. Better a Renoir than a Rubens, she thought. Or a Picasso, for that matter. He had bestowed on her the great gift of regarding herself naked with little, if any, criticism. Moira, apparently, was a floor-length flannelette and lights-out woman. Sometimes Ursula wondered if Crighton didn't exaggerate his wife's sturdy qualities. Once or twice it had crossed her mind to journey out to Wargrave to catch a glimpse of the wronged wife and find out if she really was a dowd. The problem, of course, with Moira in the flesh (Rubenesque, not Renoir, she imagined) would be that Ursula would find it difficult to betray a real person rather than an enigma.

("But she *is* a real person," Pamela puzzled. "It's a specious argument."

"Yes, I *am* aware of that." This later, at Hugh's sixtieth birthday, a rather querulous affair in the spring.)

The suite had a magnificent view of the river, from Waterloo Bridge to the Houses of Parliament and Big Ben, all shadowy now, in the encroaching twilight. ("The violet hour.") She could just make out Cleopatra's Needle, a dark finger poking skywards. None of the usual blaze and twinkle of London lights. The blackout had already begun.

"The bolt hole wasn't available then? We're out in the open?" Ursula said while Crighton opened a bottle of champagne that had been waiting for them in a sweating silver bucket. "Are we celebrating?"

"Saying our adieux," Crighton said, joining her at the window and handing her a glass.

"Our adieux?" Ursula said, bemused. "You've brought me to a good hotel and are plying me with champagne in order to end it all between us?"

"Adieu to the peace," Crighton said. "We're saying good-bye to the world as we know it." He raised his glass in the direction of the window, to London, in its dusky glory. "To the beginning of the end," he said grimly. "I've left Moira," he added, as if it were an afterthought, a nothing. Ursula was caught by surprise.

"And the girls?" (Just checking, she thought.)

"All of them. Life is too precious to be unhappy." Ursula wondered how many people across London were saying the same thing that night. Perhaps in less salubrious surroundings. And there would be others, of course, who would be saying the same words to cleave to what they already had, not to discard it on a whim.

Suddenly and unexpectedly panicked, Ursula said, "I don't want to marry you." She hadn't realized quite how strongly she felt until the words came out of her mouth.

"I don't want to marry you either," Crighton said, and, perversely, she felt disappointed.

"I've taken a lease on an apartment in Egerton Gardens," he said. "I thought perhaps you would come and join me."

"To cohabit? To live in sin in Knightsbridge?"

"If you will."

"My, you are bold," she said. "What about your career?"

He made a dismissive sound. So, she, and not the war, was to be his new Jutland then.

"Will you say yes? Ursula?"

Ursula stared through the window at the Thames. The river was almost invisible now.

"We should have a toast," she said. "What is it they say in the navy—'Sweethearts and wives—may they never meet'?" She chinked her glass against Crighton's and said, "I'm starving, we are going to eat, aren't we?"

April 1940

A car horn down in the street below broke the Sunday-morning silence of Knightsbridge. Ursula missed the sound of church bells. There were so many simple things she had taken for granted before the war. She wished that she could go back and appreciate them properly.

"Why the horn," Crighton said, "when we have a perfectly good doorbell?" He looked out of the window. "He's here," he said, "if he's a young man in a three-piece suit puffed up like a Christmas robin."

"That does sound like him." Although Ursula didn't think of Maurice as "young," had never thought of him as young, but she supposed he was to Crighton.

Hugh's sixtieth birthday and Maurice had grudgingly offered her a lift to Fox Corner for the celebrations. It was going to be a novelty, and not necessarily a good one, to spend time cloistered in a car with Maurice. They were rarely alone with each other.

"He has petrol?" Crighton had said, raising an eyebrow but really it was more a statement than a question.

"He has a *driver,*" Ursula said. "I knew Maurice would squeeze the most out of the war." "What war?" Pamela would have said. She was "marooned" in Yorkshire with only six small boys for company and Jeanette, who had turned out to be not merely a moaner but "quite the *fainéante.* I expected better of a vicar's daughter. She's so lazy, I run around all day long after her boys as well as mine. I've had enough of this evacuation lark, I think we'll come home soon."

"I suppose he could hardly turn up at home in a car *without* having given me a lift," Ursula said. "Maurice wouldn't want to be seen to be behaving badly, even by his own family. He has a *reputation* to keep up. Besides, his family are staying there and he's bringing them back to London tonight." Maurice had sent Edwina and the children to stay at Fox Corner for the Easter holidays. Ursula had wondered if he knew something about the war that the public didn't—was Easter to be a particularly hazardous time? There must be so many things that Maurice knew that others didn't, but Easter had passed off without incident and she supposed it was merely a case of grandchildren visiting grandparents. Philip and Hazel were very uninventive children and Ursula wondered how they were getting on with Sylvie's rambunctious evacuees. "It'll be horribly crowded on the way back, with Edwina and the children. Not to mention the *driver.* Still, needs must and so on."

The car horn sounded again. Ursula ignored it as a matter of principle. How wickedly satisfying it would be, she thought, to have Crighton in tow, in full naval fig (all those medals, all that gold braid), outranking Maurice in so many ways. "You could come with me, you know," she said to him. "We just wouldn't mention Moira. Or the girls."

"Is it your home?"

"Sorry?"

"You said, 'he could hardly turn up at home.' Isn't this? Your home?" Crighton said.

"Yes, of course," Ursula said. Maurice was pacing impatiently up and down on the pavement and she rapped on the window pane to get his attention and held up her index finger, mouthing "one minute" to him. He frowned at her. "It's a figure of speech," she said, turning back to Crighton. "One always refers to one's parents' place as 'home.' "

"Does one? I don't."

No, thought Ursula, you don't. Wargrave was "home" for Crighton, even if only in his thoughts. And he was right, of course, she didn't consider the apartment in Egerton Gardens to be her home. It was a point in time, a temporary stopping-off place on yet another journey that the war had interrupted. "We can argue the point if you want," she said amiably. "It's just, you know... Maurice, marching up and down out there like a little tin soldier."

Crighton laughed. He never looked for arguments.

"I would love to join you and meet your family," he said, "but I'm going to the Citadel." The Admiralty was constructing an underground fortress, the Citadel, on Horse Guards Parade and Crighton was in the process of moving his office over.

"I'll see you later then," Ursula said. "My carriage awaits and Maurice is pawing the ground."

"Ring," Crighton reminded her and Ursula said, "Oh, yes, of course, I nearly forgot." She had started wearing a wedding ring when not at work, for appearances' sake, "Tradesmen, and so on." The boy who delivered the milk, the woman who came in to clean twice a week, she didn't want them thinking she was in an illicit relationship. (She had surprised herself with this bashfulness.)

"You can imagine how many questions there would be if they saw *that,*" she said, slipping the ring off and leaving it on the hall table.

Crighton kissed her lightly on the cheek and said, "Have a nice time."

"No guarantee of that," she said.

Still not caught yourself a man?" Izzie asked Ursula. "Of course," she said, turning brightly to Sylvie, "you have—how many grandchildren now, seven, eight?"

"Six. Perhaps *you're* a grandmother, Izzie."

"What?" Maurice said. "How could she be?"

"Anyway," Izzie said airily, "it takes the pressure off Ursula to produce one."

"Produce?" Ursula said, a forkful of salmon in aspic suspended on its way to her mouth.

"Looks like you're left on the shelf," Maurice said.

"Pardon?" The fork returned to the plate.

"Always the bridesmaid..."

"Once," Ursula said. "I have been a bridesmaid once only, to Pamela."

"I'll have that if you're not eating it," Jimmy said, filching the salmon.

"I was, actually."

"Even worse then," Maurice said. "Nobody even wants you as a bridesmaid except for your sister." He sniggered, more schoolboy than man. He was, annoyingly, seated too far away for her to kick him beneath the table.

"Manners, Maurice," Edwina murmured. How many times would he disappoint you in a day if you were married to him? Ursula wondered. It seemed to her that in the search for arguments against marriage the existence of Maurice presented the very best one of all. Of course, Edwina's nose was currently out of joint on account of the *driver,* who turned out to be a rather attractive ATS girl in uniform. Sylvie, to the girl's embarrassment (her name was Penny but everyone immediately forgot this), insisted that she join them at the table when she would clearly have been more comfortable staying with the car, or in the kitchen with Bridget. She was stuck at the cramped end of the table with the evacuees and was the object of constant frosty scrutiny from Edwina. Maurice, on the other hand, studiously ignored her. Ursula tried to read some meaning into this. She wished Pamela were here, she was very good at deciphering people, although not perhaps as good as Izzie. ("So, Maurice has been a naughty boy, I see. Mind you, she's a looker. Women in uniform, what man can resist?")

Philip and Hazel sat passively between their parents. Sylvie had never been particularly fond of Maurice's children whereas she seemed to delight in her evacuees, Barry and Bobby ("my two busy bees"), currently crawling beneath the Regency Revival dining table, giggling in a rather manic fashion. "Full of mischief," Sylvie said indulgently. The evacuees, as everyone else referred to them, as if they were entirely defined by their status, had been scrubbed and polished into apparent innocence by Bridget and Sylvie but nothing could disguise their impish nature. ("What little horrors," Izzie said with a shudder.) Ursula rather liked them, they reminded her of the small Millers. If they had been dogs their tails would have been constantly wagging.

Sylvie now had a pair of real puppies as well, excitable black Labradors who were also brothers. They were called Hector and Hamish but seemed to be known collectively and indistinguishably as "the dogs." The dogs and the evacuees appeared to have contributed to a new shabbiness in Fox Corner. Sylvie herself seemed more reconciled now to this war than she had ever been to the last one. Hugh less so. He had been "pushed" into training the Home Guard and had only this morning after Sunday service been instructing the "ladies" of the local church in the use of the stirrup pump.

"Is that suitable for the Sabbath?" Edwina asked. "I'm sure God's on our side, but..." she trailed off, incapable of sustaining a theological position despite being "a devout Christian," which meant, according to Pamela, that she slapped her children hard and made them eat for breakfast what they left at tea.

"Of course it's suitable," Maurice said. "In my role organizing the civil defense—"

"I don't consider myself to be 'on the shelf' as you so charmingly put it," Ursula interrupted him irritably. Again, she experienced a fleeting wish for Crighton's be-medaled, braided presence. How horrified Edwina would be to know of Egerton Gardens. ("And how is the Admiral?" Izzie asked later in the garden, sotto voce, like a conspirator, for, of course, she knew. Izzie knew everything and if she didn't know it she could mouse it out with ease. Like Ursula, she had the character for espionage. "He's not an admiral," Ursula said. "But he is well, thank you.")

"You do all right on your own," Teddy said to Ursula. "*Contracted to thine own bright eyes,* and so on." Teddy had faith in poetry, as if merely to quote from Shakespeare would mollify a situation. Ursula thought the sonnet he was quoting from was about being selfish but didn't say so as Teddy meant it kindly. Unlike everyone else, it seemed, all of whom appeared quite fixed on her unmarried status.

"She's only thirty, for heaven's sake," Izzie said, putting in her oar again. (If only they would all be quiet, Ursula thought.) "After all," Izzie persisted, "I was over forty when I married."

"And where *is* your husband?" Sylvie asked, looking around the Regency Revival—both leaves extended to accommodate their numbers. She feigned perplexity (it didn't suit her). "I don't seem to see him here."

Izzie had chosen the occasion to turn up ("Uninvited, as usual," Sylvie said) to offer her congratulations on Hugh's six decades. ("A landmark.") Hugh's other sisters had deemed the journey to Fox Corner "too challenging."

"What a parcel of vixens they are," Izzie said later to Ursula. Izzie might have been the baby but she was never the favorite. "Hugh has always been so good to them."

"He's always been good to everyone," Ursula said, surprised, alarmed even, to find tears starting up at the thought of her father's sound character.

"Oh, don't," Izzie said, handing her a froth of lace that apparently passed as a handkerchief. "You'll make me cry as well." It seemed unlikely, it had never happened before.

Izzie had also chosen the occasion to announce her imminent departure for California. Her husband, the famous playwright, had been offered a job writing screenplays in Hollywood. "All the Europeans are going there," she said.

"You're European now, are you?" Hugh said.

"Aren't we all?"

The whole family had gathered, apart from Pamela, for whom the journey was genuinely too challenging. Jimmy had managed to wangle a couple of days' leave and Teddy had brought Nancy along. On arrival, she gave Hugh a disarming hug, said, "Happy birthday, Mr. Todd," before handing him a parcel, wrapped prettily in old wallpaper scavenged from the Shawcross household. It was a copy of *The Warden.* "It's a first edition," Nancy said. "Ted said that you liked Trollope." (A fact that none of the rest of his family appeared to know.)

"Good old Ted," Hugh said, kissing her on the cheek. And to Teddy, "What a sweetheart you have here. When are you going to pop the question?"

"Oh," Nancy said, blushing and laughing, "plenty of time for that."

"I hope so," a somber Sylvie said. Teddy had graduated now from the Initial Training School ("He has wings!" Nancy said. "Like an angel!") and was waiting to sail to Canada, to train as a pilot. When he was qualified he would head back here and take up a place in an Operational Training Unit.

He was more likely to be killed in an OTU, he said, "than on an actual bombing run." It was true. Ursula knew a girl in the Air Ministry. (She knew girls everywhere, everyone did.) They ate their sandwiches together in St. James's Park and gloomily traded statistics, despite the dead hand of the Official Secrets Act.

"Well, that's a great comfort to me," Sylvie said.

"Ow!" one of the evacuees squealed beneath the table. "Some bugger just kicked me." Everyone instinctively looked at Maurice. Something cold and wet nosed itself up Ursula's skirt. She hoped very much that it was the nose of one of the dogs and not one of the evacuees. Jimmy pinched her arm (rather hard) and said, "They do go on, don't they?"

The poor ATS girl—like the evacuees and the dogs, defined by her status—looked as if she were about to cry.

"I say, are you all right?" ever-solicitous Nancy asked her.

"She's an only child," Maurice said matter-of-factly. "They don't understand the joys of family life." This knowledge of the ATS girl's background seemed to particularly infuriate Edwina, who was gripping the butter knife in her hand as if she were planning to attack someone with it—Maurice or the ATS girl, or anyone within stabbing distance by the look of it. Ursula wondered how much harm a butter knife could do. Enough, she supposed.

Nancy jumped up from the table and said to the ATS girl, "Come on, let's go for a walk, it's such a lovely day. The bluebells will be out in the wood, if you fancy a bit of a hike." She hooked arms with her and almost pulled her out of the room. Ursula thought about running after them.

"Courtship to marriage, as a very witty prologue to a very dull play," Izzie said as if nothing had interrupted them. "Someone said that."

"Congreve," Sylvie said. "What on earth does that have to do with anything?"

"Just saying," Izzie said.

"Of course—you're *married* to a playwright, aren't you?" Sylvie said. "The one we never see."

"The journey is different for everyone," Izzie said.

"Oh, please," Sylvie said. "Spare us your cod philosophy."

"For me, marriage is about freedom," Izzie said. "For you it has always been about the vexations of confinement."

"What on earth are you talking about?" Sylvie said. (A bafflement shared by the rest of the table.) "You talk such nonsense."

"And what life would you have led otherwise?" Izzie continued blithely (or relentlessly, depending on your viewpoint). "I seem to remember you were seventeen and on your uppers, a dead, bankrupt artist's daughter. Heaven only knows what would have happened to you if Hugh hadn't charged in and rescued you."

"You remember nothing, you were still in the nursery at the time."

"Barely. And, I, of course—"

"Oh, do shut up," Hugh said wearily.

Bridget broke the tension (often her starring role at Fox Corner now that Mrs. Glover was gone), entering the dining room bearing aloft a roast duck.

"Duck *à la surprise,*" Jimmy said, for, naturally, they had all been expecting a chicken.

Nancy and the ATS girl (*"Penny,"* Nancy reminded everyone) returned in time to be handed warmed-up plates. "You're lucky there's any duck on that," Teddy said to Nancy when he handed her a plate. "The poor bird was picked clean."

"There's so little eating on a duck," Izzie said, lighting up a cigarette. "There's barely enough for two people, I can't imagine what you were thinking."

"I was thinking there's a war on," Sylvie said.

"If I'd known you planned a *duck,*" Izzie plowed on, "I would have sought out something a little more generous. I know a man who can get anything."

"I bet you do," Sylvie said.

Jimmy offered Ursula the wishbone and they both wished loudly and pointedly for a nice birthday for Hugh.

An amnesty was brought about by the advent of the cake, an ingenious confection that, naturally, relied mainly on eggs. Bridget brought it to the table. She had no flair for making an occasion of anything and dumped it in front of Hugh without ceremony. She was coerced by him into taking a place at the table. "I wouldn't if I were you," Ursula heard the ATS girl mutter quietly.

"You're part of the family, Bridget," Hugh said. No one else in the family, Ursula thought, slaved away from dawn to dusk the way Bridget did. Mrs. Glover had retired and gone to live with one of her sisters, a move prompted by George's sudden but not unexpected death.

Just as Hugh filled his lungs, rather theatrically, for there was only one token candle to blow out, there was a great commotion out in the hallway. One of the evacuees went out to investigate and ran back with the news that it was "a woman, and loads of bloody kids!"

How was it?" Crighton asked, when she finally arrived home.

"Pammy came back—for good, I think," she said, deciding on the highlight. "She looked done in. She came by train, three little boys plus a babe in arms, can you imagine? It took her *hours*."

"A nightmare," Crighton said with feeling.

("Pammy!" Hugh said. He looked enormously pleased.

"Happy birthday, Daddy," Pamela said. "No presents, I'm afraid, just us."

"More than enough," Hugh said, beaming.)

"*And* suitcases, and the dog. She's such a stalwart. *My* journey home, on the other hand, was a different kind of nightmare. Maurice, Edwina, their uninspiring offspring and the *driver.* Turned out to be a rather lovely ATS girl."

"Good God," Crighton said, "how does he do it? I've been trying to get my hands on a Wren for months." She laughed and hovered in the kitchen while he made cocoa for both of them. While they drank it in bed she regaled him with tales from the day, somewhat embellished (she felt it her duty to entertain him). What, after all, she thought, was there to distinguish them from any married couple? Perhaps the war. Perhaps not.

"I think I'm going to have to join up, or something," she said. She thought of the ATS girl. "'Do my bit,' as they say. Get my hands dirty. I read reports every day about people doing brave things and my hands stay very clean."

"You're doing your bit already," he said.

"What? Supporting the navy?"

He laughed and rolled over and pulled her into his arms. He nuzzled her neck and as she lay there it struck her that it was just possible that she was happy. Or at any rate, she thought, qualifying the idea, as happy as was possible in this life.

"Home," it had struck her on the torturous drive back to London, wasn't Egerton Gardens, wasn't even Fox Corner. Home was an idea, and like Arcadia it was lost in the past.

She had already ticketed the day in her memory as "Hugh's sixtieth birthday," one more in a roll call of family occasions. Later, when she understood that it was the last time they would all be together, she wished she had paid more attention.

She was woken in the morning by Crighton bringing her a tray of tea and toast. She had the Senior Service to thank for his domesticity rather than Wargrave.

"Thank you," she said, struggling to sit up, still worn out from yesterday.

"Bad news, I'm afraid," he said, opening the curtains.

She thought of Teddy and Jimmy, although she knew that for this morning at least they were safely tucked up in their beds in Fox Corner, sharing their boyhood room, once Maurice's.

"What bad news?" she asked.

"Norway has fallen."

"Poor Norway," she said and sipped the hot tea.

November 1940

Pamela had sent a parcel of baby clothes that Gerald had grown out of, and Ursula thought of Mrs. Appleyard. She might not have thought of Mrs. Appleyard as she hadn't kept up with the residents of Argyll Road since she left for Egerton Gardens, something she had rather regretted as she had been fond of the Misses Nesbit and often wondered how they were faring under the relentless bombardment. But then she had had a chance encounter with Renee Miller a few weeks ago.

Ursula had been "on the town," as he put it, with Jimmy, who had a couple of days' furlough in the capital. They had been stranded in the Charing Cross Hotel thanks to a UXB—sometimes she thought unexploded bombs were more of a nuisance than exploded ones—and had taken refuge in the first-floor coffee lounge.

"There's a rather tarty girl, all lipstick and teeth, over there who seems to know you," Jimmy said.

"Ye gods, Renee Miller," Ursula said when she spotted Renee waving eagerly at her. "And who on earth is that man with her? He looks like a gangster."

Renee was effusive, as though she had been best pals with Ursula in some former life ("She's a lively girl," Jimmy laughed after they'd escaped), and insisted that they join her and "Nicky" for a drink. Nicky himself seemed less than enthusiastic about the idea but nonetheless shook hands and signaled to the waiter.

Renee filled Ursula in on "the doings" in Argyll Road, although little seemed to have changed since she left a year ago for Egerton Gardens, except that the army now had Mr. Appleyard and his wife had a baby. "A boy," Renee said. "Ugly little thing." Jimmy guffawed and said, "I like a girl who knows when a spade's a spade." Nicky was rather put out by Jimmy's personable presence, especially as by the time she had downed another watery gin Renee had begun to flirt (almost professionally it seemed) with him.

Ursula overheard someone say that the unexploded bomb had been dealt with and when Renee said, "Get us another round in, Nicky," and Nicky began to glower Ursula thought it might be politic to move on. Nicky refused to let them pay, as if it were a matter of principle. Ursula wasn't sure she wanted to be beholden to someone of his caliber. Renee hugged and kissed her and said,

"Come and see the old dears, they'd love it," and Ursula promised that she would.

"Good God, I thought she was going to eat me," Jimmy said as they maneuvered around rubble on Henrietta Street.

She made good on her promise to Renee, prompted by the parcel of Gerald's old clothes. She reached Argyll Road not long after six, getting away from work early for once. She had not, after all, donned a uniform of any kind yet, as there seemed hardly enough time to eat and breathe between work and the bombs. "Your job *is* war work," Crighton pointed out, "I would have thought that you would have enough on your plate. How is the Ministry of Some Obscurity these days?"

"Oh, you know. Busy." There was so much information to be logged. Each individual incident—what type of bomb, the damage done, how many killed or injured (the tally was mounting horribly)—streamed across their desks.

Occasionally, she would open a buff folder and find what she thought of as the "raw material"—ARP typed reports or even the hand-written reports they were based on—and wonder what it was like to be in the heat of battle, for that's what the Blitz was, wasn't it? Sometimes she saw bomb-damage maps, once one that had been drawn by Ralph. He had signed it in faint, almost indecipherable pencil on the back. They were friends, she had met him at her German class, although he had made it clear that he would like them to mean more to each other. "Your other man," Crighton called him, amused.

"How kind," Mrs. Appleyard said when Ursula appeared on her doorstep with the parcel of clothes. "Please come in."

Ursula crossed the threshold reluctantly. The previous smell of boiled cabbage now mingled with the more unappetizing smells that could accompany an infant. Sadly, Renee's judgment on Mrs.

Appleyard's baby's pulchritude, or lack of it, turned out to be true—he was an "ugly little thing."

"Emil," Mrs. Appleyard said, handing him over to Ursula to hold. She could feel the dampness of him through his rubber knickers. She almost handed him straight back. "Emil?" she said to him, making a face and grinning at him with forced jollity. He stared back at her, rather truculently, his paternity not in doubt.

Mrs. Appleyard offered tea and Ursula excused herself and scurried up the stairs to the Nesbits' aerie.

They were their usual benign selves. It must be quite nice to live with one's sister, Ursula thought. She wouldn't mind living out her days with Pamela.

Ruth grasped one of her fingers with her own twig-like ones. "You're married! How wonderful." Oh darn, Ursula thought, she had forgotten to take off the wedding ring. She demurred, "Well..." and then, seeing the complexity, finally, modestly, "Yes, I suppose so." They both offered triumphant congratulations, as if she had achieved something spectacular.

"What a shame you have no engagement ring," Lavinia said.

Ursula had forgotten their penchant for costume jewelry and wished she had brought them something. She had a little box of old diamanté buckles and clips that Izzie had given her that she knew they would have appreciated.

Lavinia was wearing an enamel brooch shaped like a black cat. A little rhinestone winked for an eye. Ruth sported a weighty carbuncle of topaz pinned to her sparrow chest. It looked like it might topple her insubstantial frame.

"We're like magpies," Ruth laughed. "We love all the shiny little things."

They had the kettle on and were happily fussing over what to feed her—toast with Marmite or toast with jam—when the siren began its infernal warble. Ursula looked out of the window. No sign of any raiders yet although a searchlight was already sweeping the black sky. A beautiful new moon had stamped a crescent of light out of the blackness.

"Come along, dear, down to the Millers' cellar," Lavinia said, surprisingly chipper. "Every night an adventure," Ruth added, as they gathered up a great amount of stuff—shawls and cups, books and darning. "Torch, torch, don't forget the torch!" Lavinia said gaily.

As they reached the ground floor a bomb thudded down a couple of streets away. "Oh, no!" Lavinia said. "I forgot my knitting."

"We'll go back, dear," Ruth said and Ursula said, "No, you must take shelter."

"I'm knitting leggings for Mrs. Appleyard's baby," Lavinia said, as if that were a good enough reason to risk her life.

"Don't worry about us, dear," Ruth said, "we'll be back before you know we've gone."

"For heaven's sake, if you must have it then I'll go," Ursula said but they were already creaking their old bones up the stairs and Mr. Miller was bustling her down to the cellar.

"Renee, Dolly, everyone—look who's come to join her old pals!" he announced to the occupants as if Ursula were a music hall turn.

She had forgotten how many Millers there were, and how starchy Miss Hartnell could be and how downright odd Mr. Bentley was. And as for Renee, she seemed to have quite forgotten the ardor of their previous encounter, saying only, "Oh, lawd, another body using up the air in this hellhole." Renee was—reluctantly—dandling a fractious Emil. She was right, it was a hellhole. In Egerton Gardens they had a rather salubrious basement that they retired to, although Ursula (and Crighton too if he was there) often took her chances and stayed in her own bed.

Ursula remembered the wedding ring and thought how confused

Hugh and Sylvie would be if they saw it on her body if she were to die in a raid. Would Crighton come to her funeral and explain? She was prevented from slipping it off by Renee suddenly thrusting Emil into her arms just before a massive explosion rocked the building.

"Crikey, old Fritz is really trying to put the wind up us tonight," Mr. Miller said cheerfully.

Her name was Susie, apparently. She had no idea, she really couldn't remember anything. A man kept calling her out of the darkness. "Come on, Susie, don't go to sleep now," and "How about we have a nice cuppa when we get out of here, eh, Susie?" She was choking on ash and dust. She sensed something inside her was torn beyond repair. Cracked. She was a golden bowl. "Quite Jamesian, really," she heard Teddy say. (Had he said that?) She was a great tree (how odd). She was very cold. The man was holding her hand, squeezing it, "Come on, Susie, stay awake now." But she couldn't, the soft dark was beckoning to her with the promise of sleep, endless sleep, and the snow began to fall gently until she was entirely shrouded and everything was dark.

A LOVELY DAY TOMORROW

September 1940

She missed Crighton, more than she had let on to either him or Pamela. He had taken a room at the Savoy on the night before war was declared and she had got dressed up in her good royal-blue satin only for him to announce that they should call an end to things ("to say our adieux"). "It's going to get awfully bloody," he said, but whether he meant the war or them she wasn't sure.

Despite or perhaps because of their adieux, they went to bed together and he spent a lot of time telling her how much he would miss "this body," the "lineaments of your flesh," "this pretty face," and so on, until she got rather fed up and said, "Well, it *is* you that wants out of this, not me."

She wondered if he made love to Moira in the same way—detachment and passion in equal measure—but it was one of those questions you couldn't ask in case he were to tell the truth. What did it matter, Moira was getting him back. Soiled goods perhaps but hers nonetheless.

The next morning they breakfasted in the room and then listened to Chamberlain's speech. There was a wireless in the suite. Not long after, a siren sounded but strangely neither of them panicked. It all seemed very unreal. "I expect it's a test," Crighton said. Ursula thought that from now on everything would probably be a test.

They left the hotel and walked along the Embankment to Westminster Bridge, where air-raid wardens were blowing their whistles and shouting that the scare was over. Others were riding along on bicycles with *All-Clear* signs attached to them, and Crighton said, "Good God, I fear for us if this is the best we can muster in a raid." Sandbags were being stacked along the bridge, being stacked everywhere, and Ursula thought it was just as well there was so much sand in the world. She tried to remember the lines from "The Walrus and the Carpenter." *If seven maids with seven mops*—but they had reached Whitehall by now and Crighton broke into her thoughts by taking both her hands in his and saying, "I must go now, darling," and for a moment he sounded like a rather cheap and sentimental movie star. She decided she would live out the war as a nun. Much easier.

She had watched him walk along Whitehall and suddenly felt horribly alone. She might, after all, go back to Finchley.

November 1940

On the other side of the wall she could hear Emil complaining and Mrs. Appleyard's soothing remonstrance. She began to sing a lullaby in her own language, the mother tongue, Ursula thought. It was an extraordinarily sad song and Ursula vowed that if she ever had a child (difficult when you had decided to live as a nun) she would sing to it nothing but jolly jigs and ditties.

She felt alone. She would have liked a warm body for comfort, a dog would be better than being on her own on nights like this. A living, breathing presence.

She moved the blackout aside. No sign of bombers yet, just the long finger of a solitary searchlight poking into the blackness. A new moon hung in the sky. *Pale for weariness,* according to Shelley but *Queen and huntress, chaste and fair* for Ben Jonson. To Ursula it betrayed an indifference that made her suddenly shiver.

There was always a second before the siren started when she was aware of a sound as yet unheard. It was like an echo, or rather the opposite of an echo. An echo came afterward, but was there a word for what came before?

She heard the whine of a plane overhead and the *bang-bang-bang-bang-bang* of the first bombs dropping and she was about to replace the blackout and make a run for the cellar when she noticed a dog cowering in a doorway opposite—almost as if she'd wished it into existence. Even from where she was, she could sense its terror. She hesitated for a second and then thought, oh, damn, and raced down the stairs.

She passed the Nesbit sisters. "Ooh, bad luck, Miss Todd," Ruth giggled. "Crossing on the stairs, you know."

Ursula was going down, the sisters were coming up. "You're going the wrong way," she said, rather pointlessly.

"I forgot my knitting," Lavinia said. She was wearing an enamel brooch shaped like a black cat. A little rhinestone winked for an eye. "She's knitting leggings for Mrs. Appleyard's baby," Ruth said. "It's so cold in her apartment."

It was incredibly noisy on the street. She could hear incendiaries clattering down on a roof nearby, sounding like a giant coal scuttle being emptied. The sky was alight. A chandelier flare fell, as graceful as fireworks, illuminating everything below.

A stream of bombers was roaring overhead as she dashed across the street to the dog. It was a nondescript terrier, whimpering and shaking all over. Just as she grabbed hold of it she heard a terrific *swish* and knew she was for it, that they were both for it. A colossal growling noise was followed by the loudest bang she'd heard so far in the Blitz. This is it, she thought, this is how I die.

She took a blow to the forehead, a brick or something, but didn't lose consciousness. A blast of air, like a hurricane, knocked her off her feet. There was a horrendous pain in her ears and all she could hear was a high-pitched whistling, singing noise and she knew that her eardrums must have gone. Debris was showering down on her, cutting her and digging into her. The blast seemed to come in successive waves and she could feel a grumbling, grinding vibration in the ground beneath her.

From a distance an explosion seemed to be over almost immediately but when you were in the middle of it, it seemed to go on forever, to have a character that changed and developed as it went along so that you had no idea how it was going to end up, how *you* were going to end up. She was half sitting, half lying on the ground and tried to hang on to something but she couldn't let go of the dog (this thought uppermost in her mind for some reason) and she found herself being blown slowly along the ground.

The pressure began to decrease a little but the dirt and dust were still raining down and the blast had life in it yet. Then something else hit her on the head and everything went dark.

She was woken by the dog licking her face. It was very hard to understand what had happened but after a while she realized that the doorway where she had grabbed the dog didn't exist anymore. The door had been blown inwards, the pair of them with it, and now they were lying among debris in the passage of a house. The staircase of the house behind them, choked with broken bricks and splintered wood, now led nowhere as the upper floors had gone.

Still stunned, she struggled to a sitting position. Her head felt thick and stupid but nothing seemed to be broken and she couldn't find any bleeding, although she supposed she must be covered in cuts and bruises. The dog too, although very quiet, seemed to be uninjured. "Your name must be Lucky," she said to it but her voice hardly came out at all, there was so much choking dust in the air.

Cautiously, she got to her feet and walked down the passage to the street.

Her house had also gone, everywhere she looked there were great heaps of smoking rubble and skeletal walls. The pared fingernail of the moon was bright enough, even through the veil of dust, to cast light on the horror. If she hadn't run to save the dog she would be cinders in the Millers' cellar now. Was everyone dead? The Nesbits, Mrs. Appleyard and Emil? Mr. Bentley? All the Millers?

She stumbled into the street where two firemen were unreeling a hose. While they were attaching it to the hydrant one of them spotted her and shouted, "Are you all right, miss?" It was funny but he looked exactly like Fred Smith. And then the other fireman yelled, "Watch out, the wall's coming down!"

It was. Slowly, incredibly slowly, as if in a dream, the whole wall tilted on an invisible axis and without a single brick detaching itself it inclined toward them, as if taking a graceful bow, and fell in one piece, bringing the darkness down with it.

August 1926

Als er das Zimmer verlassen hatte wusst, was sie aus dieser Erscheinung machen solle . . .

Bees buzzed their summer afternoon lullaby and Ursula, in the shade of the apple trees, drowsily abandoned *Die Marquise von O.* Through half-open eyes she watched a small rabbit a few yards away nibbling contentedly on grass. He was either unaware of her or very bold. Maurice would have shot it by now. He was home after graduation, waiting to start his training in the law, and had spent the entire vacation being thoroughly and noisily bored. ("He could always get a summer job," Hugh said. "It's not unheard of for vigorous young men to work.")

Maurice was so bored in fact that he had agreed to teach Ursula to shoot and even agreed to use old bottles and cans as targets rather than the many wild creatures that he was forever taking potshots at—rabbits, foxes, badgers, pigeons, pheasants, even once a small roe deer, for which neither Pamela nor Ursula would ever forgive him. As long as they were inanimate, Ursula rather liked shooting things. She used Hugh's old wildfowler but Maurice had a splendid Purdey, his twenty-first-birthday present from his grandmother. Adelaide had been threatening to die for some years now but "never came good on her promises," Sylvie said. She lingered on in Hampstead, "like a giant spider," Izzie said, shuddering, over the veal cutlets *à la Russe,* although it may have been the cutlets themselves that caused this reaction. It was not one of the better dishes in Mrs. Glover's repertoire.

One of the few things, perhaps the only thing Sylvie and Izzie had in common, was their antipathy toward Hugh's mother. "Your mother too," Hugh pointed out to Izzie and Izzie said, "Oh, no, she found me by the side of the road. She often told me so. I was so naughty that even the gypsies didn't want me."

Hugh came to watch Maurice and Ursula shooting and said, "Why, little bear, you're a real Annie Oakley."

You know," Sylvie said, appearing suddenly and startling Ursula into full wakefulness, "long, lazy days like these will never come again in your life. You think they will, but they won't."

"Unless I become incredibly rich," Ursula said. "Then I could be idle all day long."

"Perhaps," Sylvie said, "but summer would still have to come to an end one day." She sank down on the grass next to Ursula and picked up the Kleist. "A suicidal romantic," she said dismissively.

"Are you really going to do Modern Languages? Your father says Latin might be more useful."

"How can it be useful? Nobody speaks it," Ursula said reasonably. This was an argument that had been rumbling genteelly all summer. She stretched her arms above her head. "I shall go and live in Paris for a year and speak nothing but French. That will be very *useful* there."

"Oh, Paris," Sylvie shrugged. "Paris is rather overrated."

"Berlin, then."

"Germany's a mess."

"Vienna."

"Stuffy."

"Brussels," Ursula said. "No one can object to Brussels."

It was true, Sylvie could think of nothing to say about Brussels and their grand tour of Europe came to an abrupt halt.

"After university anyway," Ursula said. "That's *years* away yet, you can stop worrying."

"University won't teach you how to be a wife and mother," Sylvie said.

"What if I don't want to be a wife and mother?"

Sylvie laughed. "Now you're just talking nonsense to provoke. There's tea on the lawn," she said, rousing herself reluctantly. "And cake. And, unfortunately, Izzie."

Ursula went for a walk along the lane before supper, Jock happily trotting ahead. (He was a wonderfully cheerful dog, it was hard to believe that Izzie could have chosen so well.) It was the kind of summer evening that made Ursula want to be alone. "Oh," Izzie said, "you're at an age when a girl is simply *consumed* by the sublime." Ursula wasn't sure what she meant ("No one is ever sure what she means," Sylvie said) but she thought she understood a little. There was a strangeness in the shimmering air, a sense of *imminence* that made Ursula's chest feel full, as if her heart was growing. It was a kind of high holiness—she could think of no other way of describing it. Perhaps it was the future, she thought, coming nearer all the time.

She was sixteen, on the brink of everything. She had even been kissed, on her birthday at that, by the rather alarming American friend of Maurice's. "Just one kiss," she told him before batting him away when he got too fresh with her. Unfortunately he stumbled over his huge feet and fell backward into a cotoneaster, which looked rather uncomfortable and certainly undignified. She told Millie, who hooted with laughter. Still, as Millie said, a kiss was a kiss.

Her walk took her to the station where she said hello to Fred Smith, who doffed his railwayman's cap as if she were already a grown-up.

The imminence remained imminent, receded even, as she watched his train *huff-huff-huff* off to London. She walked back and met Nancy, grubbing for things for her nature collection, and they walked companionably together before they were overtaken by Benjamin Cole on his bicycle. He stopped and dismounted and said, "Shall I escort you home, ladies?" rather in the way that Hugh might have done and Nancy giggled.

Ursula was glad that the heat of the afternoon had already made her cheeks pink because she could feel herself blushing. She grabbed some cow parsley from the hedgerow and fanned herself (ineffectually) with it. She had not, after all, been so wrong about the imminence.

Benjamin ("Oh, do call me Ben," he said. "Only my parents call me Benjamin these days") walked with them as far as the Shawcrosses' gate where he said, "Good-bye, then," and climbed back on his bicycle for the short ride home.

"Oh," Nancy whispered, disappointed on her behalf, "I thought maybe he would walk you home, just the two of you."

"Am I so obvious?" Ursula asked, her spirits drooping.

"You are rather. Never mind." Nancy patted her on the arm as if she were the elder by four years rather than Ursula. And then, "I'm late, I think, I don't want to miss dinner," she said and, clutching her foraged treasure, she skipped along the path toward her house, singing *tra-la-la.* Nancy was a girl who really did sing *tra-la-la.* Ursula wished she was that kind of girl. She turned to go, she supposed she was late for supper too, but then she heard the mad ringing of a bicycle bell announcing Benjamin (Ben!) zooming toward her. "I forgot to say," he said, "we're having a party next week—Saturday afternoon—Mother said to ask you. It's Dan's birthday, she wants some girls to dilute the boys, I think that was her phrase. She thought maybe you and Millie. Nancy's a bit young, isn't she?"

"Yes, she is," Ursula agreed quickly. "But I'd love to come. So would Millie, I'm sure. Thank you."

Imminence had returned to the world.

She watched him cycle away, whistling as he went. When she turned round she nearly bumped into a man who seemed to have appeared out of nowhere and was hovering, waiting for her. He tipped his cap and muttered, "Evening, miss." He was a rough-looking fellow and Ursula took a step back. "Tell me the way to the station, miss?" he said and she pointed down the lane and said, "It's that way."

"Care to show me the way, miss?" he said, moving closer to her again.

"No," she said, "no thank you." Then his hand suddenly shot out and he grabbed her forearm. She managed to tug her arm away and set off running, not daring to look behind until she reached her doorstep.

"All right, little bear?" Hugh asked as she flung herself into the porch. "You look all puffed out," he said.

"No, I'm fine, really," she said. Hugh would only worry if she told him about the man.

Veal cutlets *à la Russe,*" Mrs. Glover said as she put a large white china dish on the table. "I'm only telling you because last time I cooked it someone said they couldn't begin to imagine what it was."

"The Coles are having a party," Ursula said to Sylvie. "Millie and I are invited."

"Lovely," Sylvie said, distracted by the contents of the white porcelain dish, much of which would later be fed to a less discerning (or, as Mrs. Glover would have it, "less fussy") West Highland terrier.

The party was a disappointment. It was a rather daunting affair with endless games of charades (Millie in her element, needless to say) and quizzes to which Ursula knew most of the answers but was left unheard, beaten by the ferociously competitive speed of the Cole boys and their friends. Ursula felt invisible and the only intimacy that she shared with Benjamin (he no longer seemed like Ben) was when he asked her if she would like some fruit cup and then forgot to come back with any. There was no dancing but piles of food and Ursula comforted herself picking and choosing from an impressive selection of desserts. Mrs. Cole, patrolling the food, said to her, "Goodness, you're such a little scrap of a thing, where do you put all that food?"

Such a little scrap of a thing, Ursula thought as she tramped dejectedly home, that no one even seemed to notice her.

"Did you get cake?" Teddy asked eagerly when she came in the door.

"Masses," she said. They sat on the terrace and shared the large slice of birthday cake doled out on departure by Mrs. Cole, Jock receiving his fair share. When a large dog fox trotted onto the twilit lawn Ursula tossed a piece in its direction but it regarded the cake with the disdain of a carnivore.

THE LAND OF BEGIN AGAIN

August 1933

"*Er kommt! Er kommt!*" one of the girls shouted.

"He's coming? Finally?" Ursula said, glancing at Klara.

"Apparently. Thank goodness. Before we die of hunger and boredom," she said.

They were both equally bemused and amused by the younger girls' hero-worshipping antics. They had been waiting by the roadside for the best part of a hot afternoon, with nothing to eat or drink except for a pail of milk that two of the girls had fetched from a farm nearby. Some of the girls had heard a rumor that the Führer would be arriving today at his mountain retreat, and they had been waiting patiently for hours now. Several of the girls had taken a siesta on the grass verge, but none of them had any intention of giving up without a glimpse of the Führer.

There was some cheering further down the steep, crooked road that led up to Berchtesgaden and they all jumped to their feet. A big black car swept past them and some of the girls squealed with excitement but "he" wasn't in it. Then a second car, a magnificent open-topped black Mercedes, came into view, a swastika pennant fluttering on the bonnet. It drove slower than the previous car and did indeed contain the new Chancellor of the Reich.

The Führer gave an abbreviated version of his salute, a funny little flap of the hand backward so that he looked as if he were cupping his ear to hear them better as they shouted out to him. At the sight of him, Hilde, standing next to Ursula, said simply, "Oh," investing the single syllable with religious ecstasy. And then, just as quickly, it was all over. Hanne crossed her hands over her chest, looking like a rather constipated saint. "My life is fulfilled," she laughed.

"He looks better in his photographs," Klara murmured.

The girls were all in remarkably high spirits, had been all day, and under their *Gruppenführerin*'s orders (Adelheid, a blond Amazon, an admirably competent eighteen-year-old) they now quickly formed themselves into a squad and started cheerfully on the long march back to the youth hostel, singing as they went. ("They sing *all* the time," Ursula wrote to Millie. "It's all a little too *lustig* for my liking. I feel like I'm in the chorus of a particularly jolly folk opera.")

Their repertoire was varied—folk songs, quaint love songs and rousing, rather savage, patriotic anthems about flags dipped in blood, as well as the obligatory singsongs around the campfire. They especially liked *Schunkeln*—linking arms and swaying to songs. When Ursula was pushed into rendering a song she gave them "Auld Lang Syne," perfect for *Schunkeln.*

Hilde and Hanne were Klara's younger sisters, keen members of the BDM, the Bund Deutscher Mädel—the girls' equivalent of the Hitler-Jugend ("*Ha Jot,* we call them," Hilde said, and she and Hanne fell about giggling at the idea of handsome boys in uniform).

Ursula had heard of neither the Hitler-Jugend nor the BDM before arriving in the Brenner household but in the two weeks she had been living there she had heard little else from Hilde and Hanne. "It's a healthy hobby," their mother, Frau Brenner, said. "It promotes peace and understanding between young people. No more wars. And it keeps them away from boys." Klara, like Ursula a recent graduate—she had been an art student at the *Akademie*—was indifferent to her sisters' obsession but had offered to be a chaperone on their *Bergwanderung,* their summer camping trip, hiking from one *Jugendherberge* to the next in the Bavarian mountains. "You'll come, won't you?" Klara said to Ursula. "I'm sure we'll have fun and you'll see some of the countryside. And if you don't you'll be stuck in town with Mutti and Vati."

"I think it's like the Girl Guides," Ursula wrote to Pamela.

"Not quite," Pamela wrote back.

Ursula was not intending to spend long in Munich. Germany was no more than a detour in her life, part of her adventurous year in Europe. "It will be my own grand tour," she said to Millie, "although I'm afraid it's a little second-rate, a 'not quite so grand tour.' " The plan was to take in Bologna rather than Rome or Florence, Munich not Berlin and Nancy instead of Paris (Nancy Shawcross much amused by this choice)—all cities where her tutors from university knew of good homes in which she could lodge. To keep herself she was to do a little teaching, although Hugh had arranged for a modest but regular money order to be sent to her. Hugh was relieved that she would be spending her time "in the provinces," where "people are, on the whole, better behaved." ("He means duller," Ursula said to Millie.) Hugh had completely vetoed Paris, he had a particular aversion to the city, and was hardly more keen on Nancy which was still uncompromisingly *French*. ("Because it's in France," Ursula pointed out.) He had seen enough of the continent during the Great War, he said, he couldn't see what all the hullabaloo was about.

Ursula had, despite Sylvie's reservations, studied for a degree in Modern Languages—French and German and a little Italian (very little). Recently graduated and failing to think of anything else, she had applied and been given a place on a teacher-training course. She had deferred for a year, saying that she wanted an opportunity to see a little of the world before "settling down" to a lifetime at the blackboard. That was her rationale anyway, the one that she paraded for parental scrutiny, whereas her true hope was that something would happen in the course of her time abroad that would mean she need never take up the place. What that "something" was she had no idea ("Love perhaps," Millie said wistfully). Anything really that would mean she didn't end up as an embittered spinster in a girls' grammar school, spooling her way through the conjugation of foreign verbs, chalk dust falling from her clothes like dandruff. (She based this portrait on her own schoolmistresses.) It wasn't a profession that had garnered much enthusiasm in her immediate circle either.

"You want to be a *teacher?*" Sylvie said.

"Honestly, if her eyebrows had shot up any further they would have left the atmosphere," Ursula said to Millie.

"But do you really? Want to teach?" Millie said.

"Why does every single person I know ask me that question in that same tone of voice?" Ursula said, rather piqued. "Am I so clearly unsuited to the profession?"

"Yes."

Millie herself had done a course at a drama academy in London and was now playing in rep in Windsor, in second-rate crowd pleasers and melodramas. "Waiting to be discovered," she said, striking a theatrical pose. Everyone seems to be waiting for something, Ursula thought. "Best not to wait," Izzie said. "Best to *do.*" Easier for her to say.

Millie and Ursula were sitting in the wicker chairs on the lawn at Fox Corner, hoping that the foxes would come and play on the grass. A vixen and her litter had been visiting the garden. Sylvie had been putting out scraps and the vixen was half tame now and would sit quite boldly in the middle of the lawn, like a dog waiting for its dinner, while her cubs—already rangy, long-legged things by June—squabbled and somersaulted around her.

"What am I to do then?" Ursula said helplessly (hopelessly). Bridget appeared with a tray of tea and cake and placed it on a table between them. "Learn shorthand and typing and work in the civil service? That sounds pretty dismal too. I mean what else is there for a woman to *do* if she doesn't want to go from the parental to the marital home with nothing in between?"

"An educated woman," Millie amended.

"An educated woman," Ursula agreed.

Bridget muttered something incomprehensible and Ursula said, "Thank you, Bridget."

("*You* have seen Europe," she said, rather accusingly, to Sylvie. "When you were younger."

"I was not on my own, I was in the company of my father," Sylvie said. But surprisingly this argument seemed to have some effect and it was, in the end, Sylvie who championed the trip against Hugh's objections.)

Before she departed for Germany Izzie took her shopping for silk underwear and scarves, pretty lace-edged handkerchiefs, "a really good pair of shoes," two hats and a new handbag. "Don't tell your mother," she said.

In Munich she was to lodge with the Brenner family—mother, father and three daughters (Klara, Hildegard and Hannelore) and a son, Helmut, who was away at school, in an apartment on the Elisabethstrasse. Hugh had already had an extensive correspondence with Herr Brenner to assess his suitability as a host. "I'll be a terrible disappointment," she said to Millie, "Herr Brenner will be expecting the Second Coming, given the preparations that have been made." Herr Brenner was himself a teacher at the Deutsche Akademie and had arranged for Ursula to give some classes to beginners in English and had also procured several introductions to people looking for private tuition. This he told her when he met her off the train. She felt rather downcast, she hadn't set her mind to the idea of work just yet and she was exhausted after a long and decidedly trying rail journey. The *Schnellzug* from the Gare de l'Est in Paris had been anything but *schnell* and she had shared the compartment with, among others, a man who alternated smoking a cigar with eating his way through an entire salami, both actions which made her feel rather discomfited. ("And all I saw of Paris was a station platform," she wrote to Millie.)

The salami-eating man had followed her out into the corridor when she went in search of the ladies'. She thought he was going to the buffet car but then as she reached the lavatory compartment he attempted, to her alarm, to push in after her. He said something to her that she didn't understand, although its meaning seemed lewd (the cigar and the salami seemed strange preludes). "*Lass mich in Ruhe,*" leave me in peace, she said stoutly but he continued to push her and she continued to push back. She suspected their struggle, polite as opposed to violent, might have looked quite comical to an observer. Ursula wished there was someone in the corridor that she could appeal to. She couldn't imagine what the man would do to her if he succeeded in confining her in the tiny lavatory compartment. (Afterward she wondered why she hadn't simply screamed. What a dunce she was.)

She was "saved" by a pair of officers, smart in their black uniforms and silver insignia, who materialized out of nowhere and took a firm hold of the man. They gave him a stern talking-to, although she couldn't recognize half the vocabulary, and then very gallantly they found her a different carriage, one where there were only women, which she hadn't known about. When the officers had gone her fellow female travelers couldn't stop talking about how handsome the SS officers were. ("*Schutzstaffel,*" one of the women murmured admiringly. "Not like those louts in brown.")

The train was late pulling into the station in Munich. There had been some kind of incident, Herr Brenner said, a man had fallen from the train.

"How awful," Ursula said.

* * *

Despite it being summer, it was chilly and raining heavily. The gloomy atmosphere didn't lift with her arrival at the Brenners' enormous apartment, where no lamps were lit against the evening and where the rain was beating against the lace-curtained windows as if it was determined to break in.

Between them, Ursula and Herr Brenner had lugged her heavy trunk up the stairs, a somewhat farcical procedure. Surely there was someone who could help them, Ursula thought irritably. Hugh would have employed "a man"—or two—and not expected her to manage it herself. She thought of the SS officers on the train, how efficiently and courteously they would have dealt with the trunk.

The female Brenners of the house proved to be absent. "Oh, not back yet," Herr Brenner said, unconcerned. "They went shopping, I think." The apartment was full of heavy furniture and shabby rugs and leafy plants that gave the impression of a jungle. She shivered, it seemed inhospitably cold for the time of year.

They maneuvered the trunk into the room that was to be hers. "This used to be my mother's room," Herr Brenner said. "This is her furniture. Sadly, she died last year." The way that he gazed at the bed—a large, Gothic affair that looked as if it were built specifically to induce nightmares in its occupant—clearly hinted that Frau Brenner senior's demise had taken place within its downy coverlets. The bed seemed to dominate the room and Ursula felt suddenly nervous. Her experience on the train with the salami-eating man was still embarrassingly vivid and now here she was again alone in a foreign country with a complete stranger. Bridget's lurid tales of the white slave trade came to mind.

To her relief, they both heard the front door open and a great commotion taking place in the hallway. "Ah," Herr Brenner said, beaming with delight, "they're back!"

The girls spilled and tumbled into the apartment, all wet from the rain, laughing and carrying parcels. "Look who's arrived," Herr Brenner said, inducing much excitement in the youngest two girls. (Hilde and Hanne would prove to be the most excitable girls Ursula had ever encountered.)

"You're here!" Klara said, clasping both her hands in her own cold, damp ones, "*Herzlich willkommen in Deutschland.*"

While the younger girls chattered nineteen to the dozen Klara moved quickly round the apartment turning on lamps and the place was suddenly transformed—the rugs were worn but they were figured richly, the old furniture gleamed with polish, the cold jungle of plants turned into a pretty, ferny bower. Herr Brenner lit a big porcelain *Kachelofen* in the living room ("like having a big warm animal in the room," she wrote to Pamela) and assured her that tomorrow the weather would be back to normal, warm and sunny.

A table was quickly laid with an embroidered cloth and supper produced—a platter of cheese, salami, sliced sausage, salad and a dark bread that smelled of Mrs. Glover's seedcake as well as a delicious kind of fruit soup that confirmed that she was in a foreign country. ("Cold fruit soup!" she wrote to Pamela. "What would Mrs. Glover have to say about that!")

Even Herr Brenner's dead mother's room was more accommodating now. The bed was soft and inviting, the sheets edged with handworked crochet and the bedside lamp had a pretty pink glass shade that cast a warm glow. Someone—Klara, Ursula suspected—had placed a posy of marguerites in a little vase on the dressing table. Ursula was dropping with fatigue by the time she clambered into the bed (it was so high it required a small footstool) and fell gratefully into a deep, dreamless sleep, untroubled by the ghost of the previous occupant.

But of course you're going to have some holiday time," Frau Brenner said next morning at breakfast (a meal that was oddly similar to supper the night before). Klara was "at a bit of a loose end." She had finished her art course and didn't know what to do next. She was chafing at the bit to leave home and "be an artist" but "not much money in Germany to spare for art," she grumbled. Klara kept some of her work in her room, big, harsh abstract canvases that seemed at odds with her kind and temperate nature. Ursula couldn't imagine she would make a living from them. "Perhaps I shall have to teach," she said miserably.

"Fate worse than death," Ursula agreed.

Klara occasionally did some framing for a photography studio in Schellingstrasse. The daughter of one of Frau Brenner's acquaintances worked there and had put in a word for her. Klara and the daughter—Eva—had been in kindergarten together. "But framing, it's hardly art, is it?" Klara said. The photographer—Hoffmann—was the "personal photographer" of the new Chancellor, "so I am intimately acquainted with his features," she said.

The Brenners didn't have much money either (Ursula supposed that was why they were renting her a room) and everyone Klara knew was poor, but then in 1933 everyone everywhere was poor.

Despite the lack of funds Klara was determined that they should make the most of the remainder of the summer. They went to the Carlton Teehaus or Café Heck by the Hofgarten and ate *Pfannkuchen* and drank *Schokolade* until they felt sick. They walked for hours in the Englischer Garten and then ate ice cream or drank beer, their faces pink with the sun. They also spent time boating or swimming with friends of Helmut, Klara's brother—a revolving carousel of Walters, Werners, Kurts, Heinzes and Gerhards. Helmut himself was in Potsdam, a cadet, a *Jungmann* at a new kind of military school that the Führer had founded. "He's very keen on the Party," Klara said, in English. Her English was quite good and she was enjoying practicing with Ursula.

"On parties," Ursula corrected her. "We would say 'he's very keen on parties.'" Klara laughed and shook her head, "No, no, *the* Party, the Nazis. Don't you know that since last month it's the only one that we're allowed?"

"When Hitler came to power," Pamela wrote didactically to her, "he passed the Enabling Act, in Germany it's called *Gesetz zur Behebung der Not von Volk und Reich* which translates as something like the 'Law to Remedy the Distress of People and Reich.' That's a fancy title for the overthrow of democracy."

Ursula wrote blithely back, "But democracy will right itself as it always does. This too shall pass."

"Not without help," Pamela replied.

Pamela was a grouch about Germany and was easy to ignore when you could spend long hot afternoons sunbathing with Walters, Werners, Kurts, Heinzes and Gerhards, lolling lazily by the municipal swimming pool or the river. Ursula was taken aback at how these boys were near enough naked with their short shorts and disconcertingly small swimming trunks. Germans generally, she discovered, were not averse to stripping off in front of others.

Klara also knew a different, more cerebral set—her friends from art school. They tended to prefer the dark, the smoky interiors of cafés or their own scruffy apartments. They drank and smoked a great deal and spoke a lot about art and politics. ("So by and large," she wrote to Millie, "between these two groups of people I am getting an all-round education!") Klara's art-school friends were a ragged, dissident bunch who all seemed to dislike Munich, which was a seat of "petit-bourgeois provincialism" apparently, and talked all the time about moving to Berlin. They talked a lot about doing things, she noticed, but actually did very little.

Klara was in the grip of a different kind of inertia. Her life had "stalled," she was secretly in love with one of her professors from art school, a sculptor, but he was away in the Black Forest on a family holiday. (Reluctantly, she admitted that the "family" was actually his wife and two children.) She was waiting for her life to resolve itself, she said. More prevarication, Ursula thought. Although she was hardly one to talk.

Ursula was still a virgin, of course, "intact" as Sylvie would have it. Not for any moral reason, simply because she hadn't yet met anyone that she liked enough. "You don't have to *like* them," Klara laughed.

"Yes, but I want to." She seemed instead to be a magnet for unsavory types—the man on the train, the man in the lane—and worried that they could read something in her that she couldn't read herself. She felt rather stiff and English compared to Klara and her artist friends or the absent Helmut's confrères (who were actually terrifically well behaved).

Hanne and Hilde had persuaded Klara and Ursula to accompany them to an event in the local sports stadium. Ursula was under the misapprehension that it was a concert but it turned out to be a rally of Hitler-Jugend. Despite Frau Brenner's optimism, the BDM had done nothing to counter Hilde and Hanne's interest in boys.

To Ursula, these ranks of hearty, healthy boys all looked the same but Hilde and Hanne spent a lot of time animatedly pointing out Helmut's friends, those same Walters, Werners, Kurts, Heinzes and Gerhards who loafed by the swimming pool in next to nothing. Now, squeezed into their immaculate uniforms (more short shorts), they looked like very fierce and upstanding Boy Scouts.

There was a lot of marching and singing to a brass band and several speakers who attempted the same declamatory style as the Führer (and failed) and then everyone leapt to their feet and sang "*Deutschland über alles.*" As Ursula didn't know the words she quietly sang "Glorious Things of Thee Are Spoken" to Haydn's lovely tune, a hymn they had often sung in school assembly. When the singing finished everyone shouted "*Sieg Heil!*" and saluted and Ursula was almost surprised to find herself joining in. Klara was convulsed with laughter at the sight but nonetheless Ursula noticed she had her arm raised too. "I should think so too," she said, nonchalantly. "I don't want to be set upon on the way home."

No, thank you, Ursula didn't want to stay home with Vati and Mutti Brenner in hot, dusty Munich so Klara rummaged through her wardrobe and found a navy skirt and white blouse that suited requirements and the group leader, Adelheid, provided a spare khaki battle-dress jacket. A three-cornered scarf drawn through a braided leather Turk's-head knot completed the outfit. Ursula thought she looked rather dashing. She found herself regretting never having been a Girl Guide, although she supposed it was about more than just the uniform.

The upper age limit for the BDM was eighteen so neither Ursula nor Klara was qualified to join, they were "old ladies," *alte Damen,* according to Hanne. Ursula didn't think that the troop really needed to be escorted by them as Adelheid was as efficient as a sheepdog with her girls. With her statuesque figure and Nordic blond plaits she could have passed for a youthful Freyja visiting from Fólkvangr. She was perfect propaganda. At eighteen she would soon be too old for the BDM, what would she do then?

"Why, I will join the National Socialist Women's League, of course," she said. She already wore a small silver swastika pinned to her shapely bosom, the runic symbol of belonging.

They took a train, their rucksacks stowed on the luggage racks, and by evening they had arrived in a small Alpine village, near to the Austrian border. From the station they marched in formation (singing, naturally) to their *Jugendherberge.* People stopped to watch them and some clapped appreciatively.

The dormitory they were allotted was full of two-tier bunks, most of which were already occupied by other girls and they had to squeeze themselves in, sardine fashion. Klara and Ursula elected to share a mattress on the floor.

They were given supper in the dining room, seated at long trestle tables, served with what turned out to be the standard fare of soup and *Knäckebrot* with cheese. In the morning they breakfasted on dark bread, cheese and jam and tea or coffee. The clean mountain air made them ravenous and they wolfed down everything in sight.

The village and its surroundings were idyllic, there was even a small castle that they were allowed to visit. It was cold and dank, full of suits of armor and flags and heraldic shields. It seemed like a very uncomfortable place to live.

They took long walks around the lake or in the forest and then they hitched lifts back to the youth hostel on farm lorries and hay carts. One day they hiked all the way along the river to a magnificent waterfall. Klara had brought her sketch pad with her and her quick, lively little charcoal drawings were much more appealing than her paintings. "Ach," she said, "they're *gemütlich*. Cozy little sketches. My friends would laugh." The village itself was a sleepy little place where the houses had windows full of geraniums. There was an inn on the river where they drank beer and ate veal and noodles until they thought they would burst. Ursula never mentioned the beer to Sylvie in her letters, she wouldn't have understood how commonplace it was here. And even if she had, she wouldn't have approved.

They were to move on the next day, they would be living "under canvas" for a few days, a big encampment of girls, and Ursula felt sorry to be leaving the village.

A fair was taking place on their last night there, a combination of an agricultural show and a harvest festival, a lot of it incomprehensible to Ursula. ("To me too," Klara said. "I'm a city girl, remember.")

The women all wore local costume and variously garlanded farm animals were paraded around a field and then awarded prizes. Flags, again with swastikas, decorated the field. There was plenty of beer and a brass band played. A big wooden platform had been set up in the middle of the field and, accompanied by an accordion, some boys in *Lederhosen* gave a demonstration of *Schuhplattler,* clapping and stamping and slapping their thighs and heels in time to the music.

Klara scoffed at them but Ursula considered it rather clever. Ursula thought that she would quite like to live in an Alpine village ("Like Heidi," she wrote to Pamela. She wrote less to Pamela as her sister was so aggravated by the new Germany. Pamela, even at a distance, was the voice of her conscience, but then it was very easy to have a conscience from a distance).

The accordionist took his place in a band and people began to dance. Ursula was led onto the platform by a succession of terrifically shy farm boys who had an odd clodhopping way of moving around the dance floor which she recognized as the rather awkward 3/4 time of the *Schuhplattler.* Between the beer and the dancing she began to feel quite light-headed so that she was confused when Klara appeared, dragging by the hand a very handsome man who was clearly not local, saying, "Look who I found!"

"Who?" Ursula asked.

"None other than our cousin's half-cousin's cousin once removed," Klara said gaily. "Or something to that effect. May I present Jürgen Fuchs."

"Just a half-cousin," he said, smiling.

"Delighted to meet you, I'm sure," she said. He clicked his heels and kissed her hand, she was reminded of Prince Charming in *Cinderella.* "It's the Prussian in me," he said and laughed, as did the Brenners. "We have no Prussian blood at all," Klara said.

He had a lovely smile, amused and thoughtful at the same time, and extraordinarily blue eyes. He was undoubtedly handsome, rather like Benjamin Cole, except Benjamin was his dark polar opposite, the negative to Jürgen Fuchs's positive.

A Todd and a Fuchs—a pair of foxes. Had fate intervened in her life? Dr. Kellet might have appreciated the coincidence.

He is so handsome," she wrote to Millie after that encounter. All those awful words used in trashy romances come to mind—*heart-stopping, breathtaking.* She had read enough of Bridget's novels on idle wet afternoons to know.

"Love at first sight," she wrote giddily to Millie. But of course such feelings weren't "true" love (that was what she would feel for a child one day), merely the false grandeur of madness. *"Folie à deux,"* Millie wrote back. "How delicious."

"Good for you," Pamela wrote.

"Marriage is based on a more enduring kind of love," Sylvie cautioned.

"I am thinking of you, little bear," Hugh wrote, "so far away from here."

When darkness fell there was a torchlit procession through the village and then fireworks from the battlements of the small castle. It was rather thrilling.

"Wunderschön, nicht wahr?" Adelheid said, her face radiant in the light of the torches.

Yes, Ursula agreed, it's lovely.

August 1939

Der Zauberberg. The magic mountain.

"Aaw. Sie ist so niedlich." Click, click, click. Eva loved her Rolleiflex.

Eva loved Frieda. She is so *cute,* she said. They were on the enormous terrace of the Berghof, bright with Alpine sun, waiting for lunch to be brought out. It was much nicer to eat out here, *al fresco,* rather than in the big, gloomy dining room, its massive window full of nothing but mountains. Dictators loved everything to be on a grand scale, even their scenery. *Bitte lächeln!* Big smile. Frieda obliged. She was an obliging child.

Eva had persuaded Frieda out of her serviceable English hand-smocked dress (Bourne and Hollingsworth, purchased by Sylvie and sent for Frieda's birthday) and had arrayed her instead in Bavarian costume—dirndl, apron, knee-length white socks. To Ursula's English eyes (more English every day, she felt) the outfit still looked as though it belonged in a dressing-up box, or perhaps a school play. Once, at her own school (how long ago and far away that seemed now), they had put on a performance of *The Pied Piper of Hamelin* and Ursula had played a village girl, clad in much the same getup that Frieda was now attired in.

Millie had been King Rat, a bravura performance, and Sylvie said, "Those Shawcross girls thrive on attention, don't they?" There was something of Millie in Eva—a restless, empty gaiety that needed continual feeding. But then Eva was an actress too, playing the greatest part of her life. In fact her life *was* her part, there was no difference.

Frieda, lovely little Frieda, just five years old, with her blue eyes and stubby blond plaits. Frieda's complexion, so pale and wan when she had first arrived, now pink and gold from all the Alpine sunshine. When the Führer saw Frieda, Ursula caught the zealot gleam in his own blue eyes, as cold as the Königsee down below, and knew he was seeing the future of the *Tausendjähriges Reich* rolling out in front of him, *Mädchen* after *Mädchen.* ("She doesn't take after you, does she?" Eva said, without malice, she had no malice.)

When she was a child—a period in her life that Ursula seemed to find herself returning to almost compulsively these days—she had read fairy tales of wronged princesses who saved themselves from lustful fathers and jealous stepmothers by smearing their fair faces with walnut juice and rubbing ashes in their hair to disguise themselves—as the gypsy, the outsider, the shunned. Ursula wondered how one obtained walnut juice, it didn't seem the kind of thing you could just walk into a shop and buy. And it was no longer safe to be the nut-brown outsider, much better if one wanted to survive to be here, on Obersalzberg—*Der Zauberberg*—in the kingdom of make-believe, "the Berg," as they called it with the intimacy of the elect.

What on earth was she doing here? Ursula wondered, and when could she leave? Frieda was well enough now, her convalescence drawing to a close. Ursula determined to say something to Eva today. After all, they weren't prisoners, they could leave any time they chose.

Eva lit a cigarette. The Führer was away and the mouse was being naughty. He didn't like her to smoke or drink, or wear makeup. Ursula rather admired Eva's small acts of defiance. The Führer had come and gone twice since Ursula first arrived at the Berghof with Frieda two weeks ago, his arrivals and departures moments of heightened drama for Eva, for everyone. The Reich, Ursula had concluded a long time ago, was all pantomime and spectacle, *"A tale told by an idiot, full of sound and fury,"* she wrote to Pamela. "But unfortunately *not* signifying nothing."

Frieda, on a prompt from Eva, did a twirl and laughed. She was the molten core at the center of Ursula's heart, she was the better part of everything she did or thought. Ursula would be willing to walk on knives for the rest of her life if it would protect Frieda. Burn in the flames of hell to save her. Drown in the deepest of waters if it would buoy her up. (She had explored many extreme scenarios. Best to be prepared.) She had had no idea (Sylvie gave little indication) that maternal love could be so gut-achingly, *painfully* physical.

"Oh, yes," Pamela said, as if it were the most casual thing in the world, "it turns you into a regular she-wolf." Ursula didn't think of herself as a she-wolf, she was, after all, a bear.

There were real she-wolves prowling everywhere on the Berg—Magda, Emmy, Margarete, Gerda—the brood-wives of the senior party officials, all jostling for a little power of their own, producing endless babies from their fecund loins, for the Reich, for the Führer. These she-wolves were dangerous, predatory animals and they hated Eva, the "silly cow"—*die blöde Kuh*—who somehow or other had managed to trump them all.

They, surely, would have given anything to be the mate of the glorious leader rather than insignificant Eva. Wasn't a man of his stature worthy of a Brünnhilde—or at the very least a Magda or a Leni? Or perhaps the Valkyrie herself, "the Mitford woman," *das Fräulein Mitford,* as Eva referred to her. The Führer admired England, especially aristocratic, imperial England, although Ursula doubted that his admiration would stop him from trying to destroy it if the time came.

Eva disliked all the Valkyries who might be a rival for the Führer's attentions, her strongest emotions conceived in fear. Her greatest antipathy was reserved for Bormann, the *éminence grise* of the Berg. It was he who held the purse strings, he who shopped for Eva's gifts from the Führer and who doled out the money for all those fur coats and Ferragamo shoes, reminding her in many subtle ways that she was merely a courtesan. Ursula wondered where the fur coats came from, most of the furriers she had seen in Berlin were Jewish.

How it must stick in the collective craw of the she-wolves that the Führer's consort was a shopgirl. When she first met him, Eva told Ursula, when she was working in Hoffmann's *Photohaus,* she had addressed him as Herr Wolf. "Adolf means noble wolf in German," she said. How he must like that, Ursula thought. She had never heard anyone call him Adolf. (Did Eva call him *mein Führer* even in bed? It seemed perfectly possible.) "And do you know that his favorite song," Eva laughed, "is 'Who's Afraid of the Big Bad Wolf?' "

"From the Disney film *Three Little Pigs*?" Ursula said, incredulous.

"Yes!"

Oh, thought Ursula, I cannot wait to tell *that* to Pamela.

And now one with *Mutti,*" Eva said. "Hold her in your arms. *Sehr schön.* Smile!" Ursula had watched Eva gleefully stalking the Führer with her camera, hunting down a photograph of him where he hadn't turned away from the lens or pulled the brim of his hat down comically low, like a spy in poor disguise. He disliked having his photograph taken by her, preferring flattering studio lighting or a more heroic pose than the snaps Eva liked of him. Eva, on the other hand, loved being photographed. She didn't just want to be in photographs, she wanted to be in a film. "*Ein* movie." She was going to go to Hollywood ("one day") and play herself, "the story of my life," she said. (The camera made everything real somehow for Eva.) The Führer had promised, apparently. Of course, the Führer promised a lot of things. It was what had got him where he was today.

Eva refocused the Rolleiflex. Ursula was glad she hadn't brought her old Kodak, it would hardly have stood up to comparison. "I'll have copies made for you," Eva said. "You can send them to England, to your parents. It looks very pretty with the mountains in the background. Now give me a big smile. *Jetzt lach doch mal richtig!*"

The mountain panorama was the backdrop to every photo taken

here, the backdrop to everything. At first Ursula had thought it beautiful, now she was beginning to find its magnificence oppressive. The great icy crags and the rushing waterfalls, the endless pine trees—nature and myth fused to form the Germanic sublimated soul. German Romanticism, it seemed to Ursula, was writ large and mystical, the English Lakes seemed tame by comparison. And the English soul, if it resided anywhere, was surely in some unheroic back garden—a patch of lawn, a bed of roses, a row of runner beans.

She should go home. Not to Berlin, to Savignyplatz, but to England. To Fox Corner.

Eva perched Frieda on the parapet and Ursula promptly removed her. "She has no head for heights," she said. Eva was forever lolling precariously on this same parapet, or parading dogs or small children along it. The drop below was dizzying, all the way down past Berchtesgaden to the Königsee. Ursula felt rather sorry for little Berchtesgaden with its innocent window boxes of cheerful geraniums, its meadows sloping down to the lake. It seemed a long time since she was here in '33 with Klara. Klara's professor had divorced his wife and Klara was now married to him and they had two children.

"The *Nibelungen* live up there," Eva told Frieda, pointing at the peaks all around them, "and demons and witches and evil dogs."

"Evil dogs?" Frieda echoed uncertainly. She had already been scared by the irksome Negus and Stasi, Eva's annoying Scotties, without needing to hear about dwarves and demons.

And *I* have heard, Ursula thought, that it was Charlemagne who hid out in the Untersberg, sleeping in a cave, waiting to be woken for the final battle between good and evil. She wondered when that would be. Soon perhaps.

And one more," Eva said. "Big smile!" The Rolleiflex glinted relentlessly in the sun. Eva owned a cine camera too, an expensive gift from her own Mr. Wolf, and Ursula supposed she should be glad that they weren't being recorded for posterity in moving color. Ursula imagined in a future time someone leafing through Eva's (many) albums and wondering who Ursula was, mistaking her perhaps for Eva's sister Gretl or her friend Herta, footnotes to history.

One day, of course, all this would be consigned to that same history, even the mountains—sand, after all, was the future of rocks. Most people muddled through events and only in retrospect realized their significance. The Führer was different, he was consciously *making* history for the future. Only a true narcissist could do that. And Speer was designing buildings for Berlin so that they would look good when they were in ruins a thousand years from now, his gift to the Führer. (To think on such a scale! Ursula lived hour by hour, another consequence of motherhood, the future as much a mystery as the past.)

Speer was the only one who was nice to Eva and therefore Ursula afforded him a latitude in her opinion that perhaps he didn't deserve. He was also the only one of these would-be Teutonic knights who had good looks, who wasn't gimpy or toad-squat or a corpulent pig, or—worse somehow—resembled a low-level bureaucrat. ("And they are all in uniform!" she wrote to Pammy. "But it's all pretend. It's like living in the pages of *The Prisoner of Zenda.* They're awfully good at hogwash." How she wished Pammy was here by her side, how she would have enjoyed dissecting the characters of the Führer and his henchmen. She would conclude that they were all charlatans, spouting cant.)

In private, Jürgen claimed to find them all "tremendously" flawed and yet in public he behaved like any good servant of the Reich. *Lippenbekenntnis,* he said. Lip service. (Needs must, Sylvie would have said.) This was how you got on in the world, he said. Ursula supposed in this respect he was rather like Maurice, who said you had to work with fools and donkeys to advance your career. Maurice was also a lawyer, of course. He was quite senior in the Home Office these days. If they went to war would this be a problem? Would the armor of German citizenship—donned so reluctantly—be enough to protect her? (If they went to war! Could she really countenance being on this side of the Channel?)

Jürgen was a lawyer. If he wanted to practice law he had to join the Party, he had no choice. *Lippenbekenntnis.* He worked for the Ministry of Justice in Berlin. At the time he proposed to her ("a bit of a whirlwind courtship," she wrote to Sylvie) he had barely ceased being a communist.

Now Jürgen had abandoned his Leftist politics and was staunch in his defense of what had been achieved—the country was working again—full employment, food, health, self-respect. New jobs, new roads, new factories, new hope—how else could they achieve this, he said? But it came with an ecstatic faux-religion and a wrathful false messiah. "Everything comes with a price," Jürgen said. Perhaps not as high as this one. (How *had* they done it? Ursula often wondered. Fear and stagecraft mostly. But where *had* all the money and jobs come from? Perhaps just from manufacturing flags and uniforms, enough of those around to rescue most economies. "The economy is recovering anyway," Pamela wrote, "it's a happy coincidence for the Nazis that they can claim this recovery.") Yes, he said, there was violence to begin with, but it was a spasm, a wave, the Sturmabteilung letting off steam. Everything, everybody, was more rational now.

In April they had attended the parade for the Führer's fiftieth birthday in Berlin. Jürgen had been allotted seats, in the guests' grandstand. "An honor, I suppose," he said. What had he done, she wondered, to deserve the "honor"? (Did he seem happy about it? It was hard to tell sometimes.) He hadn't been able to get them tickets for the Olympics in '36 yet here they were now, rubbing shoulders with the VIPs of the Reich. He was always busy these days. "Lawyers never sleep," he said. (Yet as far as Ursula could see they were prepared to sleep throughout the Thousand Years.)

The parade had gone on forever, the greatest expression yet of Goebbels's showmanship. A great deal of martial music and then the overture provided by the Luftwaffe—an impressive, noisy fly-past along the East–West Axis and over the Brandenburg Gate by squadrons of aircraft in formation, wave after wave. More sound and fury. "Heinkels and Messerschmitts," Jürgen said. How did he know? All boys know their planes, he said.

There followed the march-past of the regiments, a seemingly inexhaustible supply of soldiers goose-stepping along the road. They reminded Ursula of high-kicking Tiller girls. *"Stechschritt,"* Ursula said, "who on earth invented that?"

"The Prussians," Jürgen laughed, "of course."

She took out a bar of chocolate and broke off a piece and offered it to Jürgen. He frowned and shook his head as though she had showed a lack of respect to the assembled military might. She ate another piece. Small acts of defiance.

He leaned in close so she could hear him—the crowd were making an abominable racket—"You really have to admire their precision, if nothing else," he said. She did, she did admire it. It *was* extraordinary. Robotic in its perfection as if each member of each regiment was identical to the next, as if they had been produced on a factory line. It wasn't quite *human,* but then it wasn't the job of armies to look human, was it? ("It was all so very *masculine,*" she reported to Pamela.) Would the British army be capable of achieving such mechanical drilling on this scale? The Soviets perhaps, but the British were less *committed* somehow.

Frieda, on her knee, was already asleep and it had hardly begun yet. All the while Hitler took the salute, his arm stiff in front of him the whole time (she could catch a glimpse of him from where they were sitting, just the arm, like a poker). Power obviously provided a peculiar kind of stamina. If it was my fiftieth birthday, Ursula thought, I would like to spend it on the banks of the Thames, Bray or Henley or thereabouts, with a picnic, a very English picnic—a Thermos of tea, sausage rolls, egg-and-cress sandwiches, cake and scones. Her family was all there in this picture, but was Jürgen part of the idyll? He would fit in well enough, lounging on the grass in boating flannels, talking cricket with Hugh. They had met and got on well. They had gone to England, to Fox Corner, in '35 for a visit. "He seems like a nice chap," Hugh said, although when he learned that she had taken German citizenship he wasn't so keen. It had been an awful mistake, she knew that now. "Hindsight's a wonderful thing," Klara said. "If we all had it there would be no history to write about."

She should have stayed in England. She should have stayed at Fox Corner, with the meadow and the copse and the stream that ran through the bluebell wood.

The machinery of war started to roll past. "Here come the tanks," Jürgen said in English, as the first of the *Panzer* appeared, carried on the back of lorries. His English was good, he had spent a year at Oxford (hence his knowledge of cricket). Then came the *Panzer* under their own steam, motorbikes with sidecars, armored cars, the cavalry trotting smartly along (a particular crowd pleaser—Ursula woke Frieda up for the horses), and then the artillery, from light field guns to massive anti-aircraft guns and huge cannons.

"K-3s," Jürgen said appreciatively, as if that would mean something to her.

The parade showed a love of order and geometry that was incomprehensible to Ursula. In this, it was no different from all the other parades and rallies—all that theater—but this one seemed so bellicose. So much weaponry was staggering—the country was armed to the teeth! Ursula had had no idea. No wonder there were jobs for everyone. "If you want to rescue the economy you need a war, Maurice says," Pamela wrote. And what did you need weaponry for if not war?

"Refitting the military has helped to rescue our psyche," Jürgen said, "given us back our pride in our country. When in 1918 the generals surrendered..." Ursula stopped listening, it was an argument she had heard too many times. "They started the last war," she wrote crossly to Pamela. "And honestly, you would think they were the only ones who struggled afterward, and that no other people were poor or hungry or bereaved." Frieda woke up again and was cranky. She fed her chocolate. Ursula was cranky too. Between them they finished the bar.

The finale was actually rather moving. The massed colors of the regiments formed a long file several ranks deep in front of Hitler's podium—a formation so precise its edges might have been cut with a razor—and then they dipped their colors to the ground in honor of him. The crowd went wild.

"What did you think?" Jürgen asked as they shuffled out of the grandstand. He carried Frieda on his shoulders.

"Magnificent," Ursula said. "It was magnificent." She could feel the beginnings of a headache worming its way into her temple.

Frieda's illness had begun one morning several weeks ago with a raised temperature. "I feel sick," Frieda said. When Ursula felt her forehead it was clammy and she said, "You don't have to go to kindergarten, you can stay home with me today."

"A summer cold," Jürgen said, when he came home. She was always a chesty child ("Takes after my mother," Sylvie said gloomily) and they were accustomed to sniffling colds and sore throats but the cold got worse very quickly and Frieda turned feverish and listless. Her skin felt as though it were ready to catch fire. "Keep her cool," the doctor said and Ursula laid cold wet cloths on her forehead and read her stories but Frieda, try as she did, could summon no interest in them. Then she grew delirious and the doctor listened to her rattling lungs and said, "Bronchitis, you have to wait for it to pass."

Late that night Frieda grew suddenly, horribly worse and they wrapped the almost inanimate little body in a blanket and rushed in a taxi to the nearest hospital, a Catholic one. Pneumonia was diagnosed. "She's a very sick little girl," the doctor said, as if somehow they were to blame.

Ursula didn't leave Frieda's bedside for two days and nights, holding on to the little hand to keep her in this world. "If only I could have it for her," Jürgen whispered across the starchy white sheets that were also helping to pin Frieda to this world. Nuns floated around the ward like galleons in their enormous, complicated wimples. How long, Ursula wondered in an absent moment when all her attention wasn't focused on Frieda, did it take them to put these contraptions on in the morning? Ursula was sure she would never have managed without making a mess of it. The headdress alone seemed a good enough reason not to be a nun.

They willed Frieda to live and she did. *Triumph des Willens.* The crisis passed and she started the long road to recovery. Pale and weak, she was going to need to convalesce and one evening when Ursula returned home from the hospital she found an envelope, hand-delivered to their door.

"From Eva," she said to Jürgen, showing him the letter when he returned from work.

"Who's Eva?" he asked.

Smile!" *Click, click, click.* Anything to help keep Eva amused, she supposed. She didn't mind. Eva had been very kind to invite them so that Frieda could breathe good mountain air and eat the fresh vegetables and eggs and milk from the Gutshof, the model farm on the slopes beneath the Berghof.

"Is it a royal command?" Jürgen asked. "Can you say no? Do you want to say no? I hope not. And it will do your headaches good too." She'd noticed recently that the more he rose through the echelons in the ministry, the more one-sided their conversations had become. He made statements, raised questions, answered the questions and drew conclusions without ever needing to involve her in the exchange. (A lawyer's way perhaps.) He didn't even seem to be aware that he was doing it.

"The old goat has a woman after all then, does he? Who would have guessed? Did you know? No, you would have said. And to think you know her. It can only be good for us, can't it? To be so close to the throne. For my career, which is the same thing as us. *Liebling,*" he added, rather perfunctorily.

Ursula thought that being close to a throne was a rather dangerous place to be. "I don't know Eva," Ursula said. "I've never met her. It's Frau Brenner who knows her, knows her mother, Frau Braun. Klara used to work at Hoffmann's sometimes, with Eva. They were at kindergarten together."

"Impressive," Jürgen said, "from *Kaffeeklatsch* to the seat of power in three easy moves. Does Fräulein Eva Braun know her old kindergarten pal, Klara, is married to a Jew?" It was the way he said the word that surprised her. *Jude.* She'd never heard him say it that way before—sneering and dismissive. It drove a nail into her heart. "I have no idea," she said. "I am not part of the *Kaffeeklatsch,* as you call it."

The Führer took up so much room in Eva's life that when he wasn't here she was an empty vessel. Eva kept nightly telephone vigils when her lover was absent and was like a dog, one ear fretfully cocked every evening for the call that brought her master's voice to her.

And there was so little to *do* up here. After a while all the tramping along forest paths and swimming in the (freezing cold) Königsee became enervating rather than invigorating. There were only so many wildflowers you could pick, only so much sunbathing on the loungers on the terrace before you went slightly mad. There were battalions of nursemaids and nannies on the Berg, all eager to be with Frieda, and Ursula found herself with much of the same empty time on her hands as Eva. She had, stupidly, packed only one book, at least it was a long one, Mann's *Der Zauberberg.* She hadn't realized it was on the banned list. A Wehrmacht officer saw her reading it and said, "You're very bold, that's one of their forbidden books, you know." She supposed the way he said "their" implied he wasn't one of "them." What was the worst they could do? Take the book off her and put it in the kitchen stove?

He was nice, the Wehrmacht officer. His grandmother was Scottish, he said, and he had spent many happy holidays in "the Highlands."

Im Grunde hat es eine merkwürdige Bewandtnis mit diesem Sicheinleben an fremdem Orte, dieser—sei es auch—mühseligen Anpassung und Umgewöhnung, she read and translated laboriously and rather badly—"There is something strange about getting this settling in to a new place, the laborious adaptation and familiarization..." How true, she thought. Mann was hard work. She would have preferred a boxload of Bridget's gothic romances. She was sure they wouldn't be *verboten.*

The mountain air had done her headaches no good at all (nor had Thomas Mann). They were, if anything, worse. *Kopfschmerzen,* the very word made her head sore. "I can't find anything wrong with you," the doctor at the hospital told her. "It must be your nerves." He gave her a prescription for veronal.

Eva herself had no intellect to sustain her but then the Berg wasn't exactly the court of an intelligentsia. The only person whom you might have called a thinker was Speer. It wasn't that Eva led an unexamined life, far from it, Ursula suspected. You could sense the depression and neuroses hidden beneath all that *Lebenslust,* but anxiety wasn't what a man looked for in a mistress.

Ursula supposed that to be a successful mistress (although she had never been one herself, either successful or unsuccessful) a woman should be a comfort and a relief, a restful pillow for the weary head. *Gemütlichkeit.* Eva was amiable, she chatted about inconsequential things and made no attempt to be brainy or astute. Powerful men needed their women to be unchallenging, the home should not be an arena for intellectual debate. "My own husband told me this so it must be true!" she wrote to Pamela. He hadn't meant it in the context of himself—he was not a powerful man. "Not yet, anyway," he laughed.

The political world was of concern only in that it took the object of Eva's devotion away from her. She was shunted rudely out of the public eye, allowed no official status, allowed no status at all, as loyal as a dog but with less recognition than a dog. Blondi was higher in the hierarchy than Eva. Her greatest regret, Eva said, was not being allowed to meet the duchess when the Windsors visited the Berghof.

Ursula frowned on hearing this. "But she's a Nazi, you know," she said unthinkingly. ("I suppose I should be more careful in what I say!" she wrote to Pamela.) Eva had merely replied, "Yes, of course, she is," as if it were the most natural thing in the world for the consort of the once and never again King of England to be a Hitlerite.

The Führer must be seen to tread a noble, solitary path of chastity, he couldn't marry because he was wedded to Germany. He had sacrificed himself to his country's destiny—at least that was the gist of it, Ursula thought she might have discreetly nodded off at this point. (It was one of his endless after-dinner monologues.) Like our own Virgin Queen, she thought, but didn't say so, as she expected the Führer would not like to be compared to a woman, even an English aristocratic one with the heart and stomach of a king. At school, Ursula had had a history teacher who had been particularly fond of quoting Elizabeth I. *Do not tell secrets to those whose faith and silence you have not already tested.*

Eva would have been happier back in Munich, in the little bourgeois house that the Führer had bought for her, where she could lead a normal social life. Here, in her gilded cage, she had to amuse herself, flicking through magazines, discussing the latest hairstyles and love lives of film stars (as if Ursula knew anything on the subject), and parading one outfit after another like a quick-change artist. Ursula had been in her bedroom several times, a pretty, feminine boudoir quite different from the heavy-handed decor of the rest of the Berghof, spoiled only by the portrait of the Führer that was given pride of place on the wall. Her hero. The Führer had not hung a reciprocal portrait of his mistress in his rooms. Instead of Eva's face smiling at him from the wall he was challenged by the stern features of his own beloved hero, Frederick the Great. *Friedrich der Grosse.*

"I always mishear 'grocer' for 'great,'" she wrote to Pamela. Grocers were not, generally speaking, warmongers and conquerors. What had the Führer's apprenticeship for greatness been? Eva shrugged, she didn't know. "He's always been a politician. He was born a politician." No, Ursula thought, he was born a baby, like everyone else. And this is what he has chosen to become.

The Führer's bedroom, adjoining Eva's bathroom, was out of bounds. Ursula had seen him sleeping though, not in that sacrosanct bedroom but in the warm postprandial sunshine on the Berghof's terrace, the great warrior's mouth slackly open in *lèse-majesté.* He looked vulnerable but there were no assassins on the Berg. Plenty of guns, thought Ursula, easy enough to get hold of a Luger and shoot him through the heart or the head. But then what would happen to her? Worse, what would happen to Frieda?

Eva sat next to him, watching fondly as one might a child. In sleep he belonged to no one but her.

She was, fundamentally, nothing more nor less than a nice young woman. You couldn't necessarily judge a woman by the man she slept with. (Or could you?)

Eva had a wonderful athletic figure, one that Ursula felt quite envious of. She was a healthy, physical girl—a swimmer, a skier, a skater, a dancer, a gymnast—who loved the outdoors, who loved *movement.* And yet she had attached herself like a limpet to an indolent middle-aged man, a creature of the night, literally, who didn't rise from his bed before midday (and yet who could still take an afternoon nap), who didn't smoke or drink or dance or overindulge—spartan in his habits although not his vigor. A man who had never been seen stripped off further than his *Lederhosen* (comically unattractive to the non-Bavarian eye), whose halitosis had repelled Ursula on first meeting and who swallowed tablets like sweets for his "gas problem" ("I hear he farts," Jürgen said, "be warned. Must be all those vegetables"). He was concerned for his dignity but he wasn't really vain, as such. "Merely a megalomaniac," she wrote to Pamela.

A car and a driver had been sent for them and when they arrived at the Berghof the Führer himself had greeted them—on the great steps, where he welcomed dignitaries, where he had welcomed

Chamberlain last year. When Chamberlain returned to Britain he said that he "now knew what was in Herr Hitler's mind." Ursula doubted that anyone knew that, not even Eva. Particularly not Eva.

"You're very welcome here, *gnädiges Frau,*" he said. "You should stay until the *liebe Kleine* is better."

"He likes women, children, dogs, really what can you fault?" Pamela wrote. "It's just a shame he's a dictator with no respect for the law or common humanity." Pamela had quite a few friends in Germany from her university days, many of them Jewish. She had a full house (well, three of a kind) of boisterous boys (quiet little Frieda would be quite overwhelmed in Finchley) and now wrote that she was pregnant again, "fingers crossed for a girl." Ursula missed Pammy.

Pamela would not fare well under this regime. Her sense of moral outrage would be too great for her to remain silent. She wouldn't be able to bite her tongue like Ursula did (a scold's bridle). *They also serve who only stand and wait.* Did that apply to one's ethics? Is this my defense? Ursula wondered. It might be better to misquote Edmund Burke rather than Milton. *All that is necessary for the forces of evil to win in the world is for enough good women to do nothing.*

The day after they arrived there had been a children's tea party for someone's birthday, a little Goebbels or Bormann, Ursula wasn't sure—there were so many of them and they were so similar. She was reminded of the ranks of the military at the Führer's birthday parade. Scrubbed and polished, each one had a special word from Uncle Wolf before they were allowed to indulge in the cake that was set out on a long table. Poor sweet-toothed Frieda (who undoubtedly took after her mother in this respect) was too heavy-lidded with fatigue to eat any. There was always cake on the Berghof, poppy-seed *Streusel* and cinnamon and plum *Tortes,* puff pastries filled with cream, chocolate cake—great domes of *Schwarzwälder*

Kirschtorte—Ursula wondered who ate all this cake. She herself certainly did her best to get through it.

If a day with Eva could be tedious it was as nothing compared to an evening when the Führer was present. Interminable hours after dinner were spent in the Great Hall—a vast, ugly room where they listened to the gramophone or watched films (or, often, both). The Führer naturally dictated the choices. For music, *Die Fledermaus* and *Die lustige Witwe* were favorites. On the first evening, Ursula thought it would be hard to forget the sight of Bormann, Himmler, Goebbels (and their savage helpmeets) all wearing their thin-lipped snake smiles (more *Lippenbekenntnis,* perhaps) while listening to *Die lustige Witwe.* Ursula had seen a student production of *The Merry Widow* when she was at university. She had been good friends with the girl who played Hanna, the lead. She could never have guessed then that the next time she would hear "Vilja, O Vilja! the witch of the wood," it would be in German and in this strangest of company. That production had taken place in '31. She hadn't seen what her own future held, let alone that of Europe.

Films were shown nearly every evening in the Great Hall. The projectionist would arrive and the great Gobelin tapestry on one wall would be rolled up mechanically, like a blind, to reveal a screen behind it. Then they would have to sit through some awful romantic schmaltz or American adventure, or worse, a mountain film. In this way Ursula had seen *King Kong, The Lives of a Bengal Lancer* and *Der Berg ruft.* On the first evening it had been *Der heilige Berg* (more mountains, more Leni). The Führer's favorite film, Eva confided, was *Snow White.* And which character did he identify with, Ursula wondered—the wicked witch, the dwarves? Not Snow White surely? It must be the Prince, she concluded (did he have a name? Did they ever, was it enough simply to *be* the role?). The Prince who awoke the sleeping girl, just as the Führer had woken Germany. But not with a kiss.

When Frieda was born, Klara had given her a beautiful edition of *Schneewittchen und die sieben Zwerge,* "Snow White and the Seven Dwarves," illustrated by Franz Jüttner. Klara's professor had long since been barred from teaching at the art school. They had planned to leave in '35 and then again in '36. After *Kristallnacht,* Pamela had written to Klara directly, although she had never met her, offering her a home in Finchley. But that inertia, that damned tendency everyone seemed to have to *wait*... and then her professor had been part of a roundup and had been transported east—to work in a factory, the authorities said. "His beautiful sculptor's hands," Klara said sadly.

("They're not really *factories,* you know," Pamela wrote.)

Ursula remembered being an avid reader of fairy tales as a child. She had put great faith not so much in the happy ending as in the restoration of justice to the world. She suspected she had been duped by *die Brüder* Grimm. *Spieglein, Spieglein, an der Wand / Wer ist die Schönste im ganzen Land?* Not this lot, that was for sure, Ursula thought, looking around the Great Hall during her first wearisome evening on the Berg.

The Führer was a man who preferred operetta to opera, cartoons to highbrow culture. Watching him holding Eva's hand while humming along to Lehar, Ursula was struck by how *ordinary* (even silly) he was, more Mickey Mouse than Siegfried. Sylvie would have made short work of him. Izzie would have eaten him up and spat him out. Mrs. Glover—what would Mrs. Glover have done? Ursula wondered. This was her new favorite game, deciding how the people she knew would have dealt with the Nazi oligarchs. Mrs. Glover, she concluded, would probably have beaten them all soundly with her meat hammer. (What would Bridget do? Ignore him completely probably.)

When the film was finished the Führer settled down to expound (for hours) on his pet subjects—German art and architecture (he perceived himself to be an architect manqué), *Blut und Boden* (the land, always the land), his solitary, noble path (the wolf again). He was the savior of Germany, and poor Germany, his *Schneewittchen,* would be saved by him whether she wanted it or not. He droned on about healthy German art and music, about Wagner, *Die Meistersinger,* his favorite line from the libretto—*Wacht auf, es nahet gen den Tag*—"Awake, the morning is here" (it would be if he went on much longer, she thought). Back to destiny—his—how it was intertwined with the destiny of the *Volk. Heimat, Boden,* victory or downfall (What victory? Ursula wondered. Against whom?). Then something about Frederick the Great that she didn't catch, something about Roman architecture, then the Fatherland. (For the Russians it was "the Motherland," was there something to be made of that? Ursula wondered. What was it for the English? Just "England," she supposed. Blake's "Jerusalem" at a pinch.)

Then back to destiny and the *Tausendjähriges.* On and on so that the headache that had begun before dinner as a dull ache was a crown of thorns by now. She imagined Hugh saying, "Oh, do shut up, Herr Hitler," and suddenly felt so homesick she thought she was going to cry.

She wanted to go home. She wanted to go to Fox Corner.

As with kings and their courtiers, they could not leave until dismissed, until the monarch himself decided to ascend to the bedchamber. At one point Ursula caught Eva yawning theatrically at him as if to say, "That's enough now, Wolfi" (her imagination was becoming rather lurid, she knew, forgivable given the circumstances). And then at last, finally, thank God, he made a move and the exhausted company rustled to its feet.

Women in particular seemed to love the Führer. They wrote him letters in the thousands, baked him cakes, embroidered swastikas onto cushions and pillows for him, and, like Hilde and Hanne's

BDM troop, lined the steep road up to the Obersalzberg to catch a delirious glimpse of him in the big black Mercedes. Many women shouted to him that they wanted to have his baby. "But what do they *see* in him?" Sylvie puzzled. Ursula had taken her to a parade, one of the interminable flag-waving, banner-toting ones in Berlin, because she wanted to "find out for myself what all the fuss is about." (How very British of Sylvie to reduce the Third Reich to a "fuss.")

The street was a forest of red, black and white. "Their colors are very harsh," Sylvie said, as though she were considering asking the National Socialists to decorate her living room.

At the Führer's approach the crowd's excitement had grown to a rabid frenzy of *Sieg Heil* and *Heil Hitler.* "Am I the only one to be unmoved?" Sylvie said. "What is it, do you suppose—mass hysteria of some kind?"

"I know," Ursula said, "it's like the Emperor's new clothes. We're the only ones who can see the naked man."

"He's a clown," Sylvie said dismissively.

"Shush," Ursula said. The English word was the same as the German and she didn't want to attract the hostility of the people around them. "You should put your arm up," she said.

"Me?" the outraged flower of British womanhood replied.

"Yes, you."

Reluctantly, Sylvie raised her arm. Ursula thought that until the day she died she would remember the sight of her mother giving the Nazi salute. Of course, Ursula said to herself afterward, this was in '34, back when one's conscience hadn't been shrunk and muddled by fear, when she had been blind to what was truly afoot. Blinded by love perhaps, or just dumb stupidity. (Pamela had seen, unblinkered by anything.)

Sylvie had made the journey to Germany so that she could inspect Ursula's unexpected husband. Ursula wondered what she had planned to do if she hadn't found Jürgen suitable—drug and kidnap her and haul her onto the *Schnellzug?* They were still in Munich then, Jürgen hadn't started working for the Ministry of Justice in Berlin, they hadn't moved to the Savignyplatz or become parents to Frieda, although Ursula was cumbersome with pregnancy.

"Fancy you becoming a mother," Sylvie said, as if it were something she had never expected. "To a German," she added thoughtfully.

"To a baby," Ursula said.

It's nice to get away," Sylvie said. From what? Ursula wondered.

Klara met them for lunch one day and afterward said, "Your mother is rather chic." Ursula had never thought of Sylvie as stylish but she supposed that compared with Klara's mother, Frau Brenner, as soft and doughy as a loaf of *Kartoffelbrot,* Sylvie was quite a fashion plate.

On the way back from lunch, Sylvie said she wanted to visit Oberpollingers and buy a present for Hugh. When they reached the department store they found the windows daubed with anti-Jewish slogans and Sylvie said, "Gracious, what a mess." The shop was open for business but a pair of grinning louts in SA uniform were loitering in front of the doors, putting people off from entering. Not Sylvie, who had marched past the Brownshirts while Ursula reluctantly trailed in her wake into the store and up the thickly carpeted staircase. In the face of the uniforms, Ursula had shrugged a cartoon helplessness and murmured rather shamefacedly, "She's English." She thought that Sylvie didn't understand what it was like living in Germany but in retrospect she thought that perhaps Sylvie had understood very well.

Ah, here's lunch," Eva said, putting down the camera and taking Frieda's hand. She led her to the table and then propped her up on an extra cushion before heaping her plate with food. Chicken, roast potatoes and a salad, all from the Gutshof. How well they ate here. *Milchreis* for Frieda's pudding, the milk fresh that morning from the cows of the Gutshof. (A less childish *Käsekuchen* for Ursula, a cigarette for Eva.) Ursula remembered Mrs. Glover's rice pudding, a creamy, sticky yellow beneath its crisp brown skin. She could smell the nutmeg even though she knew there was none in Frieda's dish. She couldn't remember the German for nutmeg and thought it was too difficult to explain to Eva. The food was the only thing that she was going to miss about the Berghof so she might as well enjoy it while she could, she thought, and helped herself to more *Käsekuchen.*

Lunch was served to them by a small contingent of the army of staff who serviced the Berghof. The Berg was a curious combination of Alpine holiday chalet and military training camp. A small town really with a school, a post office, a theater, a large SS barracks, a rifle range, a bowling alley, a Wehrmacht hospital and much more, everything but a church really. There were also plenty of young, handsome Wehrmacht officers who would have made better suitors for Eva.

After lunch they walked up to the *Teehaus* on the Mooslahner Kopf, Eva's yappy, nippy dogs running along beside them. (If only one of them would fall off the parapet or from the outlook.) Ursula had the beginnings of a headache and sank gratefully into one of the armchairs with green-flowered linen upholstery that she found particularly offensive to the eye. Tea—and cake, naturally—were brought to them from the kitchen. Ursula swallowed a couple of codeine with her tea and said, "I think Frieda's well enough to go home now."

Ursula went to bed as early as she could, slipping in between the cool white sheets of the guest room bed she shared with Frieda. Too tired to sleep, she found herself still awake at two in the morning so she put on the bedside light—Frieda slept the deep sleep of children, only illness could wake her—and she got out pen and paper and wrote to Pamela instead.

Of course, none of these letters to Pamela was ever posted. She couldn't be completely sure that they wouldn't be read by someone. You just didn't *know,* that was the awful thing (how much more awful for others). Now she wished they weren't in the dog days of heat when the *Kachelofen* in the guest room was cold and unlit, as it would have been safer to burn the correspondence. Safer never to have written at all. One could no longer express one's true thoughts. *Truth is truth to the end of reckoning.* What was that from? *Measure for Measure?* But perhaps truth was asleep until the end of reckoning. There was going to be an awful *lot* of reckoning when the time came.

She wanted to go home. She wanted to go to Fox Corner. She had planned to go back in May but then Frieda had become sick. She'd had it all planned, their suitcases were packed, stored beneath the bed, where they were usually kept empty, so Jürgen had no reason to look inside them. She had the train tickets, the onward boat-train tickets, had told no one, not even Klara. She hadn't wanted to move their passports—Frieda's luckily still valid from their trip to England in '35—from the big porcupine-quill box where all their documents were kept. She had checked they were there almost every day but then the day before they were to go she looked in the box and there was no sign of them. She thought she was mistaken, rifled through birth and death and marriage certificates, through insurance and guarantees, Jürgen's will (he was a lawyer, after all), all kinds of paperwork except for what mattered. In mounting panic she emptied the lot onto the carpet and went through everything one by one, again and again. No passports, only Jürgen's. In desperation she went through every drawer in the house, searched inside every shoebox and cupboard, beneath sofa cushions and mattresses. Nothing.

They ate supper as normal. She could barely swallow. "Are you feeling ill?" Jürgen asked, solicitously.

"No," she said. Her voice sounded squeaky. What could she say? He knew, of course, he knew.

"I thought we might take a holiday," he said. "On Sylt."

"Sylt?"

"Sylt. We won't need a passport for there," he said. Did he smile? Did he? And then Frieda was ill and nothing else mattered.

Er kommt!" Eva said happily the next morning at breakfast. The Führer was coming.

"When? Now?"

"No, this afternoon."

"What a shame, we'll be gone by then," Ursula said. Thank God, she thought. "Do thank him, won't you?"

They were taken home in one of the fleet of black Mercedes from the *Platterhof* garage, driven by the same chauffeur who had brought them to the Berghof.

The next day Germany invaded Poland.

April 1945

They had lived for months in the cellar, like rats. When the British were bombing by day and the Americans by night there was nothing else for it. The cellar beneath the apartment block in the Savignyplatz was dank and disgusting, a small paraffin lamp for light and one bucket for a lavatory, yet the cellar was better than one of the bunkers in town. She had been caught with Frieda near the zoo in a daylight raid and had taken shelter in the Zoo Station flak tower—thousands of people crammed in, the air supply gauged by a candle (as if they were canaries). If the candle goes out, someone told her, everyone has to leave, out into the open even if a raid is in progress. Near to where they were crushed against a wall, a man and a woman were embracing (a polite term for what they were doing) and as they were leaving they had to step over an old man who had died during the raid. The worst thing, even worse than this, was that as well as being a shelter the enormous concrete citadel was a gigantic anti-aircraft battery, several huge guns pounding away on the roof the whole time so that the shelter shook with every recoil. It was the closest to hell that Ursula hoped ever to come.

An enormous explosion had shaken the structure, a bomb dropped close to the zoo. She felt the pressure wave sucking and pushing her body and was terrified that Frieda's lungs might burst. It passed. Several people vomited, although unfortunately there was nowhere to vomit except on one's feet, or perhaps worse, on other people's feet. Ursula vowed never to go into a flak tower again. She would rather, she thought, die out in the street, quickly, with Frieda. That's what she thought about a lot of the time now. A swift, clean death, Frieda wrapped in her arms.

Perhaps it was Teddy up there, dropping bombs on them. She hoped it was, it would mean he was alive. There had been a knock on the door one day—when they still had a door, before the British started their relentless bombing in November '43. When Ursula opened the door she found a thin youth standing there, fifteen or sixteen years old maybe. He had a desperate air and Ursula wondered if he was looking for somewhere to hide but he pushed an envelope into her hand and ran off before she could even say a word to him.

The envelope was creased and filthy. Her name and address were written on it and she burst into tears at the sight of Pamela's handwriting. Thin papery blue sheets, dated several weeks ago, detailing all the comings and goings of her family—Jimmy in the army, Sylvie fighting the good fight on the home front ("a new weapon—chickens!"). Pamela was well and living at Fox Corner, she said, four boys now. Teddy in the RAF, a squadron leader with a DFC. A lovely long letter and at the end a page that was almost like a postscript, "I have saved the sad news to last." Hugh was dead. "In the autumn of 1940, peacefully, a heart attack." Ursula wished she hadn't received the letter, wished she could think of Hugh still alive, of Teddy and Jimmy in noncombatant roles, living out the war in a coal mine or civil defense.

"I think of you constantly," Pamela said. No recriminations, no "I told you so," no "Why didn't you come home when you could have done?" She had tried, too late, of course. The day after Germany declared war on Poland she had gone through town, dutifully doing the things that she thought you were supposed to do when war was imminent. She stocked up on batteries and torches and candles, she bought canned goods and blackout material, she shopped for clothes for Frieda in Wertheim's department store—one and two sizes bigger in case the war went on for a long time. She bought nothing for herself, passing by all those warm coats and boots, stockings and decent frocks, something she bitterly regretted now.

She heard Chamberlain on the BBC, those fateful words *We are now at war with Germany,* and for several hours felt strangely numb. She tried to phone Pamela but the lines were all engaged. Then toward evening (Jürgen had been at the ministry all day) she suddenly came back to life, Snow White awake. She must leave, she must go back to England, passport or no. She packed a hasty suitcase and harried Frieda onto a tram to the station. If she could just get on a train somehow everything would be all right. No trains, an official at the station told her. The borders were closed. "We're at war, didn't you know?" he said.

She ran to the British Embassy in Wilhelmstrasse, dragging poor Frieda by the hand. They were German citizens but she would throw herself on the mercy of the embassy staff, surely they would be able to do something, she was still an Englishwoman after all. It was growing dark by then and the gates were padlocked and there were no lights on in the building. "They've gone," a passerby told her, "you've missed them."

"Gone?"

"Back to Britain."

She had to clap a hand over her mouth to stop the wail that rose up from deep inside her. How could she have been so stupid? Why hadn't she seen what was coming? *A fool too late bewares when all the peril is past.* Something else that Elizabeth I had said.

She wept on and off for two days after receiving Pamela's letter. Jürgen was sympathetic, came home with some real coffee for her and she didn't ask where he had got it. A good cup of coffee (miraculous as that was) was hardly going to assuage her grief for her father, for Frieda, for herself. For everybody. Jürgen died in an American raid in '44. Ursula was ashamed at how relieved she felt when she was given the news, especially as Frieda was so upset. She loved her father and he loved her, which was a nugget of grace to be salvaged from the whole sorry business of their marriage.

Frieda was ill now. She had the same gaunt features and sickly pallor of most people you saw on the streets these days but her lungs were full of phlegm and she had terrible bouts of coughing that seemed as though they would never end. When Ursula listened to her chest it was like listening to a galleon at sea, heaving and creaking through the waves. If only she could sit her down by a big warm fire, give her hot cocoa to drink, a beef stew, dumplings, carrots. Were they still eating well on the Berg? she wondered. Was anyone still on the Berg?

* * *

Above their heads, the apartment block was still standing although most of the front wall had been taken away by a bomb. They still went up there to forage for anything useful. It had been saved from looting by the almost insurmountable difficulty of getting up the staircase which was filled with rubble. She and Frieda tied pieces of cushion to their knees with rags and wore thick leather gloves that had belonged to Jürgen and in this way clambered over the stones and bricks like inept monkeys.

The one thing there was nothing of in the apartment was the only thing they were interested in—food. Yesterday they had queued for three hours for a loaf of bread. When they ate it, it seemed to contain no actual flour, although it was hard to say what it did contain—cement dust and plaster? That was what it tasted of anyway. Ursula remembered Rogerson's the baker's in the village at home, how the smell of the baking bread would waft through the street and how the bakery's window was full of lovely soft white loaves burnished with a sticky bronze glaze. Or the kitchen at Fox Corner on Mrs. Glover's baking days—the big brown "health" loaves that Sylvie insisted on, but also the sponges and tarts and buns. She imagined eating a slice of the warm brown bread, thickly buttered, with the jam made from the raspberries and red currants at Fox Corner. (She tormented herself with memories of food the whole time.) There was to be no more milk, someone told her in the bread queue.

This morning, Fräulein Farber and her sister Frau Meyer who had lived together in the attic but who now rarely left the cellar gave her two potatoes and a piece of cooked sausage for Frieda, *Aus Anstand,* they said, out of decency. Herr Richter, also a cellar resident, told Ursula that the sisters had decided to stop eating. (An easy thing to do when there was no food, Ursula thought.) They have had enough, he said. They cannot face what will happen when the Russians get here.

They had heard a rumor that in the east people were reduced to eating grass. Lucky them, Ursula thought, there was no grass in Berlin, just the black skeletal remains of a proud and beautiful city. Was London like this too? It seemed unlikely, yet possible. Speer had his noble ruins, a thousand years early.

The inedible bread yesterday, two half-raw potatoes the day before that was all Ursula had in her own stomach. Everything else—for the little it was worth—she'd given to Frieda. But what good would it do Frieda if Ursula were dead? She couldn't leave her alone in this terrible world.

After the British raid on the zoo they had gone to see if there were any animals they could eat but plenty of people had got there before them. (Could *that* happen at home? Londoners scavenging in Regent's Park zoo? Why not?)

They still saw the occasional bird that was clearly not native to Berlin, surviving against the odds, and on one occasion, a cowed, mangy creature that they had taken for a dog before they realized it was a wolf. Frieda was all for trying to take it back to the cellar with them and making a pet of it. Ursula couldn't even imagine what their elderly neighbor Frau Jaeger's reaction would have been to that.

Their own apartment was like a dollhouse, open to the world, all the intimate details of their domestic life on view—beds and sofas, the pictures on the walls, even an ornament or two that had miraculously survived the blast. They had raided anything truly useful but there were still some clothes and a few books and only yesterday she had found a cache of candles beneath a pile of broken crockery. Ursula was hoping to trade them in for medicine for Frieda. There was still a lavatory, in the bathroom, and occasionally, who knew how, there was water. One of them would stand and hold up an old sheet to protect the other's modesty. Did their modesty matter that much anymore?

Ursula had made the decision to move back in. It was cold in the apartment but the air wasn't fetid and she judged that on balance that would be better for Frieda. They still had blankets and quilts they could wrap themselves in and they shared a mattress on the floor, behind a barricade formed by the dining table and chairs. Ursula's thoughts strayed constantly to the meals they had eaten at that table, her dreams full of meat, pork and beef, slabs of it grilled and roasted and fried.

The apartment was two floors up and this, combined with the partially blocked staircase, might be enough to put the Russians off. On the other hand they would be the dolls on display in the dollhouse, a woman and a girl ripe for the plucking. Frieda would soon be eleven but if even a tenth of the rumors coming from the east were true then her age wouldn't save her from the Russians. Frau Jaeger never stopped talking nervously about how the Soviets were raping and murdering their way toward Berlin. There was no wireless anymore, just rumor and the occasional flimsy piece of newssheet. The name Nemmersdorf was rarely off Frau Jaeger's lips ("A massacre!"). "Oh, do shut up," Ursula said to her the other day. In English, which she didn't understand, of course, although she must have heard the unfriendly tone. Frau Jaeger had been visibly startled to be addressed in the language of the enemy and Ursula felt sorry, she was just a frightened old lady, she reminded herself.

The east moved nearer every day. Interest in the western front had long since died, only the east was of concern. The distant thunder of guns now replaced by a constant roar. There was no one to save them. Eighty thousand German troops to defend them against a million and a half Soviets, and most of those German troops seemed to be children or old men. Perhaps poor old Frau Jaeger would be called upon to beat off the enemy with a broom handle. It could only be a matter of days, hours even, before they saw their first Russian.

There was a rumor that Hitler was dead. "Not before time," Herr Richter said. Ursula remembered the sight of him asleep on his sun lounger on the terrace on the Berg. He had strutted and fretted his hour upon the stage. To what avail? A kind of Armageddon. The death of Europe.

It was life itself, wasn't it, she corrected herself, that Shakespeare had fretting and strutting. *Life's but a walking shadow, a poor player that struts and frets his hour upon the stage.* They were all walking shadows in Berlin. Life had mattered so much once and now it was the cheapest thing on offer. She spared an idle thought for Eva, she was always blasé about the idea of suicide, had she accompanied her leader into hell?

Frieda was so poorly now, chills and fever and complaining almost constantly of a headache. If she hadn't been sick they might have joined the exodus of people heading west, away from the Russians, but there was no way she would survive such a journey.

"I've had enough, Mummy," she whispered, a terrible echo of the sisters from the attic.

Ursula left her alone while she hurried to the chemist, scrabbling over the debris that littered the streets, occasionally a corpse—she felt nothing for the dead anymore. She cowered in doorways when the gunfire seemed too close and then scurried to the next street corner. The chemist was open but he had no medicine, he didn't even want her precious candles or her money. She came back defeated.

The whole time she had been away from Frieda she had been anxious that something would happen to her in her absence and she promised herself that she wouldn't leave her side again. She had seen a Russian tank two streets away. She had been terrified by the sight, how much more terrified would Frieda be? The noise of artillery fire was constant. She was gripped by the idea that the world was ending. If it was then Frieda must die in her arms, not alone. But whose arms would she die in? She longed for the safety of her father and the thought of Hugh made the tears start.

By the time she had climbed the rubble staircase she was exhausted, weary to the bone. She found Frieda slipping in and out of delirium and lay down beside her on the mattress on the floor. Stroking her damp hair, she talked in a low voice to her about another world. She told her about the bluebells in spring in the wood near Fox Corner, about the flowers that grew in the meadow beyond the copse—flax and larkspur, buttercups, corn poppies, red campion and oxeye daisies. She told her about the smell of new-mown grass from an English summer lawn, the scent of Sylvie's roses, the sour-sweet taste of the apples in the orchard. She talked of the oak trees in the lane, and the yews in the graveyard and the beech in the garden at Fox Corner. She talked about the foxes, the rabbits, the pheasants, the hares, the cows and the big plow horses. About the sun beaming his friendly rays on fields of corn and fields of green. The bright song of the blackbird, the lyrical lark, the soft coo of the wood pigeons, the hoot of the owl in the dark. "Take this," she said, putting the pill in Frieda's mouth, "I got it from the chemist, it will help you sleep."

She told Frieda how she would walk on knives to protect her, burn in the flames of hell to save her, drown in the deepest of waters if it would buoy her up and how she would do this one last thing for her, the most difficult thing of all.

She put her arms around her daughter and kissed her and murmured in her ear, telling her about Teddy when he was little, his surprise birthday party, about how clever Pamela was and how annoying Maurice was and how funny Jimmy had been when he was small. How the clock ticked in the hall and the wind rattled in the chimneypots and how on Christmas Eve they lit an enormous log fire and hung their stockings from the mantelpiece and next day ate roast goose and plum pudding and how that was what they would all do next Christmas, all of them together. "Everything is going to be all right now," Ursula told her.

When she was sure that Frieda was asleep she took the little glass capsule that the chemist had given her and placed it gently in Frieda's mouth and pressed her delicate jaws together. The capsule broke with a tiny crunching noise. A line from one of Donne's *Holy Sonnets* came into mind as she bit down on her own little glass vial. *I run to death, and death meets me as fast, And all my pleasures are like yesterday.* She held tightly on to Frieda and soon they were both wrapped in the velvet wings of the black bat and this life was already unreal and gone.

She had never chosen death over life before and as she was leaving she knew something had cracked and broken and the order of things had changed. Then the dark obliterated all thoughts.

A LONG HARD WAR

September 1940

"See where Christ's blood streams across the firmament," a voice nearby said. *"In"* the firmament, Ursula thought, not "across." The red glow of a false dawn indicated a massive fire in the east. The barrage in Hyde Park cracked and flared and the antiaircraft guns closer to home were doing a good job of keeping up their own cacophony, shells whistling into the air like fireworks and *crack-crack-cracking* as they exploded high overhead. And beneath it all was the horrible throbbing drone of the bombers' unsynchronized engines, a sound that always made her stomach feel pitchy.

A parachute mine floated down gracefully and a basket of incendiaries rattled their contents onto what was left of the road and burst into flowers of fire. A warden, Ursula couldn't make out his face, ran across to the incendiaries with a stirrup pump. If there had been no noise it might have seemed a beautiful nightscape but there *was* noise, brutish dissonance that sounded as if someone had thrown open the gates of hell and let out the howling of the damned.

"*Why this is hell, nor am I out of it,*" the voice spoke again as if reading her thoughts. It was so dark that she could barely make out the owner of the voice although she knew without a doubt that it belonged to Mr. Durkin, one of the wardens from her post. He was a retired English teacher, much inclined to quoting. And misquoting. The voice—or Mr. Durkin—said something else, it may still have been *Faustus* but the words disappeared into the enormous *whump* of a bomb falling a couple of streets away.

The ground shook and another voice, that of someone working on the mound, yelled, "Watch out!" She heard something shifting and a noise like displaced scree rattling and rolling down a mountain, the harbinger of an avalanche. Rubble, not scree. And a mound of it, not a mountain. The rubble that comprised the mound was all that was left of a house, or rather, several houses all ground and mashed into each other now. The rubble had been homes half an hour ago, now those same homes were just a hellish jumble of bricks, broken joists and floorboards, furniture, pictures, rugs, bedding, books, crockery, lino, glass. People. The crushed fragments of lives, never to be whole again.

The rumble slowed to a trickle and finally stopped, the avalanche averted, and the same voice shouted, "All right! Carry on!" It was a moonless night, the only light coming from the masked torches of the heavy rescue squad, ghostly will-o'-the-wisps, moving on the mound. The other reason for the immense, treacherous dark was the thick cloud of smoke and dust that hung like a curtain of vile gossamer in the air. The stink, as usual, was awful. It wasn't just the smell of coal gas and high explosive, it was the aberrant odor produced when a building was blown to smithereens. The smell of it wouldn't leave her. She had tied an old silk scarf around her mouth and nose, bandit-style, but it did little to stop the dust and the stench getting into her lungs. Death and decay were on her skin, in her hair, in her nostrils, her lungs, beneath her fingernails, all the time. They had become part of her.

They had only recently been issued with overalls, navy blue and unflattering. Until now Ursula had been wearing her shelter suit, bought almost as a novelty item by Sylvie from Simpson's soon after war was declared. She had added an old leather belt of Hugh's from which she'd strung her "accessories"—a torch, gas mask, a first-aid packet and a message pad. In one pocket she had a penknife and a handkerchief and in the other a pair of thick leather gloves and a lipstick. "Oh, what a good idea," Miss Woolf said, when she saw the penknife. Let's face it, Ursula thought, despite a host of regulations, they were making it up as they went along.

Mr. Durkin, for it was indeed he, resolved himself out of the gloom and foggy smoke. He shone his torch onto his notebook, the weak light barely illuminating the paper. "A lot of people live on this street," he said, peering at the list of names and house numbers which no longer bore any relation to the surrounding havoc. "The Wilsons are at number one," he said, as if beginning at the beginning would somehow help.

"There is no number one anymore," Ursula said. "There are no numbers at all." The street was unrecognizable, everything familiar annihilated. Even in broad daylight it would have been unrecognizable. It wasn't a street anymore, it was simply "the mound." Twenty feet high, maybe more, with planks and ladders running up its sides to enable the heavy rescue squad to crawl over it. There was something primitive about the human chain they had formed, passing debris in baskets from hand to hand, from the top of the mound to the bottom. They could have been slaves building the pyramids—or in this case, excavating them. Ursula thought suddenly of the leafcutter ants that used to be in Regent's Park zoo, each one dutifully carrying its little burden. Had the ants been evacuated along with the other animals or had they simply set them free in the park? They were tropical insects, so perhaps they would not be able to survive the rigors of the climate of Regent's Park. She had seen Millie there in an open-air production of *A Midsummer Night's Dream,* in the summer of '38.

"Miss Todd?"

"Yes, sorry, Mr. Durkin, miles away." It happened a lot these days—she would be in the middle of these awful scenes and she would find that she had drifted off to pleasant moments in the past. Little slivers of light in the darkness.

They made their way warily toward the mound. Mr. Durkin passed the list of the street's residents to her and started giving a hand with the chain of baskets. No one was actually digging on the mound, instead they were clearing the rubble by hand, like careful archeologists. "A bit delicate up there," one of the rescue squad near the bottom of the chain said to her. A shaft had been cleared, going down the middle of the mound (a volcano then, rather than a mound, Ursula thought). A lot of the men in the heavy rescue squad were from the building trade—bricklayers, laborers and so on—and Ursula wondered if it felt odd to them to be scrambling over these dismantled buildings, as if time had somehow gone backward. But then they were pragmatic, resourceful men who were not much given to this kind of fantastical thinking.

Occasionally a voice would call for quiet—impossible when the raid was still going on overhead—but nonetheless everything would stop while the men at the top of the mound listened intently for signs of life within. It looked hopeless but if there was one thing that the Blitz had taught them it was that people lived (and died) in the most unlikely of circumstances.

Ursula searched in the gloom for the dim blue lights that marked out the incident officer's post and instead caught sight of Miss Woolf, stumbling purposefully over broken bricks toward her. "It's bad," she said matter-of-factly when she reached Ursula. "They need someone slight."

"Slight?" Ursula repeated. The word, for some reason, was devoid of meaning.

She had joined the ARP as a warden after the invasion of Czechoslovakia in March '39, when it suddenly seemed horribly clear to her that Europe was doomed. ("What a gloomy Cassandra you are," Sylvie said, but Ursula worked in the Air Raid Precautions department at the Home Office, she could see the future.) During the strange twilight of the phony war the wardens had been something of a joke but now they were "the backbone of London's defenses"—this from Maurice.

Her fellow wardens were a mixed bunch. Miss Woolf, a retired hospital matron, was the senior warden. Thin and straight as a poker, her iron-gray hair in a neat bun, she came with natural authority. Then there was her deputy, the aforesaid Mr. Durkin, Mr. Simms, who worked for the Ministry of Supply, and Mr. Palmer, who was a bank manager. The latter two men had fought in the last war and were too old for this one (Mr. Durkin had been "medically exempt," he said defensively). Then there was Mr. Armitage who was an opera singer and as there were no operas to sing in anymore he kept them entertained with his renditions of *"La donna è mobile"* and *"Largo al factotum."* "Just the popular arias," he confided to Ursula. "Most people don't like anything challenging."

"Give me old Al Bowlly any day," Mr. Bullock said. The rather aptly named Mr. Bullock (John) was in Miss Woolf's words "a little questionable." He certainly cut a strapping figure—he wrestled competitively and lifted weights in a local gym as well as being the denizen of several of the less salubrious nightclubs. He was also acquainted with some rather glamorous "dancers." One or two had "dropped in" on him in the shelter and been shooed away like chickens by Miss Woolf. ("Dancers my eye," she said.)

Last but not least there was Herr Zimmerman ("Gabi, please," he said, but no one did), who was an orchestra violinist from Berlin, "our refugee" as they referred to him (Sylvie had evacuees, similarly denoted by their circumstances). He had "jumped ship" in '35 while on tour with his orchestra. Miss Woolf, who knew him through the Refugee Committee, had gone to great lengths to make sure that Herr Zimmerman and his violin were not interned, or worse, shipped across the lethal waters of the Atlantic. They all followed Miss Woolf's lead and never addressed him as "Mister," always as "*Herr.*" Ursula knew that Miss Woolf called him thus to make him feel at home but it only succeeded in making more of an alien of him.

Miss Woolf had come across Herr Zimmerman in the course of

her work for the Central British Fund for German Jewry ("Rather a mouthful, I'm afraid"). Ursula was never sure whether Miss Woolf was a woman of some influence or whether she simply refused to take no for an answer. Both, perhaps.

"A cultured lot, aren't we?" Mr. Bullock said sarcastically. "Why don't we just put on shows instead of fighting a war." ("Mr. Bullock is a man of strong emotions," Miss Woolf said to Ursula. And strong drink too, Ursula thought. Strong everything in fact.)

A small hall belonging to the Methodists had been commandeered to be their post by Miss Woolf (herself a Methodist), and they had furnished it with a couple of camp beds, a small stove with tea-making equipment and an assortment of chairs, both hard and soft. Compared to some posts, compared to many, it was luxurious.

Mr. Bullock turned up one night with a green baize card table and Miss Woolf declared herself rather fond of bridge. Mr. Bullock, in the lull between the fall of France and the first raids at the beginning of September, had taught them all poker. "Quite the card sharp," Mr. Simms said. Both he and Mr. Palmer lost several shillings to Mr. Bullock. Miss Woolf, on the other hand, was two pounds up by the time the Blitz started. An amused Mr. Bullock expressed surprise that Methodists were allowed to gamble. Her winnings bought a dartboard so Mr. Bullock had nothing to complain about, she said. One day when they were clearing a jumble of boxes in the corner of the hall they discovered that a piano had been hiding there all along and Miss Woolf—who was proving a woman of many talents—was a rather good player. Although her own tastes tended toward Chopin and Liszt, she was more than game to "bash out a few tunes"—Mr. Bullock's words—for them all to sing along to.

They had fortified the post with sandbags although none of them believed that they would be of any use if they were hit. Apart from Ursula, who thought that taking precautions seemed an eminently sensible idea, they all tended to agree with Mr. Bullock that "If it's got your name on it, it's got your name on it," a form of Buddhist detachment that Dr. Kellet would have admired. There had been an obituary in the *Times* during the summer. Ursula was rather glad that Dr. Kellet had missed another war. It would have reminded him of the futility of Guy losing everything at Arras.

They were all part-time volunteers, apart from Miss Woolf, who was paid and full-time and took her duties very seriously. She subjected them to rigorous drills and made sure they did their training—in anti-gas procedures, in extinguishing incendiaries, how to enter burning buildings, load stretchers, make splints, bandage limbs. She questioned them on the contents of the manuals that she made them read and she was very keen on them learning how to label bodies, both alive and dead, so that they could be sent off like parcels to the hospital or the mortuary with all the correct information attached. They had done several exercises out in the open where they had acted out a mock raid. ("Playacting," Mr. Bullock scoffed, failing to get into the spirit of things.) Ursula played a casualty twice, once having to feign a broken leg and on another occasion complete unconsciousness. Another time she had been on the "other side" and as a warden had had to deal with Mr. Armitage simulating someone in hysterical shock. She supposed it was his experience onstage that enabled him to give such an unnervingly authentic performance. It was quite hard to persuade him out of character at the end of the exercise.

They had to know the occupants of every building in their sector, whether they had a shelter of their own or whether they went to a public one or whether they too were fatalists and didn't bother at all. They had to know if anyone had gone away or moved, married, had a baby, died. They had to know where the hydrants were, cul-de-sacs, narrow alleyways, cellars, rest centers.

"Patrol and watch," that was Miss Woolf's motto. They tended to patrol the streets in pairs until midnight when there was usually a lull, and then if there were no bombs in their sector they would have a polite argument over who should occupy the camp beds. Of course, if there was a raid in "their streets" then it was "all hands to the pumps" in Miss Woolf's words. Sometimes they did the "watching" from her apartment, two stories up with an excellent view from a big corner window.

Miss Woolf also did extra first-aid exercises with them. As well as having been a hospital matron, she had run a field hospital during the last war and explained to them ("As you will appreciate, those of you gentlemen who saw active service in that dreadful conflict") that casualties in war were very different from the routine accidents that one saw in peacetime. "Much nastier," she said. "We must be prepared for some distressing sights." Of course, even Miss Woolf had not imagined how distressing these sights would be when they involved civilians rather than battlefield soldiers, when they involved shoveling up unidentifiable lumps of flesh or picking out the heartbreakingly small limbs of a child from the rubble.

"We cannot turn away," Miss Woolf told her, "we must get on with our job and we must bear witness." What did that mean? Ursula wondered. "It means," Miss Woolf said, "that we must remember these people when we are safely in the future."

"And if *we* are killed?"

"Then others must remember *us*."

The first serious incident they attended had been at a large house in the middle of a terrace that had received a direct hit. The rest of the terrace was undamaged, as though the Luftwaffe had personally targeted the occupants—two families including grandparents, several children, two babes in arms. They had all survived the blast, sheltering in the cellar, but both the main water pipe and a large sewage pipe had fractured and before either could be turned off everyone in the cellar had drowned in the awful sludge.

One of the women had managed to claw her way up and cling on to one of the cellar walls, they could see her through a gap, and Miss Woolf and Mr. Armitage had held on to Hugh's leather belt while Ursula had dangled over the lip of what remained of the cellar. She reached out a hand to the woman, thought for a moment that she might actually manage to grasp hold of her, but then she simply disappeared beneath the feculent water as it rose to fill the cellar.

When the fire brigade finally arrived to pump out the place they recovered fifteen bodies, seven of them children, and laid them in front of the house, as if to dry. Miss Woolf ordered them shrouded as quickly as possible and stowed away behind a wall while they awaited the arrival of the mortuary wagon. "It doesn't do morale any good to see sights like that," she said. Ursula had vomited up her supper long before then. She vomited after nearly every incident. Mr. Armitage and Mr. Palmer too, Mr. Simms before. Only Miss Woolf and Mr. Bullock seemed to have strong stomachs for death.

Afterward, Ursula tried not to think about the babies or the look of terror on that poor woman's face as she had grasped in vain for Ursula's hand (and something else, disbelief perhaps that this could be happening). "Think of them being at peace now," Miss Woolf counseled stoutly afterward, dispensing scalding-hot sugary tea. "They are out of all this, just gone a little sooner." And Mr. Durkin said, *"They have all gone into the world of light,"* and Ursula thought, *they* are *all gone into the world of light.* Ursula wasn't convinced that the dead went anywhere, except into a void, black and infinite.

"Well, I hope *I* don't die covered in shit," Mr. Bullock said, more prosaically.

She thought she would never get over that first terrible incident but the memory of it had already been overlaid by many others and now she barely thought about it.

It's bad," Miss Woolf said matter-of-factly. "They need someone slight."

"Slight?" Ursula repeated.

"Slim," Miss Woolf said patiently.

"To go in there?" Ursula said, looking up in horror at the summit of the volcano. She wasn't sure she had the gumption to be lowered into the very maw of hell.

"No, no, not there," Miss Woolf said. "Come with me." It had begun to rain, quite hard, and Ursula blundered with difficulty in Miss Woolf's wake over the jagged and broken ground, littered with every kind of obstacle. Her torch was next to useless. She caught her foot in a bicycle wheel and wondered if anyone had been riding it when the bomb struck.

"Here," Miss Woolf said. It was another mound, just as big as the last. Was it another street, or the same street? Ursula had lost all sense of direction. How many mounds were there? A nightmarish scenario flashed through her mind—the whole of London reduced to one gigantic mound.

This mound wasn't a volcano, the rescue squad were going in through a horizontal shaft at the side. More robust this time, they were hacking at the rubble with picks and shovels.

"There's a kind of hole here," Miss Woolf said, taking Ursula's hand firmly in hers, as if Ursula were a reluctant child, and leading her forward. Ursula could see no sign of a hole. "It's safe, I think, you just need to wriggle through."

"A tunnel?"

"No, it's just a hole. There's a bit of a drop on the other side, we think there's someone down there. Not a long drop," she added encouragingly. "Not a tunnel," she said again. "Go head first." The rescue squad stopped hacking at the rubble and waited, rather impatiently, for Ursula.

She had to take her helmet off in order to wriggle into the hole, her torch held awkwardly in front of her. Despite what Miss Woolf said, she had been expecting a tunnel but was immediately confronted with a cavernous space. She might have been potholing. She was relieved when she felt two pairs of invisible hands attach themselves to Hugh's old leather belt. She moved the torch around trying to see something, anything. "Hello?" she shouted as she shone the torch into the drop. It was screened by a haphazard lattice of twisted gas pipes and wood, splintered like matchsticks. She concentrated on a gap in the chaotic mesh, trying to make out anything in the gloom beyond. An upturned face, a man's, pale and ghostly, seemed to rise out of the darkness like a vision, a prisoner in an oubliette. There might be a body attached to the face, she couldn't be sure.

"Hello?" she said, as if the man might reply, although now she could see that part of his head was missing.

"Anyone?" Miss Woolf said hopefully when she crawled backward out of the hole.

"One dead."

"Easy to recover?"

"No."

The rain made everything even more foul if that were possible, turning the wet brick dust into a kind of glutinous grit. A couple of hours of toiling in these conditions and they were all covered from head to toe in the stuff. It was too disgusting to give any thought to.

There was a shortage of ambulances, traffic had been snarled up by an incident on the Cromwell Road, as had the doctor and nurse who should have been there, and Miss Woolf's extra first-aid training was put to good use. Ursula splinted a broken arm, bandaged a head wound, patched an eye and strapped up Mr. Simms's ankle—he had twisted it on the rough ground. She labeled two unconscious survivors (head injuries, broken femur, broken collarbone, broken ribs, what was probably a crushed pelvis) and several dead (who were easier, they were simply dead) and then double-checked them in case she had labeled them the wrong way round and had posted the dead to the hospital and the living to the mortuary. She also directed numerous survivors to the rest center, and walking wounded to the first-aid post being manned by Miss Woolf.

"Catch Anthony if you can, will you?" she said when she saw Ursula. "Get a mobile canteen down here." Ursula sent Tony off with this errand. Only Miss Woolf called him Anthony. He was thirteen, a Boy Scout and their civil defense messenger boy, hurtling around on the rubble-and-glass-strewn streets on his bike. If Tony were her child, Ursula thought, she would have sent him far away from the nightmare instead of plunging him into the depths of it. He loved it all, needless to say.

After she'd spoken to Tony, Ursula went back through the hole again because someone thought they had heard a sound, but the pale, dead man was as quiet as before. "Hello, again," she said to him. She thought it might be Mr. McColl from the neighboring street. Perhaps he was visiting someone. Unlucky. She was dog tired, you could almost envy the dead their eternal rest.

When she emerged again from the hole the mobile canteen had arrived. She swilled her mouth out with tea and spat out brick dust. "I bet you used to be a real lady," Mr. Palmer laughed. "I'm affronted," Ursula said and laughed. "I think I spit in a very ladylike way." The rescue on the mound was still going on with no sign of any result but the rest of the night was winding down and Miss

Woolf told her to go back to the post and rest. Up on the mound a rope had been called for, to lower someone down, Ursula supposed, or pull someone up, or both. ("A woman, they think," Mr. Durkin said.)

She was all in, could barely put one foot in front of the other. Avoiding the debris as best she could, she had gone only ten yards or so when someone grabbed her by the arm and yanked her backward so hard that she would have fallen over if the same person hadn't kept his tight grip on her and kept her upright. "Watch it, Miss Todd," a voice growled.

"Mr. Bullock?" In the confines of the post Mr. Bullock alarmed her a little, he seemed so unassailable, but, curiously, out here in this benighted place he was harmless. "What is it?" she said. "I'm very tired."

He shone his torch in front of them. "Can you see?" he said.

"I can't see anything."

"That's because there's nothing there." She looked harder. A crater—enormous—a bottomless pit. "Twenty, maybe thirty feet," Mr. Bullock said. "And you nearly walked into it."

He accompanied her back to the post. "You're too tired," he said. He held her arm all the way, she could feel the strength of his muscles behind the grip.

At the post she dropped onto a camp bed and blacked out rather than fell asleep. She woke up when the all-clear sounded at six o'clock. She felt as if she'd slept for days but it had only been three hours.

Mr. Palmer was also there, pottering about making tea. She could imagine him at home, slippers and a pipe, reading his newspaper. It seemed absurd that he should be here. "There you go," he said, handing her a mug. "You should go home, dear," he said, "the rain's stopped," as though it were the rain that had spoiled her night rather than the Luftwaffe.

* * *

Instead of going straight home she returned to the mound to see how the rescue was proceeding. It seemed different in the daylight, the shape of it oddly familiar. It reminded her of something but for the life of her she couldn't think what.

It was a scene of devastation, more or less the whole street gone, but the mound, the original mound, was still its own little hive of activity. It would have made a good subject for a war artist, she thought. *The Diggers on the Mound* would be a good title. Bea Shawcross had been at art school, graduating just as the war started. Ursula wondered if she was moved to depict the war or if she was trying to transcend it.

Very gingerly, she scaled its foothills. One of the rescue squad put out a hand to help her up. A new shift had come on but, from the look of them, the old rescue squad was the one still laboring. Ursula understood. It was hard to leave an incident when somehow you felt you "owned" it.

There was a sudden buzz of excitement around the volcano's crater as the fruits of the night's delicate drudgery finally became apparent. A woman, a rope tied under her armpits (nothing delicate about this stage), was extricated by simply hauling her out of the narrow opening. She was passed by hand down the mound.

Ursula could see that she was almost black with dirt and drifting in and out of consciousness. Broken but alive, if only just. She was loaded into an ambulance waiting patiently at the bottom.

Ursula made her own way down. On the ground, a shrouded body lay waiting for a mortuary van. Ursula removed the cover from the face and found the pale-faced man from last night. In the light of day she could see that it was definitely Mr. McColl from number ten. "Hello, you," she said. He would soon be an old friend. Miss Woolf would have told her to label him but when she looked for her message pad she discovered she had lost it and had nothing to write on. Searching in a pocket she found her lipstick. *Needs must,* she heard Sylvie's voice say.

She thought about writing on Mr. McColl's forehead but that seemed undignified (more undignified than death? she wondered), so instead she unshrouded his arm and then spat on a handkerchief and rubbed off some of the dirt, as if he were a little boy. She wrote his name and address on his arm with the lipstick. Blood red, which seemed fitting really.

"Well, good-bye," she said. "I don't suppose we'll meet again."

Skirting the treacherous crater from last night, she discovered Miss Woolf sitting behind a dining table salvaged from the wreckage, as if she were in an office, telling people what they should do next—where to go for food and shelter, how to get clothes and ration cards and so on. Miss Woolf was still cheerful, yet heaven knows when she had last slept. The woman had iron in her soul, there was no doubt about that. Ursula had grown enormously fond of Miss Woolf, she respected her almost more than anyone else she knew, apart from Hugh perhaps.

The queue was made up of the occupants of a large shelter, many of whom were still emerging, blinking in the daylight like nocturnal animals, and discovering that they no longer had homes to go to. The shelter was in the wrong place, the wrong street, Ursula thought. It took her a few moments to reorientate her brain and realize that all night she had thought herself in a different street.

"They got that woman out," she told Miss Woolf.

"Alive?"

"More or less."

When she finally got back to Phillimore Gardens she found Millie up and dressed. *"Went the day well?"* she said. "There's some tea in the pot," she added, pouring it and handing Ursula a cup.

"Oh, you know," Ursula said, taking the cup. The tea was lukewarm. She shrugged. "Pretty awful. Is that the time? I have to go to work."

The following day she was surprised to find one of Miss Woolf's log entries, written in her clear matron's hand. Sometimes a buff folder would prove to be a mysterious ragbag and Ursula was never clear how some of these things turned up on her desk. *05.00 Interim Incident Report. Situation Report. Casualties 55 to hospital, 30 dead, 3 unaccounted for. Seven houses completely demolished, approximately 120 homeless. 2 NFS crews, 2 AMB, 2 HRPs, 2 LRP, one dog still operating. Work continues.*

Ursula hadn't noticed any dog. It was just one of many incidents across London that night and she picked up a sheaf of them and said, "Miss Fawcett, can you log these." She could barely wait for the tea trolley and elevenses.

They ate lunch outside on the terrace. A potato and egg salad, radishes, lettuce, tomatoes, even a cucumber. "All grown by our mother's own fair hand," Pamela said. It really was the nicest meal Ursula had eaten in a long time. "And to follow there's an apple charlotte, I believe," Pamela said. They were alone at the table. Sylvie had gone to answer the doorbell and Hugh hadn't returned from investigating an unexploded bomb that had, reportedly, fallen in a field on the other side of the village.

The boys were also dining *al fresco*—sprawled on the lawn, eating buffalo stew and succotash (or, in the real world, corned beef sandwiches and hard-boiled eggs). They had erected a fusty old wigwam that had been unearthed in the shed and had been engaged in a lawless game of cowboys and Indians until the arrival of the chuck wagon (or Bridget, bearing a tray).

Pamela's boys were the cowboys and the evacuees were more than happy to be Apaches. "I think it suits their nature better," Pamela said. She had made them cardboard headbands with chicken feathers attached. The cowboys had to make do with Hugh's handkerchiefs tied around their necks. The two Labradors were racing around in a state of canine frenzy at all this excitement, while Gerald, still only ten months old, slept obliviously on a blanket alongside Pamela's dog, Heidi, too sedate for such antics.

"He's some kind of token squaw, apparently," Pamela said. "At least it keeps them quiet. It's like a miracle. It goes rather well with the Indian summer we're having."

"Six boys in one house," Pamela said. "Thank God the school term's started. Boys never flag, you have to keep them busy all the time. I suppose this is a flying visit?"

"'Fraid so."

A precious Saturday to herself that she had sacrificed for the sake of seeing Pammy and the boys. She found Pamela drained whereas Sylvie seemed animated by the war. She had become an unlikely stalwart of the WVS.

"I'm surprised. She doesn't like other women much," Pamela said.

Sylvie now had a large flock of chickens and had stepped up egg production to wartime levels. "The poor things are forced to lay day and night," Pamela said, "you'd think Mother was running an armaments factory." Ursula wasn't sure how you could make a chicken do overtime. "She talks them into it," Pamela laughed. "A regular henwife."

Ursula didn't mention that she had been called to an incident, a house that had been hit, where the occupants had chickens in a makeshift run in the backyard and that when they arrived they had found the chickens, nearly all of them alive, with their feathers blown off. "Ready-plucked," Mr. Bullock had laughed callously. Ursula had seen people with their clothes blown off and trees in the middle of summer stripped of all their leaves, but she didn't mention these things either. She didn't mention wading in effluent from ruptured pipes, certainly didn't mention drowning in that same effluent. Nor did she mention the gruesome sensation of putting your hand on a man's chest and finding that your hand had somehow slipped *inside* that chest. (Dead—something to be thankful for, she supposed.)

Did Harold tell Pamela the things he had seen? Ursula didn't ask, even introducing the topic seemed wrong on such a pleasant day. She thought of all those soldiers from the last war who had come home and never spoken of what they had witnessed in the trenches. Mr. Simms, Mr. Palmer, her own father too, of course.

Sylvie's egg production seemed to be at the heart of some kind of rural black market. No one in the village was particularly short of anything. "It's a barter economy around here," Pamela said. "And barter they do, believe me. That's what she'll be doing now, at the front door."

"At least you're pretty safe here," Ursula said. Were they? She thought of the UXB Hugh had gone to look at. Or the previous week when a bomb had come down in a field belonging to the Hall farm and blown the cows in it to pieces. "A lot of people have been quietly eating beef around here," Pamela said. "Us included, I'm happy to say." Sylvie seemed to think this "terrible episode" had put them on a par with London's suffering. She had returned now and lit up a cigarette rather than finish her food. Ursula ate what she had left on her plate while Pamela took one of Sylvie's cigarettes from the packet and lit up.

Bridget came out and started clearing plates and Ursula jumped up and said, "Oh, no, I'll do that." Pamela and Sylvie remained at the table, smoking in silence, observing the defense of the wigwam from a raiding party of evacuees. Ursula felt rather badly done by. Both Sylvie and Pamela spoke as if they had it hard whereas she was working all day, out on patrol most nights, facing the most awful sights. Only yesterday they had been at an incident where they had worked to free someone while blood dripped on their heads from a body up in the bedroom they couldn't reach because the staircase was knee-deep in broken glass from a huge skylight.

"I'm thinking of going back to Ireland," Bridget said as they rinsed plates. "I have never felt at home in this country."

"Neither have I," Ursula said.

The apple charlotte turned out to be simply stewed apples as Sylvie refused to use precious stale bread on a pudding when it could be fed more usefully to the chickens. Nothing went to waste at Fox Corner. Scraps went to the chickens ("She's thinking of getting a pig," Hugh said in despair), after bones had made stock they were sent for salvage, as was every last tin and glass jar that wasn't being filled with jam or chutney or beans or tomatoes. All the books in the house had been parceled up and taken to the post office to be sent off to the services. "We've already read them," Sylvie said, "so what's the point in keeping them?"

Hugh returned and Bridget grumbled back outside with a plate for him.

"Oh," Sylvie said politely to him, "do you live here? I say, why don't you join us?"

"Really, Sylvie," Hugh said, more sharply than was his usual manner. "You can be such a child."

"If I am then it's marriage that's made me so," Sylvie said.

"I remember that you once said there was no higher calling for a woman than marriage," Hugh said.

"Did I? That must have been in our salad days."

Pamela raised her eyebrows at Ursula and Ursula wondered, when had their parents become so openly quarrelsome? Ursula was going to ask him about the bomb but then, "How's Millie?" Pamela asked brightly to change the subject.

"She's well," Ursula said. "She's a very easygoing person to share digs with. Although I hardly ever see her in Phillimore Gardens. She's joined ENSA. She's in some kind of troupe that goes round factories, entertaining workers in their lunch hour."

"Poor blighters," Hugh laughed.

"With Shakespeare?" Sylvie asked doubtfully.

"I think she turns her hand to anything these days. A bit of singing, comedy, you know." Sylvie didn't look as if she did.

"I have a young man," Ursula blurted out, catching them all unawares, including herself. It was more to lighten the conversation than anything. She should have known better really.

He was called Ralph. He lived in Holborn and he was a new friend, a "pal," that she had met at her German class. He had been an architect before the war and Ursula supposed he would be an architect afterward too. If anyone was still alive, of course. (Could London be erased, like Knossos or Pompeii? The Cretans and the Romans probably went around saying, "We can take it," in the heart of disaster.) Ralph was full of ideas for the rebuilding of the slums as modern towers. "A city for the people," he said, one that would "rise from the ashes of the old like a phoenix, modernist to the core."

"What an iconoclast he sounds," Pamela said.

"He's not nostalgic in the way we are."

"Are we? Nostalgic?"

"Yes," Ursula said. "Nostalgia is predicated on something that never existed. We imagine an Arcadia in the past, Ralph sees it in the future. Both equally unreal, of course."

"Cloud-capped palaces?"

"Something like that."

"But you like him?"

"Yes."

"Have you . . . you know?"

"Really! What kind of a question is that?" Ursula laughed. (Sylvie was at the door again, Hugh was sitting cross-legged on the lawn pretending to be Big Chief Running Bull.)

"It's a very good question," Pamela said.

They hadn't, as it happened. Perhaps if he were more ardent. She thought of Crighton. "And anyway there is so little time for . . ."

"Sex?" Pamela said.

"Well, I was going to say courtship, but yes, sex." Sylvie had returned and was trying to separate the warring factions on the lawn. The evacuees made very unsportsmanlike enemies. Hugh was tied up now with an old washing line. "Help!" he mouthed to Ursula but he was grinning like a schoolboy. It was nice to see him happy.

Before the war her wooing by Ralph (or his by her, perhaps) might have taken the form of dances, the cinema, cozy dinners *à deux* but now, more often than not, they had found themselves at bombsites, like sightseers viewing ancient ruins. The view from the top deck of the number eleven bus was particularly good for this, they had discovered.

It was perhaps due more to a kink in their respective characters than the war itself. After all, other couples managed to keep up the rituals.

They had "visited" the Duveen Gallery at the British Museum, Hammonds next to the National Gallery, the huge crater at the

Bank, so big that they had to build a temporary bridge across it. John Lewis, still smoldering when they arrived, the blackened mannequins from the shop windows strewn across the pavement, their clothes ripped off.

"Do you think we're like ghouls?" Ralph asked and Ursula said, "No, we are witnesses." She supposed she would go to bed with him eventually. There was no great argument to be found against it.

Bridget came out with tea and cake and Pamela said, "I think I'd better untie Daddy."

Have a drink," Hugh said, pouring her a tumbler of malt from the cut-glass decanter that he kept in the growlery. "I find myself in here more and more these days," he said. "It's the only place I can get peace. Dogs and evacuees strictly barred. I worry about you, you know," he added.

"I worry about me too."

"Is it bloody?"

"Dreadfully. But I believe it's the right thing. I think we are doing the right thing."

"A just war? You know the Coles still have most of their family in Europe. Mr. Cole has told me some dreadful things, things that are happening to the Jews. I don't think anyone here really wants to know. Anyway," he said, raising his glass and trying for a cheerful note, "down the hatch. Here's to the end."

It was dark when she left and Hugh walked her down the lane to the station.

"No petrol, I'm afraid," he said, "you should have gone earlier," he added ruefully. He had a stout torch and there was no one to yell at him to put the light out. "I hardly think I'm going to guide in a Heinkel," he said. Ursula told him how most rescue squads had an almost superstitious horror of lights even when they were in the middle of a raid, surrounded by burning buildings and incendiaries and flares. As if a small torch beam would make any difference.

"Knew a chap in the trenches," Hugh said, "lit a match, and Bob's your uncle, a German sniper shot his head clean off. Good chap," he added reflectively, "name of Rogerson, same as the bakers in the village. No relation."

"You never talk about it," Ursula said.

"I'm talking about it now," Hugh said. "Let it be a lesson to you, keep your head below the parapet and your light beneath a bushel."

"I know you don't mean that. Not really."

"I do. I'd rather you were a coward than dead, little bear. Teddy and Jimmy too."

"You don't mean that either."

"I do. Here we are, it's so dark you could walk right by the station and never see it. I doubt that your train will be on time, if there is a train at all. Oh, look, here's Fred. Evening, Fred."

"Mr. Todd, Miss Todd. So you know, this is the last train tonight," Fred Smith said. Fred had long since graduated from fireman to driver.

"It's not really a train," Ursula said, bemused. There was an engine but no carriages.

Fred looked back along the platform to where the carriages should have been, as if he'd forgotten their absence. "Ah, yes, well," he said, "last time they were seen they were hanging off Waterloo Bridge. It's a long story," he added, clearly unwilling to elaborate. Ursula was puzzled as to why the engine should be here *sans* carriages but Fred looked rather grim.

"I won't get home tonight then," Ursula said.

"Well," Fred said, "I've got to get this engine back up to town and I've got a head of steam up and I've got a fireman, old Willie here, so if you want to hop up on the footplate, Miss Todd, I think we can get you back."

"Really?" Ursula said.

"It won't be as clean as riding on the cushions, but if you're game?"

"I certainly am."

The engine was impatient to go so she gave Hugh a quick hug and said, "See you soon," and climbed the steps up to the footplate where she took up her perch on the fireman's seat.

"You will take care, little bear, won't you?" Hugh said. "In London?" He had to raise his voice above the sound of hissing steam. "Promise me?"

"I promise," she shouted. "See you later!"

She twisted round, trying to see him on the dark platform as the train chugged off. She felt a sudden stab of guilt, she had played a rowdy game of hide-and-seek with the boys after supper. Instead she should, as Hugh said, have left when it was still light. Now Hugh would have to walk back in the dark alone along the lane. (She thought suddenly of poor little Angela, all those years ago.) Hugh quickly disappeared into the dark and smoke.

"Well, this *is* exciting," she said to Fred. It didn't cross her mind that she would never see her father again.

Exciting, it was true, but also somewhat terrifying. The engine was a great metal beast roaring through the dark, the raw power of the machine come to life. It shook and rocked as if it were trying to dislodge her from its insides. Ursula had never previously thought about what went on in the cab of an engine. She had imagined, if she had imagined it at all, a relatively serene place—the driver alert to the track ahead, the fireman cheerfully shoveling coal. But instead there was nonstop activity, a continual conferring between fireman and driver over gradients and pressure, the frantic shoveling or the sudden closing down, the continual rackety noise, the almost unbearable heat of the furnace, the filthy soot from the tunnels that didn't seem to be kept out by the metal plates that had been put up to prevent light escaping from the cab. It was so hot! "Hotter than hell," Fred said.

Despite the wartime speed restrictions they seemed to be traveling at least twice as fast as when she traveled in a carriage ("on the cushions," she thought, she must remember that for Teddy who, despite now being a pilot, still harbored his childhood desire to be a train driver).

As they approached London they could see fires in the east and hear the distant pealing of guns but as they neared the marshaling yards and engine sheds it became almost eerily quiet. They slowed to a halt and all was suddenly, thankfully, peaceful.

Fred helped her down from the cab. "There you go, ma'am," he said. "Home sweet home. Well, not quite, I'm afraid." He looked suddenly doubtful. "I would walk you home but we have to put this engine to bed. Will you be all right from here?" They seemed to be in the middle of nowhere, just tracks and points and the looming shadows of engines. "There's a bomb at Marylebone. We're at the back of King's Cross," Fred said, reading her mind. "It's not as bad as you think." He switched on the weakest of torches, it illuminated only a foot or so in front of them. "Have to be careful," he said, "we're a prime target here."

"I'll be absolutely fine," she said, a little more gung ho than she felt. "Don't give me a second thought, and thank you. Good night, Fred." She set off resolutely and immediately tripped over a rail and gave a little cry of distress when she banged her knee hard on the sharp stones of the track.

"Here, Miss Todd," Fred said, helping her up. "You'll never find your way in the dark. Come on, I'll walk you to the gates." He took her arm and set off, steering her as they went, for all the world as if they were on a Sunday stroll along the Embankment. She remembered how she had been rather sweet on Fred when she was younger. It would probably be quite easy to be sweet on him again, she reckoned.

They reached a big pair of wooden gates and he opened a small door set within them.

"I think I know where I am," she said. She had no idea where she was but she didn't want to inconvenience Fred any longer. "Well, thank you again, maybe I'll see you next time I get down to Fox Corner."

"I doubt it," he said. "I start in the AFS tomorrow. Plenty of old codgers like Willie can keep the trains running."

"Good for you," she said, although she was thinking how dangerous the fire service was.

It was the blackest blackout ever. She walked with a hand in front of her face and eventually bumped into a woman who told her where she was. They walked together for half a mile or so. After a few minutes on her own again she heard footsteps behind her and she said, "I'm here," so the owner of the feet didn't walk into her. It was a man, no more than a figure in the dark who went with her as far as Hyde Park. Before the war you would never have dreamed of hooking arms with a complete stranger—particularly a man—but now the danger from the skies seemed so much greater than anything that could befall you from this odd intimacy.

She thought it must be nearly dawn when she got back to Phillimore Gardens but it was barely midnight. Millie, all dressed up, had just returned from an evening out. "Oh, my God," she said when she saw Ursula. "What happened to you? Did you get bombed?"

Ursula looked in the mirror and found that she was smudged all over with soot and coal dust. "What a fright," she said.

"You look like a coal miner," Millie said.

"More like an engine driver," she said, rapidly recounting the night's adventures.

"Oh," Millie said, "Fred Smith, the butcher's boy. He was a bit of a dish."

"Still is, I suppose. I've got eggs from Fox Corner," she said, removing the cardboard box that Sylvie had given her from her bag. The eggs had been nestled in straw, but now they were cracked and broken from the jolting of the track or when she fell in the engine yard.

The next day they managed to make an omelet from the salvaged remains.

"Lovely," Millie said. "You should get home more often."

October 1940

"It's certainly busy tonight," Miss Woolf said. A glorious understatement. There was a full-scale raid in progress, bombers droning overhead, glinting occasionally when they caught a searchlight. HE bombs flashed and roared and the large batteries *banged* and *whuffed* and *cracked*—all the usual racket. Shells whistled or screamed on their way up, a mile a second until they winked and twinkled like stars before extinguishing themselves. Fragments came clattering down. (A few days ago Mr. Simms's cousin had been killed by shrapnel from the ack-acks in Hyde Park. "Shame to be killed by your own," Mr. Palmer said. "Sort of pointless.") A red glow over Holborn indicated an oil bomb. Ralph lived in Holborn but Ursula supposed on a night like this he would be in St. Paul's.

"It's almost like a painting, isn't it?" Miss Woolf said.

"Of the Apocalypse maybe," Ursula said. Against the backdrop of black night the fires that had been started burned in a huge variety of colors—scarlet and gold and orange, indigo and a sickly lemon. Occasionally vivid greens and blues would shoot up where something chemical had caught fire. Orange flames and thick black smoke roiled out of a warehouse. "It gives one a quite different perspective, doesn't it?" Miss Woolf mused. It did. It seemed both grand and terrible compared to their own grubby little labors. "It makes me proud," Mr. Simms said quietly. "Our battling on like this, I mean. All alone."

"And against all odds," Miss Woolf sighed.

They could see all the way along the Thames. Barrage balloons dotted the sky like blind whales bobbing around in the wrong element. They were on the roof of Shell-Mex House. The building was now occupied by the Ministry of Supply, for which Mr. Simms worked, and he had invited Ursula and Miss Woolf to come and "see the view from the top."

"It's spectacular, isn't it? Savage and yet strangely magnificent," Mr. Simms said, as though they were at the summit of one of the Lakeland fells rather than a building on the Strand in the middle of a raid.

"Well, I don't know about *magnificent,* exactly," Miss Woolf said.

"Churchill was up here the other night," Mr. Simms said. "Such a good vantage point. He was fascinated."

Later, when Ursula and Miss Woolf were alone, Miss Woolf said, "You know, I rather had the impression that Mr. Simms was a lowly clerk in the ministry, he's quite a meek soul, but he must be quite senior to have been up on the roof with Churchill." (One of the fire watchers on duty on the roof had said, "Evening, Mr. Simms," with the kind of respect people felt obliged to afford to Maurice, although in the case of Mr. Simms it was less grudgingly given.) "He's unassuming," Miss Woolf said. "I like that in a man." Whereas I prefer assuming, Ursula thought.

"It really is quite a show," Miss Woolf said.

"Isn't it, though?" Mr. Simms said enthusiastically. Ursula supposed that they were all aware how odd it was to be admiring the "show" when they were so painfully conscious of what it meant on the ground.

"It's as if the gods are throwing a particularly noisy party," Mr. Simms said.

"One I would rather not be invited to," Miss Woolf said.

A familiar fearful swishing sound made them all duck for cover but the bombs exploded some way away and although they heard the explosions *bang-bang-bang-bang* they couldn't see what had been hit. Ursula found it very odd to think that up above them there were German bombers being flown by men who, essentially, were just like Teddy. They weren't evil, they were just doing what had been asked of them by their country. It was war itself that was evil, not men. Although she would make an exception for Hitler. "Oh, yes," Miss Woolf said, "I think the man is quite, quite mad."

At that moment, to their surprise, a basket of incendiaries came swooping down and crashed its noisy load right on the ministry's roof. The incendiaries cracked and sparked and the two fire-watchers ran toward them with a stirrup pump. Miss Woolf grabbed a bucket of sand and beat them to it. ("Fast for an old bird" was Mr. Bullock's estimation of Miss Woolf under pressure.)

What if this were the world's last night?" a familiar voice said.

"Ah, Mr. Durkin, you managed to join us," Mr. Simms said affably. "You didn't have any trouble with the man on the door?"

"No, no, he knew I was expected," Mr. Durkin said, as if feeling his own importance.

"Is *anyone* left at the post?" Miss Woolf murmured to no one in particular.

Ursula felt suddenly compelled to correct Mr. Durkin. *"What if this* present *were the world's last night,"* she said. "The word 'present' makes all the difference, don't you think? It makes it seem as if one's somehow in the thick of it, which we are, rather than simply contemplating a theoretical concept. This is it, the end right now, no more shilly-shallying."

"Goodness, so much fuss over one little word," Mr. Durkin said, sounding put out. "However, I obviously stand corrected." Ursula thought that one word could mean a great deal. If any poet was scrupulous with words then it was surely Donne. Donne, himself once the dean of St. Paul's, had been moved down to an ignominious berth in the basement of the cathedral. In death he had survived the Great Fire of London, would he survive this one too? Wellington's tomb was too hefty to move and had simply been bricked up. Ralph had given her a tour—he was on the night watch there. He knew everything there was to know about the cathedral. Not quite the iconoclast that Pamela had presumed.

When they emerged into the bright afternoon, he said, "Shall we try and get a cup of tea somewhere?" and Ursula said, "No, let's go back to your place in Holborn and go to bed with each other." So they had and she had felt rotten because she couldn't help thinking about Crighton while Ralph was politely accommodating his body to hers. Afterward, he had seemed abashed as if he no longer knew how to be with her. She said, "I'm just the same person as I was before we did this," and he said, "I'm not sure I am." And she thought, oh dear God, he's a virgin, but he laughed and said, no, no, that wasn't it—he *wasn't*—it was just that he was so very much in love with her "and now I feel, I don't know . . . sublimated."

"Sublimated?" Millie said. "Sounds like sentimental twaddle to me. He has you on a pedestal, heaven help him when he discovers that you have feet of clay."

"Thank you."

"Is that a mixed metaphor or is it a rather clever image?" Millie, of course had always—

"Miss Todd?"

"Sorry. Miles away."

"We should get back to our sector," Miss Woolf said. "It's strange, but one feels rather safe up here."

"I'm sure we're not," Ursula said. She was right, for a few days later Shell-Mex House was badly hit by a bomb.

She was keeping watch with Miss Woolf in her apartment. Sitting at her big corner window they drank tea and ate biscuits and could have been any two women spending the evening together if it hadn't been for the tolling thunder of the barrage. Ursula learned that Miss Woolf's name was Dorcas (which she had never liked) and that her fiancé (Richard) had died in the Great War. "I still call it that," she said, "and yet this one is the greater. At least this time we have right on our side, I hope." Miss Woolf believed in the war but her religious faith had begun to "crumble" since the start of the bombing. "Yet we must hold fast to what is good and true. But it all seems so random. One wonders about the divine plan and so on."

"More of a shambles than a plan," Ursula agreed.

"And the poor Germans, I doubt many of *them* are in favor of the war—of course one mustn't say that in the hearing of people like Mr. Bullock. But if *we* had lost the Great War and been burdened with great debt just as the world's economy collapsed then perhaps we too would have been a tinderbox awaiting the strike of a flint—a Mosley or some such awful person. More tea, dear?"

"I know," Ursula said, "but they are trying to *kill* us, you know," and as if to demonstrate this fact they heard the *swish* and *wheee* that heralded a bomb heading in their direction and flung themselves with remarkable speed behind the sofa. It seemed unlikely that it would be enough to save them and yet only two nights ago they had pulled a woman out, almost unscathed, from beneath an upturned settee in a house that was otherwise more or less destroyed.

The bomb shook the Staffordshire cow creamers on Miss Woolf's dresser but they agreed it had landed outside their section. They were both finely tuned to the bombs these days.

They were also both terribly down in spirits as Mr. Palmer, the bank manager, had been killed when a delayed-action bomb had detonated at an incident they were attending. The DA had blown him some distance and they found him half buried beneath an iron bedstead. He had lost his spectacles but looked relatively unharmed. "Can you feel a pulse?" Miss Woolf said and Ursula puzzled as to why she was asking when Miss Woolf was much more capable of finding a pulse than she was, but then she realized that Miss Woolf was very upset. "It's different when you know someone," she said, gently stroking Mr. Palmer's forehead. "I wonder where his spectacles are? He doesn't look right without them, does he?"

Ursula couldn't find a pulse. "Shall we move him?" she said. She took his shoulders and Miss Woolf his ankles and Mr. Palmer's body came apart like a Christmas cracker.

I can put more hot water in the pot," Miss Woolf offered. To cheer her up Ursula told her stories about Jimmy and Teddy when they were boys. She didn't bother with Maurice. Miss Woolf was very fond of children, her only regret in life was not having had any. "If Richard had lived, perhaps... but one cannot look backward, only forward. What has passed has passed forever. What is it Heraclitus says? One cannot step in the same river twice?"

"More or less. I suppose a more accurate way of putting it would be 'You can step in the same river but the water will always be new.' "

"You're such a bright young woman," Miss Woolf said. "Don't waste your life, will you? If you're spared."

Ursula had seen Jimmy a few weeks ago. He'd been on two days' leave in London and had bedded down on their sofa in Kensington. "Your baby brother's grown up all handsome," Millie said. Millie was inclined to think all men were handsome, one way or another. She suggested a night on the town and Jimmy readily agreed. He'd been shut up long enough, he said, "Time for some fun." Jimmy had always been good at fun. The night almost didn't get started as there was a UXB on the Strand and they took refuge in the Charing Cross Hotel.

"What?" Millie said to Ursula when they had sat down.

"What what?"

"You've got that funny look on your face, the one you get when you're trying to remember something."

"Or forget something," Jimmy offered.

"I wasn't thinking anything," Ursula said. It had been nothing, just something fluttering and tugging at a memory. A silly thing—it always was—a kipper on a pantry shelf, a room with green linoleum, an old-fashioned hoop bowling silently along. Vaporous moments, impossible to hold on to.

Ursula repaired to the ladies', where she found a girl crying noisily and rather messily. She was heavily made up and her mascara was in runnels down her cheeks. Ursula had noticed her earlier having a drink with an older man—"rather slimy" had been Millie's verdict on him. The girl looked much younger close up. Ursula helped her to repair her makeup and mop up her tears but didn't like to pry into the cause of them. "It's Nicky," the girl offered up voluntarily, "he's a bastard. *Your* young man looks lovely, fancy a foursome? I can get us in the Ritz, into the Rivoli Bar, I know a man on the door."

"Well," Ursula said doubtfully. "The young man's my brother actually, and I don't suppose—"

The girl gave her a rather sharp jab in the ribs and laughed.

"Only joking. You two girls make the most of him, eh?" She offered Ursula a cigarette which she declined. The girl had a gold cigarette case that looked valuable. "A gift," she said, catching Ursula looking at it. She snapped it shut and held it out for inspection. There was a fine engraving of a battleship on the front with the single word "Jutland" beneath. If she were to open it up again she knew she would find the initials "A" and "C" intertwined on the inside of the lid, for "Alexander" and "Crighton." Instinctively, Ursula reached out a hand for it and the girl snatched it back, saying, "Anyway, must be getting back. I'm as right as rain now. You seem a good sort," she added, as if there had been a question over Ursula's character. She stuck out her hand. "My name's Renee by the way, in case we ever bump into each other again, although I doubt we inhabit the same *endroits,* as they say." Her French pronunciation was spot-on, how odd, Ursula thought. She took the proffered hand—hard and warm as if the girl were running a temperature—and said, "Pleased to meet you, I'm Ursula."

The girl—Renee—gave herself one last look of approval in the mirror and said, "*Au revoir* then," and was off.

When Ursula went back into the coffee lounge Renee ignored her completely. "What a strange girl," she said to Millie.

"Been making eyes at me all evening," Jimmy said.

"Well, she's barking up the wrong street there, darling, isn't she?" Millie said, batting her eyelashes at him, ridiculously theatrical.

"*Tree,*" Ursula said. "Barking up the wrong *tree.*"

They went drinking, a merry trio, in all kinds of strange haunts that Jimmy seemed to know about. Even Millie, a seasoned regular of the nightclub scene, professed surprise at some of the places they found themselves in.

"Gosh," Millie said as they left a club in Orange Street to totter homeward, "that was different."

"A strange *endroit,*" Ursula laughed. She was rather drunk. It was such an Izzie word that it was bizarre to hear it from the lips of the Renee girl.

"Promise you won't die," Ursula said to Jimmy as they groped blindly home.

"Do my best," Jimmy said.

October 1940

"Man that is born of woman hath but a short time to live, and is full of misery. He cometh up and is cut down like a flower: he fleeth as it were a shadow, and never continueth in one stay."

A light drizzle was falling. Ursula felt an urge to take out her handkerchief and wipe the wet coffin lid. On the other side of the open grave, Pamela and Bridget were pillars, holding up Sylvie, who seemed to be so consumed with her grief that she could barely stand. Ursula felt her own heart harden and contract with every sob that issued from her mother's chest. Sylvie had been needlessly unkind to Hugh in the last months and now this great affliction seemed like a show. "You're too harsh," Pamela said. "No one can understand what goes on in a marriage, every couple is different."

Jimmy, shipped to North Africa the previous week, had been unable to get compassionate leave but Teddy had turned up at the last minute. Shiningly smart in uniform, he had returned from Canada with his "wings" ("Like an angel," Bridget said) and was stationed in Lincolnshire. He and Nancy clung to each other at the committal. Nancy was vague about her job ("clerical, really") and Ursula thought she recognized the fudge of the Official Secrets Act at work.

The church was packed, most of the village turned out for Hugh and yet there was something odd about the funeral, as if the guest of honor hadn't been able to come. Which he hadn't, of course. Hugh wouldn't have wanted a fuss. He had once said to her, "Oh, you can just put me out with the dustbin, I won't mind."

The service had been the usual sort—reminiscences, and commonplaces—salted with a hefty dose of Anglican doctrine, although Ursula was surprised at how well the vicar seemed to be acquainted with Hugh. Major Shawcross read from the Beatitudes, rather movingly, and Nancy read "one of Mr. Todd's favorite poems," which surprised all the women of his family who didn't know that Hugh had any inclination toward poetry. Nancy had a nice speaking voice (better actually than Millie's which was overly thespian). "Robert Louis Stevenson," Nancy said. "Perhaps appropriate for these testing times:

Tempest tossed and sore afflicted, sin defiled and care oppressed,
Come to me, all ye that labor; come, and I will give ye rest.
Fear no more, O doubting hearted; weep no more, O weeping eye!
Lo, the voice of your redeemer; lo, the songful morning near.

Here one hour you toil and combat, sin and suffer, bleed and die;
In my father's quiet mansion soon to lay your burden by.
Bear a moment, heavy laden, weary hand and weeping eye.
Lo, the feet of your deliverer; lo, the hour of freedom here."

("Tosh, really," Pamela whispered, "but oddly comforting tosh.")

At the graveside, Izzie murmured, "I feel as if I'm waiting for something dreadful to happen, and then I realize it already has."

Izzie had arrived back from California just a few days before Hugh died. She had flown, rather admirably, on a taxing Pan Am flight from New York to Lisbon and from there with BOAC to

Bristol. "I saw two German fighter planes from the window," she said, "I swear I thought they were going to attack us."

She had decided, she said, that as an Englishwoman it was wrong to be sitting out the war amid the orange groves. All that lotus eating wasn't for her, she said (although Ursula would have said it was *exactly* her). She had hoped, like her husband the famous playwright, to be asked to write screenplays for the film industry but had received only one offer, some "silly" costume drama that had been aborted before it left the page. Ursula got the impression that Izzie's script hadn't come up to scratch ("too witty"). She had continued with Augustus, however—*Augustus Goes to War, Augustus and the Salvage Hunt* and so on. It didn't help, Izzie said, that the famous playwright was surrounded by Hollywood starlets and that he was shallow enough to find them fascinating.

"In truth, we simply grew bored with each other," she said. "All couples do eventually, it's inevitable."

Izzie was the one who had found Hugh. "He was in a deckchair on the lawn." The wicker furniture had long since rotted and been replaced by the more quotidian deckchair. Hugh had been put out by the arrival of folding wood and canvas. He would have preferred the wicker chaise longue for a bier. Ursula's thoughts were full of such inconsequences. Easier to deal with, she thought, than the bare fact that Hugh was dead.

"I thought he was asleep out there," Sylvie said. "So I didn't disturb him. A heart attack, the doctor said."

"He looked peaceful," Izzie said to Ursula. "As if he didn't really mind going."

Ursula felt that he probably minded very much but that was no comfort to either of them.

She had little conversation with her mother. Sylvie seemed always to be on the point of leaving the room. "I can't settle," she said. She was wearing an old cardigan of Hugh's. "I'm cold," she said. "I'm so cold," like someone in shock. Miss Woolf would have known what to do with Sylvie. Hot sweet tea probably, and some kind words but neither Ursula nor Izzie felt like offering either. Ursula sensed they were being rather vengeful but they had their own distress to nurse.

"I'll stay on with her for a while," Izzie said. Ursula thought this was a terrible idea and wondered if Izzie wasn't just avoiding the bombs.

"You'd better get yourself a ration book then," Bridget said. "You're eating us out of house and home." Bridget had been very affected by Hugh's death. Ursula came across her crying in the pantry and said, "I'm awfully sorry," as if the loss were Bridget's, not hers. Bridget wiped her tears vigorously on her apron and said, "Must get on with the tea."

Ursula herself stayed only two more days and spent most of the time helping Bridget to sort out Hugh's things. ("I can't," Sylvie said, "I just can't." "Neither can I," Izzie said. "Then it's you and me," Bridget said to Ursula.) Hugh's clothes were so very real it seemed absurd that the man who had worn them had disappeared. Ursula took a suit out of the wardrobe and held it against her body. If Bridget hadn't taken it from her and said, "That's a good suit, someone will be grateful for it," she might have crawled into the wardrobe and given up on life. Bridget's feelings were now locked up tightly, thank goodness. There was a great deal to be said for fortitude in the face of tragedy. Certainly her father would have approved.

They parceled Hugh's clothes up in brown paper and string and the milkman put them on his cart and took them round to the WVS.

Izzie's grief had left her wide open. She trailed around the house after Ursula, trying to conjure up Hugh from memories. They were all doing that, Ursula supposed, it was so impossible to grasp that he had gone forever that they had all started trying to reconstitute him out of thin air, Izzie most of all. "I can't remember the last thing he said to me," Izzie said. "Or what I said to him, for that matter."

"It won't make any difference," Ursula said wearily. Whose bereavement was the greater after all, the daughter or the sister? But then she thought of Teddy.

Ursula tried to remember what her own last words to her father had been. A nonchalant "See you later," she concluded. The final irony. "We never know when it will be the last time," she said to Izzie, platitudinous, even to her own ears. She had seen so much of other people's distress by now that she was numb to it. Except for that one moment when she held his suit (she thought of it—ridiculously—as her "wardrobe moment") she had put Hugh's death away in some quiet place to be taken out later and considered. Perhaps when everyone else had done talking.

"And the thing is—" Izzie said.

"Please," Ursula said. "I've got an awful headache."

Ursula was collecting eggs from the nest boxes when Izzie mooched into the henhouse. The chickens were clucking restlessly, they seemed to miss Sylvie's attentions, the Mother Hen. "The thing is," Izzie said, "there's something I'd like to tell you."

"Oh?" Ursula said, distracted by a particularly broody hen.

"I had a baby."

"What?"

"I'm a mother," Izzie said, seemingly unable to resist sounding dramatic.

"You had a baby in California?"

"No, no," Izzie laughed. "Years ago. I was just a child myself. Sixteen. I had him in Germany, I was sent abroad in disgrace, as you can imagine. A boy."

"Germany? And he was adopted?"

"Yes. Well, more like given away. Hugh saw to it all so I'm sure he found a very good family. But he made him a hostage to fortune, didn't he? Poor Hugh, he was such a rock at the time, Mother would have nothing to do with it. But that's the thing, he must have known the name, where they lived, et cetera." The hens were making a dreadful racket now and Ursula said, "Let's get out of here."

"I always thought," Izzie said, taking Ursula's arm and walking her round to the lawn, "that one day I would talk to Hugh about what he did with the baby and then perhaps try and find him. My son," she added, trying out the word as if for the first time. Tears started to roll down her face. For once, her emotions seemed from the heart. "And now Hugh's gone and I'll never be able to find the baby. He's not a baby, of course, he's the same age as you."

"Me?" Ursula said, trying to grasp this idea.

"Yes. But he's the *enemy.* He might be up there in the sky"—they both automatically glanced up at the blue autumn sky, empty of friend and foe alike—"or fighting in the forces. He might be dead, or going to die if this wretched war goes on." Izzie was sobbing openly now. "He might have been brought up as a *Jew,* for God's sake. Hugh wasn't an anti-Semite, quite the opposite, he was great friends with—your neighbor, what's his name?"

"Mr. Cole."

"You do know what's happening to the Jews in Germany, don't you?"

"Oh, for heaven's sake," Sylvie said, materializing suddenly like a bad fairy. "What are you making such a fuss about?"

"You should come back to London with me," Ursula said to

Izzie. The Luftwaffe's bombs would be more straightforward for her to deal with than Sylvie.

November 1940

Miss Woolf was treating them to a little piano recital. "Some Beethoven," she said. "I'm no Myra Hess, but I thought it would be nice." She was correct on both counts. Mr. Armitage, the opera singer, asked Miss Woolf if she could accompany him if he sang *"Non più andrai"* from *The Marriage of Figaro* and Miss Woolf, particularly game this evening, said she would certainly have a go. It was a rousing performance ("unexpectedly *virile*" was Miss Woolf's verdict) and no one objected when Mr. Bullock (no surprise) and Mr. Simms (quite a surprise) joined in with a rather ribald version.

"I know this one!" Stella said, which was true of the tune but not the words as she sang enthusiastically, "Dum-di-dum, dum-di-dum, dum-di-dum-*dum*," and so on.

Their post had recently been augmented by two wardens. The first, Mr. Emslie, was a grocer and had come from another post, having been bombed out of his house, his shop and his sector. He, like Mr. Simms and Mr. Palmer before him, was a veteran of the previous war. The second addition was in possession of a more exotic background. Stella was one of Mr. Bullock's "chorus girls" and confessed (readily) to being a "striptease artiste" but Mr. Armitage the opera singer said, "We're all artistes here, darling."

"What a bloody fairy that man is," Mr. Bullock muttered, "put him in the army, that would sort him out." "I doubt it," Miss Woolf said. (And it did rather beg the question why the strapping Mr. Bullock himself had not been called up for active service.) "So," Mr. Bullock concluded, "we've got a Yid, a pansy and a tart, sounds like a dirty music-hall joke."

"It is intolerance that has brought us to this pass, Mr. Bullock," Miss Woolf reproved him mildly. They had all been decidedly tetchy—even Miss Woolf—since Mr. Palmer's death. They would be better off saving their grudges for peacetime, Ursula thought. It wasn't just Mr. Palmer's death, of course, but also the lack of sleep and the relentless nightly raids. How long could the Germans keep it up? Forever?

"And, oh, I don't know," Miss Woolf said quietly to her as she made tea, "it's just the general sense of *dirtiness,* as if one will never be clean again, as if poor old London will never be clean again. Everything is so awfully *shabby,* you know?"

It was a relief, therefore, that their little impromptu concert party was good-natured, everyone seemingly in better spirits than of late.

Mr. Armitage followed his Figaro with an unaccompanied and impassioned rendition of *"O mio babbino caro"* ("How versatile he is," Miss Woolf said, "I always thought that was a woman's aria") that they all applauded wildly. Then Herr Zimmerman, their refugee, said he would be honored to play something for them.

"And then are you going to strip, sweetheart?" Mr. Bullock asked Stella, who said, "If you want," and winked in complicity at Ursula. ("Trust me to get stuck with a load of bolshie women," Mr. Bullock complained. Frequently.)

Miss Woolf said, looking worried, "Your violin is *here?*" to Herr Zimmerman. "Is it *safe* here?" He had never brought his instrument to the post before. It was quite valuable, Miss Woolf said, and not just from a monetary point of view, for he had left his entire family behind in Germany and the violin was all he had from his former life. Miss Woolf said that she had had a "harrowing" late night "chat" with Herr Zimmerman about the situation in Germany. "Things are terrible over there, you know."

"I know," Ursula said.

"Do you?" Miss Woolf said, her interest piqued. "Do you have friends there?"

"No," Ursula said. "No one. Sometimes one just *knows,* doesn't one?"

Herr Zimmerman produced his violin and said, "You must forgive me, I am not a soloist," and then announced, almost apologetically, "Bach. Sonata in G. Minor."

"It's funny, isn't it," Miss Woolf whispered in Ursula's ear, "how much German music we listen to. Great beauty transcends all. Perhaps after the war it will heal all too. Think of the Choral Symphony—*Alle Menschen werden Brüder.*"

Ursula didn't answer as Herr Zimmerman had raised his bow, poised for performance, and a deep hush fell as if they were in a concert hall rather than a rundown post. Some of the silence was due to the quality of the performance ("Sublime," Miss Woolf judged it later. "Really beautiful," Stella said) and some out of respect perhaps for Herr Zimmerman's refugee status, but there was also something so spare about the music that it left plenty of room for one to engage deeply with one's thoughts. Ursula found herself dwelling on Hugh's death, his absence more than his death. It was only a fortnight since he died and she was still expecting to see him again. These were the thoughts she had put away for a future time and now the future was suddenly on her. She was relieved not to be embarrassed by tears, instead she was plunged into an awful melancholy. As if sensing her emotions, Miss Woolf reached out and gripped her hand firmly. Ursula could feel that Miss Woolf herself was almost vibrating with emotion.

When the music finished there was a moment of pure, profound silence, as if the world had stopped breathing, and then instead of praise and applause the peace was broken by the purple warning—"bombers within twenty minutes." It was rather odd to think that these alerts were coming from her own Region 5 War Room, sent by the girls in the teleprinter room.

"Come on then," Mr. Simms said, standing up and sighing heavily, "let's get out there." By the time they were out the red alert had come through. Just twelve minutes, if they were lucky, to dragoon people into shelters, the siren at their back.

Ursula never used public shelters, there was something about the crush of bodies, the claustrophobia, that made her skin crawl. They had attended a particularly gruesome incident when a shelter took a direct hit from a parachute mine in their sector. Ursula thought that she would rather die out in the open than trapped like a fox in a hole.

It was a beautiful evening. A crescent moon and her bevy of stars had pierced the black backcloth of night. She thought of Romeo's encomium to Juliet—*It seems she hangs upon the cheek of night/As a rich jewel in an Ethiop's ear.* Ursula was in a poetic mood, some might have said, herself included, overly poetic, as a consequence of her mournful mood. There was no Mr. Durkin to misquote anymore. He had suffered a heart attack during an incident. He was recovering, "thank goodness," Miss Woolf said. She had found time to visit him in hospital and Ursula felt no guilt that she had not. Hugh was dead, Mr. Durkin wasn't, there was little room in her heart for sympathy. Mr. Durkin's position as Miss Woolf's deputy had been taken by Mr. Simms.

The strident noises of war had begun. The boom of the barrage, the raiders' engines overhead with that monotonous, uneven beat that made her nauseous. The gun discharges, the searchlights poking their fingers into the sky, the muted anticipation of dread—all soon spoiled any idea of poetry.

By the time they arrived at the incident everyone was there, the gas and water, the Bomb Disposal Squad, heavy rescue, light rescue, stretcher parties, the mortuary van (a baker's van by day). The road was carpeted with the tangled hoses of an AFS unit as on one side of the street a building was well on fire, with sparks and burning embers spitting out. Ursula thought she had caught a glimpse of Fred Smith, his features briefly illuminated by the flames, but came to the conclusion that she had imagined it.

The rescue squad was as cautious as ever with their torches and lamps even though the fire was blazing away at their backs. Yet, to a man, they had cigarettes hanging from the corners of their mouths, despite the fact that the gas men hadn't cleared the area, not to mention that the presence of the Bomb Disposal Squad indicated a bomb that might go off at any moment. Everyone just got on with the job in hand (needs must), cavalier in the face of possible disaster. Or perhaps some people (and Ursula wondered if she included herself among them nowadays) simply didn't care anymore.

She had an uncomfortable feeling, a premonition perhaps, that things were not going to go well tonight. "It was the Bach," Miss Woolf comforted, "it was unsettling for the soul."

Apparently, the street straddled two sectors and the incident officer in charge was wrangling with two wardens who both claimed dominion over it. Miss Woolf didn't join this little fracas as it turned out that it wasn't their sector at all, but as it was obviously such a major incident she declared that their post should pitch in and get on with it and ignore what anyone said to them.

"Outlaws," Mr. Bullock said, appreciatively.

"Hardly," Miss Woolf said.

The half of the street that wasn't on fire had been badly hit and the acid-raw smell of powdered brick and cordite struck their lungs immediately. Ursula tried to think of the meadow at the back of the copse at Fox Corner. Flax and larkspur, corn poppies, red campion and oxeye daisies. She thought of the smell of new-mown grass and the freshness of summer rain. This was a new diversionary tactic to combat the brutish scents of an explosion. ("Does it work?" a curious Mr. Emslie asked. "Not really," Ursula said.) "I used to think of my mother's perfume," Miss Woolf said. "April Violets. But unfortunately now when I try to remember my mother all I can think of are the bombs."

Ursula offered Mr. Emslie a peppermint. "It helps a little bit," she said.

The closer they got to the incident the worse it proved to be (the opposite, in Ursula's experience, was rarely so).

A grisly tableau was the first thing to greet them—mangled bodies were strewn around, many of them no more than limbless torsos, like tailor's dummies, their clothes blown off. Ursula was reminded of the mannequins she had seen with Ralph in Oxford Street, after the John Lewis bomb. A stretcher-bearer, lacking as yet any live casualties, was picking up limbs—arms and legs that were sticking out of the rubble. He looked as if he was intending to piece the dead together again at a later date. Did someone do that? Ursula wondered. In the mortuaries—try and match people up, like macabre jigsaws? Some people were beyond re-creation, of course—two men from the rescue squad were raking and shoveling lumps of flesh into baskets, another was scrubbing something off a wall with a yard brush.

Ursula wondered if she knew any of the victims. Their apartment in Phillimore Gardens was a mere couple of streets away from here. Perhaps she passed some of them in the morning on her way to work, or had spoken to them in the grocer's or the butcher's.

"Apparently there are quite a lot of people unaccounted for," Miss Woolf said. She had spoken to the Incident Officer, who had been grateful, it seemed, to talk to a warden with common sense. "We're not outlaws anymore, you'll be pleased to hear."

One floor above the man with the yard brush (although there

was no floor) a dress was hanging on a coat hanger from a picture rail. Ursula often found herself more moved by these small reminders of domestic life—the kettle still on the stove, the table laid for a supper that would never be eaten—than she was by the greater misery and destruction that surrounded them. Although when she looked at the dress now she realized that there was a woman still wearing it, her head and legs blown off but not her arms. The capriciousness of high explosives never ceased to surprise Ursula. The woman seemed to have become fused with the wall in some way. The fire was burning so brightly that she could make out a little brooch still pinned to the dress. A black cat, a rhinestone for an eye.

Rubble shifted underfoot as she made her way to the back wall of this same house. There was a woman sitting propped up among the rubble, arms and legs splayed like a rag doll. She looked as if she had been tossed in the air and landed any old how—which was probably the case. Ursula tried to signal to the stretcher-bearer but there was now a stream of bombers passing overhead and no one could hear her above the noise.

The woman was gray with dust so that it was almost impossible to tell how old she was. She had a horrible-looking burn on her hand. Ursula fumbled in her first-aid pack for the tube of Burnol and smeared some of the ointment onto her hand. She didn't know why, the woman looked too far gone to be cured by Burnol. She wished she had some water, it was painful to see how dry the woman's lips were. Unexpectedly, she opened her dark eyes, her lashes pale and spiky with dust, and tried to say something but her voice was so hoarse from the dust that Ursula couldn't understand her. Was she foreign? "What is it?" Ursula asked. She had a feeling the woman was very near death now.

"Baby," the woman rasped suddenly, "where's my baby?"

"Baby?" Ursula echoed, looking around. She could see no sign of any baby. It could be anywhere in the rubble.

"His name," the woman said, guttural and indistinct—she was making a tremendous effort to be lucid—"is Emil."

"Emil?"

The woman nodded her head very slightly as if she were no longer capable of speech. Ursula looked around again for any sign of a baby. She turned back to the woman to ask how big her baby was but her head was lolling limply and when Ursula felt for a pulse she found nothing.

She left the woman there and went in search of the living.

Can you take Mr. Emslie a morphia tablet?" Miss Woolf asked. They could both hear a woman screaming and swearing like a navvy and Miss Woolf added, "To the lady that's making all the noise." A good rule of thumb was that the more noise someone was making the less likely they were to die. This particular casualty sounded as if she were ready to fight her way out single-handed from the wreckage of the house and run round Kensington Gardens.

Mr. Emslie was in the cellar of the house and Ursula had to be lowered down by two men from the rescue squad and then had to worm her way through a barricade of joists and bricks. She was aware that an entire house appeared to be resting precariously on this same barricade. She found Mr. Emslie stretched out almost horizontally next to a woman. Below the waist she was completely trapped by the wreckage of the house but she was conscious and extremely articulate about the distress she was in.

"Soon have you out of here," Mr. Emslie said. "Get you a nice cup of tea, eh? How does that sound? Lovely, eh? Fancy one myself. And here's Miss Todd with something for the pain," he continued soothingly to her. Ursula passed him the tiny morphia tablet. He seemed very good at this, it was hard to imagine him in his grocer's apron, weighing sugar and patting butter.

One wall of the cellar had been sandbagged but most of the sand had spilled out in the explosion and for an alarming hallucinatory second Ursula was on a beach somewhere, she didn't know where, a hoop was bowling along beside her in a brisk breeze, seagulls squawking overhead, and then she was back, just as suddenly, in the cellar. Lack of sleep, she thought, it really was the devil.

"About fucking time," the woman said, greedily taking the morphia tablet. "You'd think you lot were at a fucking tea party." She was young, Ursula realized, and oddly familiar. She was clutching her handbag, a large black affair, as if it were keeping her afloat in the sea of timber. "Have you got a fag, either of you?" With some difficulty, given the awkward space they were in, Mr. Emslie produced a squashed packet of Players from his pocket and then, with even more difficulty, extracted a box of matches. Her fingers tapped restlessly on the leather of the bag. "Take your time," she said sarcastically.

"Sorry," she said after she had drawn deeply on the cigarette. "Being in an *endroit* like this has an effect on the nerves, you know."

"Renee?" Ursula said, astonished.

"What's it to you?" she said, returning to her former churlish self.

"We met in the cloakroom at the Charing Cross Hotel a couple of weeks ago."

"I think you've mistaken me for someone else," she said primly. "People are always doing that. I must have one of those faces."

She took another very long drag on her cigarette and then exhaled slowly and with extraordinary pleasure. "You got any more of those little pills?" she asked. "Good black market price for them, I bet." She sounded woozy, the morphia kicking in, Ursula supposed, but then the cigarette dropped from her fingers and her eyes rolled back in her head. She started to convulse. Mr. Emslie grabbed hold of her hand.

Ursula, glancing at Mr. Emslie, caught sight of a color reproduction of Millais's *Bubbles,* hanging by a piece of tape from a sandbag behind him. It was a picture she disliked, she disliked all the Pre-Raphaelites with their droopy, drugged-looking women. Hardly the time and place for art criticism, she thought. She had become almost indifferent to death. Her soft soul had crystallized. (Just as well, she thought.) She was a sword tempered in the fire. And again she was somewhere else, a little flicker in time. She was descending a staircase, wisteria was blooming, she was flying out of a window.

Mr. Emslie was talking encouragingly to Renee. "Come on, Susie, don't give up on us now. We'll have you out of here in two shakes of a lamb's tail, you'll see. All the lads are working on it. And the girls," he added for Ursula's benefit. Renee had stopped convulsing but now she started to shiver alarmingly and Mr. Emslie, more urgently now, said, "Come on, Susie, come on, girl, stay awake, there's a good girl."

"Her name *is* Renee," Ursula said, "even if she denies it."

"I call 'em all Susie," Mr. Emslie said softly. "I had a little girl by that name. The diphtheria took her off when she was just a littl'un."

Renee gave one last great shudder and life disappeared from her half-open eyes.

"Gone," Mr. Emslie said sadly. "Internal injuries probably." He wrote "Argyll Road" on a label in his neat grocer's hand and tied it to her finger. Ursula removed the handbag from Renee's rather reluctant grasp and shook its contents out. "Her identity card," she said, holding it up for Mr. Emslie to see. "Renee Miller" it said, indisputably. He added her name to the label.

While Mr. Emslie began the complex maneuver of turning round in order to make his way back out of the cellar, Ursula picked up the gold cigarette case that had fallen out with the compact and lipstick and French letters and God knows what else that formed the contents of Renee's handbag. Not a gift but stolen property, she was sure of that. It was a difficult task for Ursula's imagination to place Renee and Crighton in the same room as each other, let alone the same bed. War did indeed make strange bedfellows of people. He must have picked her up in a hotel somewhere, or perhaps a less salubrious *endroit.* Where had she learned her French? She probably only had a couple of words. Not from Crighton anyway, he thought English was quite enough to rule the world with.

She slipped the cigarette case and the identity card into a pocket.

The debris shifted in a heart-stopping way as they were trying to back out of the cellar (they'd given up on trying to turn round). They remained paralyzed, crouched like cats, hardly daring to take a breath for what seemed an eternity. When it felt safe to move again they found that this new arrangement of wreckage had made the barricade impenetrable and they were forced to find another, tortuous exit, creeping on their hands and knees through the shattered base of the building. "Doing my back in, this lark is," Mr. Emslie muttered behind her.

"Doing my knees in," Ursula said. They carried on with weary doggedness. Ursula cheered herself up with the thought of buttered toast, although Phillimore Gardens was out of butter and unless Millie had gone out and queued (unlikely), there was no bread either.

The cellar seemed to be an endless maze and it slowly dawned on Ursula why there were people unaccounted for up above—they were all secretly cached down here. The residents of the house clearly used this part of the cellar as a shelter. The dead here—men, women, children, even a dog—looked as though they had been entombed where they had been sitting. They were completely cloaked in a shell of dust and looked more like sculptures, or fossils. She was reminded of Pompeii or Herculaneum. Ursula had visited both, during her ambitiously titled "grand tour" of Europe. She had been lodged in Bologna where she had made friends with an American girl—Kathy, a gung-ho type—and they had taken a whistle-stop tour—Venice, Florence, Rome, Naples—before Ursula left for France and the final leg of her year abroad.

In Naples, a city that frankly terrified them, they hired a loquacious private guide and spent the longest day of their lives trudging determinedly round the dry, dusty ruins of the lost cities of the Roman Empire beneath a merciless southern sun.

"Oh, gosh," Kathy said as they staggered around a deserted Herculaneum, "I wish no one had ever gone to the bother of digging 'em up." Their friendship had flared brightly for a short time and fizzled out just as quickly when Ursula went to Nancy.

"I have spread my wings and learned how to fly," she wrote to Pamela after leaving Munich and her hosts, the Brenners. "I am quite the sophisticated woman of the world," although she was still little more than a fledgling. If the year had taught her one thing it was that after having endured a succession of private students, the last thing she wanted to do was teach.

Instead, on her return—with an eye to entrance into the civil service—she did an intensive shorthand and typing course in High Wycombe, run by a Mr. Carver who was later arrested for exposing himself in public. ("A meat-flasher?" Maurice said, his lip curling in disgust, and Hugh shouted at him to leave the room and never to use such language in his house again. "Infantile," he said when Maurice had slammed his way out into the garden. "Is he really fit for marriage?" Maurice had come home to announce his engagement to a girl called Edwina, the eldest daughter of a bishop. "Goodness," Sylvie said, "will we have to genuflect or something?"

"Don't be ridiculous," Maurice said and Hugh said, "How dare you speak to your mother like that." It was a terrifically bad-tempered visit all round.)

Mr. Carver hadn't been such a bad sort really. He had been very keen on Esperanto, which had seemed an absurd eccentricity at the time but now Ursula thought it might be a good thing to have a universal language, as Latin had once been. Oh, yes, Miss Woolf said, a common language was a wonderful idea, but utterly utopian. All good ideas were, she said sadly.

Ursula had embarked for Europe a virgin, but didn't return one. She had Italy to thank for that. ("Well, if one can't take a lover in Italy, where can one take one?" Millie said.) He, Gianni, was studying for a doctorate in philology at Bologna University and was more grave and serious than Ursula had expected an Italian to be. (In Bridget's romantic novels, Italians were always dashing but untrustworthy.) Gianni brought a studious solemnity to the occasion and made the rite of passage less embarrassing and awkward than she had feared.

"Gosh," Kathy said, "you are bold." She reminded Ursula of Pamela. In some ways, not in others—not in her serene denial of Darwin, for example. Kathy, a Baptist, was saving herself for marriage but a few months after she returned to Chicago her mother wrote to Ursula to tell her that Kathy had died in a boating accident. She must have gone through her daughter's address book and written to everyone in it, one by one. What an awful task. For Hugh, they had simply put a notice in the *Times*. Poor Kathy had saved herself for nothing. *The grave's a fine and private place, But none I think do there embrace.*

"Miss Todd?"

"Sorry, Mr. Emslie. It's like being in a crypt, isn't it? Full of the ancient dead."

"Yes, and I'd quite like to get out before I turn into one of them."

As she crept gingerly forward, Ursula's knee pressed on something soft and supple and she recoiled, banging her head on a broken rafter, sending a shower of dust down.

"You all right?" Mr. Emslie said.

"Yes," she said.

"Are we stopped for something else?"

"Hang on." She had once stood on a body, recognized the squashy, meat-like quality of it. She supposed she had to look, although God knows she didn't want to. She shone her torch on what seemed to be a dusty mound of material, scraps of stuff—crochet and ribbons, wool—partly impacted into the earth. It could have been the contents of a sewing basket. But it wasn't, of course. She peeled back a layer of wool and then another one as if unwrapping a badly packed parcel or a large, unwieldy cabbage. Eventually a small almost unblemished hand, a small star, revealed itself from the compacted mass. She thought she might have found Emil. Better then that his mother was dead rather than knowing about this, she thought.

"Be careful here, Mr. Emslie," she said over her shoulder, "there's a baby, try to avoid it."

All right?" Miss Woolf asked her when they finally emerged like moles. The fire on the other side of the street was almost out now and the street was murky with the dark, the soot, the filth. "How many?" Miss Woolf asked.

"Quite a few," Ursula said.

"Easy to recover?"

"Hard to say." She handed over Renee's identity card. "There's a baby down there, bit of a mess, I'm afraid."

"There's tea," Miss Woolf said. "Go and get yourself some."

As she made her way, with Mr. Emslie, to the mobile canteen she was amazed to spot a dog cowering in a doorway further up the street.

"I'll catch up with you," she said to Mr. Emslie. "Get a mug for me, will you? Two sugars."

It was a small nondescript terrier, whimpering and shaking with fear. Most of the house behind the doorway had disappeared and Ursula wondered if this had been the dog's home, that it was hoping for some kind of safety or protection and couldn't think of anywhere else to go. As she approached it, however, it ran off up the street. Dratted dog, she thought, chasing after it. Eventually she caught up with it, snatching it up in her arms before it had a chance to run again. It was trembling all over and she held it close, talking in soothing tones to it, rather as Mr. Emslie had to Renee. She pressed her face against its fur (disgustingly dirty but then so was she). It was so small and helpless. "Slaughter of the Innocents," Miss Woolf said the other day when they heard of a school in the East End taking a direct hit. But wasn't everyone innocent? (Or were they all guilty?) "That buffoon Hitler certainly isn't," Hugh said, the last time they had talked, "it's all down to him, this whole war." Was she really never going to see her father again? A sob escaped from her and the dog whined in fear or sympathy, it was hard to say. (There wasn't a single member of the Todd family—apart from Maurice—who didn't attribute human emotions to dogs.)

At that moment there was a tremendous noise behind them, the dog tried to bolt again and she had to hold it tightly. When she turned round she saw the gable wall of the building that had been on fire falling down, almost in one piece, the bricks rattling onto the ground in a brutish fashion, just reaching the WVS canteen.

Two of the women from the WVS were killed, as was Mr. Emslie. And Tony, their messenger boy who had been scooting past on his bicycle, but not scooting fast enough unfortunately. Miss Woolf knelt down on the jagged, broken brick, oblivious to the pain, and took hold of his hand. Ursula crouched down by her side.

"Oh, Anthony," Miss Woolf said, unable to say anything else. Her hair was escaping from its usual neat bun, making her look quite wild, a figure from a tragedy. Tony was unconscious—a terrible head wound, they had dragged him roughly from beneath the collapsed wall—and Ursula felt they should say something encouraging and not let him be aware of how upset they were. She remembered he was a Scout and started talking to him about the joys of the outdoors, pitching a tent in a field, hearing a running stream nearby, collecting sticks for a fire, watching the mist rise in the morning as breakfast cooked in the open. "What fun you'll have again when the war is over," she said.

"Your mother will be awfully glad to see you come home tonight," Miss Woolf said, joining the charade. She stifled a sob with her hand. Tony made no sign of having heard them and they watched as he slowly turned a deathly pale, the color of thin milk. He had gone.

"Oh, God," Miss Woolf cried. "I can't bear it."

"But bear it we must," Ursula said, wiping away the snot and the tears and filth from her cheeks with the back of her hand and thinking how once this exchange would have been the other way round.

Bloody fools," Fred Smith said angrily, "what did they go and park the bloody canteen there for? Right next to the gable end?"

"They didn't know," Ursula said.

"Well, they should have bloody realized."

"Well then someone should have bloody told them," Ursula said, her anger flaring up suddenly. "Like a bloody fireman, for instance."

It was first light by now and they heard the all-clear sound.

"I thought I saw you earlier, and then I decided I'd imagined you," Ursula said, making peace. He was angry because they were dead, not because they were stupid.

She felt as though she were in a dream, drifting away from reality. "I'm as good as dead," she said, "I have to sleep before I go mad. I live just round the corner," she added. "Lucky it wasn't our apartment. Lucky, too, that I ran after this dog." One of the rescue squad had given her a piece of rope to tie round the dog's neck and she had hitched it to a charred post sticking out of the ground. She was reminded of the arms and legs the stretcher-bearer had been harvesting earlier. "I suppose the circumstances dictate that's what I should call him—Lucky, even though it's a bit of a cliché. He saved me, you know, I would have been drinking my tea there if I hadn't gone after him."

"Bloody fools," he said again. "Shall I walk you home?"

"That would be nice," Ursula said but she didn't lead him "round the corner" to Phillimore Gardens, instead they walked wearily hand in hand, like children, the dog trotting beside them, along Kensington High Street, almost deserted at this time in the morning, with only a slight diversion for a gas main that was on fire.

Ursula knew where they were going, it was inevitable somehow.

In Izzie's bedroom there was a framed picture on the wall opposite her bed. It was one of the original illustrations from the first *Adventures of Augustus,* a line drawing depicting a cheeky boy and his dog. It verged on the cartoon—the schoolboy cap, the gob-stoppered cheek of Augustus and the rather idiotic-looking Westie who bore no resemblance to the real-life Jock.

The picture was very much at odds with how Ursula remembered this room before it was mothballed—a feminine boudoir, full of ivory silks and pale satins, expensive cut-glass bottles and enameled brushes. A lovely Aubusson carpet had been rolled up tightly and tied with thick string and left against a wall. There had been one of the lesser Impressionists on another of the walls, acquired, Ursula suspected, more for the way it matched the decor than for any great love of the artist. Ursula wondered if Augustus was there to remind Izzie of her success. The Impressionist had been packed away somewhere safe but this illustration seemed to have been forgotten about, or perhaps Izzie didn't care so much for it anymore. Whatever the reason, it had sustained a diagonal crack from one corner of the glass to the other. Ursula recalled the night that she and Ralph had been in the wine cellar, the night that Holland House was bombed, perhaps it had sustained the damage then.

Izzie had, sensibly, chosen not to stay at Fox Corner with "the grieving widow" as she referred to Sylvie, as "we shall fight like cats and dogs." Instead, she had decamped to Cornwall, to a house on top of a cliff ("like Manderley, terrifically wild and romantic, no Mrs. Danvers though, thank goodness"), and had started "churning out" an *Adventures of Augustus* comic strip for one of the popular dailies. How much more interesting, Ursula thought, if she had allowed her Augustus to grow up, as Teddy had done.

A buttery, unseasonal sun was trying hard to nudge its way through the thick velvet curtains. *Why dost thou thus, / Through windows, and through curtains, call on us?* she thought. If she could go back in time and take a lover from history it would be Donne. Not Keats, the knowledge of his untimely death would color everything quite wretchedly. That was the problem with time travel, of course (apart from the impossibility)—one would always be a Cassandra, spreading doom with one's foreknowledge of events. It was quite wearyingly relentless but the only way that one could go was forward.

She could hear a bird singing outside the window, even though it was November now. The birds were probably as confounded as people were by the Blitz. What did all the explosions do to them? Kill a great many, she supposed, their poor hearts simply giving out with shock or the little lungs bursting with the pressure waves. They must drop from the sky like weightless stones.

"You look thoughtful," Fred Smith said. He was lying, one arm behind his head, smoking a cigarette.

"And you look strangely at home," she said.

"I am," he grinned and leaned forward to wrap his arms around her waist and kiss the back of her neck. They were both filthy, as if they had toiled all night in a coal mine. She recalled how sooty they had been when she had journeyed on the footplate that night. The last time she had seen Hugh alive.

There was no hot water in Melbury Road, no water at all, nor electricity, everything turned off for the duration. In the dark, they had crawled under the dustsheet on Izzie's bare mattress and fallen into a sleep that mimicked death. Some hours later they had both woken up at the same time and made love. It was the kind of love (lust, to be honest about it) that survivors of disasters must practice—or people who are anticipating disaster—free of all restraint, savage at times and yet strangely tender and affectionate. A strain of melancholy ran through it. Like Herr Zimmerman's Bach sonata it had unsettled her soul, disjointed her brain and body. She tried to recall another line from Marvell, was it in "A Dialogue Between the Soul and Body," something about *bolts of bones* and fetters and manacles, but it wouldn't come. It seemed harsh when there was so much soft skin and flesh in this abandoned (in all ways) bed.

"I was thinking of Donne," she said. "You know—*Busy old foole, unruly Sun.*" No, she supposed, he probably didn't know.

"Oh?" he said, indifferently. Worse than indifferent really.

She was taken off guard by the sudden memory of the gray ghosts in the cellar and of kneeling on the baby. Then for a second she was somewhere else, not a cellar in Argyll Road, not in Izzie's bedroom in Holland Park but some strange limbo. Falling, falling—

"Cigarette?" Fred Smith offered. He lit another one from the stub of his first and handed it to her. She took it and said, "I don't really smoke."

"I don't really pick up strange women and fuck them in posh houses."

"How Lawrentian. And I'm not strange, we've known each other since we were children, more or less."

"Not like this."

"I should hope not." She was beginning to dislike him already. "I have no idea what time it is," she said. "But I can offer you some very good wine for breakfast. It's all there is, I'm afraid."

He looked at his wristwatch and said, "We've missed breakfast. It's three o'clock in the afternoon."

The dog nudged itself through the door, its paws pitter-pattering on the bare wooden boards. It jumped on the bed and gazed intently at Ursula. "Poor thing," she said, "it must be starving."

Fred Smith? What was he like? Do tell!"

"Disappointing."

"How? In bed?"

"Gosh, no, not that at all. I've never... like that, you know. I think I thought it would be romantic. No, that's the wrong word, a silly word. 'Soulful' perhaps."

"Transcendent?" Millie offered.

"Yes, that's it. I was looking for transcendence."

"I imagine it finds you, rather than the other way round. It's a tall order for poor old Fred."

"I had an *idea* of him," Ursula said, "but the idea wasn't him. Perhaps I wanted to fall in love."

"And instead you had jolly good sex. Poor you!"

"You're right, unfair of me to expect. Oh, God, I think I was an awful snob with him. I was quoting Donne. Am I a snob, do you think?"

"Awful. You do reek, you know," Millie said cheerfully. "Cigarettes, sex, bombs, God knows what else. Shall I run you a bath?"

"Oh, yes, please, that would be lovely."

"And while you're at it," Millie said, "you can take that ruddy dog in the bath with you. He smells to high heaven. But he is kinda cute," she said, imitating an American accent (rather badly).

Ursula sighed and stretched. "You know I really, *really* have had enough of being bombed."

"The war's not going away anytime soon, I'm afraid," Millie said.

May 1941

Millie was right. The war went on and on. Into that dreadfully cold winter, and then there was the awful raid on the City at the end of the year. Ralph had helped to save St. Paul's from the fire. All those lovely Wren churches, Ursula thought. They had been built because of the last Great Fire, now they were gone.

The rest of the time they did the things that everyone of their kind did. They went to the cinema, they went dancing, they went to the lunchtime concerts in the National Gallery. They ate and drank and made love. Not "fucking." That wasn't Ralph's style at all. "Very Lawrentian," she had said coolly to Fred Smith—she supposed he had no idea what she was talking about—but the crude word had jarred her horribly. She was used to hearing it at incidents, it was a vital constituent of the heavy rescue squad's vocabulary, but not in the context of *herself.* She tried saying the word to her bathroom mirror but it felt shameful.

Where on earth did you get it?" he asked.

Ursula had never seen him so dumbfounded. Crighton weighed the gold cigarette case in his hand. "I thought I'd lost it forever."

"Do you really want to know?"

"Yes, of course I do," Crighton said. "Why the mystery?"

"Does the name Renee Miller mean anything to you?"

He frowned, thinking, and then shook his head. "Afraid not. Should it?"

"You probably paid her for sex. Or bought her a nice dinner. Or just gave her a good time."

"Oh, *that* Renee Miller," he laughed. After a couple of beats of silence, he said, "No, really, the name means nothing. And anyway, I don't think I have ever *paid* a woman for sex."

"You're in the navy," she pointed out.

"Well, not for a very, *very* long time then. But thank you," he said, "you know the cigarette case meant a lot to me. My father—"

"Gave it to you after Jutland, I know."

"Am I boring you?"

"No. Shall we go somewhere? The bolt hole? Shall we *fuck?*"

He burst out laughing. "If you want."

He cared less "for the niceties" these days, Crighton said. These niceties seemed to include Moira and the girls and they soon resumed their furtive affair, although less furtive now. He was so different to Ralph that it hardly seemed like infidelity to her. ("Oh, what a beguiling argument!" Millie said.) She hardly saw Ralph now anyway and it seemed to be a mutual kind of waning.

Teddy read the words on the Cenotaph. "*The Glorious Dead.* Do you think they are? Glorious?" he asked.

"Well, they're certainly dead," Ursula said. "But the 'glorious' bit is to make *us* feel better, I expect."

"I don't suppose the dead care about anything much," Teddy said. "I think when you're dead you're dead. I don't believe there's anything beyond, do you?"

"I might have done before the war," Ursula said, "before I saw a lot of dead bodies. But they just look like so much rubbish, thrown away." (She thought of Hugh saying, "Just put me out with the dustbin.") "It doesn't seem as though their souls have flown."

"I shall probably die for England," Teddy said. "And there's a chance you might too. Is it a good enough cause?"

"I think so. Daddy said he would rather we were alive and cowards than dead and heroes. I don't think he meant it, it wasn't his style to shirk responsibility. What is it that it says on the war memorial in the village? *For your tomorrow we gave our today.* That's what your lot are doing, giving up everything, it doesn't seem right somehow."

Ursula thought that she would rather die for Fox Corner than "England." For meadow and copse and the stream that ran through the bluebell wood. Well, that *was* England, wasn't it? The blessed plot.

"I am a patriot," she said. "I surprise myself with it although I don't know why. What does it say on Edith Cavell's statue, the one by St. Martin's church?"

"Patriotism is not enough," Teddy supplied.

"Do you think that really?" she said. "Personally, I think it's more than enough." She laughed and they linked arms as they walked down Whitehall. There was quite a lot of bomb damage. Ursula pointed out the Cabinet War Rooms to Teddy. "I know a girl who works in there," she said. "Sleeps in a cupboard, more or less. I don't like bunkers and cellars and basements."

"I worry about you a lot," Teddy said.

"I worry about *you,*" she said. "And none of that worrying has done either of us any good." She sounded like Miss Woolf.

Teddy ("Pilot Officer Todd") had survived his time in an OTU in Lincolnshire, flying Whitleys, and in a week or so was due to join a Heavy Conversion Unit in Yorkshire and learn how to fly the new Halifaxes and start his first tour of duty proper.

Only half of all bomber crews survived their first tour of duty, the girl in the Air Ministry said.

("Aren't the odds the same every time they go up?" Ursula said. "Isn't that how odds work?"

"Not in the case of bomber crews," the girl from the Air Ministry said.)

Teddy was walking her back to the office after lunch, she had taken a long hour. Things were not quite as hectic as they had been.

They had planned on somewhere swanky but ended up in a British Restaurant and dined on roast beef and plum pie and custard. The plums were tinned, of course. They enjoyed all of it though.

"All those names," Teddy said, gazing at the Cenotaph. "All those lives. And now again. I think there is something wrong with the human race. It undermines everything one would like to believe in, don't you think?"

"No point in thinking," she said briskly, "you just have to get on with life." (She really was turning into Miss Woolf.) "We only have one after all, we should try and do our best. We can never get it *right,* but we must *try.*" (The transformation was complete.)

"What if we had a chance to do it again and again," Teddy said, "until we finally did get it right? Wouldn't that be wonderful?"

"I think it would be exhausting. I would quote Nietzsche to you but you would probably thump me."

"Probably," he said amiably. "He's a Nazi, isn't he?"

"Not exactly. Do you still write poetry, Teddy?"

"Can't find the words anymore. Everything I try feels like sublimation. Making pretty images out of war. I can't find the heart of it."

"The dark, beating, bloody heart?"

"Maybe you should write," he laughed.

She wasn't going out on patrol while Teddy was here, Miss Woolf had taken her off the roster. The raids were more sporadic now. There had been bad raids in March and April and they seemed all the worse for their having had a bit of a breather from the bombs. "It's funny," Miss Woolf said, "one's nerves are wired so tightly when it's relentless that it's almost easier to deal with."

There had been a decided lull at Ursula's post. "I think Hitler's more interested in the Balkans," Miss Woolf said.

"He's going to turn on Russia," Crighton told her with some authority. Millie was on another ENSA tour and they had the Kensington apartment to themselves.

"But that would be madness."

"Well, the man *is* insane, what do you expect?" He sighed and said, "Let's not talk about the war." They were drinking Admiralty whisky and playing cribbage, like an old married couple.

Teddy walked her as far as Exhibition Road and her office and said, "I imagined your 'War Room' would be a rather grand affair—porticos and pillars—not a bunker."

"Maurice has the porticos."

As soon as she was inside she was pounced upon by Ivy Jones, one of the teleprinter operators just coming on duty, who said, "You're a dark horse, Miss Todd, keeping that gorgeous man a secret," and

Ursula thought, this is what comes of being too friendly with staff. "Must dash," she said, "I'm a slave to the Daily Situation Report."

Her own "girls," Miss Fawcett and her ilk, filed and collated and sent the buff folders to her so she could formulate summaries, daily, weekly, hourly sometimes. Daily logs, damage logs, situation reports, it was never-ending. Then it all had to be typed up and put into more buff folders and be signed off by her before the folders went on their journey to someone else, someone like Maurice.

"We're just cogs in a machine really, aren't we?" Miss Fawcett said to her and Ursula said, "But remember, without the cog there is no machine."

Teddy took her out for a drink. It was a warm evening and the trees were full of blossom, so that for a moment it felt as if the war was over.

He didn't want to talk about flying, didn't want to talk about the war, didn't even want to talk about Nancy. Where was she? Doing something she couldn't talk about, apparently. It seemed nobody wanted to talk about anything anymore.

"Well, let's talk about Dad," he said, and so they did and it felt as if Hugh had finally been given the wake he deserved.

Teddy caught the train to Fox Corner next morning, he was staying there for a few nights, and Ursula said, "Will you take another evacuee with you?" and handed over Lucky. He was in the apartment all day while she was at work but she often took him to the post if she was on duty and everyone treated him as a kind of mascot. Even Mr. Bullock, who did not seem like a dog lover, would come in with scraps and bones for him. There were times when the dog seemed to eat better than she did. Nonetheless, London in wartime was no place for a dog, she told Teddy. "All the noise, it must be terribly alarming."

"I like this dog," he said, rubbing the dog's head. "He's a very straightforward kind of dog."

She went to Marylebone to see them off. Teddy tucked the little dog under one arm and gave her a salute, sweet and ironic at the same time, and boarded the train. She felt almost as sad to see the dog go as she did Teddy.

They had been too optimistic. There was a terrible raid in May.

Their apartment in Phillimore Gardens was hit. Neither Ursula nor Millie was there, thank goodness, but the roof and the upper story were destroyed. Ursula simply moved back in and camped there for a while. The weather wasn't bad and in some peculiar way she quite enjoyed it. There was still water, although no electricity, and someone at work lent her an old tent so she slept under canvas. The last time she had done that was in Bavaria when she had accompanied the Brenner girls on their BDM summer expedition to the mountains and she had shared a tent with Klara, the eldest. They had grown very fond of each other but she hadn't heard from Klara since war was declared.

Crighton was sanguine about her *al fresco* arrangement, "like sleeping on deck under the stars in the Indian Ocean." She felt a pang of envy, she hadn't even been to Paris. The Munich–Bologna–Nancy axis had defined the edges of the unknown world for her. She and her friend Hilary—the girl who slept in a cupboard in the War Rooms—had planned a holiday cycling through France but war had put paid to it. Everyone was stuck on the little sceptered isle. If you thought about it too much you could start to feel quite claustrophobic.

When Millie returned from her ENSA tour she declared that Ursula had gone quite mad and insisted they find somewhere else and so they moved to a shabby place in Lexham Gardens that she knew she would never learn to like. ("You and I could live together if you wanted," Crighton said. "A little apartment in Knightsbridge?" She demurred.)

That wasn't the worst, of course. Their post received a direct hit in the same raid and both Herr Zimmerman and Mr. Simms were killed.

At Herr Zimmerman's funeral a string quartet, all refugees, played Beethoven. Unlike Miss Woolf, Ursula thought that it would take more than the great composer's works to heal their wounds. "I saw them play at the Wigmore Hall before the war," Miss Woolf whispered. "They're very good."

After the funeral Ursula went in search of Fred Smith at his fire station and they rented a room in a nasty little hotel near Paddington. Later, after the sex, which had the same compelling quality as before, they were rocked to sleep by the sound of trains coming and going and she thought, he must miss that sound.

When they woke he said, "I'm sorry I was a complete arse last time we were together." He went and found them two mugs of tea—she supposed he had charmed someone in the hotel, it didn't seem like the kind of place to have a kitchen, let alone room service. He did have a natural charm, the same way that Teddy did, it came from a kind of straightness in their character. Jimmy's charm was different, more dishonest perhaps.

They sat up in bed and drank their tea and smoked cigarettes. She was thinking of Donne's poem, "The Relic," one of her favorites—the *bracelet of bright hair about the bone*—but refrained from quoting, considering how badly it had gone down last time. How funny though it would be if the hotel were hit and no one understood who they were or what they were doing here together, conjoined in a bed that had become their grave. She had grown very morbid since Argyll Road. It had affected her in a different way to other incidents. What would she like on her headstone? she wondered idly. "Ursula Beresford Todd, stalwart to the last."

"Do you know your problem, Miss Todd?" Fred Smith said, stubbing out his cigarette. He took hold of her hand and kissed her open palm and she thought, seize this moment because it's a sweet one and said, "No, what's my problem?" and never did find out because the siren went off and he said, "Fuck, fuck, fuck, I'm supposed to be on duty," and threw his clothes on, gave her a hasty kiss and flew out of the room. She never saw him again.

She was reading through the Home Security War Diary for the awful early hours of 11 May—

Time of Origin—0045. Form of Origin—Teleprinter. In or Out—In. Subject—South West India Dock Office, wrecked by H.E. And Westminster Abbey, the Houses of Parliament, De Gaulle's headquarters, the Mint, the Law Courts. She had seen St. Clement Dane's herself—blazing like a monstrous chimney fire on the Strand. And all the ordinary people living their precious ordinary lives in Bermondsey, Islington, Southwark. The list went on and on. She was interrupted by Miss Fawcett, who said, "Message for you, Miss Todd," and handed her a piece of paper.

A girl she knew who knew a girl in the fire service had sent her a copy of an AFS report, a little note added, "He was a friend of yours, wasn't he? Sorry..."

Frederick Smith, fireman, crushed when a wall fell while attending a fire in Earl's Court.

Bloody fool, Ursula thought. Bloody, bloody fool.

November 1943

It was Maurice who brought the news to her. His arrival coincided with that of the tea trolley bearing elevenses. "Can I have a word?" he said.

"Do you want tea?" she said, getting up from her desk. "I'm sure we can spare you some of ours, vastly inferior though it must be to the Orange Pekoe and Darjeeling and whatnot that you get in your place. And I can't imagine our biscuits can hold a candle to yours." The tea lady hovered, unimpressed by this exchange with an interloper from the airy regions.

"No, no tea, thank you," he said, surprisingly polite and subdued. It struck her that Maurice was nearly always simmering with suppressed fury (what a strange condition to live your life in), in some ways he reminded her of Hitler (she had heard that Maurice ranted at secretaries. "Oh, that's so unfair!" Pamela said, "but it does make me laugh").

Maurice had never got his hands dirty. Never been to an incident, never pulled apart a man like a cracker or knelt on a matted bundle of fabric and flesh that had once been a baby.

What was he doing here, was he going to start pontificating again about her love life? It never crossed her mind that he was here to say, "I'm sorry to have to tell you this" (as if this were an official announcement) "but Ted has caught one, I'm afraid."

"What?" She couldn't untangle the meaning. Caught what? "I don't know what you mean, Maurice."

"Ted," he said. "Ted's plane has gone down."

Teddy had been safe. He was "tour expired" and was instructing at an OTU. He was a squadron leader with a DFC (Ursula, Nancy and Sylvie had been to the Palace, bursting with pride). And then he had asked to go back on ops. ("I just felt I had to.") The girl she knew in the Air Ministry—Anne—told her that one in forty aircrew would survive a second tour of duty.

"Ursula?" Maurice said. "Do you understand what I'm saying to you? We've lost him."

"Then we'll find him."

"No. Officially he's 'missing in action.'"

"Then he's not *dead,*" Ursula said. "Where?"

"Berlin, a couple of nights ago."

"He bailed out, and he's been taken captive," Ursula said, as if stating a fact.

"No, I'm afraid not," Maurice said. "He went down in flames, no one got out."

"How do you *know* that?"

"He was seen, an eyewitness, a fellow pilot."

"Who? Who was it who saw him?"

"I don't know." He was beginning to grow impatient.

"No," she said again. And then again, no. Her heart started racing and her mouth went dry. Her vision blurred and dotted, a pointillist painting. She was going to faint.

"Are you all right?" she heard Maurice say. Am I all right, she thought, am I all right? How could I be all right?

Maurice's voice sounded a long way off. She heard him shout for a girl. A chair was brought, a glass of water fetched. The girl said, "Here, Miss Todd, put your head between your knees." The girl was Miss Fawcett, a nice girl. "Thank you, Miss Fawcett," she murmured.

"Mother took it very hard as well," Maurice said, as if bemused by grief. He had never cared for Teddy the way they all did.

"Well," he said, patting her on the shoulder, she tried not to flinch, "I'd better get back to the office, I expect I'll see you at Fox Corner," almost casually, as if the worst part of the conversation were over and they could get on with some blander chat.

"Why?"

"Why what?"

She sat up straight. The water in the glass trembled slightly. "Why will you see me at Fox Corner?" She sensed Miss Fawcett still hovering solicitously.

"Well," Maurice said, "a family gathers on occasions such as these. After all, there won't be a funeral."

"There won't?"

"No, of course not. No body," he said. Did he shrug? Did he? She was shivering, she thought she might faint after all. She wished someone would hold her. Not Maurice. Miss Fawcett took the glass from her hand. Maurice said, "I'll give you a lift down, of course. Mother sounded most awfully cut up," he added.

He'd told her on the telephone? How dreadful, she thought numbly. It hardly mattered, she supposed, how one was given the news. And yet to have it conveyed by Maurice in his three-piece pinstripe, leaning against her desk, now inspecting his fingernails, waiting for her to say she was fine and he could go...

"I'm fine. You can go."

Miss Fawcett brought her hot, sweet tea and said, "I'm so sorry, Miss Todd. Would you like me to come home with you?"

"That's very kind of you," Ursula said, "but I'll be all right. Do you think you could fetch my coat for me?"

He was twisting his uniform cap in his hands. They were making him nervous, just by their very presence. Roy Holt was drinking beer from a big dimpled-glass beer mug, great drafts with every mouthful as if he were very thirsty. He was Teddy's friend, the witness to his death. The "fellow pilot." Last time Ursula was here, visiting Teddy, was the summer of '42 and they had sat in the beer garden and eaten ham sandwiches and pickled eggs.

Roy Holt was from Sheffield where the air still belonged to Yorkshire but was perhaps not so good. His mother and sister had been killed in the awful raids in December 1940 and he said he wasn't going to rest until he'd dropped a bomb directly on Hitler's head.

"Good for you," Izzie said. She had a peculiar way with young men, Ursula noticed, both maternal and flirtatious at the same time (where once she had simply been flirtatious). It was rather disturbing to watch.

As soon as she heard the news, Izzie left Cornwall posthaste for London and then commandeered a car and a fistful of petrol coupons from a "man she knew" in the government, to take them both to Fox Corner, and then, onward, to make the journey to Teddy's airfield. ("You'll never manage the train," she said, "you'll be far too upset.") "Men she knew" was generally a euphemism for ex-lovers ("What did you do to get this?" a surly garage owner had asked when they filled up at his pumps on the road north. "I slept with someone terribly important," Izzie said sweetly).

Ursula hadn't seen Izzie since Hugh's funeral, since her astonishing confession that she had a child, and Ursula thought that perhaps she should reintroduce the subject on the drive to Yorkshire (awkward to do) as Izzie had been so upset and presumably had no one else to talk to about it. But when Ursula said, "Do you want to talk more about your baby?" Izzie said, "Oh, *that,*" as if it was something trivial. "Forget I ever said anything, I was just being morbid. Shall we stop for tea somewhere, I could demolish a scone, couldn't you?"

Yes, they had gathered at Fox Corner, and no, there was no "body." By then the status of Teddy and his crew had changed from "missing in action" to "missing, presumed dead." There was no hope, Maurice said, they must stop thinking there was hope. "There's always hope," Sylvie said.

"No," Ursula said, "sometimes there really isn't." She thought of the baby. Emil. What would Teddy look like? Blackened and charred and shrunk like an ancient piece of wood? Maybe there was nothing left at all, no "body." Stop it, stop it, stop it. She breathed. Think of him as a little boy, playing with his planes and trains—no, actually that was worse. Much worse.

"It's hardly a surprise," Nancy said grimly. They were sitting outside on the terrace. They had drunk rather too much of Hugh's good malt. It felt peculiar to be drinking his whisky when he himself was gone. It was kept in a cut-glass decanter on the desk in the growlery, and it was the first time she had drunk it when it had not been poured by his own hand. ("Fancy a drop of the good stuff, little bear?")

"He'd flown so many missions," Nancy said, "the odds were against him."

"I know."

"He expected it," Nancy said. "Accepted it, even. They have to, all those boys do. I sound sanguine, I know," she continued quietly, "but my heart is split in two. I loved him so much. *Love* him so much. I don't know why I use the past tense. It's not as if love dies with the beloved. I love him *more* now because I feel so damn sorry for him. He'll never marry, never have children, never have the wonderful life that was his birthright. Not all this," she said, waving a hand around to indicate Fox Corner, the middle class, England in general, "but because he was such a *good* man. Sound and true, like a great bell, I think." She laughed. "Silly, I know. I know you're the one that understands. And I can't cry, I don't even want to cry. My tears would never do justice to this loss."

Nancy hadn't wanted to talk, Teddy had once said, and now she wanted to do nothing but talk. Ursula herself had barely talked but wept continually. She had hardly gone an hour without finding the tears streaming unstoppably. Her eyes were still swollen and sore. Crighton had been awfully good, cradling her and shushing her, making endless cups of tea, tea purloined from the Admiralty, she supposed. He didn't deliver platitudes, didn't say everything will be all right, time will heal, he's in a better place—none of that rubbish. Miss Woolf was wonderful too. She came and sat with Crighton, never questioning who he might be, and held her hand and stroked her hair and allowed her to be an inconsolable child.

That was over now, she thought, finishing her whisky. Now there was just nothing. A vast, featureless landscape of nothing, as far as the horizon of her mind. *Despair behind, and Death before.*

"Will you do something for me?" Nancy asked.

"Yes, of course. Anything."

"Will you find out if there's a scrap of hope that he's alive? Surely there's a chance, however small, that he's been taken captive. I thought you might know someone in the Air Ministry—"

"Well, I know a girl..."

"Or perhaps Maurice knows someone, someone who could be... definitive." She stood up suddenly, swaying slightly from the whisky, and said, "I have to go."

We've met before," Roy Holt said to her.

"Yes, I came up to visit last year," Ursula said. "I stayed here, at the White Hart, they have rooms, but I suppose you know that. This is 'your' pub, isn't it? The aircrew, I mean."

"We were all drinking in the bar, I remember," Roy Holt said.

"Yes, it was a very jolly evening."

Maurice was no use, of course, but Crighton had tried. It was always the same story. Teddy had gone down in flames, no one jumped.

"You were the last person who saw him," Ursula said.

"I don't think about it really," Roy Holt said. "He was a good bloke, Ted, but it happens all the time. They don't come back. They're there at tea and they're not there at breakfast. You mourn for a minute and then you don't think about it. Do you know the statistics?"

"I do actually."

He shrugged and said, "Maybe after the war, I don't know. I don't know what you want me to tell you."

"We just want to know," Izzie said gently, "that he didn't bail out. That he is dead. You were under attack, in extreme circumstances, you may not have seen the whole sorry drama play itself out."

"He's dead, believe me," Roy Holt said. "The whole crew. The plane was ablaze from front to back. Most of them were probably already dead. I could see him, the planes were very close, still in formation. He turned and looked at me."

"Looked at you?" Ursula said. Teddy in the last moments of his life, knowing he was going to die. What did he think about—the meadow and the copse and the stream that ran through the bluebell wood? Or the flames that were going to consume him—another martyr for England?

Izzie reached out and clutched her hand. "Steady," she said.

"I was only bothered about getting away from them. His kite was going out of control, I didn't want the bugger crashing into us." He shrugged. He looked incredibly young and incredibly old at the same time.

"You should get on with your lives," he said rather roughly, and then less so added, "I brought the dog. I thought you might want it back."

Lucky was asleep at Ursula's feet, he had been deliriously happy when he saw her. Teddy hadn't left him at Fox Corner, instead he had taken him north, to his base. "With a name and a reputation like his, what else could I do?" he wrote. He sent a photograph of his crew, lounging in old armchairs, Lucky sitting proudly to attention on Teddy's knee.

"But he's your lucky mascot," Ursula protested. "Isn't that like asking for bad luck? Giving him away, I mean."

"We've had nothing but bad luck since Ted went," Roy Holt

said morosely. "He was Ted's dog," he added more kindly, "faithful unto the last, as they say. He's pining something rotten, you should take him. The lads can't bear to see him hanging around on the airfield, waiting for Ted to come back. It just reminds them that it's probably going to be them next time."

I can't bear it," she said to Izzie as they drove away. It was what Miss Woolf said when Tony died, she remembered. Just how much *was* one expected to bear? The dog was sitting contentedly on her lap, sensing something of Ted about her perhaps. Or so she liked to think.

"What else is there to do?" Izzie said.

Well, one could kill oneself. And she might have done but how could she leave the dog behind? "Is that ridiculous?" she asked Pamela.

"No, not ridiculous," Pamela said. "The dog is all that's left of Teddy."

"Sometimes I feel that he *is* Teddy."

"Now that *is* ridiculous."

They were sitting on the lawn at Fox Corner, two weeks or so after VE Day. ("Now begins the hard part," Pamela said.) They hadn't celebrated. Sylvie had marked the day by taking an overdose of sleeping pills. "Selfish, really," Pamela said. "After all, we're her children too."

She had embraced the truth in her own inimitable way and lain down on Teddy's childhood bed and swallowed a whole bottle of pills, washed down with the last of Hugh's whisky. It was Jimmy's room too, but he hardly seemed to count to her. Now two of Pamela's boys slept in that room and played with Teddy's old train set, laid out in Mrs. Glover's old attic room.

They lived at Fox Corner, the boys and Pamela and Harold. To everyone's surprise, Bridget made good on her threat to return to Ireland. Sylvie, enigmatic to the last, left behind her own version of a delayed action bomb. When her will was read they discovered that there was some money—stocks and shares and so on, Hugh wasn't a banker for nothing—that was to be divided equally but Pamela was to inherit Fox Corner. "But why me?" Pamela puzzled. "I was no more of a favorite than anyone else."

"None of us were favorites," Ursula said, "only Teddy. I suppose if he'd lived she would have left it to him."

"If he'd lived she wouldn't be dead."

Maurice was incandescent, Jimmy was not back from the war and when he did return he didn't seem to care too much one way or the other. Ursula wasn't entirely indifferent to the snub (a small word for a rather large betrayal) but she thought Pamela was the perfect person to live at Fox Corner and she was glad it was in her stewardship. Pamela wanted to sell and divide the proceeds but Harold, to Ursula's surprise, talked her out of it. (And it was difficult to talk Pamela out of things.) Harold had always disliked Maurice, for his politics as much as his person, and Ursula suspected this was his way of punishing Maurice for, well, for being Maurice. It was all rather Forsterian and it would have been easy to develop a grudge but Ursula chose not to.

The contents were to be divided among them. Jimmy wanted nothing, he already had his passage booked to New York and a job secured in an advertising agency, thanks to someone he met during the war, "A man I know," he said, an echo of Izzie. Maurice, on the other hand, having decided not to contest the will ("even though I would be successful, of course"), sent a removal van and virtually looted the house. None of the contents of the van ever turned up in Maurice's own house so they presumed he sold them, out of spite more than anything. Pamela cried for Sylvie's nice rugs and ornaments, the Regency Revival dining table, some very good Queen Anne chairs, the grandfather clock in the hall, "things we grew up with," but it seemed to appease Maurice and prevented an outbreak of total war.

Ursula took Sylvie's little carriage clock. "I want nothing else," she said. "Only to be always welcome here."

"As you will be. You know that."

February 1947

Wonderful! Like a Red Cross package, she wrote and propped the old postcard of the Brighton Pavilion on the mantelpiece next to Sylvie's clock, next to Teddy's photograph. She would put the card in with the afternoon post tomorrow. It would take forever to reach Fox Corner, of course.

A birthday card for her had made it through eventually. The weather had prevented the usual celebration at Fox Corner, instead Crighton had taken her to the Dorchester for dinner, by candlelight when the electricity gave out halfway through the meal.

"Very romantic," he said. "Just like old times."

"I don't remember us being particularly romantic," she said. Their affair had ended with the war but he had remembered her birthday, a fact which touched her more deeply than he knew. For a present he gave her a box of Milk Tray ("It's not much, I'm afraid").

"Admiralty supplies?" she quizzed and they both laughed. When she got home she ate the whole box in one go.

Five o'clock. She took her plate over to the sink to join the other unwashed dishes. The gray ash was a blizzard in the dark sky now and she pulled the flimsy cotton curtain to try to make it disappear. It tugged hopelessly on its wire and she gave up before she brought the whole thing down. The window was old and ill-fitting and let in a piercing draft.

The electricity went and she fumbled for the candle on the mantelpiece. Could it get any worse? Ursula took the candle and the whisky bottle to bed, climbed under the covers still in her coat. She was so tired. Being hungry and cold created the most awful lethargy.

The flame on the little Radiant fire quivered alarmingly. Would it be so very bad? *To cease upon the midnight with no pain.* There were worse ways. Auschwitz, Treblinka. Teddy's Halifax going down in flames. The only way to stop the tears was to keep drinking the whisky. Good old Pammy. The flame on the Radiant flickered and died. The pilot light too. She wondered when the gas would come back on. If the smell would wake her, if she would get up and relight it. She hadn't expected to die like a fox frozen in its den. Pammy would see the postcard, know that she'd been appreciated. Ursula closed her eyes. She felt as though she had been awake for a hundred years and more. She really was so very, very tired.

Darkness began to fall.

She woke with a start. Was it daytime? The light was on but it was dark. She had been dreaming she was trapped in a cellar. She climbed out of the bed, she still felt quite drunk and realized it was the wireless that had woken her. The power was back on in time for the shipping forecast.

She fed the meter and the little Radiant popped back into life. She hadn't gassed herself after all then.

June 1967

This morning the Jordanians had opened fire on Tel Aviv, the BBC reporter said, now they were shelling Jerusalem. He was standing on a street, in Jerusalem presumably, she hadn't really been paying attention, the noise of artillery fire in the background, too far away to be any danger to him, yet his faux-battle-dress attire and style of reportage—excited, yet solemn—hinted at unlikely heroics on his part.

Benjamin Cole was a member of the Israeli parliament now. He had fought in the Jewish Brigade at the end of the war and then joined the Stern Gang, in Palestine, to fight for a homeland. He had been such an upstanding kind of boy that it had been odd to think of him becoming a terrorist.

They had met up for a drink during the war but it was an awkward encounter. The romantic impulses of her girlhood had long since faded whereas his relative indifference to her as a member of the female sex had turned on its head. She had barely finished her (weak) gin and lemon when he suggested they "go somewhere."

She was indignant. "Do I look like a woman of such easy virtue?" she asked Millie afterward.

"Well, why not?" Millie shrugged. "We could be killed by a bomb tomorrow. *Carpe diem* and all that."

"That seems to be everyone's excuse for bad behavior," Ursula grumbled. "If people believed in eternal damnation they might not be seizing the day quite so much." She had had a bad day at the office. One of the filing clerks had received the news that her boyfriend's ship had gone down and she had had hysterics and an important piece of paper had been lost in the sea of buff which caused more anguish, if of a different order, so she had not seized the day with Benjamin Cole, despite him pressing his suit urgently on her. "I've always sensed something between us, haven't you?" he said.

"Too late, I'm afraid," she said, gathering up her bag and coat. "Catch me next time round." She thought about Dr. Kellet and his theories of reincarnation and wondered what she would like to come back as. A tree, she thought. A fine big tree, dancing in the breeze.

The BBC turned its attention to Downing Street. Someone or other had resigned. She had heard tittle-tattle in the office but couldn't be bothered to listen.

She was eating her supper—a Welsh rarebit—off a tray on her knee. She usually ate like this in the evening. It seemed ridiculous to lay the table and put out vegetable dishes and table mats and all the other paraphernalia of dining for just one person. And then what? Eat in silence, or hunched over a book? There were people who saw TV dinners as the beginning of the end of civilization. (Did her robust defense of them indicate that perhaps she was of the same mind?) They obviously didn't live on their own. And really the beginning of the end of civilization had happened a long time ago. Sarajevo perhaps, Stalingrad at the latest. There were some who would say the end started at the beginning, in the Garden.

And what was so wrong with watching television anyway? One couldn't go out to the theater or the cinema (or the pub for that matter) every night. And when one lived alone one's only conversation inside the home was with a cat, which tended to be a one-sided affair. Dogs were different, but she hadn't had a dog since Lucky. He had died in the summer of '49, of old age, the vet said. Ursula had always thought of him as a young dog. They buried him at Fox Corner and Pamela bought a rose, a deep red, and planted it for his headstone. The garden at Fox Corner was a veritable graveyard for dogs. Wherever you went, there would be a rose bush with a dog beneath, although only Pamela could remember who was where.

And what was the alternative to television anyway? (She wasn't letting the argument die, even though it was with herself.) A jigsaw puzzle? Really? There was reading, of course, but one didn't always want to come in from a trying day at work, full of messages and memos and agendas, and then tire one's eyes out with even more words. The wireless, records, all good of course, but still *solipsistic* in some way. (Yes, she was protesting too much.) At least with television one didn't have to *think*. Not such a bad thing.

Her supper was later than usual because she had been attending her own retirement do—not unlike attending one's own funeral, except one could walk away afterward. It had been a modest affair, no more than drinks at a local pub, but pleasant and she was relieved it had finished early (where others might feel badly done by). She didn't officially retire until Friday but she thought it would be easier on the staff to get the whole thing over and done with on a weekday. They might resent giving up their Friday evening.

Beforehand, in the office, they had presented her with a carriage clock engraved *To Ursula Todd, in gratitude for her many years of loyal service.* Ye gods, she thought, what a tedious epitaph. It was a traditional kind of gift, and she didn't have the heart to say that she already had one, and a much better one at that. But they also gave her a pair of (good) tickets for the Proms, for a performance of Beethoven's Choral, which was thoughtful—she suspected the hand of Jacqueline Roberts, her secretary.

"You've helped to pave the way for women in senior positions in the civil service," Jacqueline said quietly to her, handing her a Dubonnet, her preferred drink these days. Not *that* senior unfortunately, she thought. Not in *charge*. That was still for the Maurices of this world.

"Well, cheers," she said, chinking her glass against Jacqueline's port and lemon. She didn't drink a great deal, the occasional Dubonnet, a nice bottle of burgundy at the weekend. Not like Izzie, still inhabiting the house in Melbury Road, wandering through its many rooms like a dipsomaniac Miss Havisham. Ursula visited her every Saturday morning with a bag of groceries, most of which seemed to get thrown out. No one read *The Adventures of Augustus* anymore. Teddy would have been relieved and yet Ursula was sorry, as if another little part of him had been forgotten by the world.

"You'll probably get a gong now, you know," Maurice said, "now that you're retired. An MBE or something." He had been knighted in the last round of honors. ("God," Pamela said, "what's the country coming to?") He had sent each member of his family a framed photograph of himself, bowing beneath the Queen's sword in the ballroom of the Palace. "Oh, the hubris of the man," Harold laughed.

Miss Woolf would have been the perfect companion for the Choral at the Albert Hall. The last time Ursula had seen her was there, at the Henry Wood seventy-fifth-birthday concert in '44. She was killed a few months later in the Aldwych rocket attack. Anne, the girl from the Air Ministry, was killed in the same attack. She had been with a group of female colleagues who were sunbathing on the ministry roof, eating their packed lunches. It was a long time ago now. And it was yesterday.

Ursula was supposed to have met up with her in St. James's Park at lunchtime. The Air Ministry girl—Anne—had something to tell her, she said, and Ursula had wondered if it might be some information about Teddy. Perhaps they had found wreckage or a body. She had long since accepted that he was gone forever, they would have heard by now if he was a POW or had managed to escape to Sweden.

At the last minute fate had intervened in the shape of Mr. Bullock, who had turned up unexpectedly on her doorstep the previous evening (how did he know her address?) to ask if she would accompany him to court to vouch for his good character. He was on trial for some kind of black-market fraud, which came as no surprise. She was his second choice, after Miss Woolf, but Miss Woolf had been made a District Warden and was responsible for the lives of two hundred and fifty thousand people, all of whom ranked higher in her estimation than Mr. Bullock. His black-market "escapades" had turned her against him in the end. None of the wardens that Ursula had known from her post were still there by '44.

She was rather alarmed to find that Mr. Bullock was appearing at the Old Bailey, she had presumed it was some petty misdemeanor fit only for the magistrates' court. She had waited, in vain, all morning to be called and just as the court got up to recess for lunch she had heard the dull thud of an explosion but hadn't known it was the rocket wreaking carnage in the Aldwych. Mr. Bullock, needless to say, was found innocent of all charges.

Crighton had gone with her to Miss Woolf's funeral. He was a rock, but in the end he had stayed in Wargrave.

"Their bodies are buried in peace; but their name liveth for evermore," the minister boomed as if the congregation was hard of hearing. "Ecclesiasticus 44:14." Ursula didn't think that was really true. Who would remember Emil or Renee? Or poor little Tony, Fred Smith. Miss Woolf herself. Ursula had forgotten the names of most of the dead already. And all those airmen, all those young lives lost. When Teddy died he was CO of his squadron and he was only twenty-nine. The youngest CO was twenty-two. Time had accelerated for those boys, as it had for Keats.

They sang "Onward, Christian Soldiers," Crighton had a rather fine baritone that she had never heard before. She felt sure that Miss Woolf would have preferred Beethoven to the rousing battle hymns of the church.

Miss Woolf had hoped that Beethoven might heal the postwar world but the howitzers pointed at Jerusalem seemed like the final defeat of her optimism. Ursula was now the same age as Miss Woolf had been at the outbreak of the last war. Ursula had thought of her as old. "And now *we're* old," she said to Pamela.

"Speak for yourself. And you're not even sixty yet. That's not old."

"Feels like it."

Once her children were grown enough and no longer needed her constant oversight, Pamela had become one of those women who did good works. (Ursula was not critical, quite the opposite.) She became a JP and eventually a chief magistrate, was active on charity boards and last year had won a place on the local council as an independent. And there was the house to keep up (although she had "a woman who does") and the enormous garden. In 1948, when the NHS was born, Harold had taken over Dr. Fellowes's old practice. The village had grown around them, more and more houses. The meadow gone, the copse too, many of the fields from Ettringham Hall's home farm had been sold off to a developer. The Hall itself was empty and rather neglected. (There was talk of a hotel.) The little railway station had been given the death sentence by Beeching and had closed two months ago, despite a heroic campaign to keep it going, spearheaded by Pamela.

"But it is still lovely around here," she said. "A five-minute walk and you're in open countryside. And the wood hasn't been touched. Yet."

Sarah. She would take Sarah to the Proms with her. Pamela's reward for patience—a daughter born in 1949. She was to take up a place at Cambridge after the summer—science, she was clever, an all-rounder like her mother. Ursula was enormously fond of

Sarah. Being an aunt had helped to seal over the empty cavern in her heart from Teddy's loss. She thought often these days—if only she had had a child of her own... She had had affairs over the years, albeit nothing too thrilling (the fault, the lack of "commitment," mainly on her own side, of course), but she had never been pregnant, never been a mother or a wife, and it was only when she realized that it was too late, that it could never be, that she understood what it was that she had lost. Pamela's life would go on after she was dead, her descendants spreading through the world like the waters of a delta, but when Ursula died she would simply end. A stream that ran dry.

There had been flowers too, also Jacqueline's doing, Ursula suspected. They had survived the evening in the pub, thank goodness. Lovely pink lilies that were now sitting on her sideboard, the scent perfuming the room. The living room was west-facing and soaked up the evening sun. It was still light outside, the trees in the shared gardens in their best new leaf. It was a very nice apartment, near the Brompton Oratory, and she had put all of the money that Sylvie left her into the purchase of it. There was a small kitchen and bathroom, both modern, but she had eschewed the modern when it came to decor. After the war she had bought simple, tasteful antique furniture when no one wanted that kind of thing. There were fitted carpets throughout in a pale willow green and the curtains were the same fabric as the suite covers—a Morris print, one of the more subtle ones. The walls were painted in a pale-lemon emulsion that made the place seem light and airy even on rainy days. There were a few pieces of Meissen and Worcester—sweetmeat dishes and a garniture set—also picked up cheaply after the war, and she always had flowers, Jacqueline knew that.

The only crude note was sounded by a pair of Staffordshire foxes, garish orange creatures, each of which had a dead rabbit drooping in its jaws. She had picked them up in Portobello Road for next to nothing years ago. They had made her think of Fox Corner.

"I love coming here," Sarah said. "You have such nice things and it's always so clean and tidy, nothing like home."

"You can afford to be clean and tidy when you live on your own," Ursula said, but flattered by the compliment. She supposed she should make a will, leave her worldly goods to someone. She would like Sarah to have the apartment but the memory of the debacle over Fox Corner when Sylvie died made her hesitate. Should one show such outright favoritism? Possibly not. She must divide her estate between all seven of her nieces and nephews, even the ones she didn't like or never saw. Jimmy, of course, had never married or had children. He lived in California now. "He's a homosexual, you do know that, don't you?" Pamela said. "He's always had those proclivities." It was information, not censure, but there was still a mild prurience in her words and the faintest trace of smugness, as if she were better able to cope with liberal views. Ursula wondered if she knew about Gerald and *his* "proclivities."

"Jimmy's just Jimmy," she said.

The previous week, she had come back from lunch and found a copy of the *Times* sitting on her desk. It had been neatly folded so that only the obituaries were on show. Crighton's had a photograph of him in uniform, taken before she knew him. She had forgotten how handsome he was. It was quite a big piece, mentioned Jutland, of course. She learned that his wife Moira had "predeceased" him, that he was a grandfather several times over and a keen golfer. He had always hated golf, she wondered when his conversion had taken place. And who on earth had left the *Times* on her desk? Who all these years later would have thought to tell her? She had no idea and supposed she never would now. There was a time during their affair, when he had been in the habit of leaving notes on her desk, rather smutty little *billets-doux* that appeared as if by magic. Perhaps the same invisible hand had delivered the *Times,* all these years later.

"The Man from the Admiralty is dead," she said to Pamela. "Of course, everyone dies eventually."

"Well, now there's a truism," Pamela laughed.

"No, I mean, everybody one has ever known, including oneself, will be dead one day."

"Still a truism."

"Amor fati," Ursula said. "Nietzsche wrote about it all the time. I didn't understand, I thought it was 'a more fatty.' Do you remember I used to see a psychiatrist? Dr. Kellet? He was a philosopher at heart."

"Love of fate?"

"It means acceptance. Whatever happens to you, embrace it, the good and the bad equally. Death is just one more thing to be embraced, I suppose."

"Sounds like Buddhism. Did I tell you that Chris is going to India, to some kind of monastery, a retreat, he calls it. He's found it hard to settle to anything since Oxford. He's a 'hippie' apparently." Ursula thought Pamela was very indulgent with her third son. She found Christopher rather creepy. She tried to think of another, more generous word but failed. He was one of those people who stared at you with a meaningful smile on their face, as if he was somehow intellectually and spiritually superior, when the fact was he was simply socially inept.

The scent of the lilies, lovely when they had first gone in water, was beginning to make her feel slightly sick. The room was stuffy. She should open a window. She stood up in order to carry her plate through to the kitchen and was immediately struck by a blinding pain in her right temple. She had to sit down again and wait for it to pass. She had been getting these pains for weeks now. An acute pain and then a thick, buzzy head. Or sometimes just a straightforward horrible pounding ache. She thought it might be high blood pressure but, after a battery of tests, the hospital's verdict was neuralgia, "probably." She was given strong painkillers and told that she was bound to feel better once she had retired. "You'll have time to relax, take it easy," the doctor said in the special tone of voice reserved for the elderly.

The pain passed and she stood up, gingerly.

What *would* she do with her time? She wondered about moving to the country, a little cottage, partaking in village life, perhaps somewhere in the vicinity of Pamela. She imagined St. Mary Mead, or Miss Read's Fairacre. Perhaps *she* could write a novel? It would certainly fill in the time. And a dog, time to get another dog. Pamela kept Golden Retrievers, a succession of them, one replacing another and quite indistinguishable to Ursula's eye.

She washed up her meager pots. Thought she might have an early night, make some Ovaltine and take her book to bed with her. She was reading Greene's *The Comedians.* Perhaps she did need to rest more but lately she had become rather afraid of sleep. She was having such vivid dreams that sometimes she found it hard to accept that they weren't real. Several times recently she had believed that something outlandish had really happened to her when it quite obviously, logically, had not. And falling. She was always falling in her dreams, down staircases and off cliffs, it was a most unpleasant sensation. Was this the first sign of dementia? The beginning of the end. The end of the beginning.

From her bedroom window she could see a fat moon rising. Keats's Queen-Moon, she thought. *Tender is the night.* The pain in her head came back. She ran a glass of water from the tap and swallowed a couple of painkillers.

* * *

But if Hitler had been killed, before he became Chancellor, it would have stopped all this conflict between the Arabs and the Israelis, wouldn't it?" The Six-Day War, as they had called it, had ended, the Israelis decisively victorious. "I mean, I do understand why the Jews wanted to create an independent state and defend it vigorously," Ursula continued, "and I always felt sympathy for the Zionist cause, even before the war, but, on the other hand, I can also understand why the Arab states are so aggrieved. But if Hitler had been unable to implement the Holocaust—"

"Because he was dead?"

"Yes, because he was dead. Then support for a Jewish homeland would have been weak at best..."

"History is all about 'what ifs,'" Nigel said. Pamela's first-born, her favorite nephew, was a history tutor at Brasenose, Hugh's old college. She was treating him to lunch in Fortnum's.

"It is nice to have an intelligent conversation with someone," she said. "I've been on holiday in the south of France with my friend Millie Shawcross, have you met her? No? Not that she's called that anymore, she's been through several husbands, each one wealthier than the last."

Millie, the war bride, had hotfooted it back from America just as soon as she could, her new family were "cowpokes," she reported. She had gone back to "treading the boards" and had several disastrous relationships before she struck gold in the form of the scion of an oil family in tax exile.

"She lives in Monaco. It's *incredibly* small, I had no idea. She's really quite stupid these days. I'm wittering, aren't I?"

"Not at all. Shall I pour you some water?"

"People who live on their own do tend to witter. We live without restraint, verbal at any rate."

Nigel smiled. He wore serious spectacles and had Harold's lovely smile. When he took his spectacles off to clean them on his napkin he looked very young.

"You look so young," Ursula said. "You *are* young, of course. Am I sounding like a dotty old aunt?"

"God, no," he said. "You're just about the smartest person I know."

She buttered a bread roll, feeling rather chuffed at this compliment. "I heard someone say once that hindsight was a wonderful thing, that without it there would be no history."

"They're probably right."

"But think how different things would be," Ursula persisted. "The Iron Curtain would probably not have fallen and Russia wouldn't have been able to gobble up Eastern Europe."

"Gobble?"

"Well, it *was* just pure greed. And the Americans might not have recovered from the Depression so quickly without a war economy and consequently not exerted so much influence on the postwar world—"

"An awful lot of people would still be alive."

"Well, yes, obviously. And the whole cultural face of Europe would be different because of the Jews. And think of all those displaced people, shuffling from one country to another. And Britain would still have an empire, or at least we wouldn't have lost it so precipitately—I'm not saying being an imperial power is a good thing, of course. And we wouldn't have bankrupted ourselves and had such an awful time recovering, financially and psychologically. And no Common Market—"

"Which won't let us in anyway."

"Think how strong Europe would be! But perhaps Goering or Himmler would have stepped in. And everything would have happened in just the same way."

"Perhaps. But the Nazis were a marginal party almost up until they took power. They were all fanatical psychopaths, but none of them had Hitler's charisma."

"Oh, I know," Ursula said. "He was extraordinarily charismatic.

People talk about charisma as if it were a good thing, but really it's a kind of glamour—in the old sense of the word, casting a spell, you know? I think it was the eyes, he had the *most* compelling eyes. If you looked in them you felt you were putting yourself in danger of believing—"

"You *met* him?" Nigel asked, astonished.

"Well," Ursula said. "Not exactly. Would you like dessert, dear?"

July and hot as Hades as she walked back from Fortnum's, along Piccadilly. Even the colors seemed hot. Everything was bright these days—bright young things. There were girls in her office whose skirts were like pelmets. Young people these days had so much *enthusiasm* for themselves, as if they had invented the future. This was the generation the war had been fought for and now they bandied the word "peace" around glibly as though it were an advertising slogan. They had not experienced a war ("And that's a good thing," she heard Sylvie say, "no matter how unsatisfactory they turn out"). They had been handed, in Churchill's phrase, the title deeds of freedom. What they did with them was their affair now, she supposed. (What an old fuddy-duddy she sounded, she had become the person she always thought she would never be.)

She thought she might walk through the parks and crossed the road, into Green Park. She always walked in the parks on Sundays but now she was retired every day was a Sunday, she supposed. She walked on, past the Palace, and entered Hyde Park, bought an ice cream from a kiosk next to the Serpentine and decided she might hire a deck chair. She was awfully tired, lunch seemed to have taken it out of her.

She must have dozed off—all that food. The boats were out on the water, people pedaling, laughing and joking. Oh, drat, she thought, she could feel a headache coming and she didn't have any painkillers in her bag. Perhaps she could hail a cab on Carriage Drive, she would never be able to walk home in this heat, not in pain. But then the pain grew less rather than more severe, which was not the usual progression of her headaches. She closed her eyes again, the sun was still hot and bright. She felt wonderfully indolent.

It was odd to sleep surrounded by people. It should have made her feel vulnerable but instead there was a kind of comfort. What was Tennessee Williams's line—*the kindness of strangers*? Millie's swan song on the stage, the last gasp of the dying swan, was to play Blanche DuBois in a 1955 production in Bath.

She allowed the hum and buzz of the park to lullaby her. Life wasn't about becoming, was it? It was about being. Dr. Kellet would have approved this thought. And everything was ephemeral, yet everything was eternal, she thought sleepily. A dog barked somewhere. A child cried. The child was hers, she could feel the delicate weight of the child in her arms. It was a lovely feeling. She was dreaming. She was in a meadow—flax and larkspur, buttercups, corn poppies, red campion and oxeye daisies—and unseasonable snowdrops. The oddities of the dream world, she thought, and caught the sound of Sylvie's little carriage clock chiming midnight. Someone was singing, a child, a reedy little voice keeping the tune, *I had a little nut-tree and nothing would it bear. Muskatnuss,* she thought—the German for nutmeg. She had been trying to remember that word for ages and now suddenly here it was.

Now she was in a garden. She could hear the delicate chink of cups on saucers, the creak and clatter of a lawn mower, and could smell the peppery-sweet perfume of pinks. A man lifted her up and tossed her in the air and sugar cubes scattered across a lawn. There was another world but it was this one. She allowed herself a little chuckle even though her opinion was that people who laughed to themselves in public were likely to be mad.

Despite the summer heat, snow began to fall, which was the

kind of thing that happened in dreams, after all. The snow began to cover her face, it was lovely and cool in this weather. And then she was falling, falling into the darkness, black and deep—

But here was the snow again—white and welcoming, the light like a sharp sword piercing through the heavy curtains, and she was being lifted up, cradled in soft arms.

"I shall call her Ursula," Sylvie said. "What do you think?"

"I like it," Hugh said. His face loomed into vision. His trim mustache and sideburns, his kind green eyes. "Welcome, little bear," he said.

THE END OF THE BEGINNING

"Welcome, little bear." Her father. She had his eyes.

Hugh had paced, as was tradition, along the Voysey runner in the upper hallway, barred from the inner sanctum itself. He was unsure of the details of the doings behind the door, only too grateful that he was not expected to be familiar with the mechanics of childbirth. Sylvie's screams suggested torture if not outright butchery. Women were extraordinarily brave, Hugh thought. He smoked a series of cigarettes to stave off any unmanly squeamishness.

Dr. Fellowes's dispassionate bass notes afforded some comfort to him, counterpointed unfortunately by a kind of hysterical Celtic babble from the scullery maid. Where was Mrs. Glover? A cook could sometimes be a great help at times like these. The cook in his childhood Hampstead home had been unflappable in a crisis.

A considerable commotion could be heard at one point, indicating great victory or great defeat in the battle taking place on the other side of the bedroom door. Hugh refrained from entering unless invited, which he wasn't. Eventually, Dr. Fellowes flung open the door of the birth chamber and announced, "You have a bonny, bouncing baby girl. She nearly died," he added as an afterthought.

Thank goodness, Hugh thought, that he had managed to get back to Fox Corner before the snow closed the roads. He had dragged his sister back with him on the Channel crossing, a cat after a long night on the tiles. He was sporting a rather painful bite mark on his hand and was left wondering from where his sister had acquired her strain of savagery. Not from Nanny Mills and the Hampstead nursery.

Izzie was still wearing her counterfeit wedding ring, a legacy of her shameful week in a Parisian hotel with her lover, although Hugh doubted that the French, an immoral lot, cared about such niceties. She had left for the Continent in short skirts and a little straw boater (his mother had given him a detailed description, as if Izzie were a criminal) but she returned in a gown by Worth (as she frequently told him, as if it would impress him). It was also clear that the scoundrel had been taking advantage of her for some time before their flight, as the gown, Worth or not, was straining at the seams.

He had eventually flushed his fugitive sister out from Hôtel d'Alsace in St. Germain, a degenerate *endroit,* in Hugh's estimation, the scene of Oscar Wilde's demise, which said everything you needed to know about the place.

An unseemly tussle had taken place not only with Izzie but also with the bounder from whose arms Hugh wrestled her before hauling her, kicking and screaming, into the handsome two-door Renault taxi that he had paid to wait outside the hotel. Hugh thought it would be rather fine to own a motor car. Could he afford one on his salary? Could he learn to drive one? How difficult could it be?

They had eaten some rather decent pink French lamb on the boat and Izzie had demanded champagne, which he allowed her as he was far too worn out with the whole elopement business to bother with yet another fight. It was tempting to toss her over the rails, into the dark-gray waters of the Channel.

He had telegraphed his mother, Adelaide, from Calais, informing her of Izzie's misfortune as he thought it might be best if she were prepared before setting eyes on her youngest daughter, whose condition was plain for all the world to see.

Their fellow diners on the boat presumed they were a married couple and many pretty compliments on her impending motherhood were passed Izzie's way. Hugh supposed it was better to let them think this, appalling though it was, rather than for these complete strangers to discover the truth. Thus he found himself taking part in an absurd charade for the duration of the crossing, in the course of which he was forced to deny the existence of his real wife and children and pretend that Izzie was his child bride. He became, to all intents and purposes, the very villain who had seduced a girl barely out of the nursery (forgetting, perhaps, that his own wife was only seventeen when he proposed to her).

Izzie, of course, threw herself into this mockery with glee, taking her revenge on Hugh by making him as uncomfortable as possible, addressing him as *mon cher mari* and other extremely irritating blandishments.

"What a lovely young wife you have," a man, a Belgian, chortled while Hugh was taking the air on deck and indulging in a postprandial cigarette. "Hardly out of the cradle herself and soon to be a mother. It's the best way—getting them young—then you can mold them to how you want them."

"Your English is remarkable, sir," Hugh said, throwing the stub of his cigarette into the sea and walking away. A lesser man would have resorted to fisticuffs. He might, if pressed, fight for the honor of his country, but he would be damned if he would fight for the besmirched honor of his feckless sister. (Although it would be undeniably pleasant to mold a woman to one's exact requirements, like his bespoke suits from his tailor in Jermyn Street.)

It had been difficult to find the right wording for the telegram to his mother and he had finally settled on I SHALL BE IN HAMPSTEAD BY MIDDAY STOP ISOBEL IS WITH ME STOP SHE IS WITH CHILD STOP. It was a rather bald message and he should perhaps have spent the extra money on some mitigating adverbs. "Unfortunately" might have been one. The telegram (unfortunately) had the opposite to the desired effect and when they disembarked in Dover a reply was waiting for him. DO NOT BRING HER TO MY HOUSE UNDER ANY

CIRCUMSTANCES STOP, the final STOP carrying a leaden weight of certainty which was not to be challenged. Which did rather leave Hugh at a loss as to what exactly he *should* do with Izzie. She was, despite appearances, still only a child herself, only sixteen, he could hardly abandon her on the streets. Anxious to return to Fox Corner as soon as possible, he found himself carting her along with him.

When they finally arrived, as iced as snowmen, it was an excitable Bridget who opened the door to him at midnight and said, "Oh, no, I was hoping you were going to be the doctor, so I was." His third child, it seemed, was on its way. *Her* way, he thought fondly, looking down at the tiny crumpled features. Hugh rather liked babies.

But what are we to *do* with her?" Sylvie fretted. "She's not giving birth under my roof."

"*Our* roof."

"She'll have to give it away."

"The child is part of our family," Hugh said. "The same blood runs in its veins as in my children."

"*Our* children."

"We'll say the child is adopted," Hugh said. "An orphaned relative. People won't question, why should they?"

In the end the baby *was* born beneath the roof of Fox Corner, a boy, and once Sylvie saw him she was unable to discard him so easily. "He's a delightful little thing really," she said. Sylvie found all babies delightful.

Izzie had not been allowed beyond the garden for the remainder of her pregnancy. She was being kept a prisoner, she said, "like the Count of Monte Cristo." She handed the baby over as soon as he was born and showed no more interest in him, as if the whole affair—the pregnancy, the confinement—had been a provoking task that they had coerced her into undertaking and now she had fulfilled her part of the bargain and was free to go. After a fortnight of lying around in bed being waited upon by a disgruntled Bridget she was put on a train back to Hampstead, from whence she was packed off to a finishing school in Lausanne.

Hugh was right, no one questioned the sudden appearance of this surplus child. Mrs. Glover and Bridget were sworn to secrecy, an oath that was sweetened, unknown to Sylvie, with cash. Hugh knew the value of money, he wasn't a banker for nothing. Dr. Fellowes could, one hoped, be relied upon for his professional discretion.

"Roland," Sylvie said. "I've always rather liked that name. *The Song of Roland*—he was a French knight."

"Died in battle, I expect?" Hugh said.

"Most knights do, don't they?"

The silver hare spun and shone and shimmered before her eyes. The leaves on the beech danced, the garden budded, blossomed, fruited, without any help from her at all. *Rock-a-bye baby,* Sylvie sang. *Down will fall baby, cradle and all.* Ursula was not put off by this threat and continued on her small but dauntless journey, alongside her companion, Roland.

He was a sweet-natured child and it took some time for Sylvie to notice that he was "not quite all there," as she put it to Hugh one evening when he returned from a difficult day at the bank. He knew there was no point in sharing these fiscal problems with Sylvie, yet sometimes he liked to imagine coming home from work to a wife who was fascinated by ledgers and balance sheets, the rising price of tea, the unsteady market in wool. A wife "molded" to requirements instead of the beautiful, clever and somewhat contrary one he was wedded to.

He had secluded himself in the growlery, sitting at his desk with a large malt whisky and a small cigar, hoping to be left in peace. To no avail: Sylvie swept in and sat opposite him, like a customer in the bank looking for a loan, and said, "I think Izzie's child may be a simpleton." Up until now he had always been Roland, now, apparently defective, he was Izzie's once more.

Hugh dismissed her opinion but there was no denying that as time went on Roland didn't progress the way the others did. He was slow to learn and didn't seem to possess a child's natural curiosity about the world. You could sit him on a hearth rug with a rag book or a set of wooden bricks and he would still be there half an hour later gazing contentedly at the fire (well guarded against children) or Queenie the cat sitting next to him, attending to her toilette (less well guarded and much prone to malevolence). Roland could be set to any simple task, and spent much of his time willingly fetching and carrying for the girls, Bridget, even Mrs. Glover was not above sending him on simple errands, a bag of sugar from the pantry, a wooden spoon from the jar. It seemed unlikely that he would be going to Hugh's old school or entering Hugh's old college, and Hugh grew fonder of the boy for that somehow.

"Perhaps we should get him a dog," he suggested. "A dog always brings the best out in a boy." Bosun arrived, a large friendly animal with a tendency to herd and protect, and discerned immediately that he had been put in charge of something important.

At least the boy was placid, Hugh thought, unlike his dratted mother, or his own two eldest children who fought incessantly with each other. Ursula, of course, was different to all of them. She was watchful, as if she were trying to drink in the whole world through those little green eyes that were both his and hers. She was rather unnerving.

Mr. Winton's easel was set up to face the sea. He was quite pleased with what he had so far, the blues and greens and whites—and murky browns—of the Cornish seaside. Several passersby paused in their journeys across the sands to observe the painting-in-progress. He hoped, in vain, for compliments.

A little fleet of white-sailed yachts skimmed the horizon, a race of some kind, Mr. Winton presumed. He smudged some Chinese white on his own painted horizon and stood back to admire the results. Mr. Winton saw yachts, others might have seen blobs of white paint. They would contrast rather well, he thought, with some figures on the seashore. The two little girls so intent on building a sand castle would be perfect. He bit the tip of his brush as he gazed at his canvas. How to do it best, he wondered.

The sand castle was Ursula's suggestion. They should build, she said to Pamela, the best sand castle ever. She had conjured up such a vivid image of this sandy citadel—moats and turrets and battlements—that Pamela could almost see the medieval ladies in their wimples waving to the knights as they clattered away on their horses over the drawbridge (a piece of driftwood was to be sought out for this purpose). They had set about this task with undivided energy although they were still at the heavy-engineering stage, digging a double moat that would eventually, when the tide turned, fill with seawater to protect those wimpled ladies from violent siege (by someone like Maurice, inevitably). Roland, their ever-obliging minion, was dispatched to scour the beach for decorative pebbles and the all-important drawbridge.

They were further along the beach from Sylvie and Bridget, who were immersed in their books while the new baby, Edward—Teddy—was sleeping on a blanket on the sand beneath the protection of a parasol. Maurice was dredging in rock pools at the far end of the beach. He had made new companions, rough local boys with whom he went swimming and scrabbling up cliffs. Boys were just boys to Maurice. He had not yet learned to evaluate them by accent and social standing.

Maurice had an indestructible quality and no one ever seemed to worry about him, least of all his mother.

Bosun, unfortunately, had been left behind with the Coles.

In time-honored fashion, the sand from the moat was piled up in a central mound, the building material for the proposed fortress. Both girls, by now hot and sticky from their exertions, took a moment to stand back and contemplate this formless heap. Pamela felt more doubtful now about the turrets and battlements, the wimpled ladies seemed even more unlikely. The mound reminded Ursula of something, but what? Something familiar, yet nebulous and indefinable, no more than a shape in her brain. She was prone to these sensations, as if a memory was being tugged reluctantly out of its hiding place. She presumed it was the same for everyone.

Then this feeling was replaced by fear, a shadow of a thrill too, the kind that came with a thunderstorm rolling in, or a sea fog creeping toward the shore. Hazard could be anywhere, in the clouds, the waves, the little yachts on the horizon, the man painting at his easel. She set off at a purposeful trot to take her fears to Sylvie and have them soothed.

Ursula was a peculiar child, full of troublesome notions, in Sylvie's opinion. She was forever answering Ursula's anxious questions—*What would we do if the house caught fire? Our train crashed? The river flooded?* Practical advice, Sylvie had discovered, was the best way to allay these fears rather than dismissing them as unlikely (*Why, dear, we would gather up our belongings and we would climb on the roof until the water receded*).

Pamela, meanwhile, returned stoically to digging the moat. Mr. Winton was entirely absorbed in the close brushwork necessary for Pamela's sun hat. What a happy coincidence that those two little girls had chosen to build their sand castle in the middle of his composition. He thought he might call it *The Diggers*. Or *The Sand Diggers*.

Sylvie was dozing over *The Secret Agent* and rather resented being woken. "What is it?" she said. She glanced along the beach and saw Pamela digging industriously. Distant yelling and wild whooping suggested Maurice.

"Where's Roland?" she asked.

"Roland?" Ursula said, looking around for their willing slave and failing to see him anywhere. "He's looking for a drawbridge." Sylvie was on her feet now, anxiously scanning the beach.

"A what?"

"A drawbridge," Ursula repeated.

They concluded that he must have spotted a piece of wood in the sea and obediently waded out to collect it. He had no real understanding of danger and did not know how to swim, of course. If Bosun had been on watch on the beach he would have dog-paddled out into the waves, heedless of any peril, and snatched Roland back. In his absence, *Archibald Winton, an amateur watercolorist from Birmingham,* as the local paper referred to him, had attempted to rescue the child (*Roland Todd, aged four, on holiday with his family*). He had cast aside his paintbrush and swum out to sea and pulled the boy from the water, *but, alas, to no avail.* This clipping was carefully cut out and preserved for appreciation in Birmingham. In the course of three column inches Mr. Winton had become both a hero and an artist. He imagined himself saying modestly, "Why, it was nothing," and—of course—it *was* nothing, for no one was saved.

Ursula watched as Mr. Winton waded back through the waves, carrying Roland's limp little body in his arms. Pamela and Ursula had thought the tide was going out but it was coming in, already filling the moat and lapping at the mound of sand which would soon be gone forever. An ownerless hoop bowled past, driven by the breeze. Ursula stared out to sea while behind her on the beach a variety of strangers attempted to revive Roland. Pamela came and joined her and they held hands. The waves began to trickle in, covering their feet. If only they hadn't been so intent on the sand castle, Ursula thought. And it had seemed such a *good* idea.

&

Sorry about your boy, Mrs. Todd, ma'am," George Glover mumbled. He touched an invisible cap on his head. Sylvie had mounted an expedition to see the harvest being brought in. They must rouse themselves from their torpid grief, she said. Following Roland's drowning, the summer had been subdued, naturally. Roland seemed greater in his absence than he had done in his presence.

"*Your* boy?" Izzie muttered after they had left George Glover to his labors. She had arrived in time for Roland's funeral, in stylish black mourning, and wept, "My boy, my boy," over Roland's small coffin.

"He was *my* boy," Sylvie said vehemently, "don't you dare say he was yours," although she knew, guiltily, that she mourned less for Roland than she would have done for one of her own. But that was natural, surely? Everyone seemed to want ownership of him now he was gone. (Mrs. Glover and Bridget, too, would have staked a small claim to him as well if anyone had listened.)

Hugh was very affected by the loss of "the little chap" but knew that for the sake of his family he must carry on as usual.

Izzie had lingered on, to Sylvie's annoyance. She was twenty years old, "stuck" at home, waiting for an unknown-as-yet husband to free her from Adelaide's "claws." Roland's name had been forbidden in Hampstead and now Adelaide declared his death a "blessing." Hugh felt sorry for his sister, while Sylvie spent her time casting around the countryside for an eligible landowner with enough mutton-headed patience to withstand Izzie.

* * *

In an oppressive heat they had trudged across fields, clambered over stiles, splashed through streams. Sylvie had strapped the baby to her body with a shawl. The baby was a heavy burden, although perhaps not as heavy a burden as the picnic basket that Bridget was lugging. Bosun walked dutifully by their side, he was not a dog that ran ahead, tending more to bring up the rear. He was still puzzled by Roland's disappearance and was keen not to lose anyone else. Izzie lagged behind, any original enthusiasm for the pastoral outing long since having waned. Bosun did his best to chivvy her along.

It was a bad-tempered trek, the picnic at the end of it not much better as it turned out that Bridget had forgotten to pack the sandwiches. "How on earth did you manage that?" Sylvie said crossly and as a consequence they had to eat the pork pie that Mrs. Glover had intended for George. ("For God's sake, don't tell her," Sylvie said.) Pamela had scratched herself on a bramble bush, Ursula had tumbled into a nettle patch. Even the usually happy Teddy was overheated and fretful.

George brought two tiny baby rabbits for them to look at and said, "Would you like to take them home with you?" and Sylvie snapped, "No thank you, George. They will either die or multiply, neither of which would be a happy outcome." Pamela was distraught and had to be promised a kitten. (To Pamela's surprise, this promise was kept and a kitten duly acquired from the Hall farm. A week later it took a fit and died. A full funeral was held. "I am cursed," Pamela declared, with uncharacteristic melodrama.)

"He's very handsome, that plowman, isn't he?" Izzie said and Sylvie said, "Don't. Not under any circumstances. Don't," and Izzie said, "I have no idea what you mean."

The afternoon grew no cooler and eventually they had no choice but to wend their way home in the same heat that they had journeyed there in. Pamela, already miserable from the rabbits, stepped on a thorn, Ursula was whacked in the face by a branch. Teddy cried, Izzie swore, Sylvie breathed fire and Bridget said if it weren't a mortal sin she would drown herself in the next stream.

"Look at you," Hugh smiled in greeting when they staggered home. "All golden from the sun."

"Oh, please," Sylvie said, pushing past him. "I'm going to lie down upstairs."

I think we'll have thunder tonight," Hugh said. And they did. Ursula, a light sleeper, was woken. She slipped out of bed and pattered over to the attic window, standing on a chair so that she could see out.

Thunder rolled like gunfire in the distance. The sky, purple and swollen with portent, was suddenly split open by a fork of lightning. A fox, skulking over some small prey on the lawn, was briefly illuminated, caught as though in a photographer's flash.

Ursula forgot to count and an explosive thunderclap, almost overhead, took her by surprise.

This was how war sounded, she thought.

Ursula cut straight to the chase. Bridget, chopping onions at the kitchen table, was already primed for tears. Ursula sat next to her and said, "I've been in the village."

"Oh," Bridget said, not in the least interested in this information.

"I was buying sweets," Ursula said. "In the sweet shop."

"Really?" Bridget said. "Sweets in a sweet shop? Who would have thought it." The shop sold many things other than sweets but none of those other things were of any interest to the children at Fox Corner.

"Clarence was there."

"Clarence?" Bridget said. She stopped the chopping at the mention of her beloved.

"Buying sweets," Ursula said. "Mint humbugs," she added, for authenticity, and then, "You know Molly Lester?"

"I do," Bridget said cautiously, "she works in the shop."

"Well, Clarence was kissing her."

Bridget rose from her chair, knife still in hand. "Kissing? Why would Clarence kiss Molly Lester?"

"That's what Molly Lester said! She said, 'Why are you kissing me, Clarence Dodds, when everyone knows you're engaged to be married to that maid that works at Fox Corner?' "

Bridget was used to melodramas and penny dreadfuls. She waited for the revelation that she knew must follow.

Ursula supplied it. "And Clarence said, 'Oh, you mean Bridget. She's nothing to me. She's a very ugly girl. I am just stringing her along.' " Ursula, a precocious reader by now, had also read Bridget's novels and had learned the discourse of romance.

The knife was dropped to the floor with a banshee shriek. Irish curses were thrown liberally. "The bugger," Bridget said.

"A dastardly villain," Ursula agreed.

The engagement ring, the little gypsy ring ("a trinket"), was returned by Bridget to Sylvie. Clarence's protestations of innocence went unheeded.

You might go up to London with Mrs. Glover," Sylvie said to Bridget. "For the Armistice celebrations, you know. I believe there are late trains running."

Mrs. Glover said she wouldn't go near the capital on account of the influenza and Bridget said that she hoped very much that Clarence would go, preferably with Molly Lester, and that the pair of them would catch the Spanish flu and die.

Molly Lester, who had never spoken so much as a word to Clarence beyond a guiltless "Morning, sir, what can I get you?," attended a small street party in the village but Clarence did indeed go up to London with a couple of pals and did indeed die.

"But at least no one was pushed down the stairs," Ursula said.

"Whatever do you mean?" Sylvie said.

"I don't know," Ursula said. She really didn't.

She was disturbed by herself. She dreamed of flying and falling all the time. Sometimes when she stood on a chair to look out of the bedroom window she felt the urge to clamber out and throw herself down. She would not fall to the ground with a thud and a smash like an overripe apple, instead she was sure she would be caught. (By what, though? she wondered.) She refrained from testing this theory, unlike Pamela's poor little crinoline lady, who had been tossed from the very same bedroom window by a malignly bored Maurice one winter teatime.

On hearing his approach along the passageway—loudly signaled by Indian war whoops—Ursula had hastily placed her own favorite, Queen Solange, the knitting doll, beneath her pillow where she remained safe in her refuge while the unfortunate crinoline lady was defenestrated and smashed to pieces on the slates. "I only wanted to see what would happen," Maurice whined to Sylvie afterward. "Well, now you know," she said. She was finding Pamela's hysterical reaction to this incident more than a little trying. "We are in the middle of a war," she said to her. "There are worse things happening than a broken ornament." Not for Pamela there weren't.

If Ursula had allowed Maurice the little knitting doll, made of unbreakable wood, then the crinoline lady would have been saved.

Bosun, soon to be dead of distemper, nosed his way into the room that night and laid a weighty paw on Pamela's coverlet in sympathy before groaning into sleep on the rag rug between their beds.

The next day, Sylvie, reproaching herself for her heartlessness toward her children, acquired another kitten from the Hall farm. Kittens were in continual abundance on the farm, there was a kind of kitten currency in the neighborhood, they were bartered for all kinds of emotional regret or fulfillment by parents—a doll lost, an exam passed.

Despite Bosun's best attempts to keep a guardian eye on the kitten, they had only had it a week when Maurice stepped on it, during a vigorous game of soldiers with the Cole boys. Sylvie swiftly scooped up the little body and gave it to Bridget to take elsewhere so that its death throes could take place offstage.

"It was an accident!" Maurice screamed. "I didn't know the stupid thing was there!" Sylvie slapped him on the face and he started crying. It was horrible to see him so upset, it really was an accident, and Ursula tried to comfort him which only made him furious, and Pamela, of course, had moved beyond all notion of civilization and was trying to rip Maurice's hair from his head. The Cole boys had long since scarpered back to their own house where emotional calm was the general order of the day.

Sometimes it was harder to change the past than it was the future.

Headaches," Sylvie said.

"I'm a psychiatrist," Dr. Kellet said to Sylvie. "Not a neurologist."

"And dreams and nightmares," Sylvie tempted.

There was something comforting about being in this room, Ursula thought. The oak paneling, the roaring fire, the thick carpet figured in red and blue, the leather chairs, even the outlandish tea urn—all felt familiar.

"Dreams?" Dr. Kellet said, duly tempted.

"Yes," Sylvie said. "And sleepwalking."

"Do I?" Ursula asked, startled.

"And she has a kind of *déjà vu* all the time," Sylvie said, pronouncing the words with some distaste.

"Really?" Dr. Kellet said, reaching for an elaborate meerschaum pipe and knocking the ashes out onto the fender. It was the Turk's-head bowl, as familiar somehow as an old pet.

"Oh," Ursula said. "I've been here before!"

"You see!" Sylvie said, triumphant.

"Hmm...," Dr. Kellet said thoughtfully. He turned to Ursula and addressed her directly. "Have you heard of reincarnation?"

"Oh, yes, absolutely," Ursula said enthusiastically.

"I'm sure she hasn't," Sylvie said. "Is it Catholic doctrine? What *is* that?" she asked, distracted by the outlandish tea urn.

"It's a samovar, from Russia," Dr. Kellet said, "although I'm not Russian, far from it, I'm from Maidstone, I visited St. Petersburg before the Revolution." To Ursula, he said, "Would you like to draw me something?" and pushed a pencil and paper toward her. "Would you like some tea?" he asked Sylvie, who was still glaring at the samovar. She declined, mistrustful of any brew that didn't come out of a china teapot.

Ursula finished her drawing and handed it over for appraisal.

"What is it?" Sylvie said, peering over Ursula's shoulder. "Some kind of ring, or circlet? A crown?"

"No," Dr. Kellet said, "it's a snake with its tail in its mouth." He nodded approvingly and said to Sylvie, "It's a symbol representing the circularity of the universe. Time is a construct, in reality everything flows, no past or present, only the now."

"How gnomic," Sylvie said stiffly.

Dr. Kellet steepled his hands and propped his chin on them. "You know," he said to Ursula, "I think we shall get on very well. Would you like a biscuit?"

There was one thing that puzzled her. The photograph of *Guy, lost at Arras* in his cricketing whites was missing from the side table. Without meaning to—it was a question that raised so many other questions—she said to Dr. Kellet, "Where is the photograph of Guy?" and Dr. Kellet said, "Who is Guy?"

It seemed even the instability of time was not to be relied upon.

It's just an Austin," Izzie said. "An open-road tourer—four doors though—but nowhere near as costly as a *Bentley,* goodness, it's positively a vehicle for hoi polloi compared to *your* indulgence, Hugh." "On tick, no doubt," Hugh said. "Not at all, paid up in full, *in cash.* I have a *publisher,* I have *money,* Hugh. You don't need to worry about me anymore."

While everyone was admiring the cherry-bright vehicle, Millie said, "I have to go, I have a dancing exhibition tonight. Thank you very much for a lovely tea, Mrs. Todd."

"Come on, I'll walk you back," Ursula said.

On the return home, she avoided the well-worn shortcut at the bottom of the garden and came the long way round, dodging Izzie speeding off in her car. Izzie gave a careless salute in farewell.

"Who was that?" Benjamin Cole asked, skidding his bicycle into a hedge to avoid being killed by the Austin. Ursula's heart tripped and skipped and flipped at the sight of him. The very object of her affection! The reason she had taken the long way round was on the unlikely chance that she might engineer an "accidental" meeting with Benjamin Cole. And here he was! What luck.

* * *

They lost my ball," Teddy said disconsolately when she returned to the dining room.

"I know," Ursula said. "We can look for it later."

"I say, you're all pink and flushed," he said. "Did something happen?"

Did anything happen? she thought. Did anything *happen?* Only the most handsome boy in the entire world kissed me *and* on my sixteenth birthday. He had walked her back, pushing his bicycle, and at some point their hands had brushed, they had blushed (it was poetry) and he said, "You know I do like you, Ursula," and then right there, at her front gate (where anyone could see), he had propped his bicycle against the wall and pulled her toward him. And then the kiss! Sweet and lingering and much nicer than she had expected although it did leave her feeling—well, yes . . . *flushed.* Benjamin too, and they stood apart from each other, slightly shocked.

"Gosh," he said. "I've never kissed a girl before, I had no idea it could be so . . . exciting." He shook his head like a dog as if astonished by his own lack of vocabulary.

This, Ursula thought, would remain the best moment of her life, no matter what else happened to her. They would have kissed more, she supposed, but at that moment the rag-and-bone cart appeared round the corner of the lane and the rag-and-bone man's almost incomprehensible siren moan of *Enraagnboooooone* intruded on their budding romance.

"No, nothing happened," she said to Teddy. "I was saying goodbye to Izzie. You missed seeing her car. You would have liked it."

Teddy shrugged and pushed *The Adventures of Augustus* off the table and onto the floor. "What a load of rot it is," he said.

Ursula picked up a half-drunk glass of champagne, the rim of which was adorned with red lipstick, and poured half of it into a jelly glass that she handed to Teddy. "Cheers," she said. They chinked their glasses and drained them to the dregs.

"Happy birthday," Teddy said.

&

What wondrous life is this I lead!
Ripe apples drop about my head;
The luscious clusters of the vine
Upon my mouth do crush their wine . . .

"What is that you're reading?" Sylvie asked suspiciously.

"Marvell."

Sylvie took the book from her and scrutinized the verses. "It's rather lush," she concluded.

" 'Lush'—how can that be a criticism?" Ursula laughed and bit into an apple.

"Try not to be precocious," Sylvie sighed. "It's not a pleasant thing in a girl. What are you going to do when you go back to school after the holidays—Latin? Greek? Not English literature? I don't see the point."

"You don't see the point of English literature?"

"I don't see the point of *studying* it. Surely one just *reads* it?" She sighed again. Neither of her daughters bore any resemblance to her. For a moment Sylvie was back in the past, under a bright London sky, and could smell the spring flowers newly refreshed by rain, hear the quiet comforting clink and jingle of Tiffin's tack.

"I might do Modern Languages. I don't know. I'm not sure, I haven't quite worked out a plan."

"A plan?"

They fell into silence. The fox sauntered into the silence, insouciant. Maurice was forever trying to shoot it. Either he was not such a good shot as he liked to think or the vixen was cleverer than he was. Ursula and Sylvie tended toward the latter view. "She's so pretty," Sylvie said. "And she has such a magnificent brush." The fox sat down, a dog waiting for its dinner, her eyes never leaving Sylvie. "I haven't got anything," Sylvie said, upturning her empty hands to prove this fact. Ursula bowled her apple core, gently underarm, so as not to alarm the creature and the vixen trotted off after it, picking it up awkwardly in her mouth and then turning tail and disappearing. "Eats anything," Sylvie said. "Like Jimmy."

Maurice appeared, giving them both a start. He was carrying his new Purdey cocked over his arm and said eagerly, "Was that that damned fox?"

"Language, Maurice," Sylvie reprimanded.

He was home after graduation, waiting to start his training in the law and irritatingly bored. He could work at the Hall farm, Sylvie suggested, they were always looking for seasonal workers. "Like a peasant in the field?" Maurice said. "Is that why you've given me an expensive education?" ("Why *have* we given him an expensive education?" Hugh said.)

"Teach me to shoot, then," Ursula said, jumping up and brushing off her skirt. "Come on, I can use Daddy's old wildfowler."

Maurice shrugged and said, "May as well, but girls can't shoot, it's a well-known fact."

"Girls are absolutely useless," Ursula agreed. "They can't do *anything*."

"Are you being sarcastic?"

"Me?"

Pretty good for a novice," Maurice said reluctantly. They were shooting bottles off a wall, near the copse, Ursula hitting her target many more times than Maurice. "You're sure you haven't done this before?"

"What can I say?" she said. "I pick things up quickly."

Maurice suddenly swung the barrel of his gun away from the wall and toward the edge of the copse and before Ursula could even see what he was aiming at he had pulled the trigger, blasting something out of existence.

"Got the damned little blighter at last," he said triumphantly.

Ursula set off at a run but long before she reached it she could see the pile of ruddy-brown fur. The white tip of her beautiful brush gave a little flicker but Sylvie's fox was no more.

She found Sylvie on the terrace, leafing through a magazine. "Maurice shot the fox," she said. Sylvie rested her head back on the wicker lounger and closed her eyes in resignation. "It was always going to happen," she said. She opened her eyes. They were glistening with tears. Ursula had never seen her mother cry. "I shall disinherit him one day," Sylvie said, the idea of cold revenge already drying her tears.

Pamela appeared on the terrace and raised a questioning eyebrow at Ursula, who said, "Maurice shot the fox."

"I hope you shot *him,*" Pamela said. She meant it too.

"I might go and meet Daddy off the train," Ursula said when Pamela had gone back inside.

She wasn't really going to meet Hugh. Ever since her birthday she had been seeing Benjamin Cole in secret. Ben, he was now to her. In the meadow, in the wood, in the lane. (Anywhere out of doors, it seemed. "Good job the weather's been nice for your canoodling," Millie said, with much clown-smirking and raising up and down of eyebrows.)

Ursula discovered what an excellent liar she was. (Didn't she always know that, though?) *Do you want anything from the shop?* or *I'm just going to pick raspberries in the lane.* Would it be so dreadful if people knew? "Well, I think your mother would have me killed," Ben said. ("A Jew?" she imagined Sylvie saying.)

"And my folks, too," he said. "We're too young."

"Like Romeo and Juliet," Ursula said. "Star-crossed lovers and so on."

"Except we're not going to die for love," Ben said.

"Would it be such a bad thing to die for?" Ursula mused.

"Yes."

Things had started to get very "hot" between them, a lot of fumbling fingers and moaning (on his part). He didn't think he could "hold back" much longer, he said, but she wasn't sure what he had to hold back from exactly. Didn't love mean they shouldn't hold back anything? She expected they would marry. Would she have to convert? Become a "Jewess"?

They had made their way to the meadow where they had lain down in each other's arms. It was very romantic, Ursula thought, apart from the timothy grass that was tickling her and the oxeye daisies that made her sneeze. Not to mention the way Ben suddenly shifted himself until he was on top of her so that she felt rather as if she were in a coffin filled with earth. He went into a kind of spasm that she thought might be a prelude to death by apoplexy and she stroked his hair as if he were an invalid and said, with concern, "Are you all right?"

"Sorry," he said. "Didn't mean to do that." (But what had he done?)

"I should be getting back," Ursula said. They stood up and picked off grass and flowers from each other's clothing before walking home.

Ursula wondered if she had missed Hugh's train. Ben looked at his watch and said, "Oh, they'll have been home for ages." (Hugh and Mr. Cole traveled on the same London train.) They left the meadow and climbed over the stile into the dairy herd's field that ran alongside the lane. The cows hadn't returned from milking yet.

He gave her a hand down from the stile and they kissed again. When they broke free of each other they noticed a man making his way across the field, from the other side where it led into the copse. He was heading toward the lane—a shabby creature, a tramp perhaps—hobbling along as fast as he could. He glanced round and when he saw them he hobbled even faster. He stumbled on a tussock of grass but quickly recovered and was up again, loping toward the gate.

"What a suspicious-looking fellow," Ben laughed. "I wonder what he's been up to?"

Dinner's on the table, you're very late," Sylvie said. "Where have you been? Mrs. Glover has made that awful veal *à la Russe* thing again."

Maurice shot the fox?" Teddy said, his face a picture of disappointment.

And so it went on from there, a bad-tempered argument between everyone at the dinner table just because of a dead fox, Hugh thought. They're vermin, he felt like saying but didn't want to fuel the furor of emotions that had been unleashed. Instead, he said, "Please, let's not talk about it over dinner, it's difficult enough trying to digest this stuff." But talk about it they would. He tried to ignore them, plowing his way through the veal cutlets (had Mrs. Glover ever tasted them herself? he wondered). He was relieved that they were interrupted by a knock at the door.

"Ah, Major Shawcross," Hugh said, "do come in."

"Oh, goodness, I don't want to interrupt you at table," Major Shawcross said, looking awkward, "I just wondered if your Teddy had seen our Nancy."

"Nancy?" Teddy said.

"Yes," Major Shawcross said. "We can't find her anywhere."

* * *

They didn't meet anymore in the copse, or the lane or the meadow. Hugh imposed a strict curfew after Nancy's body was found and anyway both Ursula and Ben were stricken with guilty horror. If they had come home when they were supposed to, if they had crossed that field even five minutes earlier instead of lingering, they might have saved her. But by the time they meandered ignorantly back Nancy was already dead, lying in the cattle trough in the top corner of the field. So, indeed, just like Romeo and Juliet it had ended in death. Nancy, sacrificed for their love.

"It's a terrible thing," Pamela said to her. "But you're not responsible, why are you behaving as though you are?"

Because she was. She knew it now.

Something was riven, broken, a lightning fork cutting open a swollen sky.

In the October half-term she went to stay with Izzie for a few days. They were sitting in the Russian Tea Room in South Kensington. "A terrifically right-wing clientele here," Izzie said, "but they do the most wonderful pancake things." There was a samovar. (Was it the samovar that set her off, with its shades of Dr. Kellet? It would seem absurd if it was.) They had finished their tea and Izzie said, "Just hang on a sec, I'm going to powder my nose. Ask for the bill, will you?"

Ursula was waiting patiently for her to return when suddenly the terror descended, swift as a predatory hawk. An anticipatory dread of something unknown but enormously threatening. It was coming for her, here among the polite tinkle of teaspoon on saucer. She stood up, knocking over her chair. She felt dizzy and there was a veil of fog in front of her face. Like bomb dust, she thought, yet she had never been bombed.

She pushed through the veil, out of the Russian Tea Room onto

Harrington Road. She started to run and kept on running, onto the Brompton Road and then, blindly, into Egerton Gardens.

She had been here before. She had never been here before.

There was always something just out of sight, just around a corner, something she could never chase down—something that was chasing *her* down. She was both the hunter and the hunted. Like the fox. She carried on and then tripped on something, falling straight onto her nose. The pain was extraordinary. Blood everywhere. She sat on the pavement and cried with the agony of it all. She hadn't realized there was anyone on the street but then from behind her a man's voice said, "Oh, my, how awful for you. Let me help you. You have blood all over your nice turquoise scarf. Is that the color, or is it aquamarine? My name's Derek, Derek Oliphant."

She knew that voice. She didn't know that voice. The past seemed to *leak* into the present, as if there were a fault somewhere. Or was it the future spilling into the past? Either way it was nightmarish, as if her inner dark landscape had become manifest. The inside become the outside. Time was out of joint, that was for certain.

She staggered to her feet but didn't dare to look round. Ignoring the awful pain, she ran on and on. She was in Belgravia before she finally flagged completely. Here too, she thought. She had been here before. She had never been here before. I give in, she thought. Whatever it is, it can have me. She sank to her knees on the hard pavement and curled up in a ball. A fox without a hole.

She must have passed out because when she opened her eyes she was in a bed in a room painted white. There was a big window and outside the window she could see a horse-chestnut tree that had not yet shed its leaves. She turned her head and saw Dr. Kellet.

"You broke your nose," Dr. Kellet said. "We thought you must have been attacked by someone."

"No," she said. "I fell."

"A vicar found you. He took you in a taxi to St. George's Hospital."

"But what are *you* doing here?"

"Your father got in touch with me," Dr. Kellet said. "He wasn't sure who else to contact."

"I don't understand."

"Well, when you arrived at St. George's you wouldn't stop screaming. They thought something terrible must have happened to you."

"This isn't St. George's, is it?"

"No," he said kindly. "This is a private clinic. Rest, good food and so on. They have lovely gardens. I always think a lovely garden helps, don't you?"

Time isn't circular," she said to Dr. Kellet. "It's like a...palimpsest."

"Oh dear," he said. "That sounds very vexing."

"And memories are sometimes in the future."

"You are an old soul," he said. "It can't be easy. But your life is still ahead of you. It must be lived." He was not her doctor, he had retired, he said, he was "merely a visitor."

The sanatorium made her feel as if she had a mild case of consumption. She sat on the sunny terrace during the day and read countless books and orderlies ferried food and drink to her. She wandered through the gardens, had polite conversation with doctors and psychiatrists, talked to her fellow patients (on her floor, at any rate. The truly mad were in the attic, like Mrs. Rochester). There were even fresh flowers in her room and a bowl of apples. It must be costing a fortune for her to stay here, she thought.

"This must be very expensive," she said to Hugh when he visited, which he did often.

"Izzie is paying," he said. "She insisted."

★ ★ ★

Dr. Kellet lit his meerschaum thoughtfully. They were sitting on the terrace. Ursula thought she would be quite happy to spend the rest of her life here. It was so gloriously unchallenging.

"*And though I have the gift of prophecy, and understand all mysteries, and all knowledge . . .*" Dr. Kellet said.

"*. . . and though I have all faith, so that I could remove mountains, and have not charity, I am nothing,*" Ursula provided.

"*Caritas,* of course, is love. But you will know that."

"I'm not without charity," Ursula said. "Why are we quoting Corinthians? I thought you were a Buddhist."

"Oh, I am nothing," Dr. Kellet said. "And everything too, of course," he added—rather elliptically, in Ursula's opinion.

"The question is," he said, "do you have enough?"

"Enough what?" The conversation had quite got away from her now but Dr. Kellet was busy with the demands of the meerschaum and didn't answer. Tea interrupted them.

"They do excellent chocolate cake here," Dr. Kellet said.

All better, little bear?" Hugh said as he helped her gently into the car. He had brought the Bentley to pick her up.

"Yes," she said. "Absolutely."

"Good. Let's get home. The house isn't the same without you."

She had wasted so much precious time but she had a plan now, she thought, as she lay awake in the dark, in her own bed at Fox Corner. The plan would involve snow, no doubt. The silver hare, the dancing green leaves. And so on. German, not the Classics, and afterward a course in shorthand and typing and perhaps the study of Esperanto on the side, just in case utopia should come to pass. The membership of a local shooting club and an application for an office job somewhere, working for a while, salting money away—nothing untoward. She didn't want to draw attention to herself, she would heed her father's advice, although he hadn't given it to her yet, she would keep her head below the parapet and her light under a bushel. And then, when she was ready, she would have enough to live on while she embedded herself deep in the heart of the beast, from whence she would pluck out the black tumor that was growing there, larger every day.

And then one day she would be walking down Amalienstrasse and pause outside Photo Hoffmann and gaze at the Kodaks and Leicas and Voigtländers in the windows and she would open the shop door and hear the little bell clanging to announce her arrival to the girl working behind the counter who will probably say *Guten Tag, gnädiges Fräulein,* or perhaps she will say *Grüss Gott* because this is 1930 when people can still address you with *Grüss Gott* and *Tschüss* instead of endless *Heil Hitlers* and absurd martial salutes.

And Ursula will hold out her old box Brownie and say, "I don't seem to be able to spool the film on," and perky seventeen-year-old Eva Braun will say, "Let me have a look for you."

Her heart swelled with the high holiness of it all. Imminence was all around. She was both warrior and shining spear. She was a sword glinting in the depths of night, a lance of light piercing the darkness. There would be no mistakes this time.

When everyone was asleep and the house was quiet, Ursula got out of bed and climbed on the chair at the open window of the little attic bedroom.

It's time, she thought. A clock struck somewhere in sympathy.

She thought of Teddy and Miss Woolf, of Roland and little Angela, of Nancy and Sylvie. She thought of Dr. Kellet and Pindar. *Become such as you are, having learned what that is.* She knew what that was now. She was Ursula Beresford Todd and she was a witness.

She opened her arms to the black bat and they flew to each other, embracing in the air like long-lost souls. This is love, Ursula thought. And the practice of it makes it perfect.

BE YE MEN OF VALOR

December 1930

Ursula knew all about Eva. She knew how much she liked fashion and makeup and gossip. She knew that she could skate and ski and loved to dance. And so Ursula lingered over the expensive frocks in Oberpollinger with her before visiting a café for coffee and cake, or an ice cream in the Englischer Garten where they would sit and watch the children on the carousel. She went to the skating rink with Eva and her sister Gretl. She was invited to dinner at the Brauns' table. "Your English friend is very nice," Frau Braun told Eva.

She told them that she was improving her German before she settled down to teach at home. Eva sighed with boredom at the idea.

Eva loved to be photographed and Ursula took many, many photographs of her on her box Brownie and then they spent their evenings sticking them in albums and admiring the different poses that Eva had struck. "You should be in films," Ursula told Eva and she was ridiculously flattered. Ursula had mugged up on celebrities, Hollywood and British as well as German, on the latest songs and dances. She was an older woman, interested in a fledgling. She took Eva under her wing and Eva was bowled over by her new sophisticated friend.

Ursula knew, too, of Eva's infatuation for her "older man" whom she made sheep's eyes at, whom she trailed around after, sitting in restaurants and cafés, forgotten in a corner while he conducted endless conversations about politics. Eva started to take her along to these gatherings—Ursula was her best friend, after all. All Eva wanted was to be close to Hitler. And that was all Ursula wanted too.

And Ursula knew about Berg and bunker. And really she was doing this frivolous girl a great favor by inserting herself in her life.

And so, just as they had got used to Eva hanging around, so they became accustomed to seeing her little English friend as well. Ursula was pleasant, she was a girl, she was nobody. She became so familiar that no one was surprised when she would turn up on her own and simper with admiration at the would-be great man. He took adoration casually. To have so little self-doubt, she thought, what a thing that must be.

But, ye gods, it was boring. So much hot air rising above the tables in Café Heck or the Osteria Bavaria, like smoke from the ovens. It was difficult to believe from this perspective that Hitler was going to lay waste to the world in a few years' time.

It was colder than usual for this time of year. Last night a light dusting of snow, like the icing sugar on Mrs. Glover's mince pies, had sifted over Munich. There was a big Christmas tree on the Marienplatz and the lovely smell of pine needles and roasting chestnuts everywhere. The festive finery made Munich seem more fairy-tale-like than England could ever hope to be.

The frosty air was invigorating and she walked toward the café with a wonderful purpose in her step, looking forward to a cup of *Schokolade,* hot and thick with cream.

Inside, the café was smoky and rather disagreeable after the sparklingly cold outdoors. The women were in furs and Ursula rather wished that she could have brought Sylvie's mink with her. Her mother never wore it and it was left permanently mothballed in her wardrobe these days.

He was at a table at the far end of the room, surrounded by the usual disciples. They were an ugly lot, she thought, and laughed to herself.

"Ah. Unsere Englische Freundin," he said when he caught sight of her. *"Guten Tag, gnädiges Fräulein."* With the slightest flick of a finger he ousted a callow-looking acolyte from the chair opposite and she sat down. He seemed irritable.

Es schneit, she said. "It's snowing." He glanced out of the window as if he hadn't noticed the weather. He was eating *Palatschinken.* They looked good but when the waiter came bustling over she ordered *Schwarzwälder Kirschtorte* to eat with her hot chocolate. It was delicious.

"*Entschuldigung,*" she murmured, reaching down into her bag and delving for a handkerchief. Lace corners, monogrammed with Ursula's initials, "UBT," Ursula Beresford Todd, a birthday present from Pammy. She dabbed politely at the crumbs on her lips and then bent down again to put the handkerchief back in her bag and retrieve the weighty object nesting there. Her father's old service revolver from the Great War, a Webley Mark V. She made fast her heroine heart. "*Wacht auf,*" Ursula said quietly. The words attracted the Führer's attention and she said, *"Es nahet gen den Tag."*

A move rehearsed a hundred times. One shot. Swiftness was all, yet there was a moment, a bubble suspended in time after she had drawn the gun and leveled it at his heart when everything seemed to stop.

"Führer," she said, breaking the spell. *"Für Sie."*

Around the table guns were jerked from holsters and pointed at her. One breath. One shot.

Ursula pulled the trigger.

Darkness fell.

SNOW

11 February 1910

Rap, rap, rap. The knocking on Bridget's bedroom door wove itself into a dream that she was having. In the dream she was at home in County Kilkenny and the pounding on the door was the ghost of her poor dead father, trying to get back to his family. *Rap, rap, rap!* She woke with tears in her eyes. *Rap, rap, rap.* There really was someone at the door.

"Bridget, Bridget?" Mrs. Todd's urgent whisper on the other side of the door. Bridget crossed herself, no news in the dark of the night was ever good. Had Mr. Todd had an accident in Paris? Or Maurice or Pamela taken ill? She scrambled out of bed and into the freezing cold of the little attic room. She smelled snow in the air. Opening the bedroom door she found Sylvie bent almost double, as ripe as a seedpod about to burst. "The baby's coming early," she said. "Can you help me?"

"Me?" Bridget squeaked. Bridget was only fourteen but she knew a lot about babies, not much of it good. She had watched her own mother die in childbirth but she had never told this to Mrs. Todd. Now clearly wasn't the time to mention it. She helped Sylvie back down the stairs to her own room.

"There's no point in trying to get a message to Dr. Fellowes," Sylvie said. "He'll never get through this snow."

"Mary, Mother of God," Bridget yelped as Sylvie dropped on all fours, like an animal, and grunted.

"The baby's coming now, I'm afraid," Sylvie said. "It's time."

Bridget persuaded her back into bed and their long, lonely night's labor commenced.

Oh, ma'am," Bridget cried suddenly, "she's all blue, so she is."

"A girl?"

"The cord's wrapped around her neck. Oh, Jesus Christ and all the saints, she's been strangled, the poor wee thing, strangled by the cord."

"We must do something, Bridget. What can we do?"

"Oh, Mrs. Todd, ma'am, she's gone. Dead before she had a chance to live."

"No, that cannot be," Sylvie said. She heaved herself into a sitting position on the battlefield of bloodied sheets, red and white, the baby still attached by its lifeline. While Bridget made mournful noises, Sylvie jerked open the drawer of her bedside table and rummaged furiously through its contents.

"Oh, Mrs. Todd," Bridget wailed, "lie down, there's nothing to be done. I wish Mr. Todd was here, so I do."

"Shush," Sylvie said and held aloft her trophy—a pair of surgical scissors that gleamed in the lamplight. "One must be prepared," she muttered. "Hold the baby close to the lamp so I can see. Quickly, Bridget. There's no time to waste."

Snip, snip.

Practice makes perfect.

THE BROAD SUNLIT UPLANDS

May 1945

They were at a table in the corner of a pub on Glasshouse Street. They'd been dropped in Piccadilly by the American army sergeant who'd given them a lift when he saw them hitchhiking at the side of the road outside Dover. They had crushed themselves onto an American troop transport ship at Le Havre instead of waiting two days for a flight. It was possible that, technically, they were AWOL, but neither of them gave a damn.

This was their third pub since Piccadilly and they were both agreed that the two of them were very drunk but had the capacity to get a good deal drunker yet. It was a Saturday night and the place was packed. Being in uniform they hadn't paid for a single drink all night. The relief, if not the euphoria, of victory was still in the air.

"Well," Vic said, raising his glass, "here's to being back."

"Cheers," Teddy said. "Here's to the future."

He had been shot down in November '43 and taken to Stalag Luft VI in the east. It hadn't been bad, in that it could have been worse, he could have been Russian—the Russians were treated like animals. But then at the beginning of February they were roused from their bunks with a familiar "*Raus! Raus!*" in the middle of the night and made to set out on the march west, away from the advancing Russians. Another day or two and they would have been liberated, it seemed an especially cruel twist of fate. There followed weeks of marching on starvation rations, in the freezing cold, minus-twenty degrees most of the time.

Vic was a rather cocky little flight sergeant, the navigator of a Lancaster shot down over the Ruhr. War made strange bedfellows. They had kept each other going on the march. It was a comradeship that had almost certainly saved their lives, that and the very occasional Red Cross package.

Teddy had been shot down near Berlin, only managing to escape from the cockpit at the last minute. He'd been trying to keep the plane level to give his crew a fighting chance to bail out. A captain didn't leave his ship until everyone on board had left. The same unspoken rule applied to a bomber.

The Halifax had been on fire from end to end and he had accepted that it was over for him. He had begun to feel lighter somehow, his heart swelling, and he suddenly knew that he would be all right, that death when it came would look after him. But death didn't come because his Aussie wireless operator crawled to the cockpit and clipped Teddy's parachute on his back and said, "Get out, you stupid bastard." He never saw him again, never saw any of his crew, didn't know if they were alive or dead. He jumped at the last minute, his parachute had barely opened when he hit the ground and he was lucky to fracture only an ankle and a wrist. He was taken to a hospital and the local Gestapo came and arrested him on the ward with the immortal words, "For you the war is over," which was the greeting that nearly every airman had heard when he was taken prisoner.

He had dutifully filled in his Capture card and waited for a letter from home, but nothing came. He was left wondering for two years if the Red Cross had him on their list of prisoners, if anyone at home knew he was alive.

They were on the road somewhere outside Hamburg when the war ended. Vic had taken great pleasure in saying to the guards, *"Ach so, mein Freund, für sie der Krieg ist zu ende."*

So, Ted, did you get through to your girl?" Vic asked when Teddy came back from sweet-talking the landlady behind the bar into letting him use the pub phone.

"I did," he laughed. "I'd been given up for dead, apparently. I don't think she believed it was me."

Half an hour and another couple of drinks later, Vic said, "Aye up, Ted. By the smile on her face I would say that woman who just came through the door might belong to you."

"Nancy," Teddy said quietly to himself.

"I love you," Nancy mouthed silently to him across the din.

"Oh, and she brought a little friend along for me, how thoughtful," Vic said and Teddy laughed and said, "Watch it, that's my sister you're talking about."

Nancy was clutching her hand so hard that it hurt but the pain meant nothing. He was there, he was actually there, sitting at a table in a London pub, drinking a pint of English beer, as large as life. Nancy made a funny choking sound and Ursula stopped herself from crying out. They were like the two Marys, dumb in the face of the Resurrection.

Then Teddy spotted them and a grin split his face. He jumped up, almost knocking over the glasses on the table. Nancy pushed her way through the crowd and threw her arms around him but Ursula stayed where she was, worried suddenly that if she moved it would all disappear, the whole happy scene break into pieces before her eyes. But then she thought, no, this was real, this was true, and she laughed with uncomplicated joy as Teddy let go of Nancy long enough to stand to attention and give Ursula a smart salute.

He shouted something to her across the pub but his words were lost in the hubbub. She thought it was "Thank you," but she might have been wrong.

SNOW

11 February 1910

Mrs. Haddock sipped a glass of hot rum, in what she hoped was a ladylike way. It was her third and she was beginning to glow from the inside out. She had been on her way to help deliver a baby when the snow had forced her to take refuge in the snug of the Blue Lion outside Chalfont St. Peter. It was not a place she would have ever considered entering, except out of necessity, but there was a roaring fire in the snug and the company was proving surprisingly convivial. Horse brasses and copper jugs gleamed and twinkled. The public bar, where the drink seemed to flow particularly freely, was an altogether rowdier place. A singsong was currently in progress there and Mrs. Haddock was surprised to find her toe tapping in accompaniment.

"You should see the snow," the landlord said, leaning across the great polished depth of the brass bar counter. "We could all be stuck here for days."

"Days?"

"You may as well have another tot of rum. You won't be going anywhere in a hurry tonight."

Acknowledgments

I would like to thank the following:

Andrew Janes (the National Archives in Kew)

Dr. Juliet Gardiner

Lt. Col. M. Keech (BEM R Signals)

Dr. Pertti Ahonen (Department of History, Edinburgh University)

Frederike Arnold

Annette Weber

And also my agent, Peter Straus, and Larry Finlay, Marianne Velmans, Alison Barrow and everyone at Transworld Publishers, as well as Camilla Ferrier and everyone at the Marsh Agency.

To know more about the writing of this book (including a bibliography), please visit my website, www.kateatkinson.co.uk.

KATE ATKINSON's first novel, *Behind the Scenes at the Museum,* won the Whitbread (now Costa) Book of the Year Award. She has been a critically acclaimed, bestselling author ever since, with more than one million copies of her books in print in the United States. She is the author of a collection of short stories, *Not the End of the World,* and of the novels *Human Croquet, Emotionally Weird, Case Histories, One Good Turn, When Will There Be Good News?,* and *Started Early, Took My Dog. Case Histories,* which introduced her readers to Jackson Brodie, a former police inspector turned private investigator, was made into a television series starring Jason Isaacs. Kate Atkinson lives in Edinburgh.